# The Unseen

# THE UNSEEN

## KAT MARTIN

**THORNDIKE PRESS**
A part of Gale, a Cengage Company

Copyright © 2025 by Kat Martin.
Thorndike Press, a part of Gale, a Cengage Company.

**ALL RIGHTS RESERVED**
This book is a work of fiction. Names, characters, businesses, organizations, places, events, and incidents either are the product of the author's imagination or are used fictitiously. Any resemblance to actual persons, living or dead, events, or locales is entirely coincidental.
Without limiting the author's and publisher's exclusive rights, any unauthorized use of this publication to train generative artificial intelligence (AI) technologies is expressly prohibited.
Thorndike Press® Large Print High Octane.
The text of this Large Print edition is unabridged.
Other aspects of the book may vary from the original edition.
Set in 16 pt. Plantin.

**LIBRARY OF CONGRESS CIP DATA ON FILE.**
**CATALOGUING IN PUBLICATION FOR THIS BOOK**
**IS AVAILABLE FROM THE LIBRARY OF CONGRESS.**

ISBN-13: 978-1-4205-3022-3 (hardcover alk. paper)

Published in 2025 by arrangement with Kensington Books, an imprint of Kensington Publishing Corp.

Print Number: 1    Print Year: 2026
Printed in Mexico

# The Unseen

# CHAPTER ONE

*St. Francisville, Louisiana*
*Friday, March 1*

"Look, Joey! What is that thing?" Ten-year-old Caleb pointed to a bony protrusion sticking out of a wooden box in the sandy soil. The lid had come partway off, giving them a glimpse inside.

"Wow! That's creepy." Joey knelt near the box they had unearthed as they were building a fort in a pile of fallen logs. "Looks like part of a skeleton. Some dead guy's hand." He grabbed a short stick and started digging the soil away from around the box.

"If there's a dead guy in there, we gotta call the cops," Caleb said, far less adventurous than his friend.

Joey kept digging. "You can call 'em, soon as I see what it is." He dug around the box, moving the lid enough to expose more bones, until the skeletal hand was completely revealed. It was clearly connected to the bones of an arm.

"Maybe it's a grave," Caleb said, watching Joey try to pry off the still half-buried lid. "We're gonna be in trouble if we're digging up somebody's grave."

Standing beneath a tall, moss-draped oak, Joey glanced around, but saw only thick green foliage and wild grapevines along the bayou. "This is no cemetery," he said. "Come on, Caleb. Don't just stand there, get down here and help me."

Slightly taller than his friend, dark-haired instead of blond, Caleb stood frozen beside the hole Joey was digging. "I think we should call the cops," Caleb said.

Joey just kept digging. Sand began collapsing back into the hole, enough that he had to start using the shovel to clear it away, but little by little, the box was unearthed. Joey lifted off the lid, exposing the skeletal remains inside the box.

When he spotted the skull, Joey dropped the shovel and went back down on his knees to investigate.

Caleb pulled out his cell phone. "I'm callin' 'em, Joey. We gotta tell 'em we found a dead person."

Joey paused to look at the bones he'd uncovered. "I think there's a whole body in there," he said, his gaze fixed on the pile of bones.

Caleb ignored him as the 911 police dispatcher answered. "What's your emergency?"

"We found a body out near the bayou. It musta been here a long time 'cause it's a skeleton. We figured you'd want to know."

"Who's calling?"

Caleb gave the woman his name and Joey's. He told them they had been playing near a pile of dead logs off Creek Road, near Bayou Sara.

"A patrol car is on the way. Stay there until they arrive. I'll remain on the phone with you until they get there."

"Okay," Caleb said. His parents weren't going to like it when they found out he and Joey had been playing so far from the house. They thought everything he did was dangerous. They were always worried he was going to get hurt.

He looked back into the box to find the empty eyes of the skull staring up at him.

Caleb felt a chill. Maybe this time his parents were right.

## Chapter Two

*St. Francisville, Louisiana*
*Tuesday, March 5*

Nicole Belmond pulled her white Audi convertible up in front of Belle Reve, the 1870s Greek Revival mansion that had belonged to her family for a hundred years.

Turning off the engine, she got out and headed for the front door, trying to avoid the cracks in the wide marble steps. It was tough not to notice how badly the paint was peeling off the four white fluted Doric columns stretching across the front, or that some of the plaster had fallen off the ceiling of the covered porch.

Nicole rang the bell, letting her aunt know she was coming in, then turned the knob and walked into the entry. The interior was in as much disrepair as the outside. The pink Baccarat crystal chandelier had long ago lost its gleam, and the scuffed parquet floors needed refinishing. She crossed the faded Persian carpet and continued down the center hall toward the sweeping staircase, the beautiful rosewood banisters one of the few things still in good condition.

Refusing to think of the costs involved in doing the necessary cleaning and repairs, Nicole passed the dining room on the left and the front parlor on the right, both of which showed years of neglect.

"Aunt Rachel?"

No answer. It was a warm spring day. Nicole made her way into the big open kitchen, remodeled in the 1950s by one of her great-grandmothers, but totally outdated now.

The Belmond family had purchased the house in the 1920s. Since then, it had been rebuilt a number of times, adding electricity and indoor plumbing, but in the last few decades as the family fortune dwindled, the years had not been kind.

These days there wasn't enough money to take care of a historic mansion the size of Belle Reve; and even though Nicole's career as an artist provided enough for minor repairs, and had allowed her to convert the carriage house into a residence of her own, sooner or later, something would have to be done.

Nicole tried not to think about it.

In search of her aunt, she crossed the

kitchen, shoved open the screen door at the rear of the house, and saw Aunt Rachel sitting in her usual spot on the terrace in one of the wrought iron garden chairs, which matched the round white wrought iron table. A pitcher of her aunt's homemade lemonade sat in front of her.

Aunt Rachel smiled. "How's the gallery opening coming along?" Tall and willowy, with long, softly curling black hair, she had the smooth skin, high cheekbones, and brilliant green eyes that ran in the Belmond family. At forty-four, Rachel was a beautiful woman.

"The opening's progressing right on schedule, and Anne's a terrific promoter," Nicole said, referring to the owner of Anne Winston Fine Art, one of the galleries that represented Nicole's paintings. "I'm excited about the event. Nervous, of course, but excited."

"You have nothing to be nervous about. Your paintings are incredible. You're a very talented young woman, Nicole. The opening is sure to be immensely successful."

"I hope so." The exhibit of her latest paintings was scheduled for a week from Friday in Baton Rouge. "I still need to finish the final canvas."

"You'll get it done," Rachel said. "You still

have plenty of time."

"I'd love for you to be there. I hope you'll be feeling well enough to come."

But the odds were fifty-fifty. Rachel had been born with a rare form of muscular dystrophy, which had appeared in her late teens. She'd already outlived the doctors' predictions, had even been married for a short time in her twenties — before the husband she adored had died of cancer.

But time and Rachel's illness were both relentless, and day after day, she grew weaker.

"I'm definitely planning to go," her aunt said. "At the moment, I'm feeling very well."

"That's wonderful. Sean's going. He's never been to any of my openings before. The two of you can go together."

Fifteen-year-old Sean Handley was Nicole's half-brother, the product of her parents' divorce and her mother's remarriage. When Sean's father, William Handley, had died in a car accident, their mother had overdosed on sleeping pills, leaving Sean an orphan. Nicole, fourteen years older, had stepped in to become his guardian.

"That's a great idea," Rachel said. "Sean and I can share an Uber."

Nicole smiled. Uber wasn't a concept

most people would associate with Rachel. Her aunt had a dreamy, ethereal way about her, as if she came from a long-ago, more graceful era. The house, having been built in a distant time, seemed to fit her perfectly.

"Would you like a glass of lemonade?" her aunt asked.

"Thanks, Aunt Rachel, but I'd better get to work. I want to get the painting done and have time to make changes if I need to. Why don't I bring something over for supper?"

"I just finished a big lunch. How about a piece of that chocolate cake you baked?"

"Good idea. I ate a late lunch in Baton Rouge. Cake and a big glass of milk works for me."

Rachel smiled. "That sounds perfect." Her aunt didn't have the strength to walk very far. The house was surrounded by nineteen lush green acres that backed up to Bayou Sara. Much of it was densely overgrown, all but the garden, which Rachel and her part-time gardener carefully tended.

The carriage house, constructed a few years after the main house, sat off to the side, farther along the oak-lined gravel drive. After Nicole had accepted the responsibility of raising Sean, the old building, where she had played as a child, had seemed the perfect place to make a home for the two of them. At the same time, it allowed her to keep a close eye on her ailing aunt.

Nicole headed for the carriage house, opened the door of the single-story, gable-roofed structure, and stepped inside. The building now had a living room, two bedrooms, two-and-a-half baths, a modern kitchen, and a studio workspace.

She smiled, proud of what she had accomplished. The interior, done in a style reminiscent of Belle Reve, had molded ceilings and hardwood floors covered by Persian carpets. The furniture was a comfortable mix of traditional, accented with the ornate French antiques she had rescued from rooms no longer in use in the main house.

Nicole headed for the canvas perched on an easel in her studio, the room itself a no-nonsense space with a comfortable sofa and walls lined with worktables and bookshelves. A skylight, necessary for her painting, was the only extravagance in the room.

Pulling her paint-covered smock over her head, Nicole tied the strings behind her back and went to work.

# Chapter Three

*Sunday, March 10*

It was the end of the week, a warm, sunny late afternoon when Nicole pulled into the parking lot of the Baton Rouge Youth Center. Earlier that day, she had driven Sean and Rachel to church; afterward, she'd put the top down on the Audi so she and Sean could enjoy the weather on the trip to Baton Rouge.

Pulling off the scarf tying her shoulder-length auburn hair into a ponytail, she opened her door at the same time Sean opened his and they climbed out of the car. Sean grabbed his backpack off the floor behind his seat, and the two of them set off across the lot to the front of the redbrick building Sean called home five days a week.

Sean paused. "Everything's still on for your gallery opening, right?" At five-eleven, her fifteen-year-old half-brother was tall for his age, but still coltishly thin, with thick brown hair, which always seemed in need of a trim.

"Yup. I still have to make a few last-minute changes to my final painting, but I'll get it done."

"You better," Sean teased. "I really want to go."

Nicole smiled. She and Sean were getting along much better these days than when he'd first moved in last year. He'd been grieving the death of his parents, acting out at the awful turn of fate that had destroyed his life.

Nicole had also been grieving, but she had lost her mother years earlier, when Claire Belmond had left Nicole's father for William Handley. A year later, her father had moved to California and remarried, and a young Nicole had been sent away to boarding school. She had seen little of her parents in the years after that. They had simply gone on with their lives as if she didn't exist.

"Our aunt Rachel's going to the opening, too," Nicole said. "Maybe you'd want to ask one of your friends to join us."

Sean shook his head the instant before she realized the boys at the center wouldn't be allowed to go. They had to stay with their parents or guardians on the weekends, just as Sean did. It was part of their sentencing, and it was strictly enforced.

The sound of the throaty roar of a motorcycle wheeling into the parking lot caught her attention. The big Harley pulled into a spot just a few spaces down from the Audi and the engine went off. The rider removed his helmet, tucked it beneath his arm, and started toward the front of the building.

"It's Coach Devereaux!" Excited, Sean began waving madly. "Hey, Mr. D!"

Devereaux changed direction and headed straight for them. He was maybe three inches taller than Sean, around six-two, his thick dark brown hair well cut, but slightly windblown. Dressed in blue jeans and a snug black T-shirt, he had a broad-shouldered, lean-muscled build. A pair of biceps bulged from the sleeves of his T-shirt.

He stopped right in front of them. "Hey, Sean, good to see you. You ready for a new week?"

"Yes, sir. I'll be in the gym for sure. You gonna be here?"

Devereaux smiled warmly. "I'll be here." He turned to Nicole. "Lucas Devereaux. You're Nicole. Our paths crossed a few times when Sean first arrived."

She hadn't forgotten him. The first time she had seen him, he'd been standing behind a podium, an attractive man in a dark brown suit and expensive loafers. As the founder and owner of the youth center, he'd been there to welcome new students.

He had also served as chaplain and one of the coaches, but according to Sean, he had recently hired someone to assume the chaplain's duties and increased his hours as coach.

Nicole had spoken to him briefly that first day. After that, she had seen him several times when she had picked Sean up or dropped him off at the center, but that had been a while ago.

He looked different in a T-shirt and jeans, a pair of heavy black motorcycle boots on his big feet. She had to admit he looked good. Very good. The kind of good that made a woman's stomach flutter.

"Nice to see you again." Nicole extended a hand and Devereaux wrapped his bigger hand around it. It felt warm and strong, and the interest she was feeling hiked up a notch.

Sean glanced down at his phone, checking the time. "I gotta get going." His gaze swung to Nicole. "See you Friday, sis."

"You bet." Nicole waved as the lanky teen galloped away. She looked up at Lucas Devereaux. "Sean's a good boy, Mr. Devereaux. If he hadn't lost his parents, he never would have gotten into trouble."

"Problems at home. That's the reason a lot of these kids wind up here. And it's Lucas, or Luke, whichever you prefer." He had strong, masculine features. A slight crook in the bridge of his nose only added to his masculine appeal.

"I haven't been around as much as usual," he said. "I've been spending a lot of time trying to get the new facility on the other side of town up and running. Which, if all goes well, should happen next week."

"I read an article in the *Advocate* online about it." Nicole referenced the Baton Rouge newspaper, the closest thing to local news in St. Francisville. Her hometown was half an hour north of the city.

"As soon as the facility is open, I can get back to my responsibilities here full-time." There was something in his speech, not a typical Southern accent. Not exactly French. Cajun, maybe. Whatever it was, it was intriguing.

"We've got a new chaplain, which allows me to focus on sports. They have their own staff at the other facility, and I've kind of got a personal attachment to this place, since it was my first."

"Sean will be glad to hear that. I know you've been teaching him to box. I understand it's a sport the school encourages." According to Sean, a sport at which Lucas Devereaux excelled, and was probably responsible for the slight bump in his nose.

"That's right. A lot of our students have anger issues. Boxing gives them a way to deal with it."

"I suppose," she said, not quite convinced.

"It also serves as a means of self-defense. Bullies don't do well against a kid who can protect himself."

It made sense. Sean was a big kid, but a smaller boy . . . She smiled. "I hadn't thought of it that way."

The front door opened, and someone called out to him.

"I guess I'd better go. I'm off on weekends, just like the boys, but I try to stay close in case I'm needed." He had warm brown eyes, and as they ran over her, Nicole could have sworn she caught a glimmer of heat.

"I look forward to seeing you here again," Lucas said.

"I'll be back to pick Sean up next weekend."

He nodded, his eyes not leaving her face. "Have a good week."

Nicole watched him disappear into the building and felt as if she had met a completely different man, one better suited to the image Sean had painted. According to Sean and the article in the *Advocate,* Lucas Devereaux had been a troubled teen himself, even been a member of a gang.

As she thought of him on his Harley, it wasn't hard to imagine the rebellious youth he had been. The article said that Lucas had managed to turn his life around, gone so far as to enter a seminary after high school graduation, and had eventually become a priest.

Apparently, that hadn't worked out, and five years ago, he had left the priesthood. She had no idea how he had gone from gang member to priest to opening a youth center, but she was glad he had. The center had changed Sean's life.

Heading back across the parking lot, she slid behind the wheel of the Audi, tied back her hair, and pulled out of the lot. As she drove home on the interstate, she thought of Sean and the changes he had made.

During the first few months he had lived with her, Sean had been in one scrape after another, including vandalism and underage drinking. Twice she'd picked him up at the police station. He'd been suspended from school more than once.

Six months ago, he'd been arrested for

stealing a nearly new Maserati off a street in Baton Rouge, not the first car he had stolen, just the first time he'd been caught.

Since he was underage and there were extenuating circumstances — the death of his parents — the judge had given him a choice: a year in juvenile detention or a year at the Baton Rouge Youth Center, with weekends at home with his legal guardian. Sean had been wise enough to choose the youth center.

As she wove through traffic, she thought about Lucas Devereaux. Sean talked about him incessantly and clearly admired him. Lucas had been a good influence on Sean from the start.

Nicole had to admit there was something about him that made her want to know the rest of his story.

Maybe she would run into him again.

It was the middle of the week, the hour late, Belle Reve quiet except for the croaking of a bullfrog in the pond surrounded by weeping willows behind the house. Rachel lay awake in the big four-poster bed upstairs in the master's suite. A faded peach satin canopy draped the sides of the bed, giving her a feeling of privacy in the darkness, making her feel safe.

For as long as she had lived at Belle Reve, a name that roughly translated as Sweet Dream, she had never been afraid. She had grown up roaming the halls, prowling the six big, high-ceilinged bedrooms on the second floor, playing with her dolls in the third-floor nursery next to the old servants' quarters.

She loved Belle Reve, had only lived one other place in her life. When she was twenty-one, she had fallen deeply in love with a young college student named David Trent. Worried about her health, her parents had forbidden the relationship, but there was no keeping them apart. Against her parents' wishes and the doctor's orders, she had married David and moved with him to New Orleans.

They were happy. Madly in love, and so very sure they would be together for the rest of their lives.

Then David had fallen ill with cancer. They tried every medical procedure available, but none of the doctors could save him. David slipped away in his sleep, Rachel begging him to stay, holding him fiercely in her arms.

Even after she moved back into the house and returned to her maiden name, she had continued to mourn and endlessly grieve him. With time, David's memory slowly faded, but her love for Belle Reve had never wavered, over the years had grown even stronger.

She knew every inch of the house and grounds. As she lay in the darkness, she recognized every creak and groan, the whisper of the wind against the windowpanes, a branch on the oak tree in the garden rubbing against the side of the kitchen.

She loved the old house and had never been the least bit frightened.

Until lately.

Something in the house had changed. She knew it. Could feel it. She had no idea what could have happened, but even the air she breathed felt different.

There were noises she had never heard before, noises even in the daylight hours. In the middle of the night, there were whispers she could barely hear, eerie sighs that had nothing to do with the wind. Sometimes in the darkness, she heard footsteps. Several times, she had left the bed and gone to the door to check the hallway, even gone downstairs to see if someone had broken into the house.

But each time she searched, no one was there.

Through the years, there had been rumors that Belle Reve was haunted, but it simply wasn't true. They were tales invented to entertain the children or increase tourism in the tiny town. Rachel had lived in the house long enough to be certain nothing supernatural was there.

Lately, her certainty had begun to fade.

She could no longer deny that something in the house was different. The footsteps prowling the hall, the faint movement of a door opening and closing. Sounds she didn't recognize, sounds that sent chills down her spine.

She had considered calling the police, but if they came and found nothing, they would think she was a fool. She hadn't mentioned anything to Nicole, who already spent far too much time worrying about her.

Still, Rachel had begun locking the house's doors at night, which Nicole had been pressing her to do for some time. She had finally given in and made a nightly check of doors and windows before she headed upstairs.

She was entirely certain there was no one in the house. Every night before she went to sleep, Rachel told herself that.

And yet, as she lay in bed, staring up at the faded peach satin canopy, listening to sounds she had never heard before, her nerves scraped raw by the incessant chirp of crickets that should have been familiar, but no longer seemed to belong, Rachel began to feel the first unsettling hint of fear.

## Chapter Four

Anne Winston Fine Art, in Perkins Rowe, Baton Rouge, was filled to overflowing with art patrons attending the Friday-night gallery opening featuring prominent landscape artist, Nicole Belmond.

Lucas walked into the showroom beneath expertly angled track lighting that highlighted the intense colors of the unique Impressionist landscapes to their best advantage. Easels displayed more of the artist's incredible work.

After running into Nicole at the center last Sunday, Lucas's curiosity had been piqued. He'd gone on her web page and seen an array of her colorful paintings.

As he wandered the gallery, weaving his way through men in expensive suits and women in cocktail dresses, he realized the photos on the website hadn't begun to do the paintings justice. The vivid oranges, greens, reds, and golds in each piece gave the viewer more than just a look at the lush Louisiana countryside.

The paintings revealed the ageless strength and beauty of the land. The magnificence of moss-draped oaks along an empty lane, the mystery of weeping willows around a quiet pond, the unparalleled beauty of cypress trees against the backdrop of a sunset on the bayou.

Each piece drew him in, gave him an appreciation of the land that he too often took for granted.

"You look like you could use a drink." A woman walked toward him, forties, blond, attractive in a slightly overstated way. "There's a bar in the corner. What can I get you?"

He wasn't a big drinker. Alcohol had caused him nothing but trouble as a kid. But occasionally after a long day at work, he enjoyed the relaxation of a drink. "Scotch, if you have it. Neat."

She smiled. "Coming right up." He watched her walk away, her sapphire dress showing off a slim figure and a nice pair of legs. She was only gone a few minutes. Returning, she pressed a heavy crystal rocks glass into his hand.

"Thanks."

She smiled. "I'm Anne Winston. I'm the

owner of the gallery."

He nodded, not surprised. "Pleasure to meet you. I'm Lucas Devereaux. I'm acquainted with the artist."

Her gaze ran over him. "Well, isn't she a lucky girl." She glanced around the gallery. "Why don't you wander a little, while I find her for you." She left him in front of a haunting image of Belle Reve, the historic home where Nicole and Sean lived.

Though he had never been there, curiosity, and the way Sean talked about it, calling it "that spooky old place where my aunt lives," had convinced him to go online to see what it looked like. As spectacular as the old house was in photographs, nothing could compare to the portrait of timeless grace and elegance Nicole had painted of the mansion.

She appeared at his side, clearly surprised to find him there. "Lucas. I didn't expect to see you. Thank you for coming. Sean never told me you liked art."

"Not all of it. I'm not much on contemporary art — throwing buckets of paint at a canvas doesn't do much for me. Your work, however, is incredible. I'm glad I came."

Faint color rose in her cheeks. Lucas found it charming.

"I see you already have a drink. Would you

like me to show you around?"

He nodded. "Very much." His gaze followed her as she led him away. She was wearing a simple black cocktail dress, a gold choker and earrings, and very high heels. She had a terrific figure, which the dress elegantly displayed.

"I don't see Sean," Lucas said. "But I know he must be here. He was very excited about coming."

"He's over there with my aunt." She tipped her head in that direction. "Sean is keeping her entertained while I work."

His glance went past the boy to a slender woman with long jet-black hair. She was taller than Nicole, pale, and a little too thin. Nicole's figure was fuller, more feminine, at least to Lucas.

With her thick auburn hair and big green eyes, Nicole was a very attractive woman. He had noticed the first time he had met her, been reminded on the occasions he had run into her at the center. Last Sunday, he had finally admitted to feeling the attraction, but still wasn't sure he wanted to pursue it.

She smiled as she led him around the gallery, pausing briefly in front of one painting or another. A particular canvas caught his eye, a vibrant pink-and-gold setting sun reflected on a lake through a grove of cypress trees.

"Beautiful," he said.

"Thank you."

He turned and continued walking, but Nicole caught his arm, stopping him.

"I'm not sure I'm ready for you to see the paintings in the back of the gallery."

"Why not?"

"The subject matter is new for me. I just . . . I felt like doing something different. I wasn't going to show them, but Anne liked them. She convinced me it wouldn't hurt my reputation if I painted something out of the ordinary."

"I'd like to see them." He smiled. "I promise I'll keep an open mind."

She smiled back at him, and he felt a jolt of heat, just as he had when he'd spoken to her in front of the center five days ago.

"Follow me." She led him around a movable wall to the other side, where a series of five paintings were hung. Unlike the others, which had been done in vibrant colors, these were painted in grays, blacks, and browns, all of them dark and disturbing.

"Vicksburg," he said, recognizing the image.

"Yes. I've painted the battlefield before, but this time was different."

In the eerie gray light of dawn, the empty battlefield stretched across the canvas. A row of cannon, partially hidden by earthen battlements, stood in a rising mist, an echo of the past and a prediction of an uncertain future.

The others dealt with similar dark images, all painted in grays, browns, and blacks. The Shirley House looked down from its perch above the battlefield at the horror that had played out in front of it. There was a painting of headstones marching up a grassy knoll in the Vicksburg battle cemetery.

Lucas liked history. The Civil War was a subject he had read a great deal about. He understood, perhaps better than most, what the paintings represented.

He took a sip of scotch. "Not exactly cheerful, but definitely intriguing."

Nicole's expression dimmed. "I don't really expect people to like them. I was just painting the emotions I felt as I looked at the battlefield."

He waited until her gaze returned to his. "There's a lot of feeling there. That's what makes them interesting. What made you decide on that particular subject?"

"I don't really know. As I said, I was looking for something new, something that would spark my interest. One day, I took a drive and ended up in Vicksburg."

Anne Winston walked up just then. "I'm sorry to intrude, but Martin Kohler is interested in one of your paintings. He wants to meet the artist."

"Of course," Nicole said.

"And your friend Christian Villard is here."

A hint of displeasure tightened her lips. She wiped it away and smiled as she turned to Lucas. "Thanks again for coming."

"My pleasure," he said, meaning it. He watched her walk away, watched as she approached the first man, tall, blond, and good-looking. Whatever he said had her shaking her head, her shoulders stiff as she abruptly turned away. Had to be Christian Villard. Clearly, she wasn't a fan.

Nicole continued toward a man standing next to one of the easels. He was older, sandy-haired, ruddy-complexioned, with a friendly smile that Nicole returned. Martin Kohler, a potential buyer. Lucas hoped she made the sale.

As he finished his drink and set the glass down on a coaster on one of the tables, his glance caught on another painting of Belle Reve. *Diva,* it was titled.

A golden sun was rising, shining through a row of moss-draped oaks, illuminating the front of the old historic house and exposing its secrets. In the early light, the tall white columns were faded and worn. One of the shutters at the windows was broken and tilted at an angle. It was a house that had withstood the ravages of time, and against all odds, it had endured.

*Diva.* Even in her fading beauty, she was a warrior, a fighter who could not be conquered.

The painting moved him. Lucas checked the price tag. It wasn't cheap, but he could afford it. He spoke to Anne and asked her to reserve the painting. He would pick it up tomorrow.

"Good choice," she said. "There's something special about that one."

He just nodded. As he wove his way through the well-dressed crowd to the door, his gaze went in search of Nicole.

The art buyer was gone, and Villard stood next to her. The way the man loomed over her set Lucas's teeth on edge. He found himself walking toward her, putting himself between her and the other man.

"I think there was a painting you promised to show me." His glance went from her to Villard and back. "Or are you too busy?"

She flashed him a smile of gratitude so wide, he felt a tug in his chest. "No, of course not. When I make a promise, I keep it." She took his arm. "Sorry, I'm afraid you'll have to excuse us," she said to Villard as Lucas started leading her away.

Villard's features darkened. "This conversation isn't over," he said.

Nicole's hold tightened. "Actually, it is."

When they reached the movable wall, Lucas led her around to the back, where the dark paintings were hung.

Nicole breathed a sigh of relief. "Thanks for doing that. I wasn't in the mood to deal with Christian tonight."

"Your boyfriend?"

"God, no. I stupidly went out with him a couple of times, but it didn't take long to figure out he was nothing more than a pretty face. I wasn't interested then, and I'm not interested now."

He thought of the dark look on Villard's face. "You don't think he's a threat? I could stay, make sure you get home safely."

She looked up at him and he caught a flash of interest in her pretty green eyes. She shook her head. "It's very kind of you to offer, but the truth is, I don't think Christian's really a threat. His father is a very wealthy man, and the family reputation is important to both of them."

"All right. In that case, I think I'll say

good night to Sean and then head on home."

"Thank you, Lucas, for coming tonight and for playing Sir Galahad."

His mouth edged up. With the life he'd led, he was as far from a white knight as a man could be. "No problem."

Lucas made his way over to Sean, who introduced him to his aunt. Rachel Belmond was a very gracious lady, definitely Southern born and Southern bred.

Lucas left the gallery, heading outside to his silver Lexus coupe, his gift to himself as he thought of it. In a way, he was sorry Nicole hadn't needed his help. He hadn't felt such a strong attraction to a woman in years.

On the other hand, pursuing that attraction was a bad idea. It wasn't good to mix work at the center with his personal life.

He caught a last glimpse of Nicole through the gallery window, saw her smiling at one of the customers, and his body tightened.

Since he had always made his own rules, he was going to find out if Nicole felt a similar attraction to him.

# Chapter Five

Saturday morning was sunny, but not overly humid, a pleasant spring day. As Aunt Rachel had suggested, last night, she and Sean had Ubered from the art show back to Belle Reve. Sean had wanted to stay a little longer, but he loved his aunt, and he knew she would be tiring.

*My brother's growing up,* Nicole thought. Becoming the man he was meant to be.

As she brewed a pot of coffee, she thought of the opening, which had been a tremendous success. Even two of her dark pieces had sold.

She'd been surprised to see Lucas Devereaux there. He looked almost as good in his beige, lightweight summer jacket and brown slacks as he had in jeans and a body-hugging black T-shirt. *Almost.* But it was his eyes that intrigued her.

During his brief confrontation with Christian Villard, Lucas's warm golden-brown eyes had turned so dark they looked nearly black. Beneath his polite façade, she had sensed a danger he kept carefully controlled.

That he rode a badass motorcycle no longer surprised her. Perhaps it was a way for him to release the darker side of his nature. Whatever it was, the combination of intelligence, compassion, and an edge of danger drew her to him — as a man hadn't done in a very long time.

Nicole didn't think Christian Villard was a threat, but she wasn't sure about Lucas Devereaux.

Still, spending time with him last night, her attraction to him continued to grow. When he'd stood next to Christian, she couldn't help comparing the two. Christian had taken her out to dinner a couple of times, but she'd found him a dull conversationalist who talked far too much about himself. He had pressed her to sleep with him, actually driven her to his apartment and tried to convince her to come inside, but Nicole had never felt any physical attraction to him.

She had told him earlier that night that she wasn't interested, but to Christian, *no* did not mean *no*. Which really pissed her off.

He had called her last week and apologized, promised to behave himself, and asked her to go to a party at his father's estate in Baton Rouge. Phillipe Villard was a wealthy real estate developer, a direct descendant of Pierre and Therese-Louise Villard, the original builders of Belle Reve.

Though the Villards had sold the property to the Belmonds long ago, Phillipe seemed to feel as if it should still belong to him. He wanted to buy Belle Reve and turn it into a high-end resort.

Rachel wasn't interested.

Still, Phillipe continued to press the issue, determined to end up owning the old estate.

Hearing footsteps, Nicole looked up to see Sean wandering into the kitchen. He was dressed in a navy-blue T-shirt and a pair of khaki shorts, with bedhead hair, yawning and scratching his chest.

He shuffled over to the refrigerator, took out a Pepsi, and popped the top.

"You did good last night," he said. "Sold a lot of paintings, right?"

She smiled. "I sold more than I thought I would. Even some of the dark stuff."

"That stuff is cool. I mean, they aren't like your regular paintings, but I really like them."

"Thanks." She glanced at the stove. "I'm making oatmeal. You want some?"

"I'll just have some Mini-Wheats." He grabbed a bowl, filled it, added milk, and carried the bowl over to the breakfast table.

"Coach came over and talked to me at the gallery last night," Sean said as he sat down and started to eat.

Nicole glanced in his direction.

Sean shoved in a mouthful of cereal and talked around it. "I think he likes you."

Nicole kept stirring the oatmeal. "You think so?"

"Maybe. He isn't married, you know."

"I didn't think so." She had read in the newspaper he was single, but the way he was looking at her last night made it clear. Or maybe that was just wishful thinking.

"I heard some cool stuff about him the other day."

"Oh, yeah?" She turned off the stove and poured the oatmeal into a bowl. "Like what?"

"You know he was a priest, right? Remember I told you people used to call him Father Luke."

"You might have mentioned it — only about a dozen times."

"Yeah, well, when he was a priest, he learned how to do stuff. He used to do exorcisms. You know, like when people get possessed by the devil? Father Luke could get rid of the evil."

"That's crazy."

Sean shrugged. "That's what Monty Holcomb said. Monty says sometimes Coach still does it. I guess you have to be a special kind of person, but if you are, the Church will let you do it even if you aren't a priest."

"I don't believe it."

"I do. Monty says he knows someone who knows someone who asked him to get rid of a demon and he did it."

"I still don't believe it."

"I'm going to ask him."

She glanced up. "I don't think that's a good idea — unless you think you're going to have a run-in with the devil in the near future."

Sean laughed. "No, but I'm still gonna ask him."

Nicole just smiled. Sean had homework to do; then he planned to work on his model cars. Her brother loved cars, especially fancy sports cars: Ferrari, Lamborghini, Porsche, Maserati. His favorites were McLaren and Bugatti. She had helped him make a sort of workshop from an old outbuilding where horses and wagons were kept.

She and Sean had built a wall to close off a portion of the building. There was an electric heater and a window air conditioner so he could work out there year-round. He'd made it comfortable with an old leather couch, a discarded Formica-topped table, and a couple of wooden chairs.

Until his sentence was over, the teen's movements were restricted. It was tough on a kid his age to be cooped up in the house all day. Nicole tried to make sure he had something to do to keep himself busy and out of trouble.

As for her, with the beautiful weather, she figured today was a good day to start a new painting. She collected the stuff she would need and was ready to go, but first she needed to check on Rachel.

As she crossed the gravel drive, Nicole hoped her aunt had enjoyed the gallery opening last night, since Rachel didn't go out that often. Walking up on the porch, she gave a quick knock to let her aunt know she was coming inside, then reached down to open the front door. It was locked.

*Finally.* For weeks, Nicole had been trying to persuade her aunt to keep the house locked up. The modern world was dangerous. Sad as it was, bolting your doors at night was simply the wise thing to do.

Pulling her keys out of her pocket, Nicole opened the door and stepped into the entry.

Ahead of her, the sweeping staircase climbed to the second floor. From there, a smaller staircase led up to the third floor, once the servants' quarters and the nursery.

"Aunt Rachel?"

No answer. Nicole continued past the staircase, into the kitchen, then outside to the terrace overlooking the garden, but no one was there. Rachel wasn't in the dining room. A glance across the hall into the once-elegant front parlor, past the tall grandfather clock, and Nicole spotted her aunt sitting on one of the faded velvet settees that faced each other in front of the hearth. A book sat open in her lap.

"I guess you didn't hear me calling you."

As Rachel glanced up, her face looked paler than usual, and there were smudges beneath her eyes.

"Are you all right?" Nicole asked.

"I'm sorry. I must have been engrossed in my book." Rachel's smile looked forced.

"How are you feeling?" Nicole asked. "You were out later than usual last night."

"I'm fine. I just didn't sleep very well."

Nicole sat down on the settee beside her. "Maybe you shouldn't have stayed at the gallery so long."

"It wasn't that. Sean and I got home at a reasonable hour. It was just . . . I don't know . . . I woke up and couldn't get back to sleep. My mind kept wandering around in the past." She managed another wan smile. "I'm sure I'll sleep the sleep of the dead tonight."

With her aunt's poor health, Nicole would have preferred a different metaphor. "If you want, Sean and I could come over and spend the night. We could make popcorn and watch TV."

A room off the kitchen, formerly the maid's quarters, had been converted into a den. Unlike the rest of the house that suffered from years of wear and neglect, the den had a coat of fresh paint, a big flat-screen TV, and a comfortable leather sofa and chairs, furniture Nicole had purchased.

Oddly, it was the original rooms of the house her aunt preferred.

"I appreciate your offer," Rachel said. "But after being out last night, I'm looking forward to a quiet evening to myself."

Nicole nodded. "That's probably a good idea." Her gaze ran over the threadbare Persian carpet, then moved to the pale pink walls that desperately needed painting. The heavy rose damask draperies would fall apart with any attempt to clean them. The gilded mirror over the fireplace's ornate marble-mantel needed to be resilvered.

Phillipe Villard wanted to buy the mansion and remodel it completely, build condos out back and turn the entire property into a luxury resort. The local historical society had expressed an interest, but they didn't have enough money. Sooner or later, Rachel wouldn't have any choice but to take Villard's offer.

Nicole's insides tightened. She loved the old house almost as much as her aunt did.

"I better get going if I'm planning to get any work done," she said, rising from the settee.

"What are you working on?" Rachel asked.

"I'm starting something new. I think I'll just walk around, see what's out there. I've done quite a few paintings of Belle Reve, but maybe I'll see something new that will inspire me."

"I'm sure you will. You have a wonderful eye. Perhaps some wildlife for a change. Birds or something."

"Maybe." She had always stayed with landscapes, but she was keeping an open mind. "Why don't you lie down for a while, catch a nap?"

Rachel's smile looked a little brighter. "Yes, perhaps I will."

Nicole left her in the parlor and returned to the carriage house to collect her easel, a fresh canvas, and painting supplies. She spotted Sean leaving the house on his way to his man/boy cave, as Nicole thought of it.

With the blank canvas tucked under her arm and a basket of supplies, she managed to give him a wave and kept walking, excited to see what discovery she might make.

# Chapter Six

Lucas swung aboard his Harley-Davidson cruiser, purchased after his father had died. He'd used a portion of his inheritance, along with some of what he'd made from financial investments, to open the first youth center.

He'd been riding since his bad-boy days. Since he didn't blame the motorcycle for his soiled past, he rode whenever he needed to clear his head or just get out of the city. With the sun beating down and a faint breeze blowing, he roared onto the I-110 North for the thirty-minute trip to St. Francisville.

Lucas had tried to talk himself out of it, reminded himself again it was bad to mix business with pleasure. But the lure of seeing Nicole Belmond was too tempting. He probably should have called first. She'd said Christian Villard was not her boyfriend, but that didn't mean the lady didn't have another significant male in her life.

He wove his way through the light Saturday traffic and eventually pulled onto Highway 61. It was a great day for a ride, and he could always tell her the paintings he had seen of Belle Reve last night had made him curious — which was the truth. More than that, he wanted to see Nicole, see if his attraction to her was as strong as he believed. See if her feelings ran anywhere near the same.

He had his phone in a mount on the handlebars, a map with directions pointing the way. In St. Francisville, he turned left on Commerce, left on Ferdinand, turned right onto Old Ferry Road. It wasn't much farther to Belmond Place, a paved one-lane road that came to a gravel drive on the left. He slowed and made the turn.

Cruising along beneath massive moss-draped live oaks, he spotted the white-columned house ahead. *Diva.* Just like in the painting he had picked up from Anne Winston earlier that day. The historic Greek Revival mansion was in major disrepair and, at the same time, still one of the most hauntingly beautiful places he had ever seen.

He followed the gravel drive around the side of the house and pulled to a stop across from the carriage house, the place where Sean had said he and Nicole lived. Her Audi convertible was parked in a carport off to one side, so he figured she was home.

When a knock on the door produced no results, he decided to take a quick walk around, see if she was painting somewhere on the property.

Sure enough, he spotted a lone figure in front of an easel next to a quiet pond out behind the house. As he headed in that direction, he remembered a painting of the pond he had seen last night at the gallery.

Afraid he would startle her, he called out as he drew near. "Nicole, it's Lucas." She looked up and he kept walking. "I'm interrupting. I'm sorry about that, but after last night, my curiosity got the better of me. I hope you don't mind."

"Lucas." She smiled. "No, not at all." She fiddled with the elastic scrunchie around her shiny russet ponytail. "Sean will be thrilled you decided to come for a visit."

His eyes met hers. "I didn't come to visit Sean. I came to see you."

Color rose in her cheeks. "Well . . . okay, then. I don't exactly know what to say."

"Say you're glad to see me. But only if you are."

A bright, warm smile slowly curved her

lips. They were wide and full and tempting. "I am, yes. I'm glad you came."

He made a point of glancing around. "No sign of Villard. Anyone else I should be worried about?"

"No. No one else."

He relaxed a little, moved a little closer to the canvas she was working on. One of his eyebrows went up. "Not what I was expecting to see." It was the beginning of one of her dark paintings, a bleak gray dawn, made even more grim by the weeping willow cloaked in shadow, hanging over the inky-black water in the pond.

"Where did this come from?" he asked, turning toward her.

Nicole's burnished eyebrows pulled slightly together. "I don't know. I came out to paint, and when I started drawing, this is what appeared on the page." She shook her head. "I have no idea why, but I feel like there's something I need to find out. Something I need to say."

She looked up at him. "I'm sure that sounds crazy. Now that I've seen the expression on your face when you saw the canvas, maybe I should throw it away and start over."

Lucas's gaze returned to the painting. It was dark, but also compelling. He wanted to know what the painting would reveal when it was finished.

"No, I don't think you should stop. I think you need to follow your instincts. Paint what you're feeling. Tell the story that wants to be told."

"Really?"

"Yes. But that's just my opinion. I'm no artist. Maybe I'm wrong."

She pulled off the elastic band holding back her hair and shook it free, setting off ruby highlights among the softly waving strands. He wanted to run his hands through it, let the ends curl around his fingers.

"I think I'll take a break," Nicole said. "Would you like some lunch? I've got stuff for ham and cheese sandwiches. I need to make something for Sean. Might as well feed you both."

He smiled. "All right. A ham sandwich sounds good."

He followed her back to the carriage house. She was wearing stretch jeans and a sleeveless pink knit sweater. Her arms were firm, her bottom perfectly round in the tight blue jeans.

His groin tightened. No more doubt about the attraction. He liked the way her mind worked, but along with that, he had an almost-uncontrollable urge to strip off her clothes and bed her in the lush green foliage next to the pond.

Lucas jerked his mind back from where it hadn't traveled in months. He was no longer a priest, no longer celibate, hadn't been for years. But he didn't make a practice of sleeping with a woman unless there was something more to the relationship than just a means of physical release.

He walked into the carriage house, impressed with the way she had made the place into a cozy home. It was both elegant and welcoming. He sat down on a stool at the kitchen counter as Nicole took the ingredients out of the refrigerator and set them on the counter across from him.

"How are you handling the duties of motherhood?" Lucas asked. "From what Sean told me, you've never been married, never had children of your own."

She looked across the counter to where he sat. "It was difficult at first. I had no experience with kids. Sean was deeply grieving. I had no idea how to handle it. I took him to a psychologist, but Sean disliked the man, practically on sight. I tried a woman, but it didn't go any better."

Nicole set bread out on paper plates and spread mayonnaise and mustard on each slice. "I'm almost glad Sean got into trouble.

It forced him to get the help he needed. The center changed his life."

She looked up at him. "You played a big part in it. I want to thank you for that."

"I can't take the credit. It's the counselors who do the work."

"He admires you . . . admires the way you turned your life around. Your story gave him the courage to change the direction he was heading."

"I'm honest with them about my past. At least for the most part."

Her eyes found his across the counter. "What do you mean?"

He never went further, never told people how bad it really was, yet he found himself speaking. "I was raised in Lafayette. My family had money. After my mother left, my father lavished all his attention on me. He gave me anything I wanted. Fast cars, too much money, not enough supervision."

She said nothing. She was no longer making sandwiches, just listening.

"Being in a gang was a high without the drugs — although drugs were often involved. I wasn't the leader, but I was Butch's right-hand man. I'd always been strong and athletic. I was a real tough guy back then. The worse we behaved, the better I liked it."

"What happened? You changed schools and entered a seminary. I read that in the *Advocate.* Something must have happened."

He could see it in the eye of his mind. "One night, we got into a fight with a rival gang, younger guys, not as experienced. They were trying to get street cred by taking us on."

He looked at her, but instead of Nicole's pretty face, he saw images of what happened that night, felt again the horror and pain. "One of the guys in the other gang, a kid named Bobby. He was young. Should have been home with his family. Bobby got knifed in the heart. Dropped dead right at my feet."

He heard her quick intake of breath, then felt the warmth of her hand cover his on top of the counter. He looked up to see her big green eyes luminous with tears.

He swallowed. "I wasn't the one who killed him. But it didn't matter. Bobby was dead, and in a way, I was responsible. None of us were ever caught, but I was through with all of it. I asked my father to get me transferred to another high school. As soon as I graduated, I went into the seminary. I became a priest, hoping to find forgiveness for some of the things I'd done and for what had happened to Bobby that night."

As Lucas scrubbed a hand over his face, Nicole came up behind him. He turned and she enveloped him in a brief, warm hug.

"I'm glad you told me," she said softly, stepping away. "I'm glad Sean has you in his life."

Lucas shook his head. He could still feel the warmth of her arms around him. "I have no idea why I told you that. It isn't something I share very often."

"Thank you for trusting me." She gave him a watery smile and mercifully changed the subject. "Sean's outside in his man/boy cave. It's in the building a little farther down the drive. Why don't you go get him, bring him back for lunch?"

"After what I told you, are you sure I'm still invited?"

Her smile was wide and warm. "Absolutely."

Lucas left the carriage house. As he stepped outside, the air felt fresher, the sun a little brighter. He had no idea why he'd told Nicole about the night that had changed his life. Perhaps because he had read the deep understanding revealed in her paintings.

Whatever it was, he was more attracted to her than ever.

He needed to decide what to do about it.

■ ■ ■ ■

Lunch was over. Lucas was gone. Sean was back in his man/boy cave, and Nicole had returned to her easel in front of the pond.

She tried to focus on the canvas, but all she could see was Lucas, the look on his face as he'd told her the story of his past. She had sensed the darkness inside him. It was there beneath the warmth and compassion that masked the pain he still felt.

There was more to his story. She wanted to know why he had left the priesthood, why he had decided to make another life-altering change.

Along with the intriguing mystery he posed, she was wildly attracted to him. Just being near him made her heart race and her palms go damp. She wanted to see him again, spend time with him. It was a bad idea, though.

She figured Lucas must know it. She had Sean to consider. How would her brother feel if she got involved in an affair with the man who ran his school? What would the other kids say if they found out?

Add to that, she was a dismal failure at relationships. The few times she had tried had been disasters.

On the other hand, exploring the attraction she felt to Lucas might be worth the risk. After his appearance at the gallery last night and his unexpected visit today, maybe it was Nicole's turn to take the next step. She could invite him to dinner during the week when Sean wasn't at home, give them a chance to get to know each other.

But if that happened, Lucas's honesty would require her to be equally up front. Nicole wasn't ready to talk about her past.

She glanced down at the painting, at the gray dawn spreading over the canvas, which suddenly matched her mood. Picking up a brush, she began making long strokes over the surface of the black pond water. Something was emerging. Something shadowy that pulled her in. She couldn't tell what it was, but it seemed urgent that she find out.

Her hand trembled as the painting continued to draw her into the grim world she was creating.

# Chapter Seven

The house was dark and silent. It was after midnight, no hint of a moon. The doors and windows were all securely locked. Rachel had checked before she'd gone upstairs to bed.

It took a while to fall asleep. The wind was blowing, scraping branches against the windowpanes, howling against the chimneys. Even after she drifted off, she stirred restlessly on the mattress. Faint noises intruded. Unfamiliar sounds began to nudge her awake. It took her a moment to realize something wasn't quite right. The darkness was too thick, the silence too intense.

Her heart rate increased. Someone was there, someone lurking in the silent, shadowy darkness. Someone was in her bedroom, someone Rachel couldn't see.

Her pulse raced. Her heart fluttered as if it were a bird trying to escape her chest. A rush of air drifted over her skin as whoever was there moved closer. Rachel stifled a cry of fear.

"Who . . . are you? What — what are you doing in my bedroom?"

No reply, just the sound of heavy breathing. It was impossible. She had locked the bedroom door securely. No one could have entered the room.

And yet he was there. She could feel his presence like a whisper of wind in the darkness. Her heart thrummed harder. An icy chill swept down her spine.

She felt the covers moving, being lifted, sliding off her body, then suddenly jerked away. Shock stunned her. Shock and abject fear. She tried to scream, but no sound came out. She tried to move, but her limbs were completely frozen. Inside, she trembled, but her body remained immobile. She couldn't blink. Her eyes remained open and staring at the canopy as unseen hands slid her white nylon nightgown up her body. It lifted over her head and disappeared in the darkness to land with a soft *whoosh* on the floor.

Fresh fear pooled in her belly. She lay on the mattress naked and exposed, unable to move or speak. *Who are you?* The question formed in her mind, but she couldn't make her lips say the words: *What do you want?*

*I want you* . . . , the voice in her mind said softly, seductively. She couldn't have heard a reply; the silence was as dense as before, the only sound the ticking of the brass pendulum on the ormolu clock on the mantel. A hand slid up her leg, gliding from her ankle to her knee, going higher. She tried to move, tried to escape. She tried to cry out, but her lips remained locked in a soundless plea, a cry for something she didn't understand.

*Leave me alone!* she shouted in her mind. *Get out of my room!*

*You're mine!* a man's voice commanded inside her head, deep and compelling, irresistible. She felt his touch as his hands gripped her ankles and spread her legs. She felt like crying, but there were no tears.

Her mind filled with the sound of his deep voice. *I hate you for what you did to me!*

She tried to shake her head. *No! You're wrong. It wasn't me!* Then she felt his hands on her breasts, rough, calloused, kneading them, rubbing her nipples, pinching them. Silently, she cried out in her mind, and his rough touch softened, caressing now, kneading her gently. She felt the wet brush of his mouth as he began to suckle the fullness. Impossibly, her nipples tightened. Impossibly, she felt a stirring between her legs. He touched her there, began to stroke her.

*I'll make you want me.*

She didn't understand what was happening. Couldn't remember ever feeling this way before. He probed deeper, continued to touch her with exquisite care until her heart was no longer beating in fear, but pounding with desire. She could barely recall what it felt like to want a man's touch, it had happened so long ago. Still, every time his long fingers stroked over her body, the feeling stirred through her, grew a little stronger.

He moved and she felt the weight of him on top of her, pressing her down in the mattress. She could feel his thick length against the inside of her thigh. Part of her wanted to struggle, to fight him, but another, secret, long-dead part desperately wanted him to continue.

She felt his heavy length sliding deep inside her, felt a rush of pleasure that came out of the darkness without warning. Heat burned through her. Pleasure so profound, she silently moaned.

He kept moving, thrusting in and out, until the heat and the pleasure mingled, became so intense she couldn't stop the rush of ecstasy that struck like lightning straight to her core, a rush of pleasure unlike anything she had ever known. He moved deeper, took her harder, and a second wave struck; the pleasure so intense she could taste it in her mouth.

She knew when he reached his peak a few seconds later, could feel the jerk of his body, hear the cry of his pleasure in her mind. At the end, she felt the brush of his lips over hers, a soft kiss that seemed to hold a well of longing.

Then it was over, and he was gone. Rachel's control returned and her body sagged against the mattress. Her eyes welled with tears as she glanced around the room, trying to see into the darkness, though she knew the room was as empty as before.

The tears in her eyes rolled down her cheeks and she started weeping, deep, wracking sobs that shook her whole body.

Dear God, what had just happened?

It was impossible. And yet her body felt bruised and battered, her breasts achy and her nipples tingling. She was damp between her legs.

She had only been with one man, and as much as she had loved him, he had never given her the kind of pleasure she had known tonight. Guilt wiped away the last of her fear. Whatever had happened, she had responded as she never had before. She felt as if her body had betrayed her. Climbing out of bed, she retrieved her long white nightgown, pulled it over her head, and got back into bed. Every part of her felt strange, as if she were a different woman. She was both exhausted and energized as faint ripples of pleasure continued to pulse through her.

As the minutes ticked past and she relaxed deeper into the mattress, her mind ran over what had happened. She thought of how she hadn't been able to fall asleep at first; then she had dropped into a deep, exhausted slumber. It was a dream, she suddenly realized. Some dark fantasy buried deep inside her mind. Just a dream, nothing more, nothing she had the power to control. Relief, followed by a wave of exhaustion, finally claimed her, and she fell deeply asleep.

When she awakened in the morning, she lay quietly beneath the covers and stared up at the satin canopy. In the back of her mind, she remembered the dream. Both terrifying and exhilarating, like nothing she had ever felt before. Only a dream, she repeated. Just a dream that felt too real. Rachel wondered if tonight she would dream again.

# Chapter Eight

Standing on the sidelines of the basketball court in the gym, Lucas watched the game play out. Sean passed the ball to his friend Monty Holcomb, who was taller and thinner than Sean. Monty dribbled the ball, jumped, and took the shot.

"Score!" Sean yelled, shooting a fist into the air. The buzzer sounded, and the game was over.

Lucas crossed the court as the players on both teams came together. "Good job, guys. Go ahead and hit the showers. One more class and it'll be time to head home for the weekend."

He watched Sean Handley disappear out the door. Tall and smart, the kid was a born leader. Though he'd been surly and argumentative when he'd first arrived, after a few months, he had accepted his circumstances and, instead of fighting the system, become an asset to the youth center.

Lucas liked him.

He liked Sean's sister even more. He pushed that thought aside as a group of boys walked into the gym for the last athletics class before the weekend. One of them, a kid named Hugo Rodriquez, was a real troublemaker. He was shoving one of the younger boys, the smallest kid in the center, pushing him hard enough to send him sprawling.

When he'd opened the center, Lucas had learned how to deal with boys like Hugo. One thing he would not tolerate was a bully, particularly one who used his size and strength to intimidate smaller, weaker kids.

He walked over and helped the boy to his feet. "You okay, Tim?" A bruise was beginning to form on his cheek.

"I'm okay." Tim glanced over at Hugo, standing with his arms crossed over his chest. "It was an accident."

"Is that so?" Lucas turned toward Hugo and a group of his friends a few feet away, self-satisfied smirks on their faces.

Lucas managed to hold on to his temper. "Rodriquez! Get over here!"

Hugo sauntered over. "Yeah, Coach?" At seventeen, the kid was six-two, 180 pounds of solid muscle, a real tough guy in the making. Nothing the teachers had done so far had managed to change Hugo's belligerent attitude.

"Get in the ring." Lucas turned. "Osborne, get him gloved up."

Curtis Osborne, another kid Hugo picked on, broke into a grin. "Sure, Coach."

The rest of the group stopped talking and moved closer to the ring as Lucas stripped his T-shirt off over his head and tossed it in the corner. He opened a locker and took out his own set of gloves. "Monty, give me a hand here."

"Yes, sir!" Monty grinned, and the uncertain mood in the gym turned to excitement. As their boxing coach, Lucas had sparred with students, but the kids had never seen him with someone who could pose a real threat.

Lucas made it a point to work out and stay in shape. At thirty-five, he was still in prime condition. He walked over to the ring, ducked between the ropes, and headed for Hugo's corner.

"Put your mouthpiece in and your headgear on."

Hugo looked at him standing there barechested, wearing only his jeans and sneakers. They were evenly matched in height and weight. "You and me, huh?"

"That's right. Just you and me."

A nasty grin spread over Hugo's face. Lucas turned to one of Rodriquez's friends. "Jackson, get in here and referee."

The kid just nodded and climbed into the ring, went to stand in the middle. "Let me know when you're ready," he said.

Lucas shoved in his mouthpiece, met Hugo in the middle of the ring, and held out his gloves. Hugo did the same. They bumped gloves, Jackson nodded, and Holcomb rang the bell.

The fight was on. It was clear in seconds — this was no sparring match.

As Nicole crossed the parking lot, she spotted Sean madly racing toward her. He grabbed her arm and started tugging her toward the gymnasium. "Come on, sis! Hurry! You gotta see this!" He took her hand and started pulling her faster.

"What in the world . . . ?"

"Hurry up!"

As they neared the gym, Nicole could hear male voices cheering and shouting. By the time she stepped through the door, the fight was in full swing.

"Isn't he something?" Sean whispered. "I figured he could kick some ass, but I wasn't sure he could kick Hugo's ass."

Nicole flashed her brother a quick frown

at his language, but her gaze was riveted on Lucas Devereaux and his opponent, boxing in the middle of the ring. As they danced around each other, the tall, muscular teenager's darker-skinned body was drenched in perspiration. Lucas wasn't even sweating.

"That's a guy named Rodriquez," Sean whispered. "He's a real dick."

"Sean . . ." she hissed softly. "Watch your language." The school discouraged swearing, and Sean was usually good about it, but apparently, he considered this an exception to the rule.

"Mr. D is really good."

She couldn't argue with that. She wasn't sure Rodriquez had landed a single blow. Lucas hit him with a couple of jabs that knocked the kid's head back, then drove a solid punch into his stomach. With a soft *whoosh* of air, the kid doubled over.

Both men were wearing headgear, Lucas's blows just hard enough to make it clear who was in control of the fight. Lucas was pulling his punches, careful not to do any serious damage. Hugo was definitely not of the same mind.

The kid swung a powerful punch that would have done some major damage, if it had connected. He swung again, came closer, but Lucas just danced away.

Both fighters were bare-chested; Hugo in athletic shorts, Lucas in a pair of jeans. Clearly, the encounter had not been planned. Nicole tried to ignore Lucas's muscled shoulders, powerful biceps, and six-pack abs, but it was impossible to look away.

Two more jabs, followed by a hard right punch, sent Rodriquez into the ropes. He staggered and managed to get back on his feet, but he was wheeling around the ring, swaying back and forth, clearly defeated.

"Ring the bell," Lucas commanded. "Fight's over."

One of Rodriquez's friends helped him over to a stool in the corner and urged him to sit down.

"Dude, Coach gave you a real ass-whuppin'," his friend said as Rodriquez pulled off his headgear and spit out his mouthpiece.

Lucas strode across the ring, stopping in front of them. "He doesn't need to hear that from you, Montoya. Boxing's a skill. Being good requires putting in a lot of work. It has nothing to do with having a set of balls. It's a matter of technique."

He waited until Rodriquez looked up at him. "You have everything you need to be exceptionally good at this, Hugo — if you're willing to put in the work it takes to learn."

Rodriquez tugged at the laces on his glove. "You really think I could be good . . . I mean, good as you?"

"I do. In school, I was always fighting. Sometimes I even won. I was lucky enough to run across a coach who was willing to teach me the skills required to make me a damn good boxer."

Rodriquez said nothing, but Nicole could almost see his mind spinning.

"Let me know if you're interested," Lucas finished. He grabbed the white terry cloth towel one of the boys handed him and ducked out of the ring. Nicole watched as he mopped his face and draped the towel around his neck.

"We better get going," she said to Sean, and turned to leave.

"Wait up!" Lucas called out, catching up with them.

Sean paused. "That was really somethin', Coach."

Lucas smiled at Sean. "Like I said, it's mostly a matter of learning the right skills." He looked at Nicole. "I don't suppose you two would have time for an early supper before you head home?"

Nicole forced herself not to ogle Lucas's gorgeous bare chest. He had a V-shaped body, wide shoulders, not too bulky, just lean muscle in all the right places. "I don't know . . . We probably ought to —"

"Come on, sis. I wanna talk to Coach about the fight."

Her gaze went to Lucas. "Are you sure about this?"

"If you can wait long enough for me to shower and get dressed. Won't take long. You like pizza?"

"I love pizza!" Sean said.

Nicole smiled. "So do I. Looks like we're having pizza for supper."

"I'll make it quick," Lucas promised. "Be right back." He left them standing near the door of the gym.

"Told you he likes you," Sean said.

"He's probably just being nice."

"Sure, he is. I might be your brother, but I'm also a guy. I know how guys think."

"So you wouldn't mind if Lucas and I went out on a date? What would your friends say?"

Sean frowned. "I hadn't thought of that."

Disappointment filtered through her. "Well, it's only pizza, so you really don't have to worry."

Sean made no reply. Nicole figured that was answer enough. Even if Lucas asked her out, she couldn't go. Sean had to come first. She had accepted that when she had become his guardian. In return, she had been given the gift of her brother's love — and learned how to give love in return.

Perhaps she and Lucas could just be friends. More than that was a bad idea. She couldn't afford to have a man in her life while she was trying to raise her brother.

She told herself it didn't matter.

It hadn't. Until she'd met Lucas Devereaux.

Lucas walked out of the gym, his dark hair still damp, and they headed for the parking lot. He led them over to a gunmetal-gray Jeep Wrangler and they all piled in. As Lucas started the engine and pulled out of the lot, Nicole reminded herself it was only pizza, just a short trip to a place called Rosa's Italian.

"I'll get us a table," Sean volunteered as soon as the Jeep pulled up in front. He jumped out before the engine was even turned off.

Nicole smiled. Her brother had plenty of energy — that was for sure. She cracked the passenger door and started to climb out, but Lucas was already there, helping her down from the seat.

"I've been hoping for a minute alone with you," he said. "I need to ask a favor."

She looked up at him, tried not to think how handsome he was, tried to ignore the little hum of attraction racing through her. "What kind of favor?"

"If it's too short notice, it's no big deal. I should have asked when I was out at Belle Reve last Saturday."

"What is it?"

"There's a black-tie affair tomorrow night in honor of the mayor. All the Baton Rouge notables will be there. Which means some major donors to the center. I have to go. I might actually enjoy myself if you would go with me. Is there a chance you could make it?"

She wanted to go, she realized. She wanted to see him in other circumstances besides their connection through the youth center. She wanted to pursue the attraction that grew stronger every time she was with him.

"What about Sean?" she asked.

"You think he'll object?"

*Would he?* "No, but it might cause him problems at school."

"I don't talk about my personal life at the center. If you're worried about it, why don't you tell him you're doing me a favor. I needed a date on short notice, and you agreed to help."

She mulled that over. "I'd never lie to him,

but I guess that's pretty much the truth."

When the corners of his mouth lifted in a smile, a little curl of heat slid into her stomach.

"Yes, it is," he agreed.

"Okay, then. I'll be your last-minute date to the party."

"Great. I appreciate it. I'll pick you up at seven, if that's okay. That should give us plenty of time to get there."

"All right, seven o'clock. So where are we going?"

"The party's in Mallard Lakes, at Phillipe Villard's estate." He cast her a glance. "I didn't tell you?"

## Chapter Nine

It was Saturday morning. With plenty of time before her date tonight, Nicole collected her brushes and paints, determined to finish the dark painting she had started. She was just heading for the door when she heard the crunch of gravel under tires, went to the window, and looked out to see a white SUV with *Sheriff Department West Feliciano Parish* written on the side.

The car rolled to a stop in front of the carriage house. The engine went silent, and two deputies in black uniforms got out of the vehicle. Nicole thought they might head for the big house, but most of the locals knew about Rachel's condition and came to Nicole with any problems that concerned Belle Reve.

She looked back out the window, her heart rate kicking up. She prayed it wasn't a problem with Sean, but she trusted Lucas to have called her if her brother had been in any sort of trouble.

Hoping nothing was seriously wrong, she opened the front door as the two men walked up on the porch. She recognized the sheriff from his picture in the *Advocate;* he was the taller of the two, a man in his forties, athletic build, with short, thick black hair.

"Sheriff Matt Loewen," he said, introducing himself. "I believe you know Deputy Beck."

She smiled. She had met Frank Beck and his wife at a couple of town meetings after her return to Belle Reve. The house was a historical treasure. She had gone to the meetings to make sure it was safe from the likes of Phillipe Villard or anyone else who had plans to destroy it.

"It's nice to see you, Frank." He was shorter, slightly overweight, and going bald, but a good family man, and always willing to help in any way he could. "How's Sarah-Beth?"

"She's fine. Busy with the kids. I'll tell her you asked. She loves your paintings."

"That's nice to hear." She plastered a smile on her face and returned her attention to the sheriff. "What can I do for you, Sheriff?"

"May we come in? We only need a few

minutes."

"Of course." She stepped aside, her worry kicking up another notch.

Wiping his feet on the mat in front of the door, the sheriff stepped into the foyer, followed by Deputy Beck.

"Could I get you a cup of coffee or something? A bottle of water, maybe?"

"We're fine," the sheriff said. "We have some news. We're hoping you or Ms. Rachel might know something that can help us."

Her nerves continued to build. She prayed again that Sean wasn't involved. "Why don't we sit down?"

The sheriff and Deputy Beck followed her into the living room and sat down on the sofa behind the coffee table. Nicole took one of the matching chairs.

"We're here about a discovery that was recently made," the sheriff began. "Some kids were playing off Creek Road, near Bayou Sara. Their folks' places aren't far away. The thing is, the boys uncovered an old cedar box filled with skeletal remains."

She blanched. "Do you know who it is?"

"No idea," Deputy Beck said. "We're contacting families in the area, people whose ancestors go back for generations."

"The remains are that old?"

"We have a forensic anthropologist examining them," the sheriff said. "They study the box, the condition of the bones inside it, how much they're discolored and degraded. They look at the teeth, see how much wear and tear there is, that sort of thing."

"The bones are well over a hundred years old," the deputy said.

"Closer to at least one hundred fifty," the sheriff added. "Caucasian male. Age between thirty-five and fifty."

"They did some kind of isotopic analysis that can help determine the region the person lived in," Deputy Beck said. "The test confirmed he lived in this area."

"So you know he's a local."

"That's right," the sheriff continued. "We've talked to some of the old families who live here. The Villards, of course, and the Thurbers, along with other families like yours that go back generations. We're hoping someone will have heard a story that's been passed down through the years, something that might explain the bones. It's a long shot, but worth a try."

"Do you know how he died?" Nicole asked.

"Still working on it," the deputy said. "No definite answer yet."

"What will you do with the bones?" she asked.

"We'll keep them until we figure out where they belong," the sheriff said. "The department is looking for any information that might help." He glanced out the window to the big white-columned mansion. "We'd appreciate it if you spoke to your aunt. Let her know what we've found and see if she knows anything that might help us. If either of you come across anything, please let us know."

"Yes, of course."

The men rose and Nicole walked them to the door.

"Thanks for your time," Sheriff Loewen said.

"Good luck with your search." Nicole watched as they turned the SUV around and drove away. She needed to talk to Rachel, see if she had heard some story from the past that might give the sheriff a clue.

She felt sorry for the family of the man who had been lost so long ago. She hoped the sheriff would be able to figure out who he was.

She decided to wait to speak to her aunt. Rachel had seemed more tired than usual and oddly distracted. Perhaps tomorrow she would feel better.

■ ■ ■ ■

Nicole spent the rest of the day painting. It was a good way to keep her mind off her upcoming date. As the hour drew closer, and she went into the house to change, her nerves began to fray. She shouldn't have agreed. Lucas was far too attractive, and a man in her life was the last thing she needed. Unfortunately, it was too late to back out now.

At least Sean hadn't been a problem. Just the opposite. When she'd explained this morning about her impromptu date with Lucas, Sean had seemed surprisingly unconcerned. He was more interested in getting back to work on his model car collection.

Nicole smoothed the front of the outfit she had chosen, an above-the-knee navy-blue silk cocktail dress, with narrow sequined straps that left her shoulders bare and showed a bit of cleavage.

As an art history major in college, she'd won a scholarship to the Sorbonne in Paris for her final year of study. During that time, she had realized it wasn't the history of art but the work itself that called to her.

She had returned to the States, moved into Belle Reve with her aunt, and begun painting her own stylized version of Impressionist landscapes. Anne Winston was the first gallery to successfully show and sell her work, but by the end of that year, her paintings hung in galleries all over Louisiana.

She had learned a lot about art in Paris, but she had also learned about fashion. She checked her appearance in the mirror in the entry and finger-combed the auburn hair she'd left loose around her shoulders. Rhinestone earrings flashed in her ears.

"Wow, you look great, sis!" Sean stood in the living room, shirttail out, brown hair mussed as usual.

She smiled. "Thanks."

"You're gonna rock Coach's world."

She fiddled with her bag. "It's just a favor, remember? It's not a real date."

"Yeah, right."

The doorbell rang. Nicole took a deep breath and pressed a hand over her stomach to calm her nerves. She tucked her lipstick and compact into her satin evening bag and opened the door.

Warm golden-brown eyes ran over her with obvious approval. "Looks like you're ready to go."

She moistened her suddenly dry lips and nodded. "I'm ready." She turned back to

Sean. "If you need anything, Aunt Rachel is only a few yards away. I told her I was going out tonight. She knows you'll be here alone."

"Don't worry, I'm not going to sneak out and steal another car."

Lucas spoke up from the doorway. "Your sister wouldn't have agreed to go if she didn't trust you completely."

Sean's face reddened. "Sorry. I know that. You guys have a good time."

"Thanks," Lucas said. "We won't be out late, so if you're planning to commit a crime, you better get it done in a hurry."

Sean seemed to think that was uproariously funny. Lucas was smiling as he closed the door behind them. He was good with Sean, good with the boys at the center.

Dressed in a perfectly tailored black suit, a crisp French-cuffed white shirt, and shiny black dress shoes, he led her over to a classy silver Lexus two-door coupe. He opened the passenger door and waited while Nicole slid into the plush gray leather seat.

"Nice car," she said as he rounded the hood, climbed in behind the wheel, and closed the car door.

"The Jeep's for work, hauling stuff, and maybe a little time outdoors. The motorcycle's for fun. This one's for a night like this, or just comfort driving."

"Must be nice," she teased.

Lucas smiled. "Money's never been a problem for me. Lots of other things, but never money. I finally got old enough and smart enough to understand how to handle it."

Nicole was amazed once more at how easy it was for Lucas to talk about his past and be honest about himself. It was the opposite for her. For Nicole, the past was a painful subject.

As the car rolled down the interstate toward Baton Rouge, she forced herself to say something — anything — that might give Lucas some insight into the kind of person she was.

"My family used to be wealthy — back in the twenties when they bought Belle Reve from the Villard family." As she looked at him, she noticed his strong, tanned hands, the competent way he handled the car, and felt a tug of heat as she imagined those big hands sliding over her body.

Embarrassed, she glanced away, jerking her mind back to where it belonged. "You know the Villards were the original owners."

He nodded. "After your gallery opening, I was intrigued. I went online and looked up information on the history of the house.

There was an article about Villard, his family, and his current efforts to purchase the property."

"He thinks it should be returned to his family."

"What do you think?"

"Villard wants to — and I quote — 'bring Belle Reve into the twenty-first century.' He wants to completely change it. The house would lose its historical significance entirely."

He nodded. "Belle Reve has survived for a hundred fifty years. She deserves to retain her dignity."

She caught his gaze across the console. "You think of her as a woman?"

"So do you."

"I do, but how did you know?"

"The painting you call *Diva* — I bought it."

Her eyes widened in surprise. "You did?"

"I did, indeed. There seemed to be something special about the painting. I couldn't resist."

She settled back in her seat. "That's the way I felt about it. I almost hated to sell it."

The corners of his mouth edged into a smile. "I'll give it a good home, I promise."

Nicole made no reply. She was still reeling from the thought that Lucas Devereaux had purchased one of her most personal paintings.

They reached Baton Rouge, then turned down Wood Duck Drive in Mallard Lakes, one of the most exclusive neighborhoods in the city. Lucas pulled the Lexus to a stop in front of a sprawling mansion, with a light glowing in every window.

A white-jacketed valet opened Lucas's door, while another opened the door on Nicole's side. As she stepped out of the car, Lucas was there to take her arm and guide her along the concrete walkway through a sea of manicured lawn to the opulent residence that belonged to Phillipe Villard.

At least twelve or thirteen thousand square feet, Nicole guessed, maybe more — a sprawling brick-trimmed beige house, with columns and towers and turrets that seemed to go on forever.

Nicole could barely look away. "Wow! I had no idea Villard had so much money." And the man was determined to get his hands on Belle Reve. She had known fighting him would be hard. Now she knew it was going to be nearly impossible to defeat him.

"He's one of our biggest donors," Lucas said.

"Looks like he can afford it."

Lucas paused at the front door. "You know it's likely Christian will be here."

"I know. I'd rather not see him, but I'm here with you and I refuse to let him intimidate me."

"In that case, maybe you better stay close to me." Lucas gave her a look that could melt the bricks across the front of the house, and Nicole's stomach contracted.

The man was ridiculously sexy without even trying. They were friends, she reminded herself. As long as Sean lived at the center, that was all they could be.

"We'd better go greet our host," Lucas said, guiding her through the front door. The older Villard was standing in a massive two-story entry topped by a circle of stained-glass windows. A crystal chandelier cast sparkling light onto arriving guests.

"Lucas!" Villard reached out a hand, which Lucas shook. "It's good of you to come." He was a tall man, with long arms and thin fingers, a dignified man, with silver hair and a narrow face. It was his eyes that bothered her. They were a pale ice-blue color, and full of cunning.

"Thanks for inviting me," Lucas said. He turned. "With your family connection to

Belle Reve, I assume you've met Nicole Belmond."

He turned those icy eyes in her direction. "It's nice to see you again, Ms. Belmond." He extended a thin-boned hand, which she forced herself to accept.

"Your home is lovely," Nicole said, unwilling to return the same greeting.

"I believe you and my son have spent some time together. I understand the two of you are . . . well acquainted." The subtle inference they were intimately involved could not be mistaken.

Nicole's hackles went up. "Actually, Christian and I have spent very little time together, certainly not enough to become . . . *well acquainted.* You, on the other hand, I feel as if I know very well."

She didn't bother to hide the dislike she was feeling. The man was out to destroy her family home. In that moment, she resolved to do everything in her power to keep that from happening.

She cast a glance at Lucas and caught a flash of amusement in his dark eyes.

"Why don't we get a drink?" he said to her. He looked over at Phillipe. "If you'll excuse us . . ."

"Of course," Phillipe said, but his jaw looked tight. "Enjoy your evening."

Nicole made no reply.

"Sorry you came?" Lucas asked as they approached the bar, one of several set up throughout the house, which was done in a Spanish motif, with high wood-beamed ceilings and red-tiled floors.

"Just the opposite," she said. "It's good to know your enemy. This is one of the few times I've come face-to-face with him."

"You're in line to inherit the property?"

"I'm a Belmond, so yes."

He nodded his approval. "You're going to fight to keep what's yours. Good for you."

Nicole looked up at him. "You don't believe Christian and I were ever —"

"It wouldn't matter, but no, I don't. Christian isn't your type."

She smiled. "Why not?"

"Too weak for a woman like you. You would have no respect for a man like him."

"What about a man like you?"

A faint smile touched his lips. "With any luck, we're going to find out."

Before she had time to reply, he asked, "What are you drinking?"

"A glass of white wine. Chardonnay, if they have it."

Lucas ordered the drinks: wine for her, tall scotch and soda for him.

Nicole took a sip of wine. "You were a

priest. I'm surprised you drink."

"I hate to disillusion you, but priests enjoy a drink now and then, just like anyone else." He spotted someone across the room, took her arm, and started walking. "Come on, there's someone I'd like you to meet."

He led her toward a black-haired, mustached man as tall as Lucas and about his same age.

"Nicole Belmond, meet Remy Moreau," Lucas said. "Remy and I have been friends since grammar school."

Remy smiled wide enough to lift his mustache. "Mademoiselle Belmond. My friend, as always, has exquisite taste." He took her free hand and brought it to his lips. His mustache tickled and made her smile. He was attractive in a flashy sort of way, dressed in a purple shirt and expensive black suit. Onyx hair curled over the top of his collar.

"Remy owns the Four Queens Casino and Hotel down on the river."

Her eyes met his. "I'm afraid I've never been there. I was always busy doing something besides having fun."

One of Moreau's black eyebrows went up. "Perhaps Lucas will take you. You would both be my guests, of course. The Joker's Wild is a gourmet restaurant. A little gambling . . ." He shrugged and smiled. "Who knows, you might get lucky."

Lucas flashed him a warning glance, but Remy's smile just widened. She could hear the same Cajun French she'd heard in Lucas's voice, only more pronounced.

She flicked Lucas a glance. "Do priests also gamble?"

"A former priest might, on occasion, in moderation, of course. If he was with the right companion."

She could feel her heart accelerate. "Is that an invitation?" she asked softly.

His gaze met hers and she could almost feel the heat. "Only if you're going to say yes."

Remy lifted his glass. "Then it is settled! You will pick a night and I will join you — at least for a while." He looked over Lucas's shoulder. "Now I am afraid I must leave you. I need a word with our host. *Au revoir, mes amis.*"

As Remy dashed away, Lucas sipped his drink. "Villard also dabbles in the gaming business. He owns an interest in the Golden Spike. Were you aware?"

She felt a sinking in the pit of her stomach. "I had no idea. No wonder he's got so much money."

As Lucas sipped his drink, his broad

shoulders tightened. Nicole followed his gaze and saw Christian Villard approaching. In a white dinner jacket, blue shirt, and black slacks, his blond hair perfectly groomed and gleaming beneath the overhead lights, he was an extremely attractive man — until you got to know him.

"Good evening, Nicole." His gaze ran over her, pausing a little too long on her cleavage, finally moving to her face. "I thought you said you were busy."

Nicole settled her hand in the crook of Lucas's arm. "As you can see, I am."

Christian's lips thinned. He turned and introduced himself to Lucas. "Christian Villard. I saw you at the gallery opening, but I don't believe we've met."

"Lucas Devereaux, Baton Rouge Youth Center. I'm a friend of your father's. Phillipe sponsors a number of boys in residence at the center."

"Is that so?"

"There are other donors, of course, but your father has contributed a great deal to our efforts."

"I'm sure he has . . . in the past." His eyes returned to Nicole, slid over her like cold grease. The smile he gave her didn't reach his eyes. "You've never seen the house. It's quite spectacular. Why don't I show you around?"

Her hand tightened on Lucas's arm. "Maybe some other time."

"Perhaps you're right. We'll make it another night. I'm sure there are parts of the house you'll particularly enjoy. The bedroom wing is quite impressive."

At the smirk on his face, color flooded her cheeks. For a moment, she glanced away. When she looked back, she realized Lucas had a grip on Christian's wrist and was bending his hand backward. Pain leached all the color out of his face.

"Your insinuations are insulting. You owe the lady an apology, Villard."

"It's okay," Nicole said, her nerves kicking in. "I'm sure Christian didn't mean anything by it."

"Now," Lucas said, bending the hand back even farther.

"I . . . I'm . . . sorry. I a-apologize . . . if — if I said anything that might be offensive."

Lucas let go of Christian's hand. "You can go now. I'm sure you have better things to do than stay here and chat with us."

Fury twisted Christian's features. He rubbed his sore wrist. "You'll be sorry for that. I promise you." He didn't say more, just turned and strode off into the crowd.

"I can't believe you did that," Nicole said, but she was smiling.

"He deserved it."

"I know, but he might make trouble for you with his father."

"If he does, he does." His lips twitched. "As someone I know once said, I refuse to be intimidated."

Nicole laughed. "So I guess you learned a few interesting things when you were in a gang."

Lucas smiled. "More than a few, and not all of them so civilized."

Nicole's eyebrows shot up. "You call *that* civilized? You nearly broke his wrist."

"If I had wanted to break his wrist, he would have a broken wrist." He urged her forward. "Let's mingle so I can finish what I came here to do, and then we can go home."

Nicole nodded. She thought of Lucas's past, one he had learned from and turned to his advantage. She thought of his protective streak, the way he'd stood up to Villard.

It came as a complete surprise to wish that when Lucas took her home, he wouldn't leave until morning.

## Chapter Ten

Rachel checked the doors and windows, then crossed the parlor to the hall. Sean had stopped by, around nine, to check on her. They'd shared homemade chocolate chip cookies and milk before he'd gone home to bed. He was such a sweet boy.

Yawning, Rachel climbed the sweeping staircase to the second floor and made her way down the corridor to her bedroom. She locked the door and stripped off the loose-fitting jeans and T-shirt she had been wearing as she watched Ramon working in the garden.

After he'd finished, she'd felt rested enough to spend some time working in the Villard/Belmond family cemetery, determined not to let the weeds grow over the gravestones.

The day had been cooler than expected, with the possibility of a storm. As she prepared for bed and plaited her long black hair into a single thick braid, she could hear the first patter of rain on the windows. She'd be glad when Nicole got home. She always worried when her niece was on the road late at night.

Too tired to read, she turned off the lamp next to the bed and curled into her pillow. The wind was just beginning to rattle the branches of the trees against the windowpanes. The faint hoot of an owl was the last thing she remembered as she drifted off to sleep.

She awakened to the last chimes of the clock at midnight. The wind had abated. There was only deep quiet outside. The house had fallen equally silent. When the clock on the mantel stopped ticking, she glanced toward the window, but saw only empty darkness.

Something stirred in the air and a shiver ran down her spine. She turned her head as a sound in the hallway caught her attention. Footsteps, she realized, coming toward her bedroom door. Her heart rate accelerated. She wanted to call out to whoever was there, but instead she remained silent, her instincts warning her to beware.

In the darkness, she heard the door of the armoire creak open, then slowly swing closed. She tilted her head, listening, listening. Something was there. She knew it and a tremor of fear snaked through her.

Lying beneath the satin canopy, she clutched the bedcovers with trembling hands. Around her, the darkness seemed to thicken, to throb with a disturbing rhythm that matched the increasingly frantic beating of her heart.

An invisible something moved in the shadows, stirring the air, shifting it across the bed. She thought she heard footsteps moving toward her in the darkness, heavy, the kind that could only belong to a man.

Her breath caught as the mattress dipped beneath his weight, and she could feel him beside her. She knew who it was, remembered the feel of his body on top of her, moving inside her.

*I need you,* he said inside her mind, and she felt the brush of his lips against the side of her neck.

Her eyes slid closed at the gentle touch. She was dreaming again. Dreaming of the man who had taken her before.

"Who . . . are you?" she asked into the darkness. "Why are you here?"

*Why did you do it?*

Her eyebrows pulled into a frown. "I don't understand. I didn't do anything."

*Don't lie to me!*

She'd angered him, she realized, just as she had before.

*I'll make you pay for your betrayal!*

Stark fear rose inside her. She tried to open her mouth, tried to speak, but her lips were frozen. She tried to move, but as before, her limbs were completely immobile. The covers lifted and flew across the room to hit the wall and land on the floor. Her nightgown lifted over her head and disappeared, and the fear inside her swelled.

Fear and something more.

She felt his hands on her body, rough at first, then slowly turning gentle, sliding over her skin, touching her breasts, brushing over her nipples with exquisite care.

*You want me. Say it!*

*You're wrong.* The words formed in her mind, but she couldn't force her lips to move. *I don't want you to touch me!* But as his mouth covered her breast and he began to suckle, heat speared into her core, and her breasts turned achy. Moisture gathered between her legs.

*Tell me! Say it!*

She tried to shake her head, but her body wouldn't obey. When she made no reply, he turned her over, lifted her, and she could feel him behind her, feel his arousal, feel him stroking her, then sliding deep inside.

His body was solid and all lean muscle and he felt wonderful everywhere he touched her.

It was impossible, and yet her body was responding with abandon, with a powerful rush of hunger unlike anything she had known. She felt him thrusting deep, felt a heated rush of desire. She made a sound of distress in her mind and his touch gentled as if he read her thoughts, understood exactly what she needed. The pleasure built, scorching through her, so hot and sweet her eyes welled with tears.

*It's only a dream!* she silently shouted, the last of her fear fading away as her need continued to build. He knew just how to touch her, how to please her. Her body clenched, and the ecstasy of climax broke over her like a wave. Her eyes were wet, but they were tears of joy.

She knew when he reached fulfillment, felt it in the tightening of the body she couldn't see. Felt him as he moved to lie beside her, pulled her against him so they were lying spoon fashion on the bed. It was impossible and yet she could feel him all around her.

He moved in the darkness and suddenly her braid came undone. Unseen fingers spread her hair gently around her shoulders.

*You aren't her.* In her mind, she could hear

the regret in his voice.

*No,* she said. *I'm not her.*

*I'm sorry I hurt you. I thought you were her. Who are you?*

*I'm sorry,* he said again. *But I know you wanted me and I'm glad because I wanted you so much.*

She caught a glimpse of him, just a hazy, ghostly image moving away from her. Then he turned toward her, and she saw his eyes, a brilliant, mesmerizing shade of blue. He moved closer. She felt the brush of his lips over her hair.

And then he was gone.

Her muscles relaxed and she sagged on the bed, her body once more her own. She wanted to call him back, admit to him that he hadn't hurt her. And though she had feared him in the beginning, he had brought her incredible pleasure.

It was impossible, and yet it was true.

She sank deeper into the mattress, remembering the sadness in his voice, certain he would never return. She reminded herself it was only a dream, and then she started to weep.

She didn't have much time left in this life. Little time for happiness. Perhaps she could discover a way to summon the dream again.

If she managed to work up her courage, perhaps she would try.

"Hey, Sean, wake up!"

It was Sunday night and he was back at the center. Sean felt someone shaking his shoulder and managed to pry open his eyes.

"Wake up, dude! You gotta come with us."

Sean yawned behind his hand and swung his legs to the side of the bed. He was lucky enough to have a room of his own, which you got when one became available and you'd been there long enough to qualify — and had been smart enough to follow the rules. It hadn't taken him long to figure out the benefits of behaving himself.

He rubbed his face and stared up at his best friend. Monty was sandy-haired and very tall, taller even than Sean. "Are you crazy? It's after lights-out. I'm not going anywhere."

Tim Richards was also there, along with Tim's friend Curtis Osborne.

"Come on, Sean!" Monty prodded. "Get your clothes on. He's gonna be gone before we can follow him."

"What are you talking about? We can't leave. If they catch us, we'll all get thrown in juvie."

"We aren't gonna get caught," Tim argued,

a little guy with more balls than brains. "Come on, man. Monty's brother is picking us up down the block. He's gonna drive."

"I've already had enough trouble," Sean said. "Whatever you're gonna do, count me out."

Monty gripped his shoulder. "Listen, dude, Curtis overheard Coach on the phone. He's going out to some haunted house in Denham Springs. He's gonna help them get rid of a ghost."

"You know he does that stuff, right?" Tim added.

"I guess so." Sean had heard the rumors. Everyone knew he'd been a priest. But getting busted for leaving the center meant ending up in juvenile detention. He had caused his sister enough trouble already. "You guys go on. I'm staying here."

"Chicken," Tim grumbled.

"Loser," Curtis added, shoving Tim toward the door.

But if Sean didn't go, his friends would probably come to their senses and stay where they belonged.

"Don't say I didn't warn you," Sean said as the three boys stumbled out of his dorm room.

On the other hand, if the guys actually

drove out to the haunted house, he might get to hear one heckuva story.

Lucas pulled up in a cul-de-sac at the end of the road in front of a double-wide trailer, his headlights illuminating the front porch. After the half-hour drive to Denham Springs, it was almost eleven p.m.

The screen door swung open as he turned off the engine, climbed out of the Jeep, and started across the front lawn, which badly needed mowing. Grass grew between the cracks in the walkway leading up to the house.

"Thank you so much for coming, Father Luke."

He was used to the name, though he rarely heard it these days.

He just nodded. Darla Robinson, the owner of the house, stepped back so he could walk in. She was a tall, bone-thin African-American woman with dark skin and very close-cropped black hair, a single mom whose teenage son had once been a student at the center. The kid had straightened out his life, started getting good grades, and won a basketball scholarship to Louisiana State.

"How's Jaden?" Lucas asked as Darla led him into the living room.

"Boy's stayin' out of trouble, if that's what you mean."

Lucas smiled. "That's not what I meant, but I'm glad to hear it."

They sat down on an overstuffed plush brown sofa and chairs. Brown shag carpet covered the floors, and a stack of magazines sat on the coffee table, a copy of *People* on top.

"Can I get you a cup of coffee or maybe a soda?" Darla asked.

"I'm fine, thanks. When you called, you said you were having problems in the house. You said weird things were happening, some of them very scary."

"Jaden told me about you. He said that when you was a priest you could get rid of evil spirits. Said you can still do it."

How the damnable story ever got out, he had no idea, but he couldn't deny it was true. "When I was in the Church, I worked with a priest who did exorcisms. As I was learning the rituals from him, I discovered I had an ability most men don't have. It doesn't mean I'll be able to help you. First I need to know what's going on."

Seated on the couch, Darla leaned toward where he sat in one of the overstuffed chairs. "It's been goin' on for a while now, ever since Jaden moved out. I think it was happenin' before, but I was too busy trying to raise my boy to pay attention. His friends were here, people all around. It's different now I'm alone."

"So things are happening. What kind of things?"

"They come at night. When I'm in bed, I hear noises. Men talkin' and walkin' around outside, but when I look, there's no one there. Sometimes I hear these loud bangs out behind the house, down by the river."

"Okay. Anything else?"

"Oh, yeah, sure is. A couple of times, I woke up and there was a man at the foot of my bed. Well, not exactly a man. He was hazy and sort of floating, but I could see his clothes was torn and ragged and there was blood all over him. Another time, I saw a man's face with a hole where one of his eyes shoulda been. I let out a scream loud enough to bring down the house, I can tell you. That's when the face disappeared." Darla made the sign of the cross over her heart. "I swear I'm not making this up."

Lucas nodded. "I believe you. You can't imagine some of the strange things I've seen."

"I want them gone, Father Luke. Please say you'll help me."

"Have any of the spirits been aggressive

toward you? Have they attacked you, pushed you, threatened you in any way?"

"They haven't hurt me, but they sure as all hell . . ." She stopped herself. "Sorry, Father, but they sure do scare the bejesus out of me."

He felt the pull of a smile. "I'm sure they do. From what you're telling me, I don't think what's happening here is the kind of evil I'm able to deal with — and that's a good thing. They sound like your everyday ghosts, spirits who somehow got trapped here on earth. If they are, they need help getting where they're supposed to be. Let me do some research, see if I can find out what might have happened that would cause them to get stuck here."

"Can you get them to leave?"

"I'm afraid that isn't what I do, but I know someone who might be able to help."

"I surely would appreciate anything you could do."

Lucas nodded as he rose from the chair. There was nothing he could do tonight. He figured just showing up would give Darla some comfort.

"I'll do some work on this. I'll get back to you as soon as I can — I promise. In the meantime, just remember, most ghosts are harmless."

Darla ran a thin hand over her short, curly hair. "Okay, I'll do my best to remember. But when one of 'em's standing at the foot of your bed, it ain't that easy to do."

Lucas laughed. "No, I don't suppose it is."

Darla walked him to the door and waited while he climbed into the Jeep and fired the engine. He needed to do some digging. Look into the history of the area, see what might have happened that could explain events in the house.

He didn't have the ability to communicate with spirits, but he knew someone who did. With luck, his grandmother would be able to help Darla, as well as the ghosts who needed to find their way home.

## Chapter Eleven

Today was Monday. Nicole hadn't heard from Lucas since he had brought her home Saturday night after their evening at the Villard estate. That night, as promised, he had driven up in front of the carriage house at eleven o'clock, walked her to the door, and played the perfect gentleman.

If it hadn't been for the scorching kiss they had shared on the front porch, she might have figured she wouldn't hear from him again. The kiss, however, was amazing. Lips that took control, melded perfectly with hers, and stirred her up inside. Lucas knew exactly how to take the kiss from soft and sweet to deep and erotic, how to gently end the kiss, leaving her yearning for more.

The attraction that sparked between them was undeniable. It had taken all her will not to invite him in, but Sean was there, and she had a feeling Lucas would have refused even if she had been alone.

She'd spent Sunday painting, working on the dark piece she had started at the pond. A faceless image had arisen out of the water, hazy and strangely disturbing, so she had set the painting aside, unhappy with the result.

She had spoken to Rachel, intending to tell her about the sheriff's visit of the day before, but her aunt was feeling overly tired, so Nicole had decided to wait. She had driven Sean back to the youth center, then gotten a fairly decent night's sleep. This morning, she was ready to paint, but she wanted to check on Rachel first.

Nicole rang the bell, then used her key to unlock the front door, glad her aunt was developing the habit of securing the house. There was no one around when she walked inside, and the place seemed unnaturally quiet.

"Aunt Rachel? Where are you?"

The silence stretched out. Nicole checked the lower floor, then headed upstairs. At the bedroom door, she stopped and knocked.

"Aunt Rachel? It's me." She started to open the door, but found it also locked. "Aunt Rachel, are you all right?"

She could hear footsteps as her aunt crossed the room and opened the door. She was still wearing her nightgown, her raven hair unbound and draped around her shoulders.

"Are you ill? It's almost noon and you're still in bed. You almost never get up this late. Do you want me to call the doctor?"

Rachel managed to smile. "I'm fine. I just felt like resting a bit longer."

"Are you sure? You haven't been yourself lately."

Rachel looked as if she wanted to say something, then just shook her head. "If anything, I'm feeling better than usual."

"That's good to hear."

"It's a nice day. I think I'll go out and work in the garden."

"That sounds like a good idea."

But Rachel didn't start to get dressed, just stood there without moving. "I was wondering . . ."

"Yes?"

"There are things you and I never talk about. Things that seem forbidden in some way. Of course, you've never been married, but before you became Sean's guardian, I know you dated several young men. In these modern times, I assume you slept with them."

*No,* Nicole thought, *they had definitely never had a conversation like this.* "I went with Steven Wiles for almost a year after I got back from Paris. It didn't work out." *He told me he loved me, then left me two months later.* "It didn't work out with Ryan Markley, either, but I had a physical relationship with each of them." *Not particularly satisfying, but not really their fault.* "What's this about, Aunt Rachel?"

Her aunt sat down on the bench in front of her mirror. "You're a healthy young woman. Have you ever had . . . well, an erotic dream?"

Nicole bit back a smile. "I might have. If I did, I don't remember it."

"I just wondered."

"A lot of people have them, Aunt Rachel. You're still a young woman. It wouldn't be a bad thing if you had a sexual dream. In fact, it's probably very healthy." And if Nicole thought too long about Lucas Devereaux's scorching kiss, she might have an erotic dream about him tonight.

"I suppose that must be what happened to me. It just seemed so real."

"I don't think you should worry about it. I imagine it's just part of being human."

Rachel toyed with a long strand of black hair. "I could only see his eyes. I wish I could have seen his face."

Nicole grinned. She couldn't help it. "With luck, maybe you'll see him more clearly the next time."

Rachel's expression seemed to mix hopefulness with trepidation. "Maybe." As she rose from the bench, the color returned to her cheeks. She pulled jeans and a T-shirt out of a drawer and began getting dressed. "If you need me for something, I'll be working in the garden."

Nicole nodded. "Okay. I'm going back to the pond to paint. I'll see you later." As her aunt began to braid her hair, Nicole headed downstairs and crossed to the carriage house to retrieve her easel and paints. She intended to start a new painting, but at the last minute, she picked up her unfinished canvas and carried it back out to the pond.

After the conversation with her niece, Rachel felt much better. So she'd had a sexual fantasy? So what! Other women had them. In a way, it had made her feel younger, and more womanly than she had ever felt before.

Tossing her long black braid over her shoulder, she headed downstairs in her jeans and T-shirt, grabbed her big, floppy-brimmed straw hat off the hook, and walked out the back door. Ramon was off today. Her gardener only worked part-time, all she could afford. Rachel enjoyed his company, but she also liked having time to herself.

She still hadn't finished weeding the cemetery the Villard and Belmond families shared, so she continued along the gravel drive, past the carriage house, farther on down to the parcel of land that sat on a low hill beneath a pair of live oak trees, and let herself in through the black wrought iron gate.

Most people avoided a place that housed the dead, but Rachel found the cemetery peaceful. She had brought her trowel, a pair of shears, and a big plastic bag to hold the weeds she pulled.

The sun felt warm on her back as she bent over each headstone, clearing any unwanted vegetation. She was working on the Villard family plot, some of the old tombstones taller than she was. There were several stone crosses and a beautiful granite angel over the grave of a little girl named Josephine, who had died when she was six.

Rachel always wondered about the people who were buried there. What sort of lives had they led? What had happened to them? What about the little girl? Why had she died so young?

She pulled off a vine that was making itself at home on a granite marker, with a rounded top, and read the words engraved in the stone:

IN LOVING MEMORY
Francois Etienne Villard
Beloved Son of Pierre and
Therese-Louise Villard
Born February 18, 1843
Died 1878

He would have been thirty-four or thirty-five, she realized. She noticed there was no month or day of death, only the year he was deceased.

"I wonder what your story is," she said aloud as she traced a finger through the grooves chiseled into the stone.

*I am not there.*

Rachel's head shot up and she spun around, searching for the source of the words. Her heart was beating too fast as her gaze scanned the cemetery, but no one was in sight.

She looked back down at the gravestone.

*I'm not there,* the voice said again. *I am lost. Can you help me?*

She felt lightheaded, afraid she would fall over in a faint right there in the grass. She knew that voice, knew it was the man who had come to her in her dreams. Her pulse accelerated, pounding so hard she thought her heart might beat its way through her chest.

She read the words on the gravestone. "Are you . . . Francois?"

*Yes. But I am not there.*

She started shaking. She swallowed, trying to regain her composure. "You aren't real. You can't be. You're — you're dead."

She felt a stirring in the air behind her and turned. Two beautiful blue eyes stared down at her.

*"Francois,"* she whispered.

*You are so beautiful.* Today she recognized the trace of French in the words he said inside her mind.

"I wish . . . I could see you." It was all she could think to say. She felt the faint brush of his hand against her cheek.

*I feel as if I have known you for so long.* Then he was gone.

Rachel leaned back against the headstone, her breath sawing in and out, her mind spinning. It was impossible. She was hallucinating. It was the same thing that had happened to her in her bedroom. He wasn't really there. She was imagining things that simply weren't real.

Fear gripped her. She was in ill health and failing, but her mind had always been sharp. Was something happening to her brain? Was her mind starting to fail, along with her body?

She managed to push herself up off the ground, but her legs were so weak she had to grip the gravestone to pull herself to her feet.

She left her tools where they lay and managed to make it back to the house. She was exhausted, her limbs shaky, her heart still racing. In the kitchen, she poured herself a glass of water and drank deeply, made her way across the room and sank down in a chair at the kitchen table.

If she were going crazy, why were her memories so clear? She remembered every second, every instant, of the time that she and her imaginary lover had been together. Was it possible Francois was an actual spirit? What if something had happened to him and he was trapped in this world instead of going on to the next?

Was it possible? He had certainly seemed real enough when he had been in her bed.

She stared up at the kitchen ceiling as if she could see into her room. "If you're real, come to me again. If . . . you're real, I'll help you if I can."

But there was no reply.

Rachel put her head down on the table and started to cry. She was going crazy. She needed to talk to someone, get some kind of help.

But in the darkest part of her soul, she wished Francois would come to her again.

## Chapter Twelve

Nicole got a call from Lucas on Tuesday morning. He told her how much he had enjoyed their evening at the Villard estate and said he had meant to call sooner. She had wondered if she had misread the connection, but the minute she heard that deep voice, that faint, sexy Cajun accent, she wanted to see him again.

"We finally had the official opening of the new youth center, so that's one problem out of the way."

"Congratulations."

"Thank you. I know your schedule is as busy as mine, but I was wondering if maybe you could get away for a few hours this afternoon."

"I'm at the gallery, but I'm just about finished."

"You're in Baton Rouge?"

"Yes."

"That makes things easier. I need to take

a ride down to Thibodaux. Any chance you could go with me?"

The town was a little over an hour away from the city. "Does the trip include lunch?"

"Absolutely. Homemade Cajun cooking. I need to talk to my grandmother. I promise you, Grandmere is not your typical older woman. I think you'll like her."

Nicole wondered if he'd taken a lot of different women to meet his grandmother, or if she was somehow special. "I'd love to meet her."

"How much time do you need?"

"I'm ready whenever you are."

"Good. I'm on my way."

They headed south on I-10 East, down to Highway 61, wound up in Thibodaux, and eventually pulled into a neighborhood of older wood-framed houses within walking distance to a number of small businesses and restaurants. Lucas pulled the Jeep to a halt in front of a wood-framed white house on St. Mary Street.

"Grandmere has lived here most of her life," Lucas said. "I tried to get her to move to Baton Rouge, but there was no way that was going to happen."

"She sounds like an independent woman."

"Oh, she definitely is that. She's my grandmother on my mother's side. Her married name was Brumaire, but she divorced him when he made the mistake of cheating, and she went back to her maiden name, which was Lafon."

Nicole scoffed. "Well, then, good for her."

Lucas helped Nicole out of the Jeep, and they walked up an immaculate redbrick path to a covered front porch. The yard was perfect, the house freshly painted. Pink geraniums spilled out of flower boxes on both sides of the door.

"You take good care of her," Nicole said, guessing Lucas was the one responsible for the house being so well kept.

"She's all the family I have left." He knocked on the door, and a few seconds later, a tiny silver-haired woman with intelligent brown eyes and a warm, welcoming smile pulled it open.

Lucas leaned down and hugged her, then stepped back to make introductions. "Grandmere, I'd like you to meet my friend Nicole Belmond. Nicole, this is my grandmother Gabrielle Lafon."

"It is just Gabby," the older woman said, still smiling. She looked to be in her early seventies and was robust, her cheeks glowing with color. She spoke with an accent much more pronounced than Lucas's. She glanced between the two of them. "Or you may call me Grandmere, as Lucas and his friends do."

Nicole's heart warmed. "It's wonderful to meet you . . . Grandmere," she said.

The older woman seemed pleased as she led the way through a carpeted living room that merged into a dining room, with built-in leaded-glass bookcases.

Though the sofa and chairs were relatively new, the house held a wealth of antiques Nicole recognized as French: an inlaid rosewood buffet against the wall, beneath a gilded mirror; a pair of rosewood end tables. What were clearly family heirlooms — old framed photos, cut crystal vases, and crocheted doilies — added warmth and charm.

They continued into a modern kitchen, done in soft yellow tones, where the aromas of onions, bell peppers, tomatoes, and celery filled the air.

"Shrimp gumbo," Lucas pronounced, turning toward her. "The best you've ever tasted." He sniffed. "I smell boudin in the Crock-Pot."

"Of course," Grandmere said. "We will have coffee and beignets for dessert."

Boudin was a sausage-and-rice dish, Nicole knew. She had been raised in Louisiana. She loved spicy food.

They ate in the kitchen around a beautiful, old claw-foot oak table. The food was as good as Lucas had promised, and afterward, they retired to the living room for rich, dark coffee and beignets, the deep-fried dough with powdered sugar for which Louisiana was famous.

When they finished, Grandmere set her gold-rimmed porcelain cup and saucer down on the coffee table. She arched a silver eyebrow at Lucas. "Now it is time to tell me why you have come all this way."

"It isn't that far," Lucas countered. "Only a little over an hour." He smiled. "And we were hungry."

Grandmere laughed. "Well, now you are both stuffed full. I'm guessing you have a problem you are hoping I can help you fix."

Lucas flicked a glance at Nicole, who had no idea what the two of them were talking about.

"There's a house in Denham Springs," he began. "The owner's having problems. She hears voices, says it sounds like men talking outside, but no one is there. She hears noises. As she described them, they sound like gunfire. Apparitions in bloody clothes appear at the foot of her bed."

"You've looked into it?"

"Yes. I suspected they were soldiers who had died in the war, so I did a little digging.

In May of 1862, Union troops took Baton Rouge, and the Confederates fled. But the South regrouped and returned that August. The Union lost three hundred eighty-three men, while the Confederates lost even more, a total of four hundred fifty-six. As I suspected, there was fighting near Denham Springs, along the Amite River, which runs behind Darla's house."

"Darla is the woman having the problems?" Grandmere asked.

He nodded. "Darla Robinson."

"You couldn't help her?"

"It isn't my kind of problem."

Nicole sat up on the sofa. "All right. I've been quiet long enough. Are you saying this woman in Denham Springs has ghosts in her house?"

"I can't be sure," Lucas said. "I'm hoping Grandmere will look into it. She has a certain . . . gift."

"What about you?" Nicole asked, thinking of what Sean had told her.

"My talent's not the same."

"That's it? That's all you're going to tell me?"

"Let's just say, there are things in this world none of us really understand." He turned back to his grandmother. "Will you help?"

"You know I will."

"I'll set it up for tomorrow night. I'll pick you up —"

"The house is in Denham Springs?" Grandmere asked.

"That's right."

"Bud can drive me. Let me know what time, and we will meet you there."

"So you and Bud are still . . . ?"

"Don't give me that look. I'm old, but I'm not dead yet."

Lucas flashed one of his rare, devastating grins and rose from his place next to Nicole on the sofa. When he extended his hand, she took it, and he helped her to her feet.

"It was really nice to meet you," Nicole said to Grandmere, still stunned by the strange discussion. "Thank you for the delicious meal."

"It was my pleasure. I look forward to seeing you again."

Nicole said nothing. She had no idea where her relationship with Lucas was going or if this was the last time she would see him. The thought gave her a pang.

They were halfway back to Baton Rouge when she broke the uneasy silence in the car. "Did you take me there to see my reaction when I found out you and your grandmother could . . . What do you call it? Communicate with ghosts?"

"I can't communicate with ghosts."

"But your grandmother can."

"That's right. My abilities run in a slightly different direction."

She thought again of what Sean had said. "Like what, exactly?"

He flicked her a sideways glance. "Occasionally I'm asked to deal with demons."

Nicole fell silent. Lucas passed a slow-moving vehicle, giving her a chance to think, but it didn't do any good. "I have no idea what to say to that."

His eyes met hers across the console. "Say you won't let what I do, what my family is able to do, interfere with what is happening between us."

She forced herself to ignore his handsome profile and the big, strong hands controlling the car with such ease. His knuckles were large and scarred. She knew he'd been fighting since he was a kid.

"If you have those kinds of abilities, why did you leave the priesthood?"

His hands tightened on the wheel. "What I do has more to do with the things I learned while I was a priest than it does with my abilities, though that seems to heighten the results."

"All right, then why did you leave?"

They reached Baton Rouge, headed for Perkins Rowe, and Lucas turned into the parking lot of the Anne Winston Gallery, where Nicole had left her car.

Lucas parked the Jeep and turned off the engine. "Simply put, I fell in love. I was young and stupid. I knew a lot about sex, but nothing about relationships. I refused to break my vows and sleep with her, so I left the Church. Unfortunately, once the thrill of having an affair with a priest was gone, so was Marie."

When he glanced at her, she could feel a little of his pain. "I'm sorry."

"I'm not. Clearly, Marie was the wrong woman for me. I'm lucky I escaped with only a bruised ego."

"You couldn't go back?"

"By then, I'd realized the Church was no longer where I belonged. I'd have to find redemption somewhere else."

"The work you do with the boys is extremely important."

He just nodded. "I know. What I do there feels right somehow."

Nicole thought of Marie, the woman Lucas had loved. What kind of person would play such a destructive game? But she knew the answer. The few men she had dated had little regard for the brokenhearted women they left in their wake. This was the same situation in reverse.

"Thank you for telling me," she said.

"I don't enter into affairs lightly, Nicole."

She arched an auburn eyebrow. "No sex since Marie?"

Lucas just smiled. "I never kiss and tell. I might have been a priest, but I'm not a saint. I have needs, just like any other man. Discovering how human I was is one of the reasons I left the Church."

Nicole had no doubt Lucas Devereaux was all man. The thought sent a sliver of heat into her core.

"How does it work? Being a former priest, isn't having sex before marriage condemned by the Church?"

"We're all sinners, Nicole. I try to stay true to myself and just let God guide me. That's the best I can do."

Nicole made no reply. She was drawn to the inner peace Lucas clearly enjoyed, as well as his quiet strength. He was watching her, she realized, his eyes on her face.

"I want to see you again, Nicole."

Her heart was racing. She was wildly attracted to him. She wanted to spend time with him. She wanted a lot more than that. But there was Sean to consider, and her responsibilities as his guardian, the closest thing he had to a mother. And there was her track record of relationship failures.

"I have to think about Sean," she said, giving herself a way out.

"I know, and your concern for your brother is one of the things I admire about you. That, and your incredible artistic talent. I know Sean has to be your first priority. I wouldn't do anything to change that."

The conversation was making her nervous. She didn't have time for dating. She didn't have room for a man in her life. Around the place he had parked, cars were driving in and out of the lot. Nicole had work to do when she got home, and so did Lucas, but neither of them made a move to leave.

"I want to go with you and your grandmother to Darla's house," she said, changing the subject.

For the first time, Lucas looked uncertain.

"You are who you are, Lucas. If we're going to see each other, that's the person I want to know."

She caught his faint sigh as he cracked open his door and stepped out of the Jeep. Nicole was out of the vehicle by the time he reached her door.

"All right, you can go," he said. "I'll set it up and call you with the details."

"Okay."

"You need to understand, we could go out there and wait for hours and nothing will happen." His mouth edged into the faintest of smiles. "Or it could turn out to be a very interesting evening."

She wanted to say that she would be with him, so either way it was going to be an interesting evening. "I'll keep that in mind," she said.

# Chapter Thirteen

Lucas phoned Darla after he returned from his lunch in Thibodaux. He explained what he had discovered and told her he believed the spirits she was encountering were the ghosts of soldiers killed in a Civil War battle near her home.

They arranged to meet Wednesday night. Next he phoned Grandmere, then Nicole, to finalize the plan.

"Everything's all set?" Nicole asked.

Lucas felt a pulse of desire at the sound of her voice, which made him think of warm nights and satin sheets.

"When you're working with the paranormal, nothing is ever set. But we're scheduled to be in Denham Springs late tomorrow night."

"Are you picking me up, or am I meeting you there?"

"I'll pick you up."

"All right, then. So, why don't you come

over early and I'll cook you supper?"

He hadn't liked the idea of taking her into an unknown situation, but the evening was suddenly sounding better.

"What can I bring?" he asked.

"Just your smiling face . . . and . . . maybe a bottle of red wine?"

He didn't drink while he was working, but in this case, Grandmere would be doing the work. "My pleasure. Seven o'clock okay?"

"Perfect, I'll see you then."

Wednesday afternoon seemed to drag, but now he was driving down the gravel lane that led to Belle Reve, continuing a little past the big white-columned mansion, stopping in front of the carriage house. Since he was coming directly from the center, he was driving his Jeep.

Lucas grabbed the bottle of Cabernet out from behind the seat and headed for the front door. Nicole pulled it open before he had time to knock.

"Hi," she said, smiling. "Come on in."

He held up the bottle and she took it from his hand as he walked past her into the living room.

She was wearing a pair of black stretch jeans, sandals, and an off-the-shoulder white silk blouse. As she moved, her fiery hair swirled like flames around her shoulders.

His groin tightened. Lucas tried not to wonder how long it would take him to strip her out of the clothes she looked so good in. No, he definitely wasn't a saint.

"Something smells delicious," he said.

"Nothing too exciting. Roast chicken and mashed potatoes with gravy. I made a salad and Aunt Rachel made a cherry pie. She's bringing some of it over after supper for our dessert."

"Sean introduced me to your aunt at the gallery opening. We only spoke briefly, but I could tell how proud she was of you."

"I love her very much."

"I'd say the feeling is mutual."

Nicole looked at him across the kitchen counter. "Aunt Rachel is in very ill health, Lucas. She has a rare form of muscular dystrophy. It's one of the reasons keeping the house is so important. Rachel loves Belle Reve. I'm not sure she could survive anywhere else."

"Then you'll have to make sure she keeps it."

Nicole smiled, and he wanted to kiss that wide, smiling mouth. He knew the taste of her, the feel of her womanly curves pressed against him. He wanted more.

"I'm not exactly sure what's going on with her," Nicole continued. "She seems a little off somehow. I'm worried about her."

He frowned, his thoughts turning serious. "Anything I can do to help?"

"I don't know. You were a chaplain and a priest. I could mention it, see what she says."

He would help if he could. It seemed to be his calling. As Nicole worked in the kitchen, Lucas wandered around the living room. He recognized the painting sitting on an easel in the corner, the dark landscape Nicole had been working on out by the pond.

She walked up beside him as he studied the canvas, which now contained a faint image, the face of a man standing next to the water. In the painting, which was completely done in grays, browns, and blacks, the face had a distinctive pair of brilliant blue eyes. It was the only color on the canvas. The results were startling.

"Looks like your painting has taken an interesting turn. Good-looking man. Should I be jealous?"

She sighed. "No idea who that is. It's strange, I know. I'm not sure whether to stop and move on to something else or keep going."

Lucas heard soft footfalls approaching from behind them, and turned to see the tall, willowy figure of Rachel Belmond, a foil-covered pie tin in her hand. She took one look at the painting, shrieked in terror, and dropped the pie, which landed upside down on the rug.

"Aunt Rachel!" Nicole rushed toward her as she fainted into Lucas's arms.

"Put her on the sofa," Nicole instructed. "I'll call the doctor." As she pulled out her cell and hit the doctor's contact button, Rachel's eyes fluttered open.

She took a shaky breath. "Please don't . . . Please don't call him." Rachel struggled to sit up on the sofa and Nicole ended the call to help her. "I'm — I'm all right," Rachel said. "It was just such a shock."

Nicole sat down on the edge of the sofa next to her aunt and picked up her pale, fine-boned hand.

"What's going on, Aunt Rachel? What frightened you so badly?"

"Your painting." Her gaze went to the canvas sitting on the easel. "It's — It's . . . him."

"Who?" Nicole looked back at her artwork. "Him? You mean the man in the painting? I have no idea who that is. I was just working on the canvas, and the image popped into my head."

Rachel sat up a little straighter on the sofa.

"I thought I was going crazy. I told myself I had to see someone, talk to someone. A psychiatrist, maybe, or someone else. But now . . ."

Nicole squeezed her aunt's slender fingers. "Why don't you start at the beginning?"

Rachel raked back her long black hair with a trembling hand. "At first, I thought it was a dream. He came to me while I was sleeping. I thought . . . I thought . . ." Color washed into her cheeks and she glanced away.

"Just take your time," Nicole said.

"At night, I could hear him in my room. I was frightened at first, but then I realized I was only dreaming. There was nothing to be afraid of."

"Are these the dreams we talked about?" Nicole asked, thinking of the erotic dreams her aunt had mentioned.

Rachel glanced down at the hands she clasped in her lap and nodded. "Yes. Then two days ago, I was pulling weeds out in the cemetery, and I heard his voice. It was the same voice I had heard in my dreams — only this time, I wasn't asleep. It was the middle of the day."

Rachel looked at Nicole. "He spoke to me that day. His name is Francois Villard. I wasn't sure what he looked like, but he had the most beautiful blue eyes I'd ever seen." She pointed with a trembling hand. "He's there . . . in your painting. That's Francois." Rachel burst into tears.

Nicole knelt on the floor in front of the sofa. "It's all right, Aunt Rachel. We'll figure everything out."

Lucas found a box of Kleenex in the bathroom, brought it into the living room, and pressed a tissue into Rachel's hand.

Nicole glanced at him over her shoulder as she spoke to her aunt. "Lucas is here. He knows about these things."

Rachel's tear-filled gaze locked with his. "I pray that you believe me, Lucas. Francois is real — and he needs our help."

The chicken was overcooked, the mashed potatoes too dry. Lucas helped Nicole clean the pie mess off the carpet.

"I don't think I should leave her," she said as the hours slipped past.

"I think you're right. You probably ought to stay in the big house with her tonight."

Rachel overheard them talking. "That isn't necessary. I'm feeling fine now. Seeing his face was just such a shock."

They walked her across the gravel drive to the house, and Nicole helped her get settled upstairs in her bedroom. Lucas was waiting at the bottom of the staircase when Nicole finally came back down.

"Looks like I'm going with you after all," she said.

"What about Rachel?"

"Physically, she seems to be all right. She insists I go. I think . . . she wants to be alone in case Francois comes to her tonight."

"Comes to her in a dream?"

"Sort of."

He arched an eyebrow. "Looks like there's more to the story than I know. You think she'll be okay?"

"As she pointed out while we were upstairs, she's a grown woman. She doesn't need me to make decisions for her."

Lucas grinned. "I like your aunt. Let's go."

On the drive to Darla's house, they talked about what had happened to Rachel, and her story of the ghostly visitor she had encountered in the family cemetery.

"Do you believe her?" Lucas asked.

"I believe she believes it. I'm trying to keep an open mind."

"You'll need it where we're going tonight."

Nicole mulled that over. Lucas seemed to have no problem believing her aunt's tale.

"The timing is interesting," Nicole said. "On Saturday, I got a visit from the sheriff.

He came to Belle Reve to talk to me about a box of old bones some kids dug up out on the bayou. They have a forensic anthropologist working on them. Sheriff Loewen says the bones are at least a hundred fifty years old, Caucasian male, thirty-five to fifty years of age, definitely from this area. The sheriff's looking for any information that might help them figure out who the skeletal remains belong to."

"The bones have surfaced, and now your aunt is encountering a spirit. You're right, the timing is interesting."

"I haven't told her yet. I don't want to upset her any more than she already is. I'm not sure what I should do."

"Why don't we talk to her together?"

Relief trickled through her. Lucas would be there. He had once been a priest; he would know what to say. Still, she wasn't sure any of this was real, but Rachel was convinced.

Nicole looked over at Lucas. "That would be great," she said.

## Chapter Fourteen

Lucas's Jeep pulled to a stop out front of the double-wide trailer, behind an older-model Ford pickup. After they parked, Nicole unfastened her seat belt.

"That's Bud's car," Lucas said.

"Your grandmother is already here?"

"Looks that way." They both climbed out of the vehicle, and Lucas took her hand as they headed up the sidewalk.

A tall, thin black woman wearing huge hoop earrings, a long, flowered skirt, and a white blouse, came out on the porch to greet them.

Lucas introduced her. "Darla Robinson, this is Nicole Belmond. She's a friend."

"Pleased to meet you," Darla said.

"You as well," said Nicole.

Darla spoke to Lucas. "Your grandmama is here. She's in the living room with her man-friend. I told her what's been goin' on. So far, nothin's happened. It goes that way most nights, then out of the blue — things get crazy."

"We have plenty of time. Grandmere has a way of reaching them. We'll see what happens."

Lucas kept hold of Nicole's hand as he led her into the house. Grandmere kissed both of Nicole's cheeks, then introduced her to Bud, who was a big, strapping silver-haired man, even taller than Lucas. He was polite, with intelligent brown eyes, and he was clearly enthralled with Gabrielle.

They sat down in chairs around the coffee table in the living room. Darla made a pot of coffee and served them in heavy mugs she filled with the dark French-roast brew.

Grandmere asked that they stay as quiet as possible, and the room fell silent. An hour passed. Darla warmed up their coffee and another hour passed. It was almost midnight when Grandmere rose and began to wander through the house. Speaking both French and English, referring to them as *boys,* she talked as if speaking to family.

If it hadn't been for Lucas, Nicole would have doubted the entire event. She would have figured it was all a hoax, perhaps some kind of a con. If it were, she didn't see much to gain. Clearly, Darla Robinson wasn't a wealthy woman.

At midnight, a clock began to chime in one of the bedrooms down the hall. After the twelfth note struck, an eerie silence settled over the house. In the living room, no one moved or spoke. Nicole's nerves were building, had been as the hours ticked past. Anticipation seemed to burn in the air.

Then, in the distance outside the windows, Nicole heard men's footsteps moving quietly through the darkness. The soft thud of boots in the rich, moist soil was unmistakable.

She reached out a hand to Lucas, who laced their fingers together. She could feel his solid strength and it settled her. She felt safe with him, she realized. Lucas was the first man she had ever felt she could count on, an odd thought, considering how little time she had actually spent with him.

It didn't seem to matter. As long as her hand was in his, she felt as if nothing bad could happen to her.

Grandmere was still prowling the house. Nicole could hear a smattering of French here and there, along with words in English. The soldiers who had fought in the war were a mixed lot, gathered from every part of the country.

The one-sided conversation was clear enough. Grandmere was telling them the war was over. They had died in the fighting, and now it was time to move on. She told them they were loved and missed and that they should go on to where their loved ones waited.

Nicole understood enough French to know she was repeating the story to the soldiers who had lived in the area. Quiet settled around the house. Everything seemed to be going smoothly until Grandmere told them the Confederate Army had lost the war.

Then all hell broke loose.

Nicole gasped as the double-wide started shaking. The coffee table began hopping up and down, coffee mugs jumping, moving around on the top of the table. Icy shivers ran down her spine. Her heart was racing. Outside the house, she could hear what sounded like a barrage of gunfire, then the thunderous boom of a cannon.

"This can't be real," she whispered, her grip tightening on Lucas's hand.

He leaned toward her. "Losing the war was very bad news," he whispered in her ear — so softly, only she could hear.

Another round of shaking started, causing a family photo to fall off the wall, the glass breaking as it hit the floor. It took all Nicole's will not to jump up and run screaming out of the house.

As hard as she tried to hold it in, a fearful sound escaped. Lucas quietly moved his chair closer and lifted her into his lap. Nicole leaned against him, her arms went around his neck, and she just hung on.

The battle seemed to rage for hours, though it was only minutes. In the bedroom portion of the house, she could hear Grandmere's voice, soothing, concerned, but determined.

She ordered the spirits to leave the people in the house alone. She commanded them to leave the past behind and move forward. As the brave soldiers that she knew they were, they had no other choice, she said.

Little by little, the sounds outside the house died away. Darla, sitting next to Bud, seemed to be comforted by the big man's presence. Bud seemed to take all of it in stride. He was dating a woman who talked to spirits. Nicole figured this probably wasn't Bud's first rodeo.

Grandmere walked toward them, down the hall, back into the living room. Her face was pasty white, and her legs were shaking. Lucas settled Nicole back in her chair and went to his grandmother. Gently leading her over to the sofa, he urged her to sit down, then crouched in front of her.

"Are you all right?"

She looked up at him and there were tears in the brown eyes so like her grandson's. "Those poor boys. Some of them were little more than children. Too young to die the terrible way they did." She wiped a tear from her cheek.

"You helped them," Lucas said. "They're not stuck here anymore. They're in a far better place now."

"At least most of them." A look passed between them.

Some of the soldiers in the war were very bad people. Nicole doubted the future that awaited them was going to be pleasant.

Lucas walked over to Darla. "I think it's over. We'll be leaving now. Are you going to be okay?"

"I don't know," she said, looking up at him. "Right now, my brain is whirlin' around, tryin' to make sense of all this."

"I know what you mean," Nicole said, walking up beside them.

"I don't think they'll be back," Grandmere said, her face a little less pale. "Now that they know the war is over, they've got no reason to stay."

Bud came up behind her. "Let's go home, darlin'."

Grandmere just nodded. She clung to Bud

as they left the house. Lucas made their farewells to Darla, and a few minutes later, they were on their way back to Belle Reve.

"What happened in there tonight?" Nicole asked as the Jeep rolled down the highway.

"Grandmere has a gift. It seems to be handed down from generation to generation from the female side of the family. It's unpredictable. Some of us are born with an aptitude of some kind, while others have no talent at all."

"Until tonight, I never believed in ghosts," Nicole said. "I still haven't seen one, but the voices of the soldiers and the gunfire . . . seemed completely real."

"As real as spirits can be."

"How does it work?"

"I don't think anyone knows for sure. There are scientists, Einstein among them, who believe consciousness can't be destroyed, even by death, that it can exist outside the body in the form of soul or spirit."

"Is that what you believe?"

"I've seen more than the average man. I know spirits exist, both good and evil. Most ghosts are passive, like a recording of a song that plays over and over. Some are active, the kind who can move objects, create sounds, touch you, even make brief appearances in the earthly realm. Some of them are fiercely malevolent. Those are the kind I'm occasionally asked to deal with."

The information rolled around in her head. "It sounds dangerous."

"It can be. When I'm in those situations, I stand with God. I count on Him to protect me."

Nicole made no reply. This was way over her head. She wasn't sure how to deal with it.

"So there's a chance what Aunt Rachel is experiencing is real."

"Considering everything we know, I'd say there's a very good chance."

Belle Reve was dark when they arrived, no lights shining through the windows.

"You think we should check on your aunt?" Lucas asked as they climbed out of the Jeep.

Nicole thought of the spirits outside Darla's double-wide trailer. She thought of Rachel's erotic dreams, the ghost in the graveyard, and the face in the painting.

"I think she needs time to process what's been happening to her." Just as Nicole did.

Lucas walked her to the front door of the carriage house, and she realized she didn't want him to leave. Things were happening that she didn't understand. She wanted him to stay, make her feel safe.

Instead, when they reached the front door, she turned and looked up at him. "It's been an incredible night."

"Yes," he said simply. "Does it change anything between us?"

Did it? The man believed in spirits. Then again, so did her aunt. And after tonight, she was fairly well convinced they might actually be real.

"No. It doesn't change anything."

"Then I guess we're over the first hurdle." Lucas pulled her into his arms. She felt his fingers beneath her chin as he tipped her head back and his mouth came down over hers, gentle at first, then more demanding. Nicole found herself clinging to his wide shoulders, kissing him back, making greedy little sounds of need in the back of her throat.

Very gently, Lucas broke the kiss. She had never noticed the tiny gold circles around his pupils, but they were glowing with heat tonight.

"I'll call you tomorrow," he said a little gruffly.

Nicole just nodded. "Good night, Lucas."

He caught her chin, then bent and kissed her lightly one last time. "Good night, *cher.*"

He returned to the Jeep, climbed in, and started the engine. She watched as he turned the vehicle around and drove back down the lane.

Her insides were still shaking. She wasn't sure if it was from the ghost experience she'd had that night.

Or Lucas Devereaux's amazing kiss.

## Chapter Fifteen

Sean never got to hear his friends' ghost story. By the time the guys had left his room Sunday night, Coach's car was already gone. With no idea where he was headed in Denham Springs, they gave up their screwy plan and went back to their rooms.

Sean could tell the guys were secretly glad. None of them wanted to end up spending a year in juvenile detention.

It was late on Wednesday night, and only a couple of guys still in the TV and game room, when he headed down the hall of the Spartan Wing of the dorm. The Titan Wing sat on the opposite side. There were twenty rooms, most of them doubles, plus the private rooms like the one he had, making a total of thirty kids in the center.

He smiled. At least he had some privacy. The smile slid off his face at the sight of Mickey Dugan sitting on his narrow bed.

Sean quickly closed the door behind him.

"What are you doing here? Are you crazy? What if someone sees you?"

Mick shrugged. "I just dropped by for a visit. No big deal."

"You're going to get me in trouble, Mick. Get out."

"You're already in trouble, Sean." Mick rose from the bed, a skinny guy with stringy brown hair and a bald spot on the back of his head. He walked over and draped an arm around Sean's shoulders. "Why don't we take a little walk outside? I'll explain things."

"It's almost lights-out. You need to leave right now."

"All right, fine, we'll talk right here." Mick pulled out the chair in front of the desk, spun it around, and straddled it.

Sean forced himself to ignore the nerves building inside him. "What do you want, Mick?"

"What do I want? It's not what *I* want, Sean, it's what the boss wants."

*The boss.* Sean didn't know his name, but he was the guy at the top of the organization, and no one ever went against him.

"So here's the deal," Mick said. "You owe us two cars, and the boss wants you to get 'em for us."

"No way. I'm not stealing for you again."

"Oh, I think you will. Your friend Artie got paid half in advance for four cars — your share and his — but you're the only one who delivered. That means you still owe us two more cars."

"Artie took the money and ran. I'm in here because of him. Artie is the one who owes you, not me."

"Well, the boss doesn't see it that way. Someone has to pay. You bring us two more cars and you're out. If you don't — it's going to be your sexy sister who pays."

Sean could feel the blood draining out of his face. "You leave my sister out of it."

Mick shook his head. "All that gorgeous red hair and a body that makes a man hard just looking at it. Not a chance. You don't do what we tell you, your sister's got a date with Bruno and the boys."

Nausea rolled in his stomach. He'd heard some of the things Bruno had done. He enjoyed hurting people, especially women.

"Why now?" Sean asked. "Why did you wait so long to come after me?"

"We didn't need you till now. We got some monster stuff coming in. Big convention in town. Big-dollar cars — and I mean *big*. You're young, but you're a damn good driver. You bring us two more cars — two quick runs — your debt is paid. You don't do it . . ." He shrugged. "You know what's gonna happen."

Sean said nothing. He didn't want to imagine what they would do to Nicole.

"We've got some time yet," Mick said. "Convention's not happening for a while. I'll be back to let you know when we're gonna need you."

Mick strolled to the door, checked the hallway, and stepped out of the room. As Mick's footsteps faded, Sean realized he was sweating. A few seconds later, the lights-out warning flashed.

Sean held his breath, praying Mick had gotten out of the building and left the grounds before anyone had seen him. Time ticked past. When no one came to his door, he figured for now he was safe.

He sank down on the bed, his heart still beating too fast. Why had he ever listened to Artie? He knew the guy was trouble. But Artie had offered him a way to make money and he figured he might need it if things didn't work out with his sister.

He'd been an idiot. He'd been mad at the world for taking his parents away from him. He was so damned lonesome, so depressed. His dad had been a mechanic who specialized in high-end imported automobiles. They both loved fast cars. His dad had taught him to drive.

The idea of stealing super-expensive vehicles was a real turn-on. It was the first time he'd felt alive since his parents died. His first two cars had gone down without a hitch, a Mercedes S 580 and a Porsche Cayenne. He'd gotten paid for those two and stashed the money. Most of it was still in a can buried in the yard behind his old house. He'd stayed there with an older cousin until his sister had been able to get the paperwork approved to claim him. Maybe he could go back there, find the money, and give it to Mick; then they would leave him alone.

His stomach churned. It would be impossible to leave the center long enough to retrieve the money, and even if he did, the amount they'd paid him was only part of what he owed, and nothing compared to the hundreds of thousands the cars were worth when they were sold.

*It's only two cars,* he told himself. He could do it. He'd have to. He just needed to make sure he didn't get caught this time.

Nicole stood at the kitchen sink that Friday morning. She hadn't heard from Lucas since their trip to Darla Robinson's house. Which meant she still hadn't told her aunt about the sheriff's visit.

She wanted Lucas to be there, which meant she had to call him to set up a time when they could get together. But calling a man she was attracted to was something she didn't want to do. Lucas was an extremely good-looking, virile male. She'd seen the way women looked at him. Would he think she was being too forward, pushing him to come out to Belle Reve just so she could see him?

She told herself it didn't matter. They weren't actually dating. And her aunt's condition was more important than the embarrassment she was bound to feel.

With a breath for courage, she pulled out her cell and hit his contact number. Lucas picked up on the second ring.

"Nicole," he said as her name popped up on his screen. "Everything okay?"

"I'm sorry to bother you, Lucas. I was hoping you'd still be willing to come out when I talk to my aunt about the sheriff's visit." She held her breath, praying she hadn't sounded too eager.

"Of course," he said. "I should have called sooner. Sometimes things around here just get so darned hectic I lose track of time. It's Friday. Why don't I save you a trip to Baton Rouge and drive Sean home for his weekend visit? We could all have supper together. Afterward, we could talk to Rachel."

A breath eased from her lungs. "Yes, that would work."

"You cooked last time. I'll bring supper and do the cooking. What do you say?"

She relaxed even more. "You know how to cook?"

"I've been a bachelor for a long time, *cher.*"

The endearment washed over her. Nicole found herself smiling. "Sounds wonderful."

"All right, then, I look forward to seeing you tonight."

As the call ended, Nicole felt both relieved and nervous. She began to worry about the implications of Lucas driving Sean home, then staying for supper. How would Sean react?

And what could she say to Rachel about the skeletal remains the sheriff had found — and the ghost that might or might not be haunting Belle Reve?

With a sigh of resignation, Nicole walked over and picked up her easel, paints, and brushes. The phone call had set things in motion, and there was no turning back. She'd just have to deal with whatever came.

In the meantime, she needed to paint. The world disappeared when she was immersed in her craft. As she carried the unfinished canvas and supplies toward the pond, she pushed aside all her doubts and fears. Setting the unfinished canvas on the easel, she looked into the image she had painted above the water — a face with the bluest eyes she had ever seen.

A chill went through her. She had no idea why she had painted the man's handsome face. Dear God, she was beginning to wonder if she could be more like her aunt than she'd thought. It seemed as if lately, it was getting harder and harder to tell reality from fantasy.

Nicole took a steadying breath and thought of Lucas, remembered his quiet strength. Picking up her paintbrush, she studied the dark images on the canvas and went to work.

# Chapter Sixteen

Sean stood next to the boxing ring as Coach Devereaux finished giving Hugo his first boxing lesson. Hugo had always been sullen and bitter. Today, even with Hugo's mouthpiece in and wearing his headgear, it was clear he was grinning. Sean could see his eyes shining as he danced around the ring.

After practice, both of the boxers removed their headgear and mouthpieces.

"You did good today," Coach said. "I told you, you had a natural ability. You're learning to make defensive moves that actually work. Like I said, you're doing really well."

Hugo's eyes gleamed. "Think I could ever go pro?"

Hugo was a poor kid who came from a broken home. Sean knew Coach had brought him in on a scholarship sponsored by the center. Up until now, he'd been a real a-hole, but Coach had a way of reaching even the toughest kids.

Coach slapped Hugo on the back. "Life is full of possibilities, Hugo. You just have to be ready when an opportunity arises."

Coach crossed the floor in Sean's direction. "Soon as I shower and dress, we're out of here."

"Okay." Coach would be driving him home and staying at Belle Reve for supper. Sean wasn't sure how he felt about that.

Lucas Devereaux was a real babe magnet, though he didn't seem to get it. Or maybe he just wasn't interested. He was interested in Nicole. Sean just hoped the other boys didn't find out. If they said bad things or called his sister names, he'd have to defend her, and though he was bigger than a lot of the kids, some of them were real badasses.

Worse yet, being around Coach made him feel guilty about the crime he was about to commit. He didn't want to do it. He wasn't the same kid he'd been before.

But if he refused, it was going to bring trouble to Nicole. If he did it and got caught, it was also going to bring trouble.

*Maybe the boss will change his mind about me. Maybe he'll decide to let it all just fade away.*

Sean's stomach knotted.

*Yeah, and maybe pigs could fly.*

■ ■ ■ ■

Lucas drove the Jeep up the lane to Belle Reve. Several cars were parked in front of the big house; one was a truck with a HANDY DANDY PLUMBING sign.

"I wonder what's going on," Sean said.

The boy had been quiet during the whole trip from the youth center, and he seemed to have spent more time in his room over the past couple of days. Lucas hoped it wasn't because he was seeing Sean's sister.

He didn't want to stop seeing Nicole. He'd been drawn to her from the start. Her gorgeous red hair and sexy figure would attract any red-blooded male and he certainly wasn't immune. But it was more than that. She was a talented artist, one whose paintings moved him, gave him a glimpse of the woman she was inside.

Nicole was smart and talented. And the more time he spent with her, the more he wanted her. He'd told her he didn't enter into affairs lightly and it was the truth. He wanted more from Nicole Belmond than a one-night stand or a few nights in her bed. He hoped she wanted more, too.

Lucas had a strong feeling this was the path he was supposed to follow. He was determined to find out where it led.

They got out of the Jeep to the sound of hammering and occasional swearing inside the main house. The front door stood open, and he and Sean both headed in that direction.

Nicole walked out the door in a pair of jeans, wet above the ankles, and a paint-smeared T-shirt, her hair pulled up in a ponytail. She glanced down at her watch when she saw him and her cheeks turned pink.

"Lucas! I'm sorry, I didn't realize it was getting so late."

"What's going on?"

"A water pipe broke in one of the upstairs bathrooms. It filled the room and leaked through the ceiling. The plaster fell down on the room below. It's a real mess."

"Anything Sean and I can do to help?"

Sean's head came up. He seemed surprised he would be included.

"The plumbers are here. They're working on it. We'll have to get plasterers and painters out here next week."

"Gonna cost a lot of money," Sean said.

"Yes, unfortunately, it is." Nicole walked over and hugged him. "You don't have to worry. We'll manage."

"Where's Aunt Rachel?" Sean asked as

Nicole stepped away.

"She's talking to the plumber; then she's going upstairs to change for supper. She'll be over as soon as she's finished."

Lucas made eye contact, silently asking whether she had told Rachel about the bones. Nicole faintly shook her head and started walking toward the carriage house.

"Sean, help me get the groceries out of the Jeep," Lucas said.

The boy nodded. They each grabbed a bag and started toward the carriage house. Once inside, Lucas set cans of tomato sauce, fresh tomatoes, mozzarella cheese, and angel-hair pasta on the kitchen counter. A few tins of spices, salad makings, and a bottle of Chianti came out of another bag.

Nicole surveyed the groceries and arched a dark red eyebrow. "Italian? From a Frenchman? I was expecting something more like coq au vin or beef bourguignon."

"Next time," Lucas said, smiling as he looked around the kitchen for the pots and pans he needed.

"I love Italian," Sean said.

Nicole smiled. "Me too." She helped him locate the necessary cookware, then began setting the table with red placemats and colorful red-checked napkins.

"Mind if I go out to my shop till dinner's

ready?" Sean asked.

Nicole just smiled. "We'll let you know when it's time to eat."

The boy slipped away as Lucas continued his supper preparations. "Anything going on besides household repairs?" he asked.

"Way too much at the moment. Or at least that's how it feels." They talked for a while about the sheriff's visit and what to tell Rachel about the bones that had been found.

"It all fits together with what Aunt Rachel told us," Nicole said.

"Which ties in with your painting. How's that coming along, by the way?"

"I worked on it today before disaster struck at the big house. The easel is sitting in the living room. Come, take a look."

He left the spaghetti sauce simmering and went into the living room. The face in the painting was clearer, an incredibly handsome man with high cheekbones and thick black hair.

He walked back into the kitchen, picked up the wooden spoon, and continued stirring his sauce. "You think the man in your painting is the guy they found in the cedar box?"

"I have no idea," Nicole said. "If it's Francois, maybe we could get the sheriff to let us bury him in his rightful place. I mean, if my aunt is correct and he isn't already in there." She sighed. "But I guess we'd have to dig up his grave to find out."

"Even if we do all that and manage to put his bones in their proper resting place, that might not be enough to make him leave."

"What? Why not?"

"I think finding the bones is what set all this in motion. Francois never haunted Belle Reve before. At least not that we know of. Right?"

"Right."

"Usually, the spirit remains on the earthly plane for a reason. In this case, maybe he wants to know what happened to him. How he ended up forgotten in some wooden box. Or maybe he wants other people to know. Until he has the answers, he might refuse to leave."

Nicole fell silent. There was just so much to take in. She finished setting the table and walked up to the kitchen counter. "Aunt Rachel should be here any minute. What are we going to tell her?"

"I'd say your best bet is to tell her the truth. As she said before, she's a grown woman. I know she's ill and physically fragile, but I think she's strong enough to handle the information."

"You're right. We'll talk to her as soon as

it feels right. The news is going to upset her. I'll tell Sean the whole strange story tomorrow. He already believes you can get rid of demons. Believing there's a ghost haunting Belle Reve shouldn't be much of a stretch."

"How about you? How are you doing after your run-in with the spirits at Darla Robinson's trailer?"

"I don't know. None of it seems real."

He walked around behind her, slid his arms around her waist, and pulled her back against him. "I'll show you what's real." Pulling the rubber band off her hair, he pushed the heavy strands aside and kissed the nape of her neck. Lucas didn't miss the tremor that ran through her body.

"Just something for you to keep in mind when Sean's back in school and I call you next week."

Nicole turned into his arms and looked up at him. "Maybe we should just be friends, Lucas."

He leaned down and kissed her, didn't stop until she melted against him, and her arms went around his neck. "Friends," he repeated. "With benefits?"

"I . . . I don't know. Maybe."

"I'm already your friend, Nicole. I want more than that."

A light knock sounded at the front door before she had time to reply. Lucas let her go and stepped away as her aunt opened the door and walked into the carriage house.

Rachel was a beautiful woman, Lucas thought, as he had before. Both Belmond women were amazing in more ways than just their good looks.

Lucas planned to find out a lot more about the younger one.

Rachel was exhausted. The bill for the water damage repairs was going to be huge. Even more upsetting, she had overheard the plumbers' comment that it looked like someone had been messing with the pipes, loosening them under the sink so they would leak. Who would have done something like that?

Someone trying to force her to sell Belle Reve.

She couldn't tell Nicole. It had to be Phillipe Villard, and the two of them were already oil and water. Nicole might do something rash and end up in trouble.

They already had enough trouble as it was.

She forced herself to smile as she walked into the kitchen of the carriage house. Lucas Devereaux was there, the best thing that had happened to Nicole in years. And to Sean. Lucas was just the sort of man both of them needed in their lives, a man who gave his support and affection easily, something Nicole desperately needed, though Rachel doubted her niece would admit it.

Nicole pushed men away. She didn't trust them or her own feelings.

Rachel thought of Francois and her unexpected feelings for him, and a lump formed in her throat. There had been no sign of his presence since that day in the cemetery. It was insane to wish a ghost would visit her again.

She exchanged hugs with Nicole, and Lucas bent and kissed her cheek.

"Supper in a few minutes," he said, stirring a skillet full of sauce with a wooden spoon. "How about a glass of Chianti?"

"Yes, that sounds good." She didn't drink much, but an occasional glass of wine helped her relax, and she certainly needed to relax tonight. Lucas poured all three of them a glass, and Rachel wandered into the living room.

She went dead still at the fully formed face in Nicole's dark painting. Somehow, she had known he would be very handsome. With his electric blue eyes and high cheekbones, this man was beyond good-looking. He was beautiful. Like a dark-haired Renaissance angel.

She reached out to touch him, trying not to think of the intimacy that had passed between them. She was older than he was. Perhaps he no longer desired her.

She forced the thought away. She was daydreaming about a ghost, not a live human being. The aroma of spaghetti sauce drew her back to the kitchen.

"The sauce is simmering," Nicole said. "We've got a few minutes. Let's go sit down. There's something you need to hear."

*More bad news?* Rachel thought. Bracing herself, she returned to the living room and they all sat down.

"The sheriff was here about a week ago," Nicole began.

"Sheriff Loewen?"

"Yes."

"What did he want?"

"He came to tell me about the skeletal remains of a man that were found off Creek Road, near Bayou Sara." She told Rachel the age of the bones and other clues. Combined with what Rachel had said about the writing on the tombstone in the cemetery, and the face in the painting, the discovery seemed to suggest the bones could belong to Francois.

Rachel's throat closed up. The thought of the beautiful man in the painting, abandoned and left to rot in a wooden box buried in the middle of nowhere, made her whole body ache. Rachel made a keening sound and bent over to block a sudden surge of pain.

Nicole sat down beside her and slid an arm around her waist. "If it's him, we're going to fix it." She turned. "Right, Lucas?"

Lucas crouched on the floor in front of Rachel, reached over, and took hold of her icy hand. "There's a good chance that finding the bones set all of this in motion. If it's Francois, he's here for a reason. We're going to figure out what that reason is and help him find his way to where he's supposed to be."

Tears burned Rachel's eyes and ran down her cheeks. "You can do that?"

"No, but it looks as if he's reaching out to you. If he's chosen you, once we have the information we need, *you* may be the one who can help him get on with his journey."

Rachel made no reply. How could she tell Lucas or anyone else that she didn't want Francois to leave?

"I'll do whatever I can," she said, fighting

down the terrible grief she was feeling inside.

"What would you think about digging up the grave in the cemetery with Francois's headstone on it?" Nicole asked. "You don't think he's in there. I think we need to be sure."

"I . . . I don't know. Wouldn't we need some kind of permission?"

"Technically, we'd have to convince the sheriff's department to get a warrant to exhume the body," Lucas said. "That might take a while."

"If Villard finds out what we're doing," Nicole said, "he'll likely do everything in his power to stop us. He'll do anything to cause us trouble."

Rachel straightened on the sofa. "We can't let him succeed. We need to dig up the grave and see what's inside." But Rachel already knew what they would find. Francois had told her he wasn't there.

Lucas started nodding. "Let's do some research, see what we can find out. If the grave is empty, we try to find out what happened to Francois."

"Find out why he ended up in a wooden box in the middle of nowhere," Nicole added.

Rachel made a sound of despair in her

throat. The pain was back. She didn't want to think about what might have occurred.

"We'll find out what happened," Lucas said gently. "And then we can help him go on to where he's supposed to be."

"When are we going to do it?" Rachel looked at her niece.

"The sooner, the better," Nicole said.

Rachel nodded, took a deep breath, and pasted on a smile she didn't feel. "All right, now that all that's settled, I'm getting hungry. How's supper coming?"

Lucas squeezed her hand as he rose to his feet. "Almost ready. I hope you like spaghetti."

"I love it." If she could manage to swallow a bite of Lucas's delicious-smelling meal.

"I'll go get Sean," Nicole said. "Maybe you could help Lucas dish up the plates."

"Of course," Rachel said, grateful the painful conversation was over, anxious to finish supper and get back to the house.

Praying Francois would come to her again.

If only in her dreams.

## Chapter Seventeen

It was Monday night, almost lights-out. Sean was back in school, hunched over his desk, trying to concentrate on his homework.

Yesterday was Easter Sunday. Sean, Nicole, and Aunt Rachel had attended the early-morning service at Our Lady of Mount Carmel, a little white church, one of the oldest in St. Francisville.

Aunt Rachel usually cooked, but she wasn't feeling well. Nicole baked a ham, served it with cranberry sauce, mashed potatoes, and gravy, and Sean's favorite chocolate cake with chocolate icing for dessert.

Aunt Rachel had left as soon as they'd finished eating. She seemed to be growing weaker right in front of his eyes. He and Nicole were both worried about her.

Sean thought of the story Nicole had told him: how out near Bayou Sara, someone had found in a wooden box the 150-year-old bones of a man. The weird part was his aunt believed the dead guy in the box was haunting Belle Reve.

The crazy story had distracted him for a while, but over the Easter weekend, he'd had plenty of time to think. By the time Nicole had driven him back to Baton Rouge, he had made a decision. He loved his family, even if sometimes they seemed a little crazy. He wasn't going to steal cars for anyone, not even for *the boss*. Whatever it took, he would find a way to pay the man back.

Sometimes Coach helped kids get an outside job after school. A student had to have a spotless record, which, at the moment, Sean did. He'd stayed out of trouble, studied hard, and done his best to make his sister proud of him.

If he was caught stealing, all his efforts would go down the drain. He'd be in juvie, and Nicole would feel like it was her fault. He owed her too much to let that happen.

After his parents had died, Nicole was the only person who'd offered to take him in. His cousins didn't give a big rat's ass about him — and there was no one else.

He'd been a real dick at first, blaming everyone else for his troubles. He'd been a rude smart-ass, but Nicole had never given up on him. She'd helped him turn his life around, and he wasn't going to fail her.

He went to see Coach the following morning, nervous by the time he knocked on the office door.

"Come on in." Sitting behind his desk, Coach glanced up as Sean walked in. He rolled back his chair. "Sean, what can I do for you?"

"I need a job, Coach. I know you do that sometimes, help kids get after-school work."

"Take a seat and tell me what's going on."

Sean sat down in one of the metal chairs in front of the beige metal desk. A couple of metal file cabinets sat against the wall next to the brown leather sofa Coach slept on sometimes when he worked late, and there was a tiny bathroom with a shower. A shelf filled with boxing trophies, along with pictures of Coach with some of his friends, lined another wall.

"So, why do you want a job?" Coach asked.

Sean didn't want to lie, but he couldn't tell the truth — that the men he'd worked for wanted him to steal two more cars.

"I want to help out at home," he said. "The repairs on Belle Reve cost a lot. I want to be able to help."

"Have you talked this over with your sister?"

"I was hoping I could just make some money and give it to her. I know I meet the criteria: no demerits, B plus average, no problems since I came here. What do you think?"

"I think you'd be a good candidate. I think you'd work hard and do a good job. I might be able to make it happen."

"I'd really appreciate it."

Coach propped an elbow on his desk. "I'll tell you what. I'll make some calls, see what I can do."

Relief rolled through him. Coach rose behind his desk, and Sean stood up, too.

"Thanks, Coach." Sean had a feeling Coach would find him a job. As soon as he knew for sure he'd have money coming in, he'd talk to Mick. It wouldn't be easy to convince them. The boss would rather have the cars. But stealing was no longer an option. Somehow, he'd find a way out for him and his sister.

It was Tuesday afternoon when Nicole got a call from Lucas, the first she had heard from him since last week.

"Am I catching you at a bad time?" he asked.

There was no bad time when it came to Lucas. "No, not at all."

"I was wondering if you might be free tonight. I thought I could drive up and take you to dinner. I want to talk to you about Sean, but mostly I just want to see you."

The words sent a little thrill buzzing through her.

"Is there a problem with Sean?"

"Not that I know of. Say yes and we'll talk about it tonight."

She wanted to go. Of course, she did. She told herself she was Sean's guardian — she really didn't have a choice.

"All right. Dinner sounds good."

"You pick the place — somewhere nice where we can talk — and make a reservation. I'll be there at seven to pick you up."

"Seven's perfect. I'll see you then."

Nicole spent an hour trying to decide what to wear. It was ridiculous. It was only dinner, and Lucas was there to talk to her about her brother. In truth, she was tired of lying to herself, tired of being controlled by the past. She was fiercely attracted to Lucas Devereaux. She wanted to see where that attraction might lead.

She chose an off-the-shoulder dress made

of soft, flowy fabric in a rich olive-green color. The belt at the waist was stretchy, with a small gold buckle. Gold hoop earrings and heeled gold sandals finished the look.

Lucas showed up right on time, as she had known he would. She had made a reservation at the Saint, located in the St. Francisville Inn, one of the town's historic homes. The restaurant was quiet and charming, with high ceilings and antique furnishings, candlelight and linen-draped tables, one of the finest restaurants in town.

"Nice choice," Lucas said as the hostess seated them in one of several intimate dining rooms and took their drink orders, a glass of Cabernet for each of them. "You look beautiful, by the way. In case I forget to tell you later."

*Later.* A nervous twinge combined with a feeling of anticipation. Nicole smiled up at him. "Thank you."

Lucas looked beyond gorgeous. Tall and solid, with a pair of wide shoulders and narrow hips that perfectly filled out the white dress shirt and black slacks.

"You said you wanted to talk about Sean," Nicole reminded him as the drinks arrived.

"I do, but mostly that was an excuse to take you to supper."

A slice of warmth curled in the pit of her stomach. The server returned with their glasses of wine and took their orders, steak for Lucas and redfish in cream sauce for her.

"Sean wants me to get him a job after school," Lucas said. "He hasn't been in any trouble since he arrived, and he's one of the center's top students. I have some contacts. I'd be happy to vouch for him. It would only be a couple of hours a day during the week, but I'd like your opinion before I go any further."

Sean had a small allowance, the amount the youth center suggested. It never occurred to her that he might need more.

"Do you think Sean having money of his own could be a problem?" she wondered.

"If it is, it's one he's going to have to deal with after he gets out."

Which was less than six months away.

"I think it might be good for him," Nicole said. "Make him feel more independent."

Lucas nodded. "That was my thought as well."

Dinner was served and the food was delicious. They made light conversation and shared bread pudding for dessert. Nicole relaxed more and more as the evening progressed. Lucas had a way of doing that to people.

Now it was time to go home.

Nicole's nerves built as the silver Lexus rolled back toward Belle Reve. Did she have the nerve to invite him in for a drink or a cup of coffee before he made the drive back to Baton Rouge?

Rachel would be in bed by now. The lights were all off in the big house as the car approached. Lucas parked in front of the carriage house. Rounding the vehicle, he opened the passenger door, then escorted her up to the front porch.

It was now or never. "I know it's late, but would you like to come in for a brandy or a cup of coffee?"

Lucas's gaze slid over the curves the soft material of the dress revealed, and his eyes turned dark. His hands wrapped around her waist.

"I don't need brandy or coffee. I don't need anything but you." As he pulled her against him, his mouth came down over hers.

Nicole gripped his shoulders. For a moment, she stood immobile, then her body softened into his and her arms slid around his neck.

The kiss lengthened and deepened. Heat

flashed through her, stunning in its force. Every synapse in her body was hopping, passing signals to other parts of her body. She was moaning, pressing herself against him, when Lucas gently ended the kiss.

## Chapter Eighteen

"Give me your key."

Nicole fumbled in her purse to find it and hand it over.

Lucas took the key, let them into the house, and closed the door. She wasn't sure what to say, what to do. It had been years since she'd felt any real desire for a man, and she'd never felt this kind of heat.

Her nervousness swelled. She wanted him to kiss her again. Wanted him to hold her. She just plain wanted him.

He must have sensed her uncertainty because he pushed her up against the wall and his mouth claimed hers once more. Nicole made a little sound in her throat as damp heat pulsed through her. Her nipples turned hard where they brushed against his white dress shirt.

He nibbled the side of her neck. "Stop me now if this isn't what you want."

She could barely swallow, barely form the

words. She wanted more of him, not less, wanted to follow where he was leading, but she didn't know how to ask. Since she wasn't sure what to say, she just went up on her toes and kissed him.

Lucas growled low in his throat and kissed her back — hot, wet, and deep. Heat raged between them. Reaching behind her, he unzipped her dress and slid it off her shoulders; popped the clasp on her bra, slid it off, and tossed it away. His hands cupped her breasts, and her knees went weak. Lucas's arm went around her waist to hold her up as he bent his head and took the fullness into his mouth.

Nicole made a soft sound in her throat and Lucas swept her up in his arms. "Where's your bedroom?"

"Down the hall on your right." As he started in that direction, doubt gripped her. She wasn't a virgin, but suddenly she felt like one. It had been so long — and it had never been very good. She thought of Sean and how he would feel if he found out she was sleeping with the man who ran his school, a man he practically idolized.

Her stomach knotted.

Lucas carried her into the bedroom and set her on her feet; then he bent and took off her heeled sandals. Pushing the dress down over her hips, he left her in only a plain white thong. As he started unbuttoning his shirt, she sat down on the edge of the bed and crossed her arms over her bare breasts. As his shirt fell open, she caught a glimpse of the tantalizing muscles on his chest; then he paused.

He must have read the nerves building inside her, making her mouth feel dry and her heart pound for an entirely different reason than the lust she had felt before.

"I can stop right now," he said. "If that's what you want. Is it?"

She swallowed, her arms still over her breasts. "No . . . Yes . . . I don't know." She pressed her lips together. "I'm sorry, Lucas. I'm not the type of woman who would lead you on and then say no. It's just that . . ."

He reached down and his hand cradled her cheek. "Tell me, *cher.*"

Her eyes burned. This wasn't supposed to be happening. "You said you knew a lot about sex, and, well, I don't. Every time I've been in an intimate relationship, it's been a disaster." Her eyes filled, then overflowed onto her cheeks. Feeling like an idiot, she wiped the tears away with the tips of her fingers. She should never have started this.

"I'm sorry," she said again. "I knew I

would screw this up."

He sat down on the bed, lifted her, and then set her on his lap. "You haven't screwed anything up. We've barely gotten started." She could feel his erection beneath her. At Darla's house, she'd been too terrified to notice.

"I want you," he said. "You can feel exactly how much. I was hoping if we got this out of the way, you'd be more willing to trust me. You know my life story and I know almost nothing about you. I'd like that to change."

Lucas wanted to know about her. The men she'd known only wanted to talk about themselves. But did she want to tell him? He'd tried to draw her out at supper, but she had always been good at dodging questions.

"Most men hate the after-sex talk."

He took her hand and brought her fingers to his lips. "All right, then, so we'll talk about it now. You're a beautiful woman, *cher.* Why has it been so difficult for you to be with a man?"

She didn't want to discuss this. Too many unwanted memories. "I told you, I always screw it up."

"There's got to be more. Tell me."

It sounded like a request, but it was more

a demand, and she couldn't seem to resist. Resigned, she released a slow breath.

"I have trust issues. My parents divorced. When my mother moved away and married Sean's father, I was sent to a girls' boarding school. I rarely saw either one of them, even on holidays. I was on my own by the time I finished boarding school."

"At least you were smart enough to stay out of trouble."

Nicole made no reply. She had never been in trouble. She had just been lonely most of her life. Fortunately, she had an aunt she cared about and now she had a brother. And though she tried to deny it, she was coming to care for Lucas.

"What happened to your father?"

"He died when I was in college. I got a phone call from his second wife. He'd already been cremated. There was no memorial service. I hadn't even talked to him in a couple of years."

She expected a look of pity, but it was more like understanding.

"What about college?" Lucas asked. "You told me you went to Louisiana State."

"That's right. I studied art history, even got a scholarship for a year at the Sorbonne in Paris. That's when I realized I didn't want to study works of art. I wanted to paint them."

"You must have dated," he said, still holding her hand. "I imagine you had an endless stream of male admirers."

"I was busy with my painting, and I didn't really care about dating. The few men I went out with were just like my parents. They didn't really give a damn about me. They just wanted sex. It didn't take me long to figure that out. Three years ago, I met an artist from New Orleans. He was handsome and well-traveled. I thought it might be different with Ryan Markley. Turned out he was just the same. We lasted less than six months. He said I was a lousy lover. He said I wasn't responsive. He was right."

One of Lucas's dark eyebrows went up. "Maybe he was the problem, not you."

She thought of the way she'd felt when Lucas kissed her. No man had ever made her feel that way. "You really think that's possible?"

"You liked it when I kissed you."

"I liked it. Yes . . . very much."

"Why don't we find out what else you might like?"

He was asking for permission. She wanted him to make love to her so much, she ached with it. But she was terrified she would fail again.

"I don't want to disappoint you."

His mouth edged up. "Just looking at you makes me hard, sweetheart. There's nothing you could do to disappoint me."

She knew he was attracted to her. The problem lay with her.

His gaze met hers as he traced a finger over her trembling lips. "You don't need to worry. I think I know what your problem has been." Lucas slid his fingers into her thick auburn hair, pulled her head back, and his mouth came down over hers.

The kiss started softly and slowly, urging her to trust him. Seconds later, he took possession, the pressure of his lips turning hot and fierce, then deeper and even more demanding. Nicole clutched his shoulders as heat burned through her, flashed like kindling into flame.

Lucas kissed her and kissed her; taking, then giving; soft and coaxing, then hard and deep. She felt his hand cupping her breasts, teasing her nipples. His clever hands moved lower, sliding over her most sensitive places. The more he touched her, the more she wanted; and all the while, he kissed her.

Her hands trembled as she worked the last button on his shirt, pulled it out of his waistband, and slid it off his shoulders. His body was lean, not an ounce of fat, and he was hard — everywhere. Pecs, abs, biceps. He was a fighter, once part of a gang.

It occurred to her that the guys she had dated were boys. Lucas Devereaux was a man.

She felt his hands again, stroking over her flesh as if he owned every inch of her. He knew just where to touch her, how to bring her pleasure. She stifled a cry as an unexpected orgasm ripped through her, wild and erotic, completely unstoppable.

For a moment, she rested her head on his shoulder, fighting to catch her breath. Then he moved, and she felt his mouth on her breasts, teasing and tasting, demanding a response, and a second climax struck, something that had never happened before.

She heard the buzz of his zipper. He lifted her astride him before she had time to think, kissed her deeply, and gripped her hips to hold her in place as he drove himself deep.

Nicole whimpered and held on to him tighter. Lucas kissed her in that soft way he had that made her feel safe, urging her to relax, and then he began to move.

The pleasure started building again. He touched her and kissed her and didn't stop until she was poised on the edge, then sailing over the brink, biting back the sound of his name on her lips. Lucas followed her to release.

For long seconds, she just sat there, her head on his shoulder, her body still wrapped around him, tiny ripples of pleasure pulsing through her.

She felt his lips on the top of her head.

"All right?" he asked.

She wanted to grin. She wanted to dance for the sheer joy of it. She wanted to weep.

"Thank you," she said stupidly, and felt a faint rumble of laughter in his chest. He kissed her softly one last time.

"Now do you believe it wasn't you?"

"Maybe." She looked up at him. "I guess being with you changes things."

Lucas said nothing. Reality was setting in. Maybe it hadn't been as good for him as it was for her. The thought made her stomach ache.

Lucas lifted her away and rose from the edge of the bed. With his height and narrow-hipped, broad-shouldered build, he looked as good from the back as he did from the front as he headed into the bathroom to dispose of the condom she hadn't realized he'd put on.

When he returned, he grabbed his shirt

off the floor, and she figured he was leaving. Her eyes burned, but she clenched her jaw. *He's just like Ryan,* she thought.

"Drive safely," she said.

Lucas turned. "You think I'm leaving?"

Nicole made no reply.

Lucas just smiled. He tossed the shirt over a chair, then bent and swept her up. He settled her in the bed.

"You're staying?"

"Yes, and if you're going to freak out again, I'll just have to start over."

He was staying, but for how long?

And what about Sean? Her brother came first, and no man wanted to be second.

And Rachel? Whatever was happening, Rachel was in trouble.

Her family depended on her. They had to be her priority.

And she still wasn't certain if she should trust him. She looked up at him, a question in her eyes.

"I'm staying," he said as he stripped off the rest of his clothes. "Get used to it." Then he climbed onto the bed beside her and pulled her into his arms.

## Chapter Nineteen

Rachel listened as the wind picked up. She had been tossing and turning, unable to sleep, when the headlights of a car coming up the driveway flashed through the windows.

She always worried when her niece went out in the evenings, but knowing she was with Lucas eased her mind. There was something about Lucas Devereaux that earned people's trust. She wondered if Nicole felt it, too.

She shifted in the bed, trying to get comfortable. A storm was coming in, a light rain pelting the windows. The temperature had risen that afternoon, making the wet wind humid. The ceiling fan slowly rotated, stirring a cooling breeze. Staring up at the satin canopy, she listened to the soft, slow whir of the wooden blades.

The light caress of air against her skin made her think of Francois, and her eyes welled with tears. She wasn't supposed to care about a man who wasn't really there, but she couldn't seem to stop herself. She yearned to see his beautiful eyes, to feel his touch and the pleasure only he could bring.

The tears in her eyes spilled over onto her cheeks as she thought of the terrible fate he had suffered. She imagined his beautiful, dark angel face. Night after night, she had silently called out to him, but he had never come.

She told herself it was impossible to feel an ache in her heart for a man who didn't exist in her world. Closing her eyes, she listened to the soft patter of the rain and finally drifted to sleep.

It was dark and silent when she awakened, disoriented, though she was in her own bed. She blinked, then blinked again as something moved toward her in the darkness. Something as light and invisible as the air stirred by the ceiling fan. Something that made her heart beat faster.

Time seemed to slow. The blades stopped spinning.

"Francois?" She should have been afraid. She shouldn't be feeling this desperate need for him to touch her. She spoke to him and prayed he could hear her. Prayed, as she had every night.

A featherlight touch caressed her cheek.

Rachel's throat closed up. "Francois . . . I've been hoping . . . I've been waiting for you."

The air swirled gently around her. *I hurt you. I'm sorry.*

She remembered that he had thought she was someone else, and an unexpected rush of jealousy burned through her. "Who was she?"

She could sense him struggling to recall, but he made no reply.

"It's all right," she said softly. "I'm here . . . and I . . . I want you to stay."

When only silence filled her mind, she thought that he had gone, returned to wherever he had come from.

Instead, the air stirred as he moved closer, and she looked into the beautiful face Nicole had painted. His face and his brilliant blue eyes, nothing more. The mattress dipped beside her.

She reminded herself he wasn't really there. It was impossible. Francois had been dead for close to 150 years. And yet she could feel him lying next to her on the mattress, feel him moving closer until he was curled around her.

She felt the press of his lips against the top of her head and closed her eyes. She wanted him to take her, make her feel the things she had felt before, but she was just so weak and tired. So very tired.

His warmth surrounded her. Whether he was real or not, Rachel had never felt more at peace. Her eyes slowly closed. Little by little, she drifted into a deep, untroubled sleep.

In the morning when she awakened, the rain had stopped, and Francois was gone.

Loneliness swept over her. Rachel curled into herself and began to weep.

Lucas awoke to an overcast sky and Nicole curled asleep against him. It was early, plenty of time to get back to his condo in Baton Rouge, change clothes, and get to the center on time.

He glanced down at the woman whose fiery hair spread over his chest. Though they had made love for hours last night, he was hard for her again this morning.

In his early years, his wild days, he'd been with an endless stream of women, none of whom meant more than a means of sexual release. Years later, there was Marie. He'd fallen in love for the first time in his life, but he'd only been a curiosity to Marie.

After the pain of her betrayal, he'd learned to keep his emotions locked down. It hadn't been difficult until now. None of the few women he'd been involved with since he'd left the priesthood had moved him as Nicole had.

He wasn't sure what it was about her. He just knew he was on the path God meant for him to follow — exactly what he intended to do — though he was fairly certain Nicole wasn't ready to hear *that* news.

He almost smiled.

As quietly as possible, he slid out of bed and pulled on his clothes. He considered just leaving her a note, but somehow that didn't feel right. Instead, he went into the kitchen and brewed a pot of coffee.

The rich aroma drifting through the house must have awakened her. Nicole padded barefoot into the kitchen in a white terry robe, her soft curls around her shoulders. She looked well-tumbled, and so tempting he wanted to take her again, right there on the kitchen counter.

He'd always been a man of considerable passions, a problem that had been part of the reason he had left the Church.

"I thought you were gone," she said, surprise in her voice.

"I thought I'd fix you a cup of coffee before I took off."

The smile that broke over her face tightened something in his chest. He filled a mug and handed it over.

Nicole cradled the mug in both hands. "Thanks."

"My pleasure." The night they'd shared flashed through his head. Lucas forced down a surge of hunger.

Nicole walked toward him, her eyes on the unbuttoned opening at the top of his wrinkled white dress shirt. She lifted out the medal the size of a quarter he wore on a gold chain around his neck.

"What's this? I noticed it last night."

"St. Michael's medallion." On the front of the circle of gold, a huge, winged angel wielded a massive sword against Satan.

" 'St. Michael Protect Us,' " she read aloud. She looked up at him. "The Archangel Michael."

"That's right. The defender of humankind against evil."

Her gaze caught on the quarter-size scar underneath the medallion. Nicole ran her fingers over it, studied it for several long moments. "The image of St. Michael is burned into your skin. How could that happen?"

He caught her hand and brought it to his lips. "Long story. I promise to tell you sometime soon. Right now, I've got to get back to Baton Rouge."

He looked down at Nicole, wanted to see her again, and mentally ran over his options. He didn't want to scare her away. But she didn't need another man in her life who had no idea how to handle a strong woman like her.

"Unless you have an objection, I'll be back tonight. We can eat here, or we can go out. Your choice."

He didn't miss the trapped-animal look that flashed in her pretty green eyes. "I know you have a lot to do," she said. "Running two youth centers, as well as coaching the boys, takes up a lot of your time."

"True enough." He took a sip of his coffee. "Does that mean you have plans for tonight?"

She worried her full bottom lip, and he felt a tug in his groin. Going slow wasn't going to be easy.

Nicole sipped her coffee, giving herself time to think. A knock at the door interrupted her reply.

*Saved by the bell* was the look on her face. Lucas turned and walked into the living room to see who was there. Nicole raced up beside him as he peered out the window.

He arched a brow in question. "It's your aunt. You want me to disappear into the bedroom?"

She made a sound of frustration in her throat. "By now, Aunt Rachel has seen your car. We might as well let her in."

Lucas inwardly smiled. Pulling open the door, he stepped back as Rachel walked into the living room, her heavy black hair pulled into a single long braid down her back.

"I saw your car," she said to him. "I'm glad you're here."

Nicole's glance went from Lucas to Rachel and back. "You are?"

"Yes."

"You want a cup of coffee?" Lucas asked.

"You aren't supposed to have caffeine," Nicole reminded her.

Rachel ignored her. "Yes, please."

Lucas poured her a cup and handed it over as Nicole sat down on one of the barstools at the kitchen counter.

"Okay, Aunt Rachel, what's going on?"

Rachel sat down on the stool beside her. "I'm afraid it's Francois. He . . . umm . . . came to me last night. It was late, well after midnight. This time, I . . . umm . . . saw his face."

"You saw his face?" Nicole responded.

"Yes. As I guessed, he looks exactly like the black-haired man in your painting."

"You don't think what you saw in the

painting could have influenced your thinking?"

"I don't believe so. I think it's more likely Francois came into your mind, and you painted his portrait."

For a moment, Nicole fell silent. "So . . . when Francois came to you last night, did he speak to you?"

"Not exactly. I hear him in my head."

"Like when you were working in the cemetery."

"That's right. Francois needs our help and you both promised to help him."

"Yes, we did," Lucas agreed. "It's been a week, past time we got started. I'll get on the computer as soon as I get back to Baton Rouge and see what I can turn up."

Nicole looked resigned. "You two are an impossible combination to resist. You know that, right?"

Lucas just smiled.

Nicole took a sip of coffee. "I have more free time than you do, Lucas. I'll start here in town. We have lots of historical information in St. Francisville. Maybe I can find something that will help."

For an instant, Rachel's eyes glistened. "Thank you. Thank you, both of you. I'm not very good at this sort of thing or I would try to do it myself."

Nicole leaned over and hugged her. "Don't worry, Aunt Rachel. We're going to do the very best we can."

"If you need to talk to someone," Lucas said to Rachel, "I've dealt with this kind of thing before. Nothing you tell me will come as a surprise."

Rachel's cheeks flushed. "I'm not so sure of that."

Though she had piqued his curiosity, he didn't press for more. "Do you have your phone with you?"

"Yes." She pulled it out of the pocket of her jeans, and Lucas took it from her hand. He added his number to her contacts.

"If you need me, I'm just a phone call away. Call me anytime."

Rachel took the phone back. "Thank you, Lucas."

He turned to Nicole. "I've got to go." He bent and gave her a brief kiss on the lips. "I'll see you tonight."

Nicole's eyes widened, but she didn't say a word. He had expected uncertainty, maybe even anger, but he could swear he caught a hint of fear. He'd deal with it. In the meantime, hoping she wanted to see him again as much as he wanted to see her, Lucas headed for the door.

One thing for sure. His life was never boring.

# Chapter Twenty

Blocking thoughts of Lucas from her mind, as soon as his Lexus disappeared down the driveway, Nicole headed for the family cemetery. Carrying a notepad, she copied information off the tombstones in the Villard side of the cemetery, concentrating on Pierre and his wife, Therese-Louise, and their offspring, two boys, Francois Etienne and Jules Claude, the younger brother.

Francois, born in 1843, had died sometime in 1878 at age thirty-four or thirty-five. Jules, born a year later, in 1844, had died in 1894 at the age of fifty.

Another tombstone belonged to Jules's wife, Simone, six years younger than Jules. Born in 1850, she had been eighty when she'd died in 1930.

Jules and Simone had two children. Andre, the oldest, lived to be thirty-eight, but Josephine, the little girl buried beneath the statue of an angel, had died when she was only six. There were other gravestones, Andre's descendants, but they had lived at a later time.

Aside from the curious gravestone that belonged to Francois, which gave no day and month of death, nothing else stood out among the markers of the dead.

Nicole headed back to the carriage house, then drove to the West Feliciana Parish Library on Burnett Road, just a few miles from Belle Reve.

The modern brick structure was family friendly, the floors carpeted in warm tones that matched the light wood furniture. Even better, Nicole knew Winnie Bonner, who had worked in the library since Nicole was in grade school, before she'd been sent away to boarding school.

"Mrs. Bonner?"

In a flowered blouse and navy polyester pants, her gray hair pulled back in a tight bun at the nape of her neck, the stout librarian turned at the sound of her name.

"I'm Nicole Belmond. You probably don't remember me, but —"

"Of course, I remember you! You used to borrow books to write reports for your classes. I might have forgotten for a while, but these days, your beautiful landscape paintings have made you a local celebrity."

Nicole smiled. "That's wonderful to hear. If you think it would be appropriate, I would love to gift the library one of my pieces."

"Oh, my, yes! That would be splendid."

Nicole's smile widened. "All right, I'll pick something and drop it off. In the meantime, I'm working on a project that involves the history of Belle Reve. I was hoping you might be able to help me."

"I'll certainly do my best. Belle Reve is something of a landmark, so visitors are often interested in its history."

"I know Pierre and Therese-Louise Villard built the house back in the 1870s. I'm looking for information on their children, particularly Francois, the oldest son. I'm hoping I can find an article in an old newspaper, or perhaps someone in the area wrote something about the Villard family. They were extremely wealthy, important people in the community back in their day."

Winnie started nodding. "The Villards meant a great deal to the people of St. Francisville. They were in the shipping trade, moving goods along Bayou Sara through the town, down the Mississippi to New Orleans. Of course, the town of Bayou Sara was washed away years ago in a tragic flood, but before that, Villard Shipping provided a lot of jobs. The family was well-liked and known to be great philanthropists. There's a book by a man named Charles La Tour about Pierre Villard and his descendants."

Nicole felt a rush of excitement as Winnie started walking toward the section that dealt with local history. Winnie pulled a leather-bound volume off the shelf and handed it to Nicole.

"Though there may be other copies in existence," Winnie said, "this, unfortunately, is the only copy we have. As you can see, it's in very rough condition. It was badly damaged in the flood of 1927 when some of the pages were destroyed. You're welcome to read it, but we can't let you take it out of the library."

Nicole looked down at the worn, stained, faded red leather-bound volume: *BELLE REVE: The Tragic History of a Beautiful Dream.*

As Nicole read the title, a shiver of unease moved through her.

"Thank you," she said. "This is a perfect place to begin."

"We also have old copies of the *Baton-Rouge Gazette* on microfiche. It became the *Baton Rouge Tri-Weekly Gazette and Comet,* but that was years later. You're welcome to take a look."

"I think I'll go through La Tour's book first. That should give me an idea of what I still need to know."

Nicole carried the volume over to one of the library tables, sat down, and took out her notepad. She began to skim the fragile, water-stained pages. At the cemetery, she had learned that Francois's parents, Pierre and Therese-Louise, had died about a year or so after their elder son's death.

Nicole wanted to know what had happened to them. More than that, she wanted to know what had happened to Francois.

She was tired by the time she finished reading La Tour's account, her notepad full of information she had jotted down. She knew a good deal more about the family, discovered it had been Pierre's dream to build the spectacular mansion as a gift for his beloved wife.

The first few years had been good ones. Villard Shipping had been an extremely successful business. With the help of Pierre's two sons, that success had continued. Several pages with crumbled edges and print too faded to read left a time gap in the family history. The frayed edges of a couple of missing pages looked as if they might have been torn out.

The next entry she could discern talked

about the disappearance of the Villards' oldest son: Francois had ridden out one morning in 1878 on his way to the docks, but never arrived. There was speculation, of course. Rumors surfaced that he and his brother had argued, and he had simply ridden away. Another version said the argument was between Francois and his father, the result the same. Francois left without word, never to return.

The most common theory was that he had been attacked by thieves around the docks, an area known for criminal activity. That he had been murdered, his body never found.

The book went on to describe the grief his parents felt at their loss. His father began drinking and his mother was bedridden for a time.

Pierre and Therese-Louise were overjoyed when, a year later, after an acceptable period of mourning, the daughter of one of Pierre's best friends, Simone St. Denis, became engaged to Jules Villard. The couple was married that summer.

There were more damaged pages. The family history resumed with the terrible news that Pierre and Therese-Louise had been killed a few months after the wedding when their carriage overturned on a bridge and fell into the water.

For a moment, Nicole paused, feeling a rush of sadness for the couple whose lives had ended so tragically, people to whom she felt a special connection through the magnificent house they had loved.

She went back to reading, trying to make out water-damaged paragraphs, some of which described the ups and downs of the Villard family over the decades that followed. Jules and Simone suffered one misfortune after another, including several miscarriages and two stillborn births, and then the tragic death of their six-year-old daughter, Josephine, the little girl buried beneath the angel in the cemetery. Only one son had survived to carry on the family line.

According to the book, unlike Pierre, neither Jules nor Jules's son, Andre, had the business acumen necessary to run the company. Jules's mismanagement began the company's long slide toward bankruptcy, and Andre's ineptitude had made the problem worse. Villard descendants were forced to sell Belle Reve to the Belmond family in 1925.

The story ended there, and Nicole closed the damaged leather volume. She rubbed the back of her neck as she rose from her chair and carried the book back up to the front counter.

"Thanks so much, Mrs. Bonner. I really appreciate your help."

"Please call me Winnie, and you're very welcome, dear."

Nicole smiled. "I'll be back with that painting and to look at those old newspapers. Thanks again."

Ten minutes later, she turned the Audi down the lane leading to Belle Reve and pulled into the carport just as her cell phone rang. She grabbed the phone, saw Lucas's name on the screen, and pressed the phone against her ear.

"I hope I'm not interrupting," he said.

"Not at all."

"I wanted to let you know I was able to get Sean a part-time job at a place called Dave's Home Supplies. I figured a kid who liked to build model cars would be comfortable dealing with all the parts and pieces they sell in a hardware store. It's only two hours a day after school and it's close enough to walk from the center."

"That sounds perfect," Nicole said. "I'm sure he's excited."

"Seems to be."

"Were you able to find any information about Francois?"

"I had a little luck, found an article online

in the *Baton Rouge Tri-Weekly Gazette.* Nothing about Francois, but there was an announcement in the society pages about his brother Jules's engagement to a young woman named Simone St. Denis."

"Yes, I read something about it in the library."

"I look forward to exchanging notes. Unfortunately, I won't be able to drive out tonight. A problem's come up with one of the boys."

Disappointment warred with uncertainty. He'd slept with her. Maybe this was just an excuse.

Lucas continued. "One of Hugo's friends was caught shoplifting in a convenience store a few blocks from the center. Looks like he'll be spending the rest of his time in juvenile detention. I need to speak to his family and his attorney. Can I have a rain check for tomorrow?"

Nicole sighed, feeling relief and renewed disappointment. "I'm afraid I'm busy. I have a meeting with Anne Winston tomorrow night." She wasn't sure whether not being able to see him was good news or bad. She wanted to be with him — way too much. That was the problem.

"That might work out even better," he said. "I'll pick you up after you're finished.

What time will you be done?"

He wasn't asking, wasn't giving her a choice. He wanted to see her. It was scary how much she wanted that, too. "I should be done by seven."

"I'll be there to pick you up. Bring an overnight bag."

"But —"

"I gotta run. See you tomorrow." Lucas hung up the phone.

*Bring an overnight bag.* Her abdomen clenched with desire. She knew what it was like to make love with Lucas Devereaux. She wanted more of it, but she was afraid.

The truth was, she not only had trust issues, she also had abandonment issues. Her parents. Friends she cared about who had disappeared from her life. Men she had dated. *Ryan.*

But she had made her decision — at least for now. She would be spending tomorrow night with Lucas. Her body was ready. She just had to get her mind on board.

# Chapter Twenty-One

Lucas drove the Jeep from the youth center to the Anne Winston Fine Art gallery on Thursday night. He was taking Nicole out to supper at a quiet little restaurant that was one of his favorites. She had mentioned French food. In a small vintage white cottage tucked away off the beaten path, Maison Lacour wouldn't disappoint.

He tried not to think what would happen after, when he drove her back to his town house. The memory of making love to Nicole made his groin thicken and desire race through his blood.

He was smiling as he turned into the parking lot. The gallery must have just closed. The lights were turned off inside, the windows in the redbrick building dim. As he pulled the Jeep into one of the spaces in the empty lot, his glance went to two men near the back door who stood over a third person lying on the ground. One was tall, about Lucas's height, with stringy brown hair and a bald spot; the other shorter, muscular, with a sleeve of tats down each arm.

Unable to mistake the fiery hair that belonged to Nicole, Lucas slammed on the brakes, jammed the car into Park, and was out of the vehicle and on the move while the engine was still running.

"Tell your brother that Bruno says hello." The taller man toed Nicole in the ribs. "Next time, he'll be paying you a visit in person." He flashed a vicious smile the instant before Lucas spun him around and punched him in the face.

The musclehead with the tats leaped toward him, swinging a vicious blow that clipped Lucas's jaw and knocked him a few steps backward. He let the momentum carry him, then whirled toward the first man, punching him in the stomach, doubling him over, throwing a hard uppercut to the jaw, which sent the guy's head jerking back as his body crashed against the rough brick wall.

The musclehead ran toward him. Lucas hit him with two left jabs and a solid right cross, which sent him flying. The instant the guy hit the ground, he was up and running, his partner already on the move, both of them racing across the parking lot, disappearing around the corner, out of sight.

Lucas ran to Nicole, who lay curled on her side on the pavement. She moaned as he knelt beside her, reached out, and took hold of her hand.

"They're gone," he said. "Don't move. I'm calling an ambulance."

"No. Please don't do that." Ignoring his instructions, she struggled to sit up.

"Take it easy, honey. We don't know how badly you're hurt." He pulled his cell phone out of his pocket.

"No ambulance," she repeated more firmly. "I'm — I'm okay. Just . . . a little bruised. Give me a minute and I'll be all right."

"What about your ribs? They must be hurting."

"They're sore, but I can tell nothing's broken. I'll be okay."

He caught her chin and looked at her. Her lip was split, and she was going to have one helluva shiner.

"You might have a concussion, baby. You need to get checked out." He looked into her eyes, but her pupils didn't look dilated. "Do you have a headache?" He held up three fingers. "How many?"

"Three. A headache, but not that bad."

She tried to get to her feet, but he forced her back down.

"All right, no ambulance." He shoved the phone back into his pocket. "I'll drive you to the emergency room and we'll see what the doctors have to say."

Nicole shook her head, wincing as her fiery hair swirled around her shoulders. "I'm not going to the hospital." She looked up at him. "Take me to your house. That was our plan. Right?"

That wasn't exactly his plan, but close enough. He sighed. "All right. My house. But if you start feeling dizzy or nauseated, I'm taking you in."

When she didn't argue, Lucas took it as a win. "Stay here. I'll get the Jeep."

A few seconds later, he pulled the vehicle up to where she sat, got out, retrieved her purse from where it had landed near the back door, and helped her into the passenger seat. He fastened her belt and tilted the seat back a little.

"It'll take us a few minutes to get there. Just relax, okay?"

Nicole nodded.

Opening the glove box, he plucked out a Burger King napkin and pressed it gently against her lip to stop the bleeding. Nicole took it from his hand. "Thanks."

His town house on Fiero Street was fifteen minutes away. As he drove the route, Nicole closed her eyes, but she seemed to be breathing normally. He pulled into his garage, parked next to his Lexus, and turned off the engine.

He went around to help Nicole out of the car. "Can you walk?"

She took hold of his arm to steady herself. "I'm okay. Really. Let's go."

Lucas led her past his Harley, through the garage door into the kitchen, glad he had stocked up the fridge a few days ago. Guiding her along the hardwood floors into the high-ceilinged living room, he urged her down on the navy-blue sofa. A glass-topped coffee table sat in front, a matching navy-blue chair at each end.

The whole place was done in white: walls, cabinets in the kitchen, granite countertops. Navy blue was the accent color throughout, giving the place a clean, masculine feel.

He eased Nicole down on the sofa, went to the entry closet, and took down a pillow and a lightweight throw. He returned and placed the pillow under her head and spread the throw over her.

"How are you doing?" he asked.

"My cheek hurts where he punched me, and my lip feels twice its size. My ribs are a little sore. Apart from that, not too bad."

He almost smiled. She was tougher than she looked. "That's good. Time to tell me what happened. Are you feeling well enough to do that?"

Nicole sighed. "I'm not exactly sure what happened. It's all kind of a blurry haze. Anne let me out the back door, locked it, then went out through the front. I didn't see the men until they were right on top of me. I got in a couple of good kicks, but it didn't do anything to stop them."

"You were outnumbered, and they were waiting for you. You get well and I'll show you some self-defense moves that might even the score a little."

Nicole managed a half-hearted smile.

"What did they want? Money? Did they rob you?"

"They didn't rob me." She glanced away. "That was probably their intention, but you got there before they had a chance."

She was lying and she wasn't very good at it.

"I don't think they wanted your money. The attack had something to do with Sean, didn't it? The guy with the stringy hair said to tell your brother that Bruno says hello. I know you don't want to get Sean in trouble, but not telling me the truth could land him in the same situation you were just in — or worse."

She closed her eyes for a moment, collecting herself. "I honestly don't know what's going on, Lucas. Sean's never mentioned anyone named Bruno, but it was clearly a warning of some kind."

"We need to talk to Sean as soon as possible."

"Does it have to be tonight?" she asked, her face still pale.

Lucas took hold of her hand and brought it to his lips. "Not tonight, *cher*. He's safe at the center. I'll drive him out to Belle Reve tomorrow after class lets out for the weekend. We can talk to him then."

Tears glistened in her eyes. "Thank you. And thank you for standing up to those men tonight. I don't know what would have happened if you hadn't come along when you did."

"They got their message delivered. I think, for tonight, that's all they wanted." But what was waiting for Nicole and Sean down the road?

"I planned to take you out to a nice French restaurant," Lucas said, "but it looks like you'll be getting a bowl of chicken noodle soup instead."

Her eyes slid closed, and he could tell she

was hurting. He didn't offer her a pain reliever, since there was a chance she had a concussion. Unconsciously, his hand fisted. It didn't matter that his knuckles were scraped raw. He wanted to throw half-a-dozen more punches at the men who had hurt her.

She looked up at him with those big green eyes that never failed to move him. "Chicken noodle soup sounds perfect," she said.

And sinner that he was, he wanted to carry her upstairs right then, strip off her clothes, and take her. He wanted to spend the night with her in his bed. He wouldn't, of course. She could barely move, and he had more urgent matters to worry about than satisfying the sexual need for her that rode him like a hungry beast.

He had to find out who Bruno was, the meaning of the warning the men had delivered, and how he could stop whatever they had planned, before someone else got hurt.

It didn't matter that the night was moonless, dark, quiet, and still, that the pleasant chirp of crickets seeped through the paned glass windows to comfort her. Rachel's mind wouldn't stop spinning, wouldn't let her rest.

Staring up at the canopy above the bed,

she thought of Francois and what Nicole had told her about the discoveries she had made at the library. Rachel now knew a lot more about the family of the man who came to her in dreams. Dreams that were real and made her feel desire as she never had before.

She couldn't stop thinking about him, imagining his beautiful face, his gorgeous blue eyes, wishing he were there with her now. If she could only fall asleep, perhaps he would come to her as he had before.

But the brass pendulum on the clock kept ticking off the seconds, the minutes, the hours; and though she closed her eyes, sleep would not come.

Time dragged. Her restless mind finally began to calm and she fell into a deep, dreamless slumber. Dreamless, until she heard a voice calling to her in the darkness, whispering her name.

Rachel opened her eyes, her gaze searching the empty bedroom. "Francois?"

He made no sound, but she could feel him moving toward her, feel his weight settle on the mattress.

*Ma belle.*

He was there, as she had prayed he would be. She felt the soft brush of his lips against the side of her neck, just the gentlest of touches, then settling lightly over her lips as if he asked permission. She opened to him without reservation, allowing him to deepen the kiss, wanting everything he could give her, wanting to claim these few impossible moments for herself.

Her nightgown brushed against her skin as it lifted away and disappeared into the darkness. She could feel the wet heat of his kisses moving over her skin, along her throat and shoulders, down to her breasts. A soft moan escaped as she arched upward, silently asking for more.

Around her, the world narrowed to the soft caress of his lips, the glide of his hands over her skin. Desire rose up, hot and fierce, as he claimed her body and invaded her soul. She saw his beautiful blue eyes as he began to move inside her and felt a rush of love for him.

It was impossible. She couldn't love a man she had never really known, a man who wasn't actually there. And yet as they reached the pinnacle together, she knew her feelings for him were real. He stayed with her for a while, there on the mattress beside her. Finally at peace, her eyes drifted closed. The soft brush of his lips in a farewell kiss, and then he was gone.

"Francois!" she called after him, trying to

draw him back, but silence was her only reply, and the room remained empty.

Her heart ached. She told herself that this time with Francois was a gift from God. She believed it with all her heart, and the knowledge comforted her. Rachel closed her eyes and gave in to the sleep her frail body so desperately needed.

She dreamed of Francois and prayed he would come to her again.

## Chapter Twenty-Two

Classes were over, the boys preparing to depart for the weekend. Lucas had informed Sean that he would be giving him a ride to Belle Reve after school.

Lucas had been considering how to handle the situation with Nicole and the beating she had suffered because of her brother, and had to clamp down on the anger that stretched the limits of his control. It was unusual for him, a man who had once been a priest. He had learned years ago how to discipline himself, to keep his feelings in check. The rage he felt now was a measure of how much he had come to care for Nicole.

A knock on the door drew his attention. He checked his watch and figured it was Sean. "Come on in."

Sean opened the door and walked into the office, a wide smile on his face. "My first day at work was great. Thanks, Coach."

Classes ended at three, followed by two hours of athletics, or in this case an after-school job.

Lucas had meant to hold off on this conversation, but the smile on Sean's face changed his plans.

"Sit down, Sean."

Reading the tension in Lucas's body, the boy's smile slid away. He sat down hard in the chair on the opposite side of the desk. "What's going on?"

"Why don't you tell me? By the way, Bruno says hello."

Sean's eyes widened and he reeled in his seat.

"Your sister's lucky she isn't in the hospital. As it is, she took a beating. It was a warning, Sean. From your good friend Bruno."

Sean's breathing quickened, the air moving too fast in and out of his lungs. "Is she all right?"

"She's been better. I want the truth, Sean. Tell me what's going on."

Sean's eyes squeezed closed for an instant. He took a shaky breath and slowly released it. "Bruno . . . is one of the guys who paid me to steal cars. I don't know his last name. They call him the boss, but I'm pretty sure he works for someone else. But one of his men, a guy named Mickey Dugan, showed up in my dorm room last week. Mick says . . . he says I still owe them two more cars."

"Go on."

"Mick threatened to hurt Nicole if I didn't agree to steal them. He said Bruno would go after her." Sean looked at him, his eyes full of worry. "Bruno's a really bad dude, Coach. He likes to hurt people, especially women. I didn't want Nicole getting hurt, so I said I'd do it."

Sean's eyes glistened with unshed tears. "I didn't want to. I thought if I got a job, I could pay back the money and we would be even. After you got me the job at the hardware store, I called Mick and told him I wasn't going to steal anything. I said I'd pay the boss back; I just needed a little time. Mick didn't argue. I guess they just went after Nicole."

"What happened to the money you were paid?"

"Some of it's still buried in the yard behind my old house, but that was for the first cars. I never got paid for the next ones. Artie took the money and ran. I haven't seen him since."

"Artie was the guy who brought you in?"

"Yeah. It was after my parents died, right

after I moved in with Nicole. I wasn't sure things would work out, you know? And I was . . . It seemed like I was just mad at the world."

It was a story Lucas had heard before. Loss and pain pushing a kid into trouble. "And now?"

Sean sat up straighter in his chair. "Nicole took me in when no one else wanted me. I'd never do anything to hurt her. I'll do whatever it takes to keep her safe — no matter what happens to me."

Lucas read the sincerity in Sean's eyes and relief filtered through him. "Then I guess we better figure out what to do to protect your sister and keep you out of jail."

Nicole wiped her hands on the apron Sean had given her for her birthday: MAY THE FORKS BE WITH YOU. She smiled at the memory as she continued preparing supper for Lucas and Sean. Lucas had driven her home this morning. He hadn't wanted to leave her alone, but he said he was taking care of it, whatever that meant. After school, he would be driving Sean home for the weekend.

Knowing she would still be sore from the attack last night, Lucas had offered to pick up takeout. Nicole had declined. She had never imagined herself the domestic type. She was too career driven, too immersed in her painting, and she had long ago accepted being single for the rest of her life. Then Sean had come along, and she had discovered the nurturing side of her nature.

Her work would always be a priority, but she enjoyed cooking for Sean and other people she cared about, especially if the meal was appreciated. She glanced at the clock above the oven, caught her reflection in the glass door, and winced at her black eye and the bruise on her cheek.

She wondered what Sean would say when he saw her. Lucas had phoned earlier to tell her he had talked to her brother before they left Baton Rouge. Apparently, the men that Sean had been involved with in the car theft ring had reappeared. They were demanding her brother continue to steal for them. Sean had refused. Hurting her was a way to force him to comply. Lucas was going to help Sean deal with the situation.

Nicole silently thanked God for the man who had come into their lives when they needed him so badly. In a way she wished she hadn't slept with him. When they parted, she would lose a man who had become a very good friend to both of them.

She tried not to think of the night they

had spent together, a memory that sent desire pulsing through her. She tried and failed to convince herself she didn't want it to happen again.

Nicole sighed.

Finished seasoning the pork roast, she shoved it into the oven. The apples were peeled and cooking, sending the spicy aroma of cinnamon into the air. At the sound of a car approaching along the gravel drive, she walked over to the window above the sink. Her stomach knotted at the sight of the white sheriff's SUV rolling down the lane toward the house. Tall, black-haired Sheriff Loewen sat behind the wheel, the only person in the vehicle.

Untying her apron, she tossed it over a chair at the breakfast table and hurried to the front door. She walked out just as Lucas's Jeep pulled in behind the sheriff's vehicle.

Relief filtered through her. As Lucas and Sean climbed out of the vehicle, Sean spotted her black eye, beginning to turn several shades of yellowish purple, and the blood leached out of his face.

"I'm so sorry, sis. This is all my fault."

Nicole leaned down and hugged him, careful not to hurt her ribs. "It isn't your fault." But Sean clearly didn't believe her.

Nicole was grateful when Lucas sent him off to his man/boy cave.

Lucas stood at her side as the sheriff walked toward her. "Sheriff Loewen. Nice to see you." She plastered a smile on her face. "Sheriff, this is Lucas Devereaux. He runs the Baton Rouge Youth Center."

Beneath a black bill cap with the sheriff's department logo on the front, Loewen's gaze went from Lucas to Nicole's battered face, and his jaw hardened.

"I can see what you're thinking, Sheriff," Nicole said. "But Lucas isn't responsible for the way I look. In fact, if he hadn't shown up when he did, I'd probably look a whole lot worse."

The sheriff's gaze caught the scabs crusted on Lucas's knuckles, and he apparently understood what they meant. He extended his hand. "Nice to meet you." Lucas accepted the handshake. "Did you file a report after the assault?"

"It happened in Baton Rouge," Lucas answered. Not the sheriff's jurisdiction. "There were two men involved. Attempted robbery, I figure. We exchanged a few punches. Nothing serious. Nicole was my priority. When they took off running, I let them go."

The sheriff focused on Nicole. "Keeping

the police in the loop might still be a good idea."

She just nodded. "I'll think about it." But there was no way she was filing a report. Neither she nor Lucas wanted Sean's name brought up.

"What can we do for you, Sheriff?" Lucas asked, resting a protective hand at her waist.

"I brought news about the bones we found."

"You found out who it is?"

"Not yet, but the case has gotten more interesting. Turns out there was a hole in the back of the skull. The forensic experts believe it was caused by a club or tool of some kind. They're listing blunt force trauma as the cause of death. They've concluded whoever is in the box was murdered."

Silence fell.

It made sense. If, as Aunt Rachel believed, the bones belonged to Francois Villard, the assumption at the time of his disappearance was that criminals around the docks had murdered him. This was just more evidence that her aunt was right. It was past time they dug up Francois's grave.

"Forensics also found it interesting that the box was made of cedar, a long-lasting wood. The dead man wasn't just tossed into a pit and left to rot, he was treated with what appears to be respect."

"Interesting," Lucas said.

"It's just another piece of the puzzle."

"Thank you for letting us know," Nicole said.

"We're still trying to identify the remains. We'd appreciate a call if you run across anything that might be useful."

"We'll do that, Sheriff," Lucas said.

Loewen touched the bill of his cap and returned to his SUV.

"Let's go inside." As the sheriff drove away, Lucas urged her back into the house, toward the delicious smells coming from the kitchen. He explained the conversation he'd had with Sean before they had set off for Belle Reve.

"Your brother was trying to do the right thing. They wanted him to steal more cars, but he refused. He wanted a job so he could pay them the money they told him he still owed. He thought he had the situation under control. He was devastated when he found out they had hurt you."

"He's a good boy," she said, her eyes filling with tears.

Lucas eased her into his arms. "Yes, he is. That's the reason we're going to help him."

Nicole swallowed. She rested her head on

Lucas's shoulder. It felt so good just to have him hold her. *It's only for a moment,* she told herself.

Lucas kissed the top of her head the instant before she pulled away.

"Thank you for being here," she said. "For helping Sean." *And me,* she silently added. She had no idea how to deal with the kind of thugs who had brutally assaulted her in the parking lot, the kind who were threatening Sean.

Lucas tipped her chin up. "We're going to figure it out." He wiped tears from her cheeks. "Okay?"

She nodded. She was sure he would have kissed her if Sean hadn't opened the front door just then and walked into the house.

Her brother's lanky gait propelled him into the kitchen. He took another look at her black eye and the bruise on her cheek, and his face blanched once more.

"Jeez, sis. I'm so sorry those bastards did that to you." He walked over for a closer look. Nicole winced as he reached up and gently touched her cheek. "I thought I could work things out without getting you involved. I thought I had it handled. Instead, you wound up getting hurt instead of me."

Nicole could read the regret and pain in the green eyes much like her own. "It wasn't your fault. You did what you thought was right."

He carefully hugged her, then flicked a glance at Lucas. "Coach is going to help me."

Nicole managed to smile. "I know."

"I need a couple of days," Lucas said. "I have some friends I want to talk to."

Sean's gaze shifted between Nicole and Lucas. "What if they come to Belle Reve?"

"I'm glad you asked," Lucas said. "The answer is, if they show up here, they're going to have to deal with me."

Nicole wasn't sure whose eyes widened more, hers or Sean's.

"You're staying here?" Sean asked.

"Unless that's a problem for you."

"No!" her brother said quickly. "You can have my room. I can sleep out in my studio. I do that sometimes. I've got it fixed up so it's comfortable."

Lucas turned to Nicole. "What about you? You all right with my staying?"

The bruise throbbed in her cheek. "It never occurred to me those men might show up here. I'd be grateful if you stayed."

As Sean headed back out the door to his workshop, Lucas flashed Nicole a teasing smile. "Tonight might not be a good idea, but once you're feeling better, I'm sure I can think of a way for you to show me your gratitude."

The hint of a smile touched her lips. She ignored the faint color rising in her cheeks and went back to the subject they needed to be discussing. "You think Sean will be okay out there?"

"Those men want your brother's help. If they hurt him, that isn't going to happen."

Relief trickled through her. And Lucas would be there if trouble arrived. She relaxed a little as she headed for the oven to check on the pork roast.

Aunt Rachel wouldn't be joining them. She liked her privacy, and she was feeling tired tonight. Nicole planned to take a plate over to the house a little later, when she could tell her aunt about the sheriff's visit.

News of the murder would not be welcome. As impossible as it sounded, her aunt had tender feelings for the man who had died so long ago. If Rachel agreed, tomorrow Sean and Lucas would dig up Francois Villard's grave and discover the truth.

She cast a quick glance at the handsome man across from her, taking in his lean-muscled build, the combination of virile male strength and a surprising amount of tenderness. They needed to go into Baton Rouge and pick up her car. Then they would be back.

A thread of heat slipped into her core. Nicole tried not to think about where Lucas was planning to sleep that night.

## Chapter Twenty-Three

For Sean's sake, Lucas slept in the boy's bedroom, where colorful posters of race cars covered the walls: Bugatti Chiron, McLaren Speedtail, Bentley Continental GT, and Porsche Spyder. Sean's dad had been a high-end auto mechanic. The kid knew plenty about cars and speed, clearly the reason the bad guys were pressing him so hard to steal for them again.

Nicole insisted on putting clean sheets on Sean's bed as Lucas grabbed his overnight bag out of the Jeep. He settled in, turning on the bedside lamp and cracking open a Harlan Coben novel. He read till midnight, then set the book aside and turned out the lamp. Grabbing his robe, he padded down the hall.

He didn't bother to knock. He had waited too long already. He turned the knob and pushed open the door, expecting Nicole to be asleep. Instead, he caught the gleam of her eyes in the darkness, open and watching as he walked into her bedroom.

"If I'd known you were waiting, I would have come sooner."

"We shouldn't be doing this."

One of his eyebrows went up. "Why not?"

"I need to think of Sean. And Aunt Rachel is getting weaker every day."

"As long as I'm here, I'll help you with both of them."

"I know. But you won't always be here. We both know that."

"Do we?" He walked toward her. He'd been aroused since he'd heard the sound of her voice.

It was warm in the room, the ceiling fan rotating slowly, stirring the air. The frosted glass lamp beneath the blades cast a soft yellow glow over the room. Lucas drew back the covers, leaving Nicole naked in the middle of the bed.

He smiled at the erotic sight. "I'm glad to see you were waiting for me."

"No, I just . . . It was warm in here."

He felt the pull of a smile. "*Cher,* you have no idea how much it pleases me to know you desire me."

She said nothing as he stripped off the robe and climbed into bed beside her. "I'm happy just to hold you. I know you must be still hurting."

She made a little sound of disappointment in her throat and his mouth edged up. "Looks like I'll just have to be careful."

He gently pulled her up on top of him so she sprawled over his chest. A long, hot kiss followed, wringing a response that had both of them squirming. He'd been replaying the last time they were together, remembering how good it was. When he caught her hips and positioned her over him, he felt the rush, the fierce need to be inside her.

Kissing led to touching, caressing her beautiful breasts, stroking her damp flesh until she was begging him to take her. She was every bit as fiery as he remembered, but she was injured. He was determined to let her set the pace.

"Please . . . ," she whimpered.

"Anytime you're ready. Tonight I'm leaving it up to you." He usually preferred to take charge, but he didn't want to hurt her, and he wanted to boost Nicole's confidence, give her a chance to experiment with her sexuality. He understood his own all too well.

Casting him a long, uncertain glance, she sat up over him and adjusted herself. Her nipples were taut as she eased his hard length inside. "Okay?"

He couldn't hold back a groan. This was taking far more willpower than he had imagined. "Better than okay."

Nicole began to move, rising, then lowering back down. Lucas clamped hard on his control until she was moaning, her head tilted back, the fiery strands of her hair shifting around her shoulders. He held on as long as he could, but the moment he felt the start of her climax, the tightening of her body around him, he cradled her hips in his hands to hold her in place, surged deep, and let himself go.

Nicole moaned as she came again, her body shaking with the force of it. Slowly her tremors began to fade, and she slumped over his chest. Lucas smoothed a hand over her soft curls as the rush of pleasure slowly faded. Lifting her off him, he settled her on the mattress beside him.

"I didn't hurt you?"

"No." She gave him an impish grin. "But if you had, it would have been worth it."

He smiled into the silence and tucked her a little closer against him. His smile slipped away. He was getting in deep with this woman. It occurred to him that for the second time in his life, he was risking himself, risking the heartache he had felt after losing Marie. He was fearful yet determined to follow the path God had put in front of him — unlike what he had done before.

Or perhaps it had been God's will for him to leave the priesthood, which had led him to the work that seemed to fit him so much better.

Lucas smoothed a hand over Nicole's hair. He wanted more of her, more of everything. But she needed her sleep to heal. The night was long. He closed his eyes, hoping he'd be able to sleep as well.

He was still awake when he felt her hand on his thigh, small and warm, a little uncertain.

*"Cher,"* he said, and turned to her, thankful she wanted him again.

Nicole cooked bacon and eggs for breakfast on Saturday morning. Last night, the subject of the sheriff's visit hadn't come up. Both Sean and Lucas were focused on solving Sean's problems.

This morning as they shoveled in fluffy scrambled eggs and crisp maple bacon, Nicole told her brother the reason for the sheriff's visit, news that the man whose bones had been found in the cedar box had been murdered.

"Aunt Rachel believes the murdered man

is Francois Villard," Nicole said. "His grave is in the Villard side of the family cemetery."

"Wow. Aunt Rachel thinks he's the guy who's haunting Belle Reve?"

"Something like that," Lucas said.

"Do you believe it's true?"

"I think it's possible."

"Cool. Maybe we'll get to see him."

Lucas smiled. "Not unless he wants us to."

Sean's cell rang just then. Swallowing the last bite of eggs on his plate, he pulled the phone out of the pocket of his jeans, jumped up from the table, and headed for the living room.

Nicole flashed Lucas a glance. Even from a distance, they could see the color draining from Sean's face. The call ended abruptly, and her brother walked back into the kitchen.

"I take it that call came from your friends," Lucas said.

Sean's head came up. "They *aren't* my friends."

"You're right. I'm sorry. What did they want?"

"They said I needed to be ready. The cars will be there the end of the week."

"Did they give you a location?"

"No. I'm supposed to call them on Wednesday night."

"You'll have to use the phone on the wall in the hallway. If the police get involved, your cell phone could show a connection between you and the guys in the car theft ring."

"I know. They don't care if I go to jail or not."

"I care," Nicole said. "Lucas, what are we going to do?"

"If I'm going to help you, I need more information. I need to know their names and everything you know about them."

Nicole was sure Lucas had read the police file before Sean arrived at the youth center. But Sean had told the police as little as possible, hoping to end any future trouble. Clearly, that hadn't worked.

Her brother scrubbed a hand through his dark hair. "I don't know that much. Artie said he would handle things. He told me which cars to steal and where to drop them. It went smooth for a while, but then everything fell apart."

"What happened?" Lucas asked.

"I think Artie gave me the wrong drop site on purpose. The cops were waiting. Artie was nowhere around when I got there. He stole the money, I took the blame, and Artie disappeared."

"What's his full name?"

"Arthur Whatley. But maybe he lied about it."

"You mentioned a guy named Mickey Dugan and there's someone named Bruno. What do they look like?"

"Mick's a tall, skinny guy, with stringy brown hair and a bald spot on the back of his head."

"I think we've met," Lucas drawled.

Nicole looked at Sean. "He was one of the guys who attacked me in the parking lot."

Sean's lips thinned.

"What about Bruno?" Lucas asked.

"I've never seen him, but he's got a reputation as a real bad dude."

"There was another guy in the parking lot," Lucas said. "Short, muscled, a sleeve of tats on each arm."

Sean's eyes widened. "That's Ollie Martinez. I only met him once. He was cleaning his nails with a switchblade. It was Mick's way of telling me I'd better do my job and keep my mouth shut or bad things would happen."

"I need details," Lucas said. "How you knew where to find the vehicles and where you dropped them."

"Artie told me where to find the cars. He gave me a device that opened the car door and started the engine."

"There's such a thing?" Nicole asked.

Sean nodded. "You can look it up on the internet. If you have the right tech, you wouldn't believe how easy it is to steal a car, even one that costs hundreds of thousands of dollars."

"Okay," Lucas said. "After you got the car, where did you take it?"

"A different place each time, but usually somewhere a few miles out of town, down a dirt road somewhere. There was a moving van parked there. I drove the car up a ramp into the van, and when I came out, Artie was there to pick me up. He drove me back home and I waited until he called me for the next run."

"Anything else I need to know?"

"These are bad people, Coach. I was crazy to ever get involved with them. I was almost glad when I got arrested. I thought at least I would be out of it."

"But that didn't happen," Lucas said.

Sean looked down at his feet. "I guess not."

Lucas clamped him on the shoulder. "We'll figure it out, okay?"

Sean just nodded.

"In the meantime, we have some work to do this morning."

Interest flashed in Sean's green eyes. "What kind of work?"
"We're going to dig up a grave."

## Chapter Twenty-Four

The moist warmth of an early April day surrounded them as they stood in the family cemetery. The sun beating down from a clear blue sky helped Nicole face the gruesome task ahead.

She stood silently next to Rachel as Lucas drove the blade of the shovel into the earth, stepped on it, filled the blade, then tossed the dirt over a muscled shoulder. Working on the other side of the grave, Sean repeated the motion.

The temperature had both men sweating. Lucas peeled his black T-shirt over his head and Nicole's gaze slid over the hard muscles that bunched and flexed as he moved. Even the gristly task they were completing couldn't block memories of what that hard body had felt like last night.

She glanced away, afraid one of them would notice the warm color rising in her cheeks.

Following Lucas's lead, Sean stripped off his white T-shirt and continued working. When Lucas's shovel made an eerie thump as it struck something solid, Nicole felt a chill. Next to her, Rachel shifted and hugged her arms around her, but her gaze remained fixed on the deep hole in the ground.

A little more digging unearthed the rotting wooden casket that had been Francois Villard's final resting place.

*Or not.*

Lucas jumped into the hole and cleared away enough of the remaining dirt to expose the tarnished brass latches on the lid of what had once been a beautiful rosewood coffin. The wood itself was faded to an indistinct gray and was soft enough that Lucas could push his finger through it.

He looked up at Rachel, whose face was as pale as wax. Nicole moved close enough to put an arm around her aunt's thin shoulders.

"Are you sure you want to be here for this?" Nicole asked gently.

Rachel pressed her lips together and nodded.

"If you're right, we won't find anything inside."

"Please," Rachel said, "I need to know."

Standing in the grave, Lucas took a deep

breath. The muscles in his arms and shoulders flexed as he lifted the heavy lid off the casket. Inside, the ivory satin lining was stained an ugly dark yellow, tattered, and half-eaten by insects. Nicole's stomach churned. But there were no human remains in the coffin.

Rachel started crying. Nicole's hold tightened around her. "We're finished here. Why don't we go back to the house?"

Rachel nodded and started to turn, but Lucas's voice stopped her.

"There's something inside," he said.

They turned back to the grave as he pulled a small, oval, tarnished silver picture frame out of the bottom of the coffin. Lucas grabbed his T-shirt off the ground and used it to wipe the glass, studied the old photo inside the frame, then handed the picture to Rachel.

Her fingers trembled as she touched the face beneath the glass. "It's him. Dear God . . . it's Francois." She turned to Nicole, fighting to hold back more tears. "He's just as beautiful as you painted him."

Nicole studied the faded sepia photo, the beautiful face of the man she had painted on the canvas, and worry filtered through her. Feeling her aunt's pain, Nicole's throat tightened. "This is all so hard to believe."

Rachel clutched the picture to her breast. "The proof is right here in the picture."

"Yes, it is," Lucas said, having no trouble at all believing it. Since Nicole believed in Lucas, she had to keep an open mind.

"Do we leave the hole like it is or fill it back in?" Sean asked.

"For now, we'll leave it open," Lucas said. "It's looking more and more like the bones found in the wooden box belong to Francois Villard. The family will want them buried where they belong."

"The sheriff might be pissed we dug up the grave," Sean said.

"Maybe. He wants to identify the remains. This is part of the solution, not the problem."

But Sean was right, Nicole thought. There were rules — and digging up someone's grave was breaking those rules.

Sean tossed his shovel aside and Lucas did the same. "Let's get back to the house," Lucas said.

Nicole and Rachel led the way to the main house, going through the back door into the kitchen. Lucas and Sean followed, taking seats at the round oak table. Rachel retrieved a pitcher of lemonade from the refrigerator, while Nicole filled tall glasses with ice.

"I could use a cold drink," Lucas said as Rachel poured the lemonade into the glasses and set them on the table, then sat down to join them.

"Rachel, you doing okay?" Lucas asked.

She toyed with the frosted side of her glass. "I knew Francois wouldn't be in there, but still . . . it was . . . difficult."

Sean's eyebrows drew together. "You can talk to him, right?"

"I can hear his voice in my head."

Sean grinned. "That is so cool, Aunt Rachel."

Nicole reached over and covered Rachel's hand, where it rested on the table. "You were right. You said the grave would be empty. After what the sheriff told us, and the book I read at the library, we can be pretty sure the remains found near Bayou Sara belong to Francois."

Rachel glanced away.

"We have a problem," Lucas said. "We can't tell the sheriff we dug up Francois Villard's grave to see if it was empty and found out it was."

"No, and we can't say Francois spoke to Aunt Rachel and told her he wasn't in his grave."

"We need more information," Lucas said. "Something that will help us figure out what happened all those years ago. The more information we have, the better chance of helping Francois move forward."

"You don't think he was attacked and murdered by criminals?" Nicole asked.

"It's possible, but I don't think a bunch of thieves working the docks would have gone to the trouble of transporting his body to a different location when they could have weighed it down and tossed it into the river. And I don't think Francois would still be hanging around if the question of his death had been resolved."

Rachel sat up a little straighter. "Charlotte Villard is still alive and living in St. Francisville. She must be nearly a hundred. She might remember something she heard or read about the family that will help us."

"Good idea," Nicole said. "I'll give her a call, see if she'll talk to us. And I want to go back to the library. They have copies of old newspapers on microfiche. I want to see what else I can find."

"I'll go with you," Lucas said. "My laptop is in the car. I have plenty to do to keep me busy."

Sean finished his glass of lemonade. "I've got stuff to do in my shop. I'll see you guys later." The screen door slammed behind him as he headed back out to his studio.

Rachel finished her lemonade and rose from the table. "I think I'll go upstairs and lie down for a while."

As Rachel walked away, Lucas turned to Nicole. "Unless you have plans for tonight, we're meeting Remy Moreau for dinner at the Joker's Wild. We need to know who's behind the car theft ring, and Remy has been putting his connections to work to see what he can find out."

"Are you sure Rachel and Sean will be all right while we're gone?"

"As much as I think they'll be safe, I'm not taking any chances. I've got a friend coming over. Former military. Works security for Remy. His name is Josh Randall. He'll be here any minute."

Nicole's eyes widened. "You really think that's necessary?"

"Josh is a professional. You won't even know he's here."

Nicole said nothing. Her face still hurt from the beating she had taken. *I suppose we're better safe than sorry,* she thought as they entered the carriage house to wait for Lucas's friend.

Josh Randall showed up ten minutes early. When his black Suburban rolled down the drive, Lucas walked outside to greet him.

Josh turned the SUV around for an easy exit, probably out of habit, and got out of the vehicle.

He was about six feet, auburn hair a shade darker than Nicole's, a good-looking man who kept himself in shape, a necessity when you worked security for Remy Moreau.

"Thanks for coming," Lucas said. The men shook hands.

"After you told Remy what happened to your lady, he was worried," Josh said. "He told me to stay for as long as you need me."

Lucas nodded. "I'll be spending the nights here until this is over, but I'm gone most days and I don't want to leave Rachel or Nicole alone. Or Sean, for that matter. Most of the time, the boy will be in school, but he's here on weekends. I've got things to do at the youth center and some leads I need to follow. I want you to watch out for them whenever I'm gone."

Josh flipped open his dark blue windbreaker to reveal the Glock semiauto holstered at his waist. "I came prepared. Hopefully, I won't need it, but Remy says these guys are not fooling around."

"I'm sure Remy will fill me in tonight. Nicole and I are meeting him for supper, eight o'clock at the Joker's Wild."

Lucas glanced up to see Nicole walking

over to join them.

"Josh, this is Nicole Belmond." Lucas set a possessive hand at her waist. *I might as well make things clear from the start.* "Nicole, meet Josh Randall."

"Pleasure," Josh said, his mouth edging up as he received Lucas's message loud and clear.

"We appreciate your help," Nicole said.

"Why don't we introduce Josh to your aunt and Sean?" Lucas urged Nicole toward the house. "Then we'll head for the library."

Nicole smiled at Josh as the three of them walked toward Belle Reve, and Lucas felt a thread of jealousy he hadn't experienced since his days with Marie. It told him just how deep his feelings ran for Nicole.

They left Josh prowling the grounds, assessing the area, preparing for possible trouble. Nicole retrieved one of her paintings, sunset reflected on the water through a cluster of cypress, and they headed outside.

"It's a gift for the library," she explained as Lucas stashed it behind the seat of the Jeep.

"I'm sure they'll be grateful." He helped Nicole into the seat, then rounded the hood and slid in behind the wheel.

Nicole clicked her seat belt into place.

"Your friend Josh seems nice."

Lucas fastened his seat belt and started the engine. "Josh is one of the good guys. He's worked for Remy for years. He'll take care of your family."

"Remy sent him here?"

"I asked for a favor. Whenever I'm not around, Josh will take care of things."

Nicole made no reply.

Though all of this was foreign to her, she was handling it better than he'd expected. They drove in silence to the library. Lucas parked the Jeep and carried Nicole's landscape inside.

He left the painting at the front desk. "I'll be right over there, whenever you're ready to go." He pointed to one of the tables off by itself, leaving Nicole with the silver-haired woman behind the counter. The woman smiled broadly and thanked her for the gift of the painting.

As Lucas set up his laptop, he saw the librarian leading Nicole over to the microfiche area. After some brief instruction, she sat down and went to work.

Lucas had plenty of work to do himself. He ran two youth centers, and though he had a school administrator in each place, there were always accounts to check, bills paid that needed to be examined, and emails to answer. He flicked a last glance at Nicole and began pulling up files.

## Chapter Twenty-Five

Nicole sorted through one old newspaper after another. She didn't know the exact date of Francois's death, just that sometime in 1878 he had simply disappeared. In various publications of the Baton Rouge newspapers, she found references to Villard Shipping, including bills of lading that showed the contents of the vessels that traveled up and down the Mississippi.

She found no reference to the death of Francois Villard or any mention of his disappearance. Since his body was never found, she figured that made sense. He could have just ridden off to live somewhere else.

After an hour and a half of searching, she put away the last of the microfiche and walked over to where Lucas's dark head was bent over his laptop. She hated to disturb him, but Charlotte Villard had returned her call and agreed to see them this afternoon.

Lucas glanced up. His gaze took in her

stretch jeans and the sleeveless mint-green sweater that hugged her breasts. The gold in his eyes began to glow with what she had come to recognize as desire. Her pulse quickened as her thoughts went to Lucas's magnificent bare chest as he had worked in the sun, and the hours she had spent with him in bed.

Her cheeks warmed. Lust was new to her. She hoped he wouldn't notice.

"Finished already?" he asked, his expression back to normal.

She smiled. "Time flies when you're having fun."

He chuckled. "Find anything new?"

"Not exactly. In a way, the fact the newspapers never reported Francois's death is information in itself. People must have believed he just rode off and went on with his life someplace else."

"Which supports the theory that he fought with either his father or his brother — which would have been a motive for his departure."

"Unfortunately, from what we've learned, that doesn't appear to be what happened."

"No."

"The good news is, Charlotte Villard returned my call. She's willing to talk to us this afternoon." Nicole pulled her cell phone out and checked the time. "We've got about fifteen minutes to get there."

He closed his laptop. "Let's go."

Ten minutes later, the Jeep pulled up in front of a white-trimmed, wood-framed light blue house, with a big wraparound porch. It was one of the historic properties in the area.

When they knocked on the front door, Charlotte Villard pulled it open. She smiled. "Nicole, it's so good to see you." Charlotte's hair was completely white and so fine her pale pink scalp showed through. Her face was badly wrinkled, but her shoulders remained straight, her strength apparent, along with the family pride.

"It's good to see you, too, Charlotte." Nicole leaned over and hugged her. "This is my friend Lucas Devereaux. He owns the Baton Rouge Youth Centers."

Charlotte's gaze met Lucas's, ran over his handsome face and broad-shouldered, lean, muscled build, and a smile of approval touched her lips. "It's nice to meet you. Please come in."

Nicole walked into the entry, Lucas behind her, and Charlotte closed the front door. "I've made us some tea," the old woman said.

"That sounds wonderful." Nicole followed her into a living room that held decades of memories. Hooked rugs over polished hardwood floors, a room filled with family heirlooms and precious knickknacks handed down through generations.

Nicole sat down on a burgundy sofa and Lucas took a seat beside her. The aroma of fresh-cut flowers filled the room as Charlotte poured tea from a gold-rimmed blue porcelain teapot into matching cups and saucers. She offered sugar and cream from a silver serving set, but both of them declined. Charlotte passed the cups and saucers around and settled herself in a chair across from them.

Nicole took a sip of her tea. "Delicious."

Charlotte's lined mouth curved into a smile. "It's jasmine. My favorite."

Nicole returned the smile. "Mine too."

Charlotte sipped her tea. "After you called, I started thinking about my family. Phillipe and Christian are both living in Baton Rouge, not that far away, but I don't see either of them very often."

Nicole made no reply. She wasn't surprised the Villard men had no time for an old woman who couldn't do anything to benefit their social status or business interests.

"On the phone, you mentioned you were concerned with the original owners of Belle Reve," Charlotte continued. "Of course, I wasn't alive back in the days when Pierre Villard founded the family shipping empire, but I remember my grandmother talking about him and his wife. It was a love match, quite a story at a time when arranged marriages were the standard."

"I understand Pierre built the house as a gift for Therese-Louise."

"According to my grandmother, he loved her very much. She said Therese-Louise went against her parents' wishes to marry him."

Charlotte shook her head. "Sadly, they were killed in a tragic accident not long after the marriage of their younger son, Jules. I remember my grandmother said the Villard family was cursed. Grandmother was a Fontaine before she wed. She said her husband told her that at some point in the glory days, the older Villard son had vanished without a trace. Trouble had followed the family ever since."

"You believe the Villards are cursed?" Lucas asked.

"Not really. My life has been blessed. Alain Villard was a wonderful husband. We raised three children, who now have children and grandchildren of their own. But Alain and I never lived at Belle Reve, so perhaps that is the difference."

"Anything's possible," Lucas said, and Nicole knew he believed exactly that.

Charlotte rose from her chair and walked over to the antique sideboard against the wall. "Alain's grandmother gave him a book that had been handed down through the Villard side of the family for generations. I know the library has a copy, but I wasn't sure if you had seen it."

"Winnie Bonner found it for me. I read it while I was there, but the library copy is in very bad condition. Water damaged a lot of the pages. They're either illegible or missing. It was difficult to follow some of what happened."

"Then perhaps this will help." Charlotte opened one of the paned-glass doors on the front of the sideboard and pulled out a small red leather volume.

She crossed the room and handed the book to Nicole. She recognized the title: *BELLE REVE: The Tragic History of a Beautiful Dream.*

The same book, but in extremely fine condition.

"Thank you, Charlotte. I know how much this must mean to you and your family."

"Yes, it does mean a lot."

"I'm hoping this will fill in the blanks in the story."

Beside her, Lucas shifted forward on the sofa. "I'm looking forward to a chance to read the book myself," he said. "I promise you, Ms. Charlotte, we'll take very good care of it."

"Thank you. It truly is a family treasure. Sad as the tale may be."

Nicole set her cup and saucer down on the coffee table. She held the book gently as she rose from the sofa. "This is so kind of you, Charlotte."

"Let me know if you discover something interesting I might have missed," the old woman said.

Nicole smiled. "I will, I promise. I'll bring it back as soon as we're finished."

Charlotte escorted them to the front door. "It was good to see you, my dear." She turned. "Nice to meet you, Lucas."

"You as well, Ms. Charlotte. Thanks again."

They left the house and returned to Belle Reve to change clothes and join Remy for supper. As they turned down the lane toward the house, the flashing red lights of a fire truck parked in the driveway sent a shot of fear down Nicole's spine.

"Lucas." She gripped his arm.

He turned off the engine. "Let's go see what's going on."

A pair of firemen, one tall and thick-chested, the other shorter and dark-skinned, walked out the front door as Lucas and Nicole hurried toward them. Both men wore full turnout gear: yellow striped bunker pants and coats, helmets, and high rubber boots.

Lucas stopped the closest man, the taller of the two. His name tag read Burrows. "Ms. Belmond lives here." Lucas tipped his head toward Nicole. "What's going on?"

"My aunt is ailing," Nicole added anxiously. "Is she all right?"

"Your aunt is fine."

Nicole breathed a sigh of relief.

"An electrical problem shorted out the wiring and started a small fire in the laundry room."

"You got everything under control?" Lucas asked.

The shorter man, named Jackson, nodded. "There wasn't much damage. We were just heading back to the station."

"We appreciate your help," Lucas said.

"You're going to need an electrician," Burrows said. "Once the repairs are made, the city will probably require an inspection to be sure the residence is safe."

"In a house this age, it could get expensive," Jackson added.

Nicole's shoulders slumped.

"The important thing is no one was hurt," Lucas reminded her. "Thanks again," he said to the firemen as he took Nicole's hand and started forward. "Let's go check on your aunt."

Rachel sat in the front parlor with Sean, whose face was still slightly flushed from the adrenaline rush. Rachel looked a little shaken, but resigned.

Nicole hurried toward her and took hold of her aunt's hands. "Are you okay?"

"I'm fine. The electrical box must have sparked, then caught fire. I smelled hot wiring, and it led me to the laundry room. The fire had just gotten started. If it hadn't jumped to the curtains, I would have been able to put it out myself."

"I heard the fire trucks and came running over," Sean said. "Those guys were great. They had everything under control in only a few minutes."

Nicole squeezed one of her aunt's fine-boned hands. "I'm so glad you weren't injured."

"They got here very quickly. I was never in any real danger."

"Maybe not," Nicole said, "but according to the firemen, you'll probably need to have the city inspect the electrical system after it's repaired. If they decide to make us upgrade, it won't be cheap."

Rachel sighed. "Nothing that's happened lately has been cheap."

"We'll get it done," Nicole promised. "The plumbers didn't take as long as we thought. We'll get this handled, too. Until the repairs are made, maybe you should stay in the carriage house." She flicked Lucas a glance and he nodded. Rachel's safety came first.

"I asked if it was safe to stay in the house," Rachel said. "The firemen said there was only one panel affected and they shut that one down. The rest should be okay, but we'll need to get someone out here to get the laundry room working again. As far as staying with you, I'd rather not. You know how much I like my privacy."

"I know, but maybe in this case —"

"Honestly, I think it's fine. Besides, you and Lucas will be right next door."

"Or Sean or Josh," Lucas added.

Rachel smiled. "Yes, that handsome friend of yours arrived at the same time as the fire truck. He went back outside after the firemen took charge."

"Josh is a good man," Lucas said.

Now that the excitement was over, Sean wandered back to his studio. When Lucas and Nicole left the house, they found Josh standing guard outside.

"Looks like we had a little emergency," Lucas said to him.

"By the time I realized there was a problem, Rachel had everything under control. She'd already called the fire department. The fire truck was here in minutes. I went back outside as soon as they arrived. I figured if it was any kind of a setup, I'd be more useful keeping watch out here."

Lucas nodded. "Good call. Sounds like it was just an old-house problem." But in truth, he was starting to wonder. The electrical fire was small, had happened midday, and was easily handled. If it had been sabotage, it wasn't meant to hurt anyone, though there was always a chance that could have happened.

Mostly, it was the cost of repair that was the problem.

Each incident drained more of Nicole and Rachel's money. He could help them financially — if they would allow it — but if the situation continued to worsen, sooner or later, they would be forced to sell.

His jaw tightened. Fairly easy to guess who would benefit most from the sale.

Lucas tamped down his suspicions and filed the information away. He needed to get ready for his dinner meeting with Remy. At the moment, Sean's troubles took precedent over everything else.

# Chapter Twenty-Six

They wouldn't be staying out late, Lucas promised, and Josh would remain at Belle Reve until they returned. In the meantime, Nicole focused on what it would take to keep her little brother out of jail.

She sat back in the passenger seat of the Jeep for the thirty-minute ride to the Four Queens Casino on the Mississippi River in Baton Rouge. As the car drew near, lights on the front of the building glowed in neon reds, greens, blues, and purples. The club wasn't as big as one of the massive casinos in Vegas, but plenty of gaming action went on inside.

The Jeep pulled up beneath the wide portico in front of the entrance, where a fountain bubbled in welcome. A white-jacketed valet opened the passenger door and helped Nicole out of the car. Lucas took her arm and they pushed through the gleaming brass-and-glass front doors into the pandemonium on the gaming floor: the bells, whistles, laughter, and music that made the Four Queens a success.

Lucas guided her past rows of slot machines, lights flashing, chimes ringing; past a spinning roulette wheel; heading straight for the restaurant at the rear of the club. Players shouting numbers crowded around craps tables, and blackjack dealers flipped cards, keeping players hopeful.

A purple neon sign outlined in gold read: JOKER'S WILD. Nicole felt Lucas's hand at her waist, guiding her through the door. Inside, the lighting in the room had touches of the same purple and gold. The hostess, a long-legged, voluptuous blonde, smiled as they approached.

"Lucas. It's nice to see you." A look of interest gleamed in her pretty blue eyes. "Remy is expecting you."

"His usual table?" Lucas asked, and Nicole wondered just how well he knew the woman.

"Of course. I'll show you the way in case you've forgotten."

Lucas made no comment, just urged Nicole forward, and they fell in step behind the buxom hostess in the silver sequined dress. Nicole glanced over at Lucas, but the hostess's interest in him didn't appear to be returned.

She relaxed, determined to enjoy herself, even if they were there on very serious business.

Remy slid out of the booth to greet them, a tall handsome man behind his black mustache. He leaned down and kissed her cheek. "*Cherie,* you are looking quite lovely tonight."

She'd chosen a simple white silk sheath, with gold jewelry and very high heels. She'd wanted to look good for Lucas. She thought it was one of her most flattering outfits.

"Thank you."

Remy seated her in the curved, high-backed booth surrounding a linen-draped table. Through the windows across the room, the Mississippi River sluggishly made its way to the sea. As Lucas and Remy slid into the booth, one on each side of her, a young male server appeared, tiny diamond studs in his ears. He carried a bottle of wine.

"Red wine all right?" Remy asked Nicole. "Unless you prefer something else?"

"Red wine is perfect," Nicole said. Either white or red worked for her, and she recognized the label as an expensive brand.

The server pulled the cork, poured Remy a taste, which he approved, then poured each of them a glass and set the bottle on a silver coaster on the table. The men ordered steak medium rare — no surprise there — and Nicole ordered halibut and risotto.

"Time to get down to business," Remy said as the server quietly disappeared.

Lucas took a sip of wine and set the glass back down on the table. "We discussed the situation when I called, so you know what's going on. Nicole's younger brother is in a bad situation. I'm hoping you've had time to find out something that could help us."

"Something, yes. Unfortunately, not enough." Remy took a drink of wine. "I figured out what sparked all of this. There is a car auction coming up at Casino Rouge Chateau. It's a smaller version of a Barrett-Jackson event. Though the number of attendees will be fewer, it is expected to draw some of the most expensive cars in the world in every category: Ferrari, McLaren, Bugatti, classic Mercedes, Aston Martin, and Jaguar. Some of these cars go for twenty, thirty, forty million dollars."

"Wow," Nicole said. "I had no idea."

"If you are a collector, you understand how big an industry it is."

"You don't think they're expecting Sean to steal multimillion-dollar cars?" Lucas said.

"No."

"Thank God," Nicole said.

"Unfortunately, it is nearly as bad. This kind of an auction attracts big-money buyers. They don't drive Fords and Chevys. They drive cars worth hundreds of thousands of dollars. Rolls, Bentleys, Porsches — anything and everything big money can buy."

"No chance Sean's getting away with it," Lucas said.

"I wouldn't be so sure. This setup must have been in the planning stages for months. Most likely, Sean is not the only driver. My guess is, they have several people lined up."

Nicole's stomach knotted. Sean was in even worse trouble than she had imagined.

Lucas picked up his wineglass. "We need to find out who's behind this. Any luck locating the infamous Bruno?"

"Not yet — but chances are, I will," Remy said. "I don't think Bruno is that high up in the chain of command. His name is bandied about too casually. There are definitely people above him, maybe several tiers before you reach the man at the top."

Not good news.

Their meals arrived, but Nicole's appetite had waned. When Lucas realized she was only pushing the food around on her plate, he leaned over and spoke to her softly.

"Everything's going to be all right. Remy has the contacts to get the information we need. We're going to keep Sean safe."

"It is only a matter of time before we figure out what is going on," Remy added.

Nicole fought to hold back tears. "Then what happens? How do we stop them?"

A look passed between the two men. "We will find a way," Remy said. "In the meantime, *cherie,* if you wish to keep that beautiful figure, and you do not want to insult my chef, as well as me, you must eat."

At the confidence in Remy's voice and the concern in Lucas's golden-brown eyes, she nodded. "You're right. We need to stay positive." She managed to smile. "And it's ridiculous to waste this delicious food."

Both men relaxed and dug back into their meals. Nicole was surprised to discover her appetite had returned. She trusted Lucas and she was coming to trust his best friend.

She took a sip of the rich red wine and began to enjoy her dinner.

Sitting in front of the gilded mirror above the dressing table in her bedroom, Rachel brushed her long black hair. As her mother had also done, she counted the strokes: ninety-eight, ninety-nine, one hundred.

Finished, she tossed the heavy strands over her shoulder. In the mirror, she looked thin and a little too pale. It wasn't just her deteriorating health, she knew. It was worry.

Things were happening at Belle Reve. Things she couldn't control. Like the plumbing leak and the electrical fire, problems she was coming to believe had been caused on purpose.

Unlike the sounds in the night that came strictly from the house's past.

She gasped when she looked in the mirror and saw a figure looming over her shoulder. She saw Francois's high cheekbones, gleaming jet-black hair, and brilliant blue eyes. She took a deep breath and managed to calm her nerves.

"I hoped you would come," she said into the mirror, afraid to turn and look at him, afraid he would disappear.

*I missed you.*

The words rang clearly in her head, and her eyes misted. "I missed you, too."

*I am lonely. I ache for you. Come to bed with me.*

Dear God, it was insane. None of this could be real, and yet she found herself rising from the upholstered velvet bench, turning toward him, hoping he would reach out and touch her. His face was clearly visible above the faint, transparent figure of a man.

With a whisper of silk, her white negligee slipped off her shoulders. The tie at the neck of the matching white nightgown unwound and the gown slid into a puddle at her feet. Naked, she felt embarrassment wash over her. She wanted to cross her arms over her small, pointed breasts.

*No. You are beautiful.*

Her breath froze as her body lifted and he carried her across the room. The covers turned back and he settled her on the mattress. Gentle hands roamed over her. She felt the brush of his lips and closed her eyes.

The lights dimmed. She could feel him there, pressing her down on the mattress. His lips melded with hers as his hands roamed over her, caressed her, began to stir the incredible yearning she had felt before. At her small sound of encouragement, his lips pressed against the pulse throbbing at the base of her throat.

She wanted this, wanted him, for as long as she could draw air into her lungs.

*Francois,* she said in her mind, no longer wanting to disturb the moment with the sound of her voice.

*Rachel.*

It was the first time he had used her name, and love for him swelled inside her. She wondered if he knew.

He touched her as he had before, pleasing her, pleasing both of them. Soft French words whispered over her as he joined with her and brought her to fulfillment. When they were finished, he kissed her one last time and she closed her eyes, giving in to the weariness that pulled her under.

Minutes passed, perhaps longer. A noise, something out of place in the room, caught her attention. The sound of heavy breathing sent chills down her spine and her eyes flashed open. She felt Francois ease away from her, though she knew he remained nearby.

The sounds increased, the rustle of movement, a harsh, grating sound as the breathing grew louder. Something cold touched her face.

*What's happening?* she thought. *Francois?*

*He is mine!* A woman's voice, loud and demanding.

Shock rolled through her as the bed began to shake and the windows began to rattle, thumping so hard she thought they were going to shatter. A shrieking noise filled the air, and fear pooled in her stomach.

Rachel grabbed the covers and pulled them over her naked body. "What — what is happening?" she said into the empty room.

Looking out from beneath the canopy, she could see the crystal chandelier in the center of the room shooting back and forth. The faucet in the bathroom suddenly exploded with gushing water, then turned abruptly off, turned on again, then off.

The lights flickered, then went off, flashed on again, went off, and then back on. Her fear mushroomed into terror. The chandelier began to circle, spinning faster and faster. The bedroom door swung open and slammed closed.

A whimper escaped her throat. She heard movement, felt the air thicken with some powerful force. The hum of energy filled the air.

*Leave her alone!* Francois's command rang with authority, deep and strong, harsh with warning.

She felt a rush of air as he moved toward the threat. The bedroom door swung open and slammed loudly closed. The dresser drawers shot open, spilling the contents onto the floor.

*Mine!* the voice shouted.

*Get out!* Francois demanded.

A sound like thunder rolled across the bedroom, a violent warning. Footsteps raced toward the door, which swung violently open; then the steps shot out into the hall. Another pair of footsteps followed, heavier, a man — Francois. The door shuddered on its hinges, then slammed shut, and the room fell silent.

Shivering, with shaking hands, Rachel clutched the covers up to her neck. She thought it must be the woman Francois had wanted to punish the first time he had come into her room. Who was she? Was it someone he had loved?

Rachel's thoughts returned to the female ghost or spirit — whatever it was — and the terrifying moments she had just experienced. Her heart was still racing, her breath sawing in and out of her lungs. Her throat tightened. She tried to swallow, but the muscles in her neck were cutting off her air supply.

No longer was it fear, but the disease from which she suffered. Her head was spinning. She prayed she wouldn't black out.

A knock on the door focused her attention. She tried to speak, but it came out more of a moan.

An instant later, the door burst open and Josh rushed into the room. "Rachel!" He ran to her bedside. "What's going on? Are you all right? What can I do to help you?"

When she whimpered and lay immobile on the bed, he pulled out his cell and called 911. Rachel closed her eyes and willed her body to relax. Usually, the episode would pass, but she could never be sure.

"Just take it easy," Josh said. "An ambulance is on its way."

She managed a faint nod and lay as still as possible, her breath sawing in and out. A few seconds later, she heard Nicole and Lucas rushing up the stairs.

Her niece ran into the bedroom. "Aunt Rachel!" One look at her pale face and labored breathing and Nicole understood what was going on. She hurried to Rachel's bedside. "Just lie still."

She took hold of Rachel's hand. "We were almost home when Josh called." Nicole flicked him a grateful glance.

"Ambulance should be here any minute," Josh said.

The pressure in Rachel's chest lessened. She dragged in a deep, sluggish breath of air. "I had . . . an episode." She patted Nicole's hand. "It's . . . easing. I'll be all right in a minute. It's . . . almost over now."

"I heard noises," Josh explained. "Saw the light going off and on in Rachel's room. I used the key to the front door Lucas gave me and let myself in. Rachel was in distress when I found her."

"It's ongoing," Rachel said. Which was true, and all the explanation they were going to get. No way was she mentioning Francois or the woman or the terror she had felt. "I just . . . I need some sleep and I'll be all right."

"The EMTs will be here any minute." Lucas stood near the open bedroom door. "Just take it easy until they get here."

"I don't want . . . to go to the . . . hospital," Rachel said. "This . . . happens sometimes. I'm feeling . . . much better now."

"We'll talk to the paramedics," Nicole said. "See what they have to say."

Red lights flashed through the windows. The ambulance had arrived. Josh went down to let them in, then continued with his duties outside. A young EMT and an older paramedic hurried upstairs into the bedroom to examine her.

Half an hour later, satisfied she was no longer in danger, the men — at Rachel's insistence — deemed her well enough to stay home.

As the ambulance turned around and rolled back down the lane, Rachel felt the strain of her worry and fear. Exhaustion settled in and her eyelids felt heavy.

Standing next to the bed, Nicole stared down at her. "I'll be spending the rest of the night in the room next door, and don't even think of arguing about it."

"Fine," Rachel said, too tired to resist. Nicole spotted her white nightgown tossed over the chair, but didn't mention it. Nicole said something to Lucas, who kissed her cheek as she herded him out of the bedroom and closed the door. Nicole grabbed the nightgown and helped her put it on, plumped her pillows and pulled up the covers.

"Something happened to bring all of this on," Nicole said. "What was it?"

"I had a bad dream, that's all."

"A bad dream."

"Yes."

"Fine. If that's the way you want it, we'll leave it at that — for now. If you start feeling ill again, I'll be right next door."

"I just need some sleep."

"You're sure you're okay?"

Rachel nodded. As good as she was going to get, considering the disease that weakened her more every day. Add to that, her encounter with a vicious ghost.

"If you're sure you're all right, I'll see you in the morning." Nicole leaned over and kissed her cheek, then left the bedroom and carefully closed the bedroom door.

For a while, Rachel could hear her moving around in the other room, but before long, the room fell silent.

Rachel prayed the malicious spirit wouldn't return.

She thought of Francois — and her heart twisted. Perhaps he had returned to the woman. Perhaps he loved her. She wondered if she would ever see him again.

# Chapter Twenty-Seven

Lucas awoke to the gray light of dawn creeping through the bedroom window of the carriage house. Josh had gone home after the medical team departed. Sean was asleep in his studio. Nicole was still at Belle Reve.

Lucas couldn't blame her for being worried about her aunt. Muscular dystrophy was a killer. Rachel had already lived a longer life than many of its victims.

Grabbing a black T-shirt and a pair of jeans out of the overnight bag he'd brought with him, he left Sean's room, padded down the hall to the guest bathroom, showered, dressed, and went into the kitchen to brew a pot of coffee.

As he sat down at the breakfast counter, he spotted the red leather volume that documented the Villard family history. Lucas took a sip of coffee, carefully opened the book, and began skimming the pages.

Most of it was information he and Nicole had discussed. How it had been Pierre's dream to build Belle Reve as a gift for his wife. How his sons, Francois and Jules, had helped him make Villard Shipping a success.

A paragraph caught his eye: *It was assumed Francois would announce his engagement to Simone St. Denis, the eldest daughter of Victor St. Denis, the wealthy owner of the adjacent estate and a close friend of the family. The two had been courting for nearly a year.*

But Lucas remembered it was Jules who had married the girl.

He reread the paragraph. Definitely not what he had expected. Instead of announcing his engagement, Francois had ridden out one morning on his way to the docks and simply disappeared. At the time, there were rumors that an argument between the brothers had driven Francois away. If there had been a quarrel, Lucas wondered if it could have been over this woman.

In another theory, the argument occurred between Francois and his father. Perhaps Francois had refused to marry Simone, ending Pierre Villard's dream of a very beneficial union with the St. Denis family. Could his disappointment have somehow been involved in Francois's disappearance?

The most common belief was that Francois had been murdered, his body never found. That much, they now knew, was true.

Lucas glanced up at the sound of the front door opening. Sunlight followed Nicole into the living room, setting off highlights in her fiery hair. Desire pulsed through him, reminding him of the empty bed he had slept in last night.

Nicole smiled. "I smell coffee — thank the Lord. Aunt Rachel is still asleep, and Sean never gets up this early."

Lucas walked over and very softly kissed her. "Maybe that's where we should be. Back in bed."

She slid her arms around his neck. "It wouldn't take much to persuade me." She brushed a light kiss over his lips. "What about church?"

"We'll go to a later service." His mouth claimed hers, lingered. Nicole made a little purring sound when he pressed his lips against the side of her neck, then took her mouth again. Lucas pulled her close enough to feel his arousal and she melted against him with a little sigh of pleasure.

Damn, he wanted this woman. He couldn't seem to get enough. Then she glanced over at the red leather volume lying open on the counter.

"You've been reading," she said, and he knew he had waited too long. "Find anything exciting?"

"Actually, I did." Resigned, he walked over to the coffeepot on the counter, next to the sink, and poured her a mug. "I find it extremely interesting that Jules's wife, Simone, was originally involved with Francois. Apparently, he courted her for nearly a year. Instead of proposing, he was murdered, and she ended up marrying his brother."

"Wow, I didn't see that one coming."

"Neither did I." He handed her the steaming mug and Nicole took a sip.

"Delicious. You're a life saver." She took another sip. "I don't want to sound suspicious, but I also find it interesting that Francois's parents died just a few months after Jules's wedding."

"Leaving Jules and Simone to inherit Belle Reve."

She sipped her coffee. "Could just be coincidence."

"Could be."

"Or not."

He stood up and took the mug from her hand, then set it on the counter and pulled her into his arms. "Now that I've got your thoughts churning, where were we?" Lucas kissed her and she kissed him back; in minutes, they were heading down the hall to the bedroom.

For the moment, thoughts of Francois, Jules, and Simone slid away.

Sean still hadn't appeared when Nicole went back to Belle Reve to check on her aunt. When she'd looked in on Rachel earlier, she had been deeply asleep. Figuring a good night's rest was probably the best treatment, Nicole had left her alone.

With the morning slipping away, she climbed the curving staircase to the second floor, knocked softly on Rachel's door, and heard her aunt's voice inviting her in.

"Good morning." Nicole smiled as she walked into the room. "How are you feeling?"

"Much better than I did last night." Rachel did look better, rested and somehow refreshed. She was dressed in a flowing, mid-calf, flowered pale blue skirt and blue cotton blouse. Ready for church, it appeared.

"I was worried. I'm glad you're feeling more yourself." Remembering the dresser drawers that had been standing open last night, clothes scattered over the floor, she glanced around, but everything was back in place.

"What happened last night, Aunt Rachel? Was it Francois?"

Rachel glanced away.

"I don't like the idea that whatever he's doing is making you ill."

"It wasn't his fault."

"Then whose was it?" Irritation trickled through her. "Lucas and I are trying to help you, Aunt Rachel. We can't do that if you don't tell us what's going on."

Rachel sat down on the upholstered bench in front of the mirror positioned above her dressing table. "I'm not exactly sure. There was someone else in the room last night. A woman."

"A woman? A female ghost? Seriously?"

Rachel sighed. "That's right. A ghost, some sort of spirit, I don't know. She was nothing like Francois. She was . . . Whatever she was, she was evil. Things began to happen. The room was shaking, drawers flying open, the chandelier spinning. Francois told her to leave, but she was very powerful. It was frightening."

Nicole remembered the terror she'd felt in Darla Robinson's house. "I can imagine."

"I know it sounds crazy."

"Yes, it does. I guess some things are out

of our control."

"You said Lucas knows about these things," Rachel said. "Ghosts and spirits."

"Yes. And just as crazy, his grandmother seems able to communicate with dead people."

Rachel pleated a fold in her flowered skirt. "Do you think she would come out to Belle Reve? Maybe she could talk to the woman, make her leave us alone."

"By *us,* you mean you and Francois."

"Yes."

Nicole blew out a breath. "I don't know. I don't know how any of this works. I'll talk to Lucas, see what he has to say." A thought occurred and she glanced over at her aunt. "Did the woman tell you her name?"

"No, but . . ."

"But what?"

"She said Francois belonged to her."

"Wow! And what did Francois have to say about that?"

"I don't think he likes her."

Nicole frowned. "I think I hear a *but* in there."

Rachel sighed. "I don't think he likes her, but I'm not sure."

Nicole dragged a hand through her hair, shoving it back from her face. "This is insane. All of it. It can't be real, and yet somehow it is."

Rachel said nothing.

Nicole managed to smile. "You're dressed for church. You look nice. Lucas is going to drive us."

Rachel smiled back. "I'll put on my shoes and meet you downstairs."

Nicole just nodded. She was worried about her aunt.

And she was worried about her brother.

She just wished things would get back to normal.

Unfortunately, she no longer had any idea what *normal* actually was.

The weekend came to an end. Nicole had spoken to Lucas about Rachel and the spirit of a woman who had made a violent appearance in her bedroom. Lucas told Nicole he would reach out to his grandmother and would try to arrange a meeting.

Nicole had returned the family history to Charlotte on late Sunday afternoon, then driven Sean back to the youth center hoping to prevent any uncomfortable gossip that might become a problem for her brother.

It was early Monday morning. As soon as Josh arrived to stand guard, Lucas headed for the youth center. Josh was prowling around somewhere on the property, alert for any sign of trouble. Nicole had no idea exactly where he was, but she was grateful for his discretion.

She had work to do for a show coming up in New Orleans. The Winston Gallery in the French Quarter was another venue Anne Winston owned. Slightly different from Anne Winston Fine Art, the gallery specialized in more abstract and figurative works of art.

Recently, however, Anne had approached Nicole about doing a show, certain there was an audience who would be interested in her unique Impressionist landscapes, including her dark pieces. Nicole had agreed. Now she was determined to make the show a success.

She sighed as she carried her easel and paints out the front door of the carriage house. With everything that had been happening, she was behind schedule. And being trapped at Belle Reve — for her protection — wasn't helping. She needed to get away, find new inspiration, see what intriguing subject matter she could discover.

Disgruntled, and with no other choice, she carried her art supplies toward the bayou that ran along the edge of the property. With all the overgrown vines and vegetation, it wasn't an easy trip, but she wanted something different, and she had painted the pond so many times she could see it with her eyes closed.

She needed something intriguing to inspire her. When she reached the edge of the water, she walked the sandy bank until she found a subject that looked promising.

At a spot surrounded by heavy foliage beneath the low-hanging branches of a tree, she set up her easel facing a sagging wooden dock, where an old pirogue was tied. She remembered the place from her childhood.

On the opposite bank, built on stilts that held it off the ground, sat the remains of what had once been a cabin. After years of decay, it had been reduced to weather-beaten gray boards and a falling-down screened-in porch beneath a rusted corrugated tin roof. The shack was almost entirely overgrown with wild grapevines and leafy, junglelike green vegetation.

In the past, more than once, she had painted the old cabin in full sunlight, but today the sky was overcast. Heavy, dark clouds completely changed the feel of the landscape.

The murky, brooding weather shrouded the shack in gray lifeless tones, creating an eerie feeling that drew her in and made her wonder about its past.

She let her mind wander and began to sketch, letting the scene unfold, pulling her deeper. She felt herself becoming more and more immersed in a time she couldn't see.

# Chapter Twenty-Eight

Lucas ended the workday and got ready to head back to Belle Reve. He had called Nicole earlier in the day, but the call had gone to voicemail. A second call, a little later, had the same result.

Worried, he'd phoned Josh, who told him Nicole was painting. The security guard was staying nearby, but she insisted he not interrupt while she was working.

That had been hours ago. Lucas had been about to leave the center to head back to the house, but a problem came up between a student and a teacher. He was forced to stay and resolve the situation. He phoned Nicole several more times, still couldn't reach her, and then phoned Josh again.

"I'm glad you called," Josh said. "It's getting late and dark, but Nicole is still painting. I'm starting to get worried."

"I'm almost there," Lucas said as he pulled down the gravel lane. Josh was waiting when he climbed out of the Jeep.

"I didn't want to leave her, but she's in a fairly secluded spot and there's no way you could find her unless I showed you."

Lucas nodded, his worry accelerating. "Let's go." They strode down the overgrown trail. The sky was growing darker by the minute and a mist had started to fall. Josh stopped at the edge of the small clearing, where Nicole stood behind her easel.

"I'll take over from here," Lucas said. "Thanks for watching out for her."

"Just doing my job," Josh said. "I'll see you in the morning."

Josh walked away, and for several seconds, Lucas just stood watching her. She was totally immersed in her work. Her brush moved across the canvas, as if it had a will of its own. Lucas frowned. In the lessening light, she looked pale, and the hand that held the brush was shaking. There was a bottle of water at her feet, but it was still half full.

"Nicole," he called out softly, not wanting to frighten her. "It's Lucas."

She seemed unable to hear him.

"Nicole, honey, it's Lucas." Moving slowly, he came up beside her and took hold of her arm, stilling the movement of the brush. One of her dark paintings, he saw, a picture of the shack he could see across the quiet surface of the water.

He turned her to face him and she blinked, as if waking from a dream.

"Lucas?"

He put his arms around her. "It's getting dark out here, sweetheart. Time to go in." She didn't resist when he took the brush from her hand and set it on the palette.

"Are you all right?" he asked.

As if her legs were too weak to hold her up, she relaxed against him. "I don't know. I feel shaky."

Lucas silently cursed. Picking up the bottle of water, he cranked off the cap. "Drink the rest of this."

She took the bottle with a trembling hand and downed the contents. After a few long swallows, she seemed a little more in control.

"Let's go inside, baby."

"What about my painting?"

"I'll bring it in for you." Keeping her close beside him, he grabbed the canvas and they headed back to the house. Once inside, he set the painting against the wall in the entry, led her over to the sofa, and eased her down.

"Did you eat anything today?"

She looked up at him, a line forming

between her russet eyebrows. "I can't remember."

Fresh worry filtered through him. He went into the kitchen and grabbed another bottle of water. He opened it for her and carried it over to the sofa.

"I've got supper in the car. Drink some of this while I go get it." He was glad he had picked up some Italian food on his way home. Clearly, she was in no shape to cook dinner.

She tipped up the plastic bottle as he headed out to the Jeep. Carrying the food back inside, he set it on the kitchen counter.

"Feeling better?" he asked as he returned to the living room.

Nicole gazed up at him, still looking a little dazed. "Yes . . . much better. Thank you."

"What happened out there today?"

She rubbed her palms over her jeans. "I'm not exactly sure. I was looking for something to paint. I remembered the old shack down on the bayou. I had painted it before, but it had been years ago. Today when I went out there, it looked different, strangely intriguing. Once I started, I couldn't seem to stop. Images rushed into my head so fast I could barely get them drawn on the canvas." She glanced toward the painting leaning against the wall in the entry. "I don't remember how far along in the process I was when you showed up."

Lucas walked over and retrieved the canvas. He carried it over and set it up where they could easily see it.

Nicole shot forward on the sofa. "Oh, my God, Lucas!"

The old shack was there in all its grim glory, the remnant of a past that would never be revealed. But there was something more.

"It's a face," Nicole said. A vague image hovered above the cabin, a face wreathed in pale blond hair that softly curled. The woman had lush blue eyes and ruby lips. She was beautiful.

"Do you think she could be the ghost who appeared in Rachel's room on Saturday night?" Nicole asked. "It has to be more than coincidence."

His mind ran over the possibilities. "So far, the only woman with a connection to Francois is Simone St. Denis."

"Yes, and Francois is the only other face I've painted."

"True."

"Apparently, whatever entity was in the room with Rachel on Saturday night made it clear she believed Francois still belonged to her." Nicole looked at the canvas, at the face that dominated the scene. "Maybe she was sending a message."

"Or a warning," Lucas said.

Nicole's attention swung back to him, worry in her big green eyes.

"Any idea what the shack might have to do with it?" Lucas asked.

"None whatsoever." Nicole leaned back on the sofa. "The painting's not quite finished. Once it's done, maybe we'll know more." She blew out a weary breath and sat up straighter. "I don't understand *why* any of this is happening. *How* is it happening?"

"It's the house," Lucas said. "Finding Francois's bones unleashed all of this, but Belle Reve is the focus."

"How do we stop it?"

"I don't know. I'm hoping my grandmother can help us. I called her today. She's in Lafayette visiting friends. She'll be home the end of the week. She's planning to come over as soon as she gets back. I'll be in touch with her to set up a time."

Nicole took a drink from the bottle of water, then put the cap back on. She glanced toward the kitchen. "Something smells good. What's for supper?"

He could tell she was ready for a change of subject. "Lasagna. It's not homemade, but it's from Rosa's, so it should be good."

Nicole managed a smile, but it didn't look completely sincere. "I hope you're hungry, because I'm starved."

Lucas's gaze ran over her, the ivory complexion, the few faint freckles across her nose and forehead, the fiery copper hair. He was hungry, but not for food.

Then he thought of the image in the dark painting, thought of the violence unleashed in Rachel's room, and worry took the place of the need she aroused in him.

He'd take off early tomorrow, he decided, send Josh home and look after Nicole himself. He'd make sure she didn't exhaust herself finishing the painting. He'd feel better if he was near.

There was danger in the spirit world. At the moment, that danger was focused on Belle Reve. Lucas had seen things few people would believe: the raging power, the violence, the fierce destruction. Human life was frail in comparison.

Lucas was determined that nothing, human or otherwise, was going to hurt Nicole.

The following day, Nicole was working on the painting of the shack on the bayou when she heard a vehicle driving up the lane. Thinking it was Lucas, she pulled herself away from the hold the painting seemed to have over her and started hurrying back along the overgrown path to the house.

As she stepped out into the open, a man unwound himself from inside a black-trimmed white Porsche. Tall, blond, *Christian Villard.*

Nicole clenched her teeth. Tempted to turn and run back into the trees, she forced herself to continue toward the house. There was no way she was letting Christian intimidate her. Still, the sooner she got rid of him, the better.

He turned at the sound of her approach and gave her what he believed was a charming smile. "Nicole. I was hoping I would catch you at home."

"I'm in the middle of something, Christian. What can I do for you?"

He glanced around, as if to make sure she was alone. She didn't mention Josh, who wouldn't interfere, but was somewhere nearby in case she needed him.

"I'm here to discuss a possible offer on Belle Reve," Christian said. "Why don't we go inside, where we can talk it over?"

"My aunt owns Belle Reve, and she isn't interested in selling. You and your father both know that. I'm sorry you wasted your time driving up here."

Christian kept his phony smile in place. "Unless you want me to go over to the main house and speak to your aunt, we need to go inside so you can at least hear me out."

She didn't want to go anywhere with Christian, but she didn't want him making a scene that would involve Aunt Rachel. Brushing past him, she led him into the carriage house and closed the door.

Nicole turned to face him. "All right, let's hear it — then you can leave."

Christian lounged back against the wall in the entry. "How about a cup of coffee?"

"No."

He sighed. "All right, here are the facts. We both know it's only a matter of time until your aunt passes and you inherit Belle Reve. Rachel is extremely ill. It's in her best interest to end the stress of owning a house that's in constant need of repair. Perhaps we could make some kind of arrangement for her to remain on the property until the time of her death. A life estate, of sorts. A condo, maybe — something like that."

"My aunt is only forty-four. She could live many more years. However long it is, she wishes to remain at Belle Reve, the house our family has owned for over a hundred years. She has no interest in selling. I intend to make sure her wishes are fulfilled."

She hadn't noticed him moving closer, until she felt a slight tug and realized he had wrapped a curl of her hair around his finger.

Nicole pulled away.

Christian just smiled. "How much will it take for you to convince your aunt to do what's in her best interest? We're willing to pay you a considerable sum as a brokerage fee — say, a hundred thousand dollars? That would be on top of the purchase price, of course. You'd have money in the bank, and your aunt would have enough to last till the end of her life. What do you say?"

"You aren't listening, Christian. The Belmond family isn't interested in selling. Now please leave. You aren't welcome here again."

He glanced around. She had made the mistake of letting him in, but she had never really been afraid of him. At the predatory gleam in his eyes, she realized her error and her pulse kicked up. She could scream, and Josh would come running, but she didn't want to do that unless she had to.

"If I were you and all alone out here," Christian said, an edge to his voice, "I think I'd be a little more friendly." He moved closer, blocking her escape, backing her up against the wall. He tried to kiss her, but she turned her face away.

"Get away from me, Christian."

"If I decide to have you, nothing you do is going to stop me."

"Try it and I'll call the police. Attempted rape would be a nasty blow to the Villard family name."

He gave her a feral smile. "People have seen us together. There have been rumors. Who do you think people will believe? You, a woman with financial troubles, in desperate need of a man's protection. Or me, a Villard, the son of a very powerful man."

Christian pinned her with his body, caught her jaw to hold her in place, and lowered his head. Nicole twisted and tried to knee him in the groin just as the door slammed open and Lucas burst in.

He took one look at the scene and, in an instant, he was on Christian, dragging him off her, spinning him around and smashing a fist into his face. Blood flew, spattering the front of Christian's pristine white shirt. Lucas delivered another crushing blow, this one to the stomach. Christian choked and doubled over, wheezing and trying to catch his breath. Lucas jerked him up and hit him again, sending him flying backward against the wall, slamming into it, sliding down and sprawling on the floor. Christian groaned.

When Lucas grabbed his shirt and hauled him up, then drew back a powerful arm for another blow, Nicole grabbed his bicep and hung on. "Lucas, stop it! That's enough!"

He swung around, as if facing another foe, his fist still clenched.

"Lucas!"

He shuddered, the muscles in his arm trembling with the effort it took to regain control. She had seen this side of him before — the dark, dangerous side that he had managed to leave in the past. *Mostly.*

His body slowly relaxed, and a little at a time, he became himself once more. He nudged Christian with the toe of his low-topped leather boot. "Get up."

Nicole hurried into the kitchen and grabbed a dishtowel, returned to the living room and handed it to Christian, who pressed the cloth against his bleeding nose. He staggered to his feet.

"Time for you to leave," Lucas said.

"You'll be sorry for this." Christian reeled back a few steps, then managed to regain his balance. He wove his way to the door.

"Don't come back," Nicole said as Christian staggered outside.

"You won't like what will happen next time," Lucas warned, a dark look on his face.

Christian turned back to them. "You'll pay for this, Devereaux." His glare shifted to Nicole. "You're both going to pay." Slamming the front door closed behind him, he headed for his car.

Lucas pulled her into his arms. "You okay?"

She nodded, though she was still shaking. The roar of the Porsche's engine and the screech of tires throwing up gravel signaled Christian's departure.

"What are you doing here?" Nicole asked, leaning against Lucas's chest. "Where's Josh?"

"I sent Josh home when I arrived. Why didn't you call him when Villard first got here?"

She sighed. "Stupid, I guess." She looked up at him. "I should have. I thought I could handle it myself."

"Maybe you could have." He tipped her chin up and gently kissed her. "I don't like the idea that you had the problem in the first place."

She kissed him back. "Thanks for playing Sir Galahad again."

He sighed. "The problem is, I get carried away when I see someone hurting you. It hasn't happened to me in a very long time. I don't like it."

She understood. He was a different person now than when he was younger. "With any luck, nothing like that will happen again."

"With any luck," he said. But the dark look remained on his face.

## Chapter Twenty-Nine

By the end of that day, just before the predicted April storm arrived, Nicole finished painting the dilapidated cabin. As the first few drops of rain began to fall, Lucas helped her carry her canvas and paints back to the house.

He set up the easel in the living room and stood in front of it, arms crossed over his powerful chest.

"You've added a degree of depth to the scene," he said. "The dark tones and the fading light seem to compel more emotion. But the woman's still there, hovering above the shack." He tilted his head to look at the painting from a different angle and his gaze sharpened. "There's a subtle change in her face . . . in her eyes. They seem to reflect a look of anticipation."

"*Anticipation* — yes, that's it. But I feel as if there's something more."

Lucas shifted, studied the painting again.

"Yes. It's there in the way you've drawn her eyebrows, the faint downward tilt of her lips. As if she's doing something she shouldn't be, something she knows is wrong."

"That's exactly how I felt when I painted it."

"Perhaps at one time, it was a place she visited."

"A secret place." Nicole suddenly had the thought — though she had no idea why. "A place she didn't want anyone to know about."

"We need to show this to Rachel."

Nicole sighed. "I know. I called her while you were setting up the easel. I told her a little about the painting and asked her to come over and take a look. She should be here any minute."

"There's a chance the woman looking down at the shack is the entity who came into her bedroom. You think Rachel will be able to handle it?"

Nicole thought it over, then nodded. "My aunt's being visited by spirits — not all of them friendly. I imagine she wants to know as much about what's happening as we do."

A light knock sounded, then the knob turned, and the door swung open. "May I come in?"

Nicole smiled. "Of course."

Dressed in loose-fitting jeans and a printed pink blouse, Rachel closed her umbrella and stepped into the entry.

"How are you feeling?" Nicole asked as Rachel approached.

"All right, I guess. I'm still a little shaky after my latest episode, but there's not much I can do about it."

"I think you should see Dr. Marlowe. You haven't had a checkup in a while."

"I have an appointment with him the end of the month."

Nicole felt a glimmer of relief. "That's good news."

"I guess we'll find out."

The end of the month was still weeks away, but it was better than if Rachel refused to go at all.

"Well, let's see what you've got." Her aunt walked into the living room. She spotted Lucas next to the easel and gave him a hug. "Thanks for being so patient with all of this."

"Not a problem." Lucas led her over to the sofa. "You ready to take a look?"

"I'm definitely curious." Rachel sat down on the sofa in front of the canvas. She flicked a glance at Nicole. "One of your dark paintings, I see."

"I'm afraid so."

"I wouldn't have expected anything else." Rachel studied the canvas, her sleek black brows pulling into a frown. "I recognize the old cabin." She reached toward the painting, her slender fingers hovering just over the image of the face. "You painted the woman."

"The woman who came to your bedroom?" Nicole asked. "You think that's who she is?"

"It must be." Rachel studied the painting and her eyes misted with tears. "She's beautiful."

Lucas seemed to understand. "So are you, Rachel."

"But she's so young."

Lucas's gaze sharpened on Rachel's face. "After death, her age, *your* age, what we look like — it's all unimportant. It's the soul that matters."

Nicole sat down next to Rachel on the sofa, reached over, and took her hand. "We think the woman's name might be Simone St. Denis. Her family owned the estate adjoining Belle Reve. It looks as if Francois was supposed to marry her, but something changed and the engagement never happened."

Rachel looked back at the painting. "He must have loved her very much."

"Maybe," Nicole said. "Maybe not. For whatever reason, the engagement never took place. Instead, Francois disappeared."

"Francois was murdered," Rachel said darkly.

Nicole looked at the painting. "Here's the interesting part. According to the Villard family history, a year after Francois's disappearance, Simone married Jules."

The frown returned to Rachel's face. "If she was married to Jules, what would she be doing here at Belle Reve?"

Nicole's gaze returned to the painting. "The entity said Francois belonged to her. Maybe Simone still loved him after he disappeared."

Rachel's eyes glistened.

"Even if she did," Lucas added, "you told Nicole that Francois didn't seem to like her."

Rachel's tight features softened. "That's true."

"At least now, we have more information," Lucas said. "I'm hoping my grandmother can provide something else when she comes to the house at the end of the week."

"She's agreed to come?" Rachel's expression seemed both hopeful and wary.

"Her name is Gabrielle Lafon, and yes, she's agreed to come. She's out of town at the moment, but she's planning to be here Saturday night."

"What will I have to do?"

"There are no set rules. Grandmere reaches out and we see what happens. If Francois is receptive, she may be able to help him move forward. Or you may."

Rachel said nothing.

Nicole looked at her aunt and some of her worry eased. At least her aunt hadn't freaked out over the latest speculation.

The conversation ended when Lucas's phone rang. He headed into the kitchen to answer the call. Lucas recognized Remy's number and pressed the phone against his ear.

"I've got news," Remy said.

"Tell me."

"I'd rather talk in person. When can we meet?"

"How about tonight?"

"You and Nicole?" Remy asked.

"This involves her brother. She needs to understand what's happening."

"Tonight, then," Remy said. "Joker's Wild. Supper is on me. I will join you after."

"I'll call Josh, make sure he's available to watch the house tonight. I'll text to confirm."

The line went dead. Remy was a busy man.

By the time Lucas returned to the living room, Rachel had gone back home. Nicole sat on the sofa, studying the painting. The patter of rain on the roof of the carriage house penetrated the quiet inside.

"That was Remy," Lucas said. "He has information. He wants us to meet him tonight at the club."

"You think that's good or bad?"

"I guess we'll find out tonight." Lucas phoned Josh, who agreed to come out to the house, then texted Remy to confirm the meeting. He shoved the phone back into his pocket and turned to Nicole. "At least we won't have to cook supper."

She gave him a faint smile. "There is that."

The hours slipped past. Josh arrived, and Lucas and Nicole climbed into the Jeep and headed for Baton Rouge. Driving south on US 61, the windshield wipers battling the rain, he took Exit 3A, made a couple of turns toward the Mississippi River, and the brilliant, colored lights of the Four Queens appeared ahead.

A valet parked the car, and Lucas guided Nicole inside the casino. Surrounded by the clatter and clang of slot machines and the excitement of the gaming tables, they made their way to the rear of the club where the gold and purple neon sign read *Joker's Wild.* In minutes, they were seated in Remy's favorite booth at the rear of the club, looking over menus the server handed them. They both ordered small portions and stuck with water, more interested in what Remy had to tell them than in indulging in a gourmet meal.

Elegant in all black — suit, shirt, and tie — Remy arrived just as their empty dinner plates were being cleared.

"I'm sorry I could not join you sooner." He reached for Nicole's hand and brought it to his lips. Lucas felt a twinge, even though Remy was his best friend, a man he would trust with his life.

"*Cherie,* it is good to see you. I hope my friend has been treating you well."

"Very well," Nicole said, smiling.

Lucas could have sworn faint color rose in her cheeks. Perhaps she was remembering last night's passionate lovemaking. His groin tightened. He planned to treat her even better when they got home tonight.

"So, what news?" Lucas asked.

A waiter arrived with a glass of red wine for Remy. "Join me?"

"Not tonight," Lucas said, anxious to get on with it.

Remy sipped his wine. "The man you are interested in . . . Bruno Takov is his name."

"Russian?"

"Yes. Unfortunately, he is not the man at the top of the organization, though he has plenty of influence. Enough to cause Nicole and Sean a great deal of trouble."

Lucas glanced at Nicole and read the worry in her face. "What do we do about it?"

"You're not going to like what I am going to say."

Lucas waited.

"I believe Sean has no choice but to steal the cars."

"What?" Lucas shook his head. "No. The boy will end up in the system, and that's exactly what we're trying to prevent."

"Please hear me out."

Lucas waited.

"First you need to understand that the men Sean is involved with are ruthless in the extreme. If the boy does not do as he is told, they will come after him — and Nicole. There is no limit to what they might do."

Lucas bit back a swear word he hadn't even thought in years.

Remy's long fingers toyed with the stem of his wineglass. "What I am about to tell you can go no further than here."

Lucas flicked a glance at Nicole.

"Of course not," she said.

"I have a friend, a detective in the police department. He has been working undercover. He and several other officers have been trying to bring these criminals to justice for over a year. If Sean will work with this man, and the police are able to make an arrest, this can all go away."

Nicole started shaking her head. "It's too dangerous. I can't risk my brother's life."

"His life and yours are already at risk, *cherie*."

Nicole looked up at Remy. Lucas could read the worry in her face. "Are you sure there is no other way?"

"I am sorry," Remy said to her.

Nicole's hand shook as she took a drink of water and set the glass back down. "How would it work?"

"Sooner or later, Sean will get a phone call giving him the information — which cars to steal, where to find them, where to deliver them. The police are certain it will happen during the auction at Casino Rouge Chateau. Sean will give you the information, Lucas, and you will relay it to the undercover officer."

When Lucas said nothing, Remy continued.

"Sean will pick up the first car and drive it to the delivery site, where the police will be waiting. He will be arrested, along with the others, and taken into custody. It will look as if the plan went awry, and Sean had nothing to do with it."

"Will he have to testify?" Lucas asked.

"The boy will be able to give a written statement meant to stand up in court. The detective will be the primary witness. He has been involved since the beginning."

Lucas didn't like it. Not one bit. But he had known men like these, knew how ruthless they could be. Once they made a threat, it was a matter of honor to see it through. They would go after Sean and Nicole. There would be no place safe for them, no place to hide.

"Anything more?" he asked.

"It is likely the boy will not be able to escape the consequences entirely. His story would not look credible if he did. My friend believes Sean will be able to get off with only an extension of the sentence he is now serving."

Nicole's eyes filled.

"Do you understand this?" Remy asked her.

Lucas reached over and took her hand.

Nicole wiped away a tear with the tip of her finger. "Yes, I understand. The men at the top of the theft ring have to believe Sean wasn't involved."

"Exactly."

"Anything else?" Lucas asked.

"If there is, I will call."

Lucas slid out of the booth, and Nicole slid out beside him. He settled a hand at her waist. "We'll talk it over and get back to you."

"Remember what is at stake, my friend. You do not have much time."

Lucas made no reply, just urged Nicole toward the door of the restaurant and out into the casino. Remy understood, just as Lucas did. There was no other way.

The rain continued to fall as they drove back to Belle Reve. "Tell me what you're thinking."

"I'm frightened, Lucas."

"You have every right to be."

"Sean could get killed."

"If he doesn't do it, he could also get hurt. In that event, both of you could get injured. As far as receiving an extended sentence, he's doing very well at the center. A few more months shouldn't be too difficult for him."

Lucas pulled down the lane toward Belle Reve and drove up in front of the carriage house.

"You think he should do it," Nicole said as he turned off the engine. It wasn't a question, and it was the truth.

"I think we need to talk to Sean about it. I'll see him tomorrow at school. As Remy said, we don't have much time."

Josh appeared out of the shadows beneath the eaves as they climbed out of the car. He was dressed in black, head to foot, and wearing a black rain slicker. Lucas waved, Josh waved back, and headed for his SUV.

Lucas and Nicole hurried into the house and Lucas closed the front door. Wordlessly, Nicole walked straight down the hall to her bedroom. As much as he wanted her, he understood. He knew how worried she was about her brother, understood she needed something different tonight.

She stopped at the bedroom door and turned back to him.

"I'll sleep in Sean's room," he said as he approached. "You get some rest."

"You don't have to do that."

He reached out and cradled her cheek. "It's up to you, love."

"I'd rather have you next to me."

Something warm filtered through him. He pulled her into his arms. "Then that's where I'll be."

It was dark in the room and quiet as they lay, side by side, in bed. The rain had paused, the wind gone still. He intended to let Nicole sleep, but then she reached for him.

"I need you," she said.

Lucas felt a tug in his heart. He knew how hard it was for Nicole to say those words. She didn't want to need anyone. She didn't want to trust anyone to be there if she did.

"I'm right here, honey."

"Lucas . . ."

He pulled her into his arms and kissed her. They made slow, easy love, then slept in each other's arms.

Thoughts of the dark days ahead kept him awake well into the night, but Lucas didn't mind. It made it easier for him to watch over her.

# Chapter Thirty

Nicole slept deeply, lulled by the sound of the rain on the roof and the warmth surrounding her. It was dawn Wednesday morning when she awakened, her eyes opening slowly, taking a moment for awareness to settle in.

She was cradled in Lucas's arms, her head against his shoulder. His eyes were closed, his body relaxed in sleep, his breathing deep and even. She had never been held by a man this way — as if it were completely natural, as if she belonged there.

Her heart jolted. She had never allowed herself to get this close to a man, to trust a man the way she trusted Lucas. She was falling in love with him — and that was something she could not do.

She had Sean to think of and the terrible trouble he was facing. She had Rachel's health and uncertain future to worry about. And Belle Reve. The family home was her heritage. She had to fight for it against men like Phillipe and Christian Villard.

Even against unseen forces.

Lucas stirred beside her and she realized his eyes were open and watching her.

"I should get up," she said.

"We should both get up," he said, kissing the side of her neck. "I've got to get to the center."

But neither of them moved. Nicole realized she didn't want to leave the bed, leave Lucas's arms. She wanted to stay right there forever.

She tossed back the covers. "You're right, we have too much to do." She bolted from the bed and headed for the shower. Turning on the water, she waited a few seconds, then ducked beneath the warm, misty spray.

She had just shampooed and rinsed her hair when the shower door opened and Lucas stepped in behind her. He had the most gorgeous body — all lean, corded muscle and wide, solid shoulders. Just looking at him made her feel hot all over.

He eased her back against his chest, reached around her for the soap, lathered his hands, then slid them over her body.

A soft moan escaped, and Nicole arched her back, giving him better access. His clever fingers caressed her breasts, then moved lower, stroking and teasing, arousing her as it seemed so easy for him to do.

"Put your palms flat on the wall," he whispered in her ear, pressing his mouth against the nape of her neck.

Imagining his intentions, Nicole bit back a moan and did as she was told. She felt him behind her, gripping her hips, pulling her against him, sliding deep inside.

Pleasure tore through, hot and fierce. Her back bowed as he began to move, slowly increasing the rhythm. Heat enveloped her, tightened her insides, until a fierce rush of pleasure sent her spinning into climax.

Knowing how to please her, Lucas continued, driving deep, his hands sliding over her — teasing, stroking, and moving in rhythm to his body. Shivers erupted on her skin, along with a fresh rush of pleasure. Nicole cried out as she came again and Lucas followed, both of them shaking with the force of their release. Turning her into his arms, he held her as they spiraled down.

The water was growing cold when he stepped out of the shower. Quickly toweling himself dry, he wrapped her in the folds of a fresh towel and kissed her.

"I've got to go. Josh will be outside by now. I'll talk to Sean and see you tonight."

Nicole said nothing. She was getting in

deeper with every passing second. She knew Lucas was attracted to her. He wanted her and she wanted him. But love? He was probably still in love with Marie.

Her stomach rolled at the thought.

Dressing quickly, she grabbed a cup of coffee and headed into her studio. She needed to start another painting, something more cheerful, one of the bright-colored landscape paintings she was known for, something besides the dark images that seemed to be haunting her lately.

The rain was still falling. She would paint from memory today. It might not turn out to be her best work, but with luck, at least it would keep her entertained.

Standing in the sidelines of the basketball court in the gym, Sean saw Coach striding toward him.

"We need to talk," Coach said. "Come to my office before you leave for work."

Sean nodded. "Okay." Nerves filtered through him as he watched Coach disappear out the door. He collected his gear, prepared to leave for his after-class job at Dave's Home Supplies, but headed instead to Coach's office.

He knocked, saw the door stood partly open, and walked inside.

"Close the door and take a seat," Coach said.

Sean sat down on the edge of one of the padded metal chairs in front of the desk. "What's going on?"

"I'd rather we talked somewhere else, but there just isn't time. I'll be blunt. It looks like the only way out of this mess for you is to cooperate with the police."

Sean's stomach lurched, tightened. "If the men find out, they'll kill me."

"We aren't going to let them find out. Here's the way it's going to work."

Coach laid it all out. As soon as Sean received instructions from Mickey, he would text Coach on a burner phone. Coach would relay the message to the Baton Rouge cops working the case. They knew some of the men involved: Mickey, Ollie, and Bruno.

"I don't think Bruno's the guy at the top," Sean said. "What do we do about that?"

"I'm sure the police are hoping one of the men caught up in the sweep will be willing to make a deal."

"They think one of the guys will rat on the rest of the people involved?"

"I'd say that's the plan."

"What if it doesn't work?"

"The cops know you're innocent. They know you were forced to cooperate. Whatever happens, that puts you in the clear."

Sean blew out a breath. "I guess that's something."

"Unfortunately, there's going to be consequences. It's the only way the whole scenario is believable."

The knot in his stomach went tighter. "What kind of consequences?"

"You'll probably end up with an extended sentence here at the center. I'll do everything in my power to make it as minimal as possible. Unfortunately, it looks like it's the only choice we have."

A few more months at the center. He had friends who would still be here. If he could end all of this, it wouldn't be so bad. "You think Nicole will be okay?"

Coach's jaw flexed. "No matter what it takes, I'll look out for Nicole. You can count on that. We just need to make sure you'll also be okay."

Their gazes met. There was steel in the depths of Coach's dark eyes. Sean thought Lucas Devereaux was falling for his sister and he would do whatever it took to protect her. But he was also concerned for Sean's safety.

Everything inside him settled. He could do this. It was easier knowing he had people who cared about him.

"I think they'll call tonight or it could be tomorrow," Sean said.

"The sooner, the better. More time to set things up."

Sean nodded. "I should go. I don't want to do anything out of the ordinary."

"You're right. The less contact we have from now on, the better." Coach rose from behind the desk, walked around, and handed Sean a burner phone. "I have one, too. I programed my number into yours. Put this one somewhere safe and text me as soon as you have something to report."

Sean just nodded. His stomach felt shaky. One thing he had learned at the youth center, no matter how young or old you were, the decisions you made would determine the rest of your life.

He hoped he'd be able to survive his previous bad decisions.

And that they wouldn't end up getting his sister killed.

Lucas was back at Belle Reve that Wednesday night, sitting with Nicole in the living room of the carriage house, when he received a text from Sean.

The plan was in motion. Tomorrow night, Sean would sneak out of the center an hour after lights-out and make his way to a spot two blocks away. Mickey Dugan would be waiting. Mick would drop him at Casino Rouge Chateau, where an exclusive reception was being held for participants and bidders at the car auction taking place there on Friday night, Saturday, and Sunday.

Participants' and bidders' personal autos would be parked in a special section of the parking garage, protected by cameras and security guards. For a few brief moments, a distraction would lure guards away and cameras would shut down.

Drivers, armed with digital devices, would enter the structure, start their vehicles, and exit the garage, heading for their assigned rendezvous points.

Unfortunately, drivers wouldn't receive the drop site information until just before they arrived at the casino.

Lucas felt Nicole's presence behind him, reading Sean's text over his shoulder. "I'm so worried about him. Anything could happen."

"I don't like it, either, but there's nothing else we can do." He turned and cupped her cheek. "I'll be staying in town tomorrow night. After the police pick Sean up, you and I will be the first people they call. Starting from different locations, we'll arrive at different times in two separate vehicles. No reason to connect us. Josh will be here. He'll stay to watch out for Rachel after you leave."

Nicole just nodded.

Lucas's jaw clenched. He'd be glad when tomorrow night was over. He prayed God would keep all of them safe.

It was happening. Sean rode in the passenger seat of the old Toyota Mick Dugan was driving. They hadn't spoken three words since Sean had climbed into the vehicle. As the car rolled along, he spotted the lights of Casino Rouge Chateau up ahead. Still some distance away, Mick pulled off the road into a dark grove of trees, beneath a cluster of low-hanging branches.

It was a moonless night, rolling, flat-bottomed storm clouds blocking the stars. A light mist was falling, making the roads slick and treacherous. He could handle the roads. They were the least of his problems.

"I'll see you at the drop site," Mick said.

"I'll be there." Sean cracked the car door and climbed out of the Toyota.

"Don't screw up." The car drove away and Sean started walking toward the garage, careful to stay in the shadows. He was right on schedule, the digital key Mick had handed him riding in his pocket.

As soon as Mick had given him the drop site location, Sean had managed to text the information to Lucas on the burner phone without being seen. He prayed the message had been received.

Dressed head to foot in black, a black balaclava over his head, Sean waited in the darkness outside the parking garage until he heard the distant clang of a fire alarm going off at the far opposite end of the multistoried casino-hotel complex.

The lights in the garage went off, the signal for him to move, and he raced inside. He had memorized the layout. Even in the dim interior lit only by emergency lighting, he knew where to look for his target. He spotted the car in a back corner and couldn't suppress a thrill of excitement.

"Lamborghini Diablo VT Roadster." He grinned. "Sweet." As he hurried toward the car, he noticed movement from the corner of his eye as three other black-clad figures spread out over the garage.

In less than a minute, Sean was in the car, the engine fired up, the wheels rolling toward the exit. No one tried to stop him. He pulled out of the garage onto the street and hit the gas, careful not to squeal the tires — a definite temptation — and followed the instructions he had been given.

He saw no sign of the other stolen cars, figured they had each been given a different route to their drop locations. He kept his gaze watchful and his speed under control. He just wanted to get the job done and get his life back in order.

His heart began to pound when he spotted a patrol car parked at the side of the road, red and blue lights flashing. Instead of driving straight past, he made a turn, changing the route, carrying him out of sight, and hit the gas. The rush of speed was like a drug. Adrenaline flooded his veins as he drove farther and farther away. He had to force himself to brake and bring his speed back under control.

Once more driving the designated route, he turned the Lambo down a little-used dirt road, tossed the burner phone out the window, and just as in the past, he spotted a big Lyons moving van, or what had been painted to look like one. A ramp placed at the rear provided easy access, and another car, a beautiful Ferrari V12 coming from a different direction, drove up the ramp in front of him. Sean followed.

Worry slid through him as he climbed out of the stolen vehicle, and the other driver did the same. He was shorter than Sean, but beefier, also dressed in black. They headed for the rear of the van and wordlessly moved down the ramp.

*Where are the cops?* His palms were damp, his pulse hammering.

As he walked out of the van, he saw the hulking figure he recognized as Bruno standing next to the driver's-side door. Mick stood next to his old Toyota, parked not far away. Sean headed in that direction. Still, no cops.

His worry shot up. Suddenly his heart jerked at the sound of sirens cutting through the night. Swooping toward them from all directions, police cars, with their flashing red lights, surrounded them.

"What the fuck!" Mick roared.

Sean roared right back. "You bastard! What's going on, Mick! You said this was all arranged!"

Police cars screeched to a halt and doors flew open. Uniformed officers scrambled out, guns drawn and pointed in their direction. "Down on your knees! Hands on your heads! Do it now!"

Sean dropped to his knees and clasped his hands over the back of his head. Mick dropped to the ground beside him. The Ferrari driver did the same. The van door opened and the driver got out, hands on his head.

Bruno was the last man standing, a look of burning fury on his butt-ugly face. Sean didn't see the gun that seemed to magically appear in Bruno's hand. At the staccato blast of gunfire, Sean dove to the ground. A hard jolt against his skull and a burning sensation told him he had been hit.

Sean's breath hitched. He thought of his sister and prayed Lucas Devereaux would keep her safe. Then everything went black.

## Chapter Thirty-One

Rachel lay in the darkness, unable to fall asleep. Though Nicole always tried to shelter her, her niece had told her a little of what was happening with Sean.

The boy was in trouble. Rachel prayed Lucas would be able to help him navigate the murky waters he found himself in.

It was quiet in the bedroom, just the ticking of the pendulum on the ormolu clock on the mantel and the wind beating through the branches of the trees outside the windows. She was tired and she was worried. And she was lonely. She hadn't heard from Francois since the night the ghost woman had come into her room.

Maybe now that the two of them had found each other, he was with her, back in time where they both belonged. Her eyes stung. If they were together, she hoped he was happy.

She thought of the beautiful woman in

Nicole's painting. Simone — was that her name? Had Francois died before he could marry her?

The thought was a knife in her heart.

Her eyelids felt heavy. She hadn't told Nicole, but she had been feeling weaker every day. She drifted on the edge of sleep, listening to the fury of the storm building outside. The rain thundered in waves against the rooftop. The wind continued to howl.

She slept for a while, but it was a restless slumber interrupted by bouts of fear for her family, for Sean and Nicole, and for Belle Reve.

Slowly, a little at a time, awareness trickled through her, and her eyes slowly opened. The remnants of fear slipped away, and a warm feeling sifted through her as she realized he was there.

"Francois?" she whispered.

He moved closer. *Mon amour.*

Her heart squeezed. "I wasn't sure I would see you again. I thought you would be with . . . the woman."

Francois said nothing, just moved up beside where she lay on the bed. This time, she could see him fully: a tall man dressed in the clothes of his time — frock coat, snug black breeches, full-sleeved shirt, and white stock. He was as magnificently handsome as the man Nicole had painted.

Her breathing quickened. She moistened her lips. "The woman . . . Simone? Did you love her?"

The air in the bedroom stirred violently, a furious swirling mass that forced strands of hair back from her face. The curtains shot out into the bedroom, the windows rattled, but didn't break.

*Love her? She killed me!*

Her heart lurched. *Oh, dear God. Francois . . .*

No more words were needed as he came to her, as he had before — no longer a man, just an invisible masculine presence that settled beside her, drawing her into unseen arms.

She wanted to tell him she loved him, but she was afraid he wouldn't want to hear it, that he might go away and never return. Instead, she gave herself over to him, as she had before, and let him work his magic.

The call came at midnight. Lucas was awake, sitting in his living room, dressed and ready to leave for the police station, where Sean would be taken after the arrest.

"Lucas Devereaux?" the caller asked.

"That's right."

"This is Detective Mark York, Baton

Rouge PD. One of your students has been arrested. He was attempting to steal an expensive automobile from Casino Rouge Chateau. Unfortunately, one of the other men involved resisted and began firing at police officers. Your student Sean Handley was wounded. He's been taken to Our Lady of the Lake hospital."

Lucas felt the words like a blow. He felt dizzy, his mouth cotton dry. "What's his condition?"

"I'm sorry, I don't know."

"I'm on my way. If you have questions, I'll be at the hospital." Lucas hung up before the officer could continue. As he grabbed his keys off the kitchen counter and headed out to the garage, he pulled his cell and hit the contact button for Nicole. She picked up on the first ring.

"Have you spoken to the police?" he asked. Sliding behind the wheel of the Jeep, he punched the garage door opener, then began backing into the driveway.

"One of the detectives just called. I'm just getting in the car to go to the hospital."

"Josh is staying with Rachel?"

"Yes." He could hear the tears in her voice. "I'm scared, Lucas. The police . . . They won't . . . They won't tell me how bad he is."

Guilt stabbed into Lucas's chest. This was his fault. He had known how dangerous it could be. "I don't think they know," he said, clamping down on his emotions. Now was not the time. Nicole and Sean needed him.

"Oh, God, Lucas . . ." Her voice broke. "This wasn't supposed to happen."

He ignored the pain her words caused. "I'm closer to the hospital than you are. I'll be there when you get there. Just stay strong, love. And pray for Sean."

Lucas hung up the phone and pressed down on the accelerator, taking the roads as fast as he dared without getting stopped. A delay was the last thing he wanted.

Taking his own advice, he began to pray for the boy who had been injured trying to protect his sister. Lucas prayed for strength for Nicole.

And he prayed for strength for himself.

Nicole hurried down the hospital corridor toward the ICU. The thirty-mile drive from Belle Reve to Baton Rouge seemed to take hours. Knowing Lucas was at the hospital with Sean was the only thing that kept her from breaking down.

She spotted him up ahead, tall and imposing, striding down the hall in her direction. When she reached him, he simply opened his arms. Nicole stepped into them, and they closed protectively around her.

Nicole clung to him. "They told me . . . They said Sean's in the ICU."

"That's right."

"How bad is he?"

Lucas eased her a little away. "I'm sorry, *cher*, but his condition is critical. The bullet creased the side of his head. The impact was great enough to cause a severe concussion."

Nicole made a sound in her throat.

"The good news is, the skull wasn't pierced."

She blinked back tears. "That is good news."

"Yes, it is. They think there's a chance the swelling will go down on its own and they won't have to operate to relieve the pressure."

"When will they know?"

He cupped her cheek in his hand. "They aren't sure. They'll know a little more by morning."

Nicole made a sound in her throat. For an instant, she closed her eyes, fighting for control. "What happened out there?"

Lucas's jaw hardened. "Apparently, there were a number of people involved in the theft and two different drop-off locations.

At Sean's site, there was another driver, plus the guy driving the van being used to pick up the cars. Mick Dugan was there, along with Bruno. Apparently, Bruno resisted arrest, started firing at police, and they returned fire. At this point, they aren't sure where the bullet that hit Sean came from. Could have been Bruno or the police."

Her knees felt weak. She didn't realize she was shaking until Lucas led her over to a bench along the wall and eased her down on the seat.

"I'm sorry," she said. "I'm just so worried."

He sat down beside her and took hold of her hand, bringing it to his lips. "If anyone's sorry, it's me. I was the one who convinced Sean to cooperate with the authorities. I knew it was dangerous. At the time, I didn't see any other way."

She looked up at him. "What about now?"

He shook his head. "I don't know. Maybe there was something I missed."

Nicole glanced away. It would be so easy to blame Lucas. Part of her wanted to do so. If something happened to her brother, she wasn't sure she could ever get over it. Another part knew how unfair blaming Lucas would be.

"I want to talk to the doctor," she said,

some of her strength returning.

"His name is Ed Mathias. I told him you were on your way. He said he'd be back to see you as soon as you arrived."

Twenty minutes later, Dr. Mathias appeared, a thin, black-haired man wearing horn-rimmed glasses. A white lab coat flapped around his knees as he walked down the hall. Nicole and Lucas both rose to greet him. Mathias introduced himself and shook Nicole's hand.

"Your brother's condition is still critical," the doctor said. "But at this point, we continue to remain optimistic. Many severe cases of head trauma resolve themselves. However, if things take a turn for the worse, we'll need to operate to reduce the pressure on the brain."

Nicole clamped down on the sound of fear trying to claw its way out of her throat. She felt Lucas's hand at her waist, easing her closer. Mathias gave her a more technical description of Sean's head injuries, but her mind seemed to fuzz out and go completely numb. After he left, she could barely remember what he'd said.

"The main thing is to focus your thoughts on Sean," Lucas told her. "You're a strong woman. Will your brother some of your strength."

Her eyes burned with unshed tears. She blinked them away and said a silent prayer for Sean.

A noise in the corridor drew her attention. She looked up to see a man striding toward them. He was in his late thirties, dark brown suit, worn leather shoes. He introduced himself as Detective Mark York, the man who had phoned with the news of Sean's arrest and the injuries he had sustained as a result.

"I know the timing isn't good," the detective said. "But I have a few questions I need you to answer."

Nicole looked up at Lucas.

The hand at her waist tightened. "I'm sorry, Mark, but considering the situation, I think it's better if Ms. Belmond has an attorney present when she talks to you."

Since she had no attorney, she had no idea what Lucas intended, but she stayed silent, as he advised.

Unhappy but resigned, the detective blew out a slow breath. "I'd rather do it now, but I understand. I'll be in touch again tomorrow." The detective turned and strode off down the hall.

Nicole looked at Lucas. "I don't have an attorney. What should I do?"

"You don't need to worry about it yet.

Tomorrow we'll know more and so will the police. York's been straight with us so far, but it's better to take precautions. If you need an attorney, I know several who represent kids like Sean."

It was better than facing the police alone. "All right."

"If you're okay with waiting here by yourself, I'd like to go down to the chapel for a while. I want to spend some time asking God for His help healing Sean."

Nicole's heart twisted. She had known from the start that Lucas had a strong connection to God. That he was willing to use it to help heal her brother made her feelings for him swell. Even if she wanted to blame him for Sean's injuries, she couldn't.

"I appreciate any help you can give him," she said softly.

Lucas led her to the door of the ICU waiting room and brushed a gentle kiss over her lips. "If you need me, you know where I am."

It was quiet in the room when she stepped inside. Eventually she learned that the white-haired elderly woman waited for word on her husband, who'd had a stroke, and the dark-haired mother of a teenage boy was waiting for news of the son who had been in a car accident.

An hour later, when Lucas hadn't returned, she asked a nurse where to find the chapel and headed in that direction.

The room was modern, with light beige walls, a few rows of blond wood chairs, and stained-glass windows in a contemporary design up front. It was nondenominational, just an intimate, quiet place for contemplation.

Lucas sat in a row at the back, facing forward, his head bowed, his lips moving in silent prayer. Nicole's throat swelled. She could no longer deny the love she felt for this man. The strength and compassion surrounding him made him impossible to resist.

It was a terrifying truth. At the moment, the only thing she could do was set aside the knowledge until her brother was out of danger.

She sat down beside Lucas in the pew, but didn't disturb him. Sean needed his prayers.

Nicole started praying, too.

## CHAPTER THIRTY-TWO

Nicole hadn't left the hospital since her arrival. Her clothes were wrinkled, her hair a bedraggled mess. Her muscles ached, and a headache throbbed behind her eyes.

Friday was passing in a haze of worry. Remy phoned Lucas to check on Sean's condition, but given the circumstances, he thought it best to stay away. Just before noon, Aunt Rachel arrived with Josh, who had driven her to Baton Rouge from Belle Reve.

"How's our sweet boy?" she asked, leaning over to hug Nicole, then taking a seat next to her in the waiting room.

"No change. He's still in the ICU. They may have to operate, but so far, the doctors are hopeful that won't have to happen."

Rachel glanced around. "Where's Lucas?"

"He just left. He tried to get me to go home, while he stayed here, but I just couldn't leave. He's gone to shower and change. He had some things to do at the youth center, but then he'll be back."

"I'll stay until he gets here," Rachel remarked.

"Are you sure you're feeling up to it?"

Her aunt looked worried, but at the same time oddly serene. "I feel fine. I had a restful night." She smiled as she said the words and color rose in her cheeks.

"You are positively glowing. Did he come to you last night? Your Francois?"

A soft smile touched her lips. "Yes."

Having no idea what to say to that, Nicole merely nodded. With Sean in the hospital, Lucas had phoned his grandmother and postponed their session at Belle Reve. Which meant Simone could reappear and then Rachel would be in a far different kind of danger.

One more thing to worry about.

The doctor finally allowed them to see Sean for a brief moment in the ICU, where he lay pale as death in an induced coma. Nicole's eyes teared up at the sight of him, hooked up to an IV, a heart monitor beeping a much steadier rhythm than the erratic pulse pounding in her own ears.

Aunt Rachel stayed until Lucas returned, and Josh drove her home. He was a good man, Nicole thought, more than just conscientious about his job. Clearly, he cared about the people under his protection.

Late Saturday morning, after a sleepless Friday night, Nicole was sitting next to Lucas in the hall outside the ICU when Dr. Mathias arrived. Lucas took hold of her hand and both of them stood up. There was nothing in the doctor's expression to tell if the news was good or bad.

Her heart rate kicked up. *Please let Sean be okay,* she silently implored.

Her hold tightened on Lucas's hand. "Is he —"

"Sean's out of danger. The swelling subsided and everything is heading back to normal." The doctor's thin face lit with a smile.

"Thank God." Relief washed over her, so strong her legs felt weak. As if he knew, Lucas's hand tightened around her waist.

The doctor's smile widened. "In time, aside from a powerful headache, your brother should be fine. We'll be keeping him overnight for observation. But if there are no unexpected complications, we'll be releasing him in the morning."

"Thank you, Doctor. Thank you so much."

Lucas shook Mathias's hand. "We can't

thank you enough, Doctor."

The man just smiled and nodded.

Sean's improving condition was eventually changed to stable, and a few hours later, he was moved into the private room Lucas had insisted upon and was paying for.

Sean was sleeping when the two of them walked into his room, their arrival rousing him enough to open his eyes.

"Hey," Sean said drowsily. His head was partially shaved and bandaged, the side of his face bruised, one of his eyes puffy.

Nicole's heart squeezed. "Hey, yourself." She leaned over and kissed his cheek, pasted on what she hoped would pass for a smile. She hoped he wouldn't notice the smudges beneath her eyes. "Welcome back."

"Yeah . . . thanks."

"How do you feel?" Lucas asked.

Sean managed a faint, lopsided grin. "Like someone shot me." The grin slid away. "The doctor says I can go home tomorrow."

"That's right," Lucas said. "He says you're out of danger." Lucas then told the boy not to speak to the police, that he'd have an attorney to handle things for him.

Sean just nodded and drifted back to sleep.

By late Sunday afternoon, Sean had been

released from the hospital and was back at Belle Reve. He was resting comfortably in his bedroom, rapidly recovering, a huge worry lifted from Nicole's shoulders. He would be staying home through the week, then returning to school the following Monday.

Lucas told Nicole that until the situation was resolved with the police, and he was certain she and Sean would be safe, he planned to sleep on the sofa in the living room. This was a conversation her brother must have overheard.

Sean called Nicole and Lucas into his bedroom.

"Listen, you guys, I know the two of you are together. I'm old enough to handle it. There's no reason for Coach to sleep in the living room."

Nicole blushed. Sex wasn't a subject she had ever discussed with her brother.

"You know how I feel about your sister," Lucas said.

"Yeah, I guess so."

Lucas's gaze locked with Nicole's. When she made no protest, he swung his attention back to Sean. "First I think it's time you called me Luke, or Lucas, at least when we're not at school, and we'll accept your offer with our thanks."

Nicole wasn't sure she liked the idea. Her feelings for Lucas were confusing and uncertain at best. At times, they were terrifying. She wasn't ready to face them, though it was beginning to look as if she had no choice.

For the moment, she was just happy her brother was going to be all right.

As promised, on Monday morning, Lucas contacted an attorney named Diego Reyes to represent Sean in the arrest proceedings. Unfortunately, a total of four vehicles had been stolen that night before the police had interceded. The other two, an Aston Martin DB12 and a customized Porsche Carrera, had not been recovered. That made cutting a deal more difficult.

Reyes presented Sean's written statement to the court, in which he swore that Bruno Takov had threatened his sister's life. She had already suffered a beating, the results of which Lucas had wisely photographed on his cell phone. Under the circumstances, Reyes said, Sean felt he had no choice but to cooperate.

In the end, after a session with the judge, Reyes was able to negotiate a simple six-month extension of Sean's time at the youth center and keep the teen's role in exposing the car theft ring a secret.

In other good news, Mick Dugan, in exchange for a lighter sentence, identified the head of security at Casino Rouge Chateau, Roman Cormack, as the man behind the thefts. Cormack had taken the heat and refused to cooperate, preferring to go to prison rather than incriminate anyone else.

Lucas tried to convince himself it was over, but Cormack's silence felt like a loose end that remained unresolved.

Lucas didn't like it.

Late in the afternoon the following Sunday, Rachel sat on the terrace overlooking the garden.

It was the third week of April, sunny, the temperature in the eighties; as it was this time of year, the humidity, still tolerable, was climbing. Pulling off her wide-brimmed straw hat, she tossed it on the white wrought iron table and leaned back in the chair, letting the sun warm her face as she thought of the time she had spent this week with the ghost of the man she loved.

Francois had been with her, in one form or another, three nights in a row. And though they communicated by touch, they knew each other's thoughts. Rachel knew Francois's heart and soul as she had never known another man.

She felt him watching over her, even now, as she sat on the terrace. He was worried about her, worried that Simone might harm her. So far, he had been able to keep the malicious spirit away.

She looked up to see Nicole approaching in the loose-fitting, wide-legged floral pants and white silk blouse she had worn to church. She was just back from returning Sean to the youth center.

"How did it go?" Rachel asked, wondering how difficult it would be for Sean, after being arrested, to fit in again with his friends.

Nicole sighed as she sat down at the table. "I'm not sure." She picked up the pitcher of lemonade and filled one of the empty glasses for herself. "I think his friends are torn between condemning him and admiring him."

Rachel nodded. "He committed a crime, but he also saved his family from being harmed."

"Exactly."

"Sean's a smart boy. He'll know how to handle the situation."

"I hope so." Nicole took a drink of lemonade. "It looks like Sean's out of danger. What about you? How are things going at

Belle Reve?"

Rachel toyed with her glass. "You mean with Francois?"

"Actually, I'm more worried about Simone. She doesn't seem nearly as . . . friendly."

"Simone hasn't been here since that first night."

"I guess that's good. Hard to tell what's good and bad when you're dealing with a ghost."

Rachel said nothing.

"Lucas talked to his grandmother this morning. We both thought it was better to wait until Sean was back in school before Gabrielle came out to the house. She's free any night this week."

Rachel rubbed her temple. "That's kind of her, but I'm not feeling quite up to it right now." Not exactly the truth, but she managed to smile. "You have a show in New Orleans this coming weekend, right?"

"That's right. I've been painting all week, getting ready for it. I'm working on something . . . I don't quite know how it's going to turn out, but it should be finished very soon."

"Why don't we wait for Gabrielle's visit until after the show? Perhaps I'll be feeling a little stronger." And it would give her more time with Francois.

Nicole eyed her with suspicion. "What if Simone comes back?"

Rachel just shrugged. "Maybe she's gone for good."

Nicole took a sip of lemonade. "I suppose that's possible. Anything is possible. That's what Lucas always says."

This time, Rachel's smile was sincere. "All right, it's settled. We'll plan to have Gabrielle out here after your show."

Or at least they could discuss it again at that time. As far as Rachel was concerned, she was happy the way things were.

"I suppose that will work," Nicole said. "I just hope nothing happens in the meantime."

Rachel hoped so, too. For now, she had Francois and she was happy.

They made pleasant conversation as Nicole finished her lemonade; then her niece headed back to her studio.

Rachel stayed to enjoy the sunshine a few minutes more. Lately she had been suffering the growing effects of her disease — weakness in her arms and shoulders that made lifting difficult, weakness in her legs that made it harder and harder to climb the stairs. She hadn't mentioned it. Nicole had enough problems of her own.

Thank God for Lucas. Rachel prayed her niece was smart enough to appreciate the gift that she had been given in a man who cared so much about her.

## Chapter Thirty-Three

The art show at the Winston Gallery in the French Quarter was a bohemian affair: visitors to the city with an interest in art, locals wearing everything from paisley yoga pants to designer cocktail dresses, and even a Jamaican man in a satin frock coat and breeches, with a purple plumed hat.

It was Nicole's first show in Anne's New Orleans gallery. Which meant she was nervous, not unusual, and glad to have Lucas beside her.

"You look gorgeous," he said, his warm brown eyes sweeping over the sea-green silk dress, with the flirty skirt, she was wearing with a pair of strappy gold high-heeled sandals. She'd left her auburn hair loose around her shoulders — the way he liked it.

He wrapped a curl around his finger. "I don't tell you that often enough."

She grinned. "I like what I see in your eyes even better than your words."

He laughed. "You're making me want to drag you off to our hotel room, and I can't do that quite yet."

Facing a two-hour drive back to St. Francisville after the show, they had decided to spend the night in the city. Lucas had booked a suite at the Hotel Monteleone, a luxurious old French Quarter landmark. The heated look in his eyes promised the extravagant price he had paid would be worth it.

They had arrived in the city late Thursday afternoon. Beneath a sullen gray sky, the precursor of a storm, Lucas had helped her carry the last of her paintings from the Lexus into the showroom.

Several new landscapes now hung on the walls, and the dark paintings of Vicksburg that hadn't sold before; the painting of the pond that included the faint image of Francois, and the shack on the bayou with the eerie portrait of Simone, sat covered on easels near the front of the room. Her latest painting, which she had barely finished in time and hadn't shown to anyone but Lucas, sat with the others, ready to be unveiled during the show.

"You look nervous." In a white silk cocktail dress trimmed with gold Egyptian symbols, Anne Winston walked up beside her. Gold bands ringed her upper arms, while gold earrings dangled from her ears. The outfit set off her blond hair and blue eyes spectacularly. Of course, everything Anne Winston did was spectacular.

She leaned in to give Nicole air kisses on both cheeks. "You needn't worry, darling. The show's going to be wildly successful." She turned and smiled. "Lucas." More air kisses. "It's good to see you again."

He glanced around the spacious room beneath perfectly positioned track lighting. "Looks like you've got everything under control."

The gallery sat on Royal Street, in one of the many centuries-old buildings in the French Quarter. Completely remodeled, only the antique crystal chandelier in the middle of the room remained, which, combined with the ultramodern décor, provided a stunning contrast.

"Everything's perfect," Anne said. She glanced down at her diamond-faced gold wristwatch. "People are continuing to arrive. Time for me to go to work. Smile, darlings." Anne headed off in a hip-swinging gait, and Nicole inhaled a steadying breath.

"They're going to love what you've done," Lucas said. "The new work is bright and cheerful, a memorable vision of the Louisiana landscape. And your dark work — well, it's mesmerizing. There's no other way to put it. Especially the Spirit pieces." That was the description she had now given them.

Nicole leaned up and brushed a light kiss over his lips. "Thank you." She looked toward the covered paintings perched on the easels. "I titled the first two *Francois* and *Simone*. *Francois* isn't for sale. It was a gift to my aunt. She's loaning it to me for the show."

He nodded. "That's where it belongs, I think. And the new one?"

Another Spirit painting of the shack. This time, a man's face rose above it, and it wasn't Francois.

"I'm not sure who he is, but I'm guessing it might be Jules."

Lucas's gaze went to the painting. "Handsome. Looks a little like Francois, only . . ."

"Only what?"

"Softer, less mature, perhaps more malleable."

"Yes, that's it. And rash. As if he lacks self-control." She shook her head. "No idea why I feel that way."

"It's there," Lucas said. "All of it's there in the painting."

"I named it *Rendezvous.* Again, no idea why."

His gaze returned to the Spirit painting, and he nodded. Lucas always seemed to understand. It was one of the things she loved about him. Nicole blocked the thought. Loving someone was dangerous, and now wasn't the time — not with people pouring in, filling the gallery.

There was a bar set up along one wall, next to a table of gourmet hors d' oeuvres. The storm had arrived outside, but no one seemed to mind. They just closed their umbrellas and stacked them next to the door. Nicole looked at the people clustered around her landscape paintings and her nerves continued to build.

"Why don't I get you a glass of champagne?" Lucas suggested. "Maybe it'll help you relax."

She smiled. "Thanks, I could use it."

Nicole hadn't seen them come in, but as Lucas walked away, she spotted Phillipe Villard standing next to the bar. Christian stood a few feet away, speaking to a pretty little blonde. Nicole wasn't surprised to see them there. Phillipe was one of Anne's most important clients, and Christian couldn't resist an opportunity to mingle with beautiful, sophisticated women.

Carrying two champagne flutes, Lucas paused to speak to Phillipe, ignored Christian, and continued across the room. He handed her a glass of champagne.

"Thanks." Nicole took a sip, enjoying the bubbles on her tongue. As the alcohol slid through her system, some of the tension in her shoulders began to ease.

"I guess you noticed two of your not-so-favorite people are here," Lucas said.

"They're Anne's clients. I'm not really surprised."

"Maybe Phillipe will buy a painting."

"Maybe. I'm not completely sure I want him to own one."

Lucas nodded his understanding.

Half an hour later, the gallery was packed as Anne walked up to the front and someone clinked a spoon against a wineglass, calling for quiet. Little by little, the crowd fell silent. The rain beating on the tall glass windows at the front of the gallery was the only sound in the room.

"Welcome to the Winston Gallery." Anne flashed a bright white smile. "I hope you're all enjoying the work of our featured artist, Nicole Belmond. Ms. Belmond is one of the premier Impressionist landscape artists in Louisiana. Many of you already own pieces of her work."

Anne flashed her perfect smile. "Fortunately for us, lately she's been experimenting, giving her artistic talent free rein. Tonight we're unveiling what Nicole calls her Spirit pieces. They're quite different from her usual paintings, a glimpse into a world only she can see."

She turned to her assistant. "Frederick, if you would . . ."

Frederick Thompson, Anne's latest companion, a handsome, intelligent dark-skinned man, began lifting away the covers to reveal the paintings beneath.

There was a moment of quiet, a subtle stirring, and then applause broke out. The crowd began to move toward the easels, making comments about the work. Nicole relaxed a little more at the murmurs of interest and compliments she could hear among the patrons.

"I told you not to worry," Lucas said softly.

Nicole smiled. "So you did."

But the atmosphere in the room was shifting, people nervously moving away from the Spirit pieces.

"Something's happening," she said as the patter of the rain increased, turning into a heavy downpour. The weather was getting worse, the rain falling in sheets, turning into a roar. A brilliant white flash lit the sky. A zigzag bolt of lightning struck outside the gallery windows. Thunder cracked so loud someone screamed.

The windows shook as the driving rain increased — pounding, pounding — lashing in great heaving waves against the glass. The floor began to shake, and people, already nervous, began to move toward the front door.

"What's going on?" one of the men asked as an icy chill pervaded the room, so cold Nicole's skin rose with goose bumps.

"Stay calm, everyone," Anne said. "This building has been in the French Quarter since the 1700s. It's survived thousands of storms. You're all perfectly safe."

As if to prove exactly the opposite, the painting of Simone started shaking, then hopping up and down. It tilted onto its side and shot off the easel, bladelike, cutting through the air with vicious force. Nicole bit back a cry as people ducked and screamed and the canvas hit the wall.

"Let's get out of here!" someone shouted.

"Everyone, take it easy." Frederick picked up the painting. Amazingly, it seemed undamaged in its lovely gilt frame. "The wind must have caught the canvas," he said, returning the painting to the easel. "It's all right, everything is fine."

But everything wasn't fine. The beautiful overhead crystal chandelier began to shake violently. Beams of light bounced off the glass prisms, shooting colored rays around the room. The usually musical notes rattled with a grim clatter that sounded more like a dirge. The noise gave just enough warning for people to move out from underneath before the chandelier crashed to the floor.

Everything inside Nicole screamed a warning.

"We're leaving!" someone shouted. "Come on, let's go!" People started pushing and shoving, trying to reach the front of the gallery.

Lucas reached for her and Nicole gripped his arm as Frederick raced ahead to the door and pulled it open, allowing the crowd to pour out onto the sidewalk. Some of them took time to grab their umbrellas, others just ran outside and disappeared into the storm.

Phillipe glanced around for his son, who stood a few feet away, staring at the Spirit paintings. His father grabbed his shoulder and spun him around.

"We're leaving."

Christian shook his head, as if trying to clear it, and the two of them ran out the door. Nicole held on to Lucas as he led her to the front of the gallery, where *Simone* sat once more on the easel.

"What happened?" she asked. "Was it . . . Could it be . . . her?"

"Yes." Lucas covered the paintings while Frederick urged people out of the gallery. Anne was assuring them it was just some sort of electrical phenomena caused by the unexpected violence of the lightning storm. Nicole figured most people would believe it. Until recently, she would have been one of them.

Once the crowd had left the gallery, she and Lucas pitched in to help clean up the mess, picking up cocktail napkins and dirty dishes, while Frederick swept up the broken glass shards of the chandelier.

"It was beautiful," Nicole said to Anne, looking down at the shattered crystal sparkling beneath the track lighting.

"It was very old." Anne shook her head. "Such a terrible loss." Anne looked at Nicole. "I wonder what happened."

Nicole's stomach knotted. "There's no way to know for sure, but . . . I'm taking the Spirit pieces back home with me, Anne. For now, things seemed to have settled down. If it's okay with you, we'll come by and pick them up in the morning."

One of Anne's blond eyebrows arched up. "You don't actually believe those paintings had anything to do with what happened tonight?"

"I don't know. Some odd things have been happening at Belle Reve. It never occurred to me the paintings could be dangerous, but I don't want to take any chances."

Anne sighed. "I don't believe it. Not one word. But I suppose you know best." She glanced around. "We've got this now. You two, go on and enjoy the rest of your evening. I'll see you in the morning."

Nicole looked over at Lucas.

"Anne's right. There's nothing more we can do here. We'll come back for the paintings tomorrow as soon as the gallery opens."

# Chapter Thirty-Four

Lucas led Nicole out the back door to the Lexus and drove the short distance to the hotel a few blocks away. Having checked in that afternoon, he handed the valet his car keys and led Nicole through the polished brass front doors into the Monteleone's spectacular lobby: gleaming marble floors, crystal chandeliers, stately Corinthian columns, and beautiful high molded ceilings. Built in 1886 in the Beaux-Arts style, the hotel was a historical treasure, Lucas's favorite place to stay in the city.

He glanced over at Nicole, who clung to his arm as if it was all that was keeping her upright. "I'd offer to buy you a drink in the bar, but from the look on your face, I think I'll pour you something from the bar in our suite."

She nodded. "Yes, please."

They took the elevator up to the Vieux Carre Suite, elegant quarters done in cream and gold throughout, a bedroom with a king-size bed and a luxurious marble bathroom. Lucas led Nicole over to the sofa in the living room and urged her down on the comfortable seat, then headed for the bar in the antique rosewood armoire.

"Brandy all right?"

"Yes. Thank you."

He opened two small bottles and poured the liquid into heavy crystal rocks glasses, carried them over, and handed a glass to Nicole, who took a hefty swallow.

"Feeling better?" He took a seat beside her. Nicole didn't answer, her mind clearly on what had happened in the gallery.

"How can you be sure it was her? I thought it was your grandmother who could communicate with spirits."

He had hoped to avoid the subject. At least for now. Apparently, that wasn't going to happen.

"I told you once, my talent was different from hers. From what I saw tonight — and what I felt — Simone isn't just a lost soul. She's progressed far beyond that."

Nicole looked up at him with the big green eyes that had captured him from the start. "What do you mean?"

"The entity you got a glimpse of tonight in the gallery is pure evil. She's powerful.

And she's determined. She won't be easy to defeat."

"Defeat?"

"Get rid of."

Nicole took a nervous sip of brandy. "Is that what we have to do? Find a way to get rid of her?"

"I know the way. We need Grandmere to come to the house and see what other information she can find out. Every little bit will help us."

"You're scaring me, Lucas."

He took the brandy glass from her hand and set it on the table, slid a hand into her glorious mane of auburn hair and tipped her head back, then set his mouth over hers. It was meant to be a gentle kiss, but the fire that always leaped between them took over, turning the kiss from gentle to hot, went deeper, more demanding.

"I'm going to make you forget about Simone for a while," he promised, kissing the side of her neck. "After we're finished, I'll call down to Criollo." The elegant hotel restaurant. "Have them send supper up to the room. How does that sound?"

"Perfect."

Lucas's finger ran down Nicole's smooth cheek. His thumb slid over her plump bottom lip, moist from his kiss, and he felt her tremble. He could see the rapid pulse beating at the base of her throat; he leaned down and pressed his mouth there, inhaling the fragrance of her soft perfume.

Lucas kissed her and Nicole slid her arms around his neck. He nibbled and tasted. Didn't stop until she was moaning. Didn't stop as he carried her into the bedroom. Didn't stop until both of them were naked in bed and lying in each other's arms.

Afterward, sated and content, they rested for a while, their limbs entwined. Lucas felt the touch of Nicole's finger tracing lines across the muscles in his chest.

"Keep that up and we're going to be starting all over again."

Nicole laughed. "I wouldn't mind — though I admit I'm getting hungry."

Lucas softly kissed her. "I'm going to feed you. I promise."

He started to get up, but she pulled him back down.

"I want you to know, Lucas, that being with you has been a very special gift."

One of his eyebrows went up. "Is that so . . ."

"From the start, I knew you were an extremely virile man. You once told me your sexuality was part of the reason you left the Church."

"That's true. I was never cut out to be celibate. Though it took me a while to accept that."

Her fingertip continued its journey, circling his navel, making his groin tighten. "I was worried I would never be able to keep up with you, that my own needs would never match yours. You showed me I was wrong."

He leaned over and kissed her. "You're a very sensual woman, Nicole. I'm glad I was the man to awaken that sensuality." He brought her hand to his lips. "We're good together. I'm glad you're beginning to see that."

He swung his legs to the side of the bed and tugged on her hand. "Time for a shower and — since you still seem interested — other things."

Nicole laughed as he led her into the luxurious bathroom. Tonight was theirs. A long-overdue special evening together.

Tomorrow they would talk. Lucas would try to explain about demons and how to get rid of them, a subject better addressed in the daylight. He would try to prepare Nicole for what was going to happen in the very near future, explain that all hell was about to break loose at Belle Reve.

■ ■ ■ ■

Nicole rode silently in the passenger seat as Lucas drove back to St. Francisville. Earlier in the day, they had driven to the Winston Gallery to pick up the Spirit pieces now covered in the trunk of the Lexus, harmless it would seem.

After what had happened last night, Nicole knew it wasn't true.

Aside from the disappointment of her failed art show — and the fear she had experienced — they'd had a wonderful evening. The sex had been spectacular, as it always was between them. She had finally accepted that being with Lucas made the difference, bringing out a part of her that she had never known.

She didn't want to imagine what her life would be like without him, and yet some part of her believed that day would come.

As the miles slipped past, her gaze swung to the handsome man behind the wheel. In profile, she could see the slight bump on his nose and it somehow reassured her. He was, after all, only a man. When he left, she would find a way to live without him, alone as she always had been. She reminded herself that she had a brother now, but it wouldn't be long before Sean went away to college. And Aunt Rachel — she didn't want to think about losing her beloved aunt.

She shoved the depressing thoughts away and focused on their current problem. It was time to discuss the trouble waiting for them at Belle Reve.

"I think it's time we talked about it, don't you? You said you would explain about ghosts, about spirits and demons. I need to understand what's happening, Lucas."

His gaze slanted toward her and she remembered last night, his lips moving hotly over hers, the thrill of his amazing lovemaking. He had taken her as if he claimed her, as if she were his and always would be.

If only that were true.

She forced herself to concentrate on the subject she so desperately needed to understand. "Tell me," she pressed. "Please, Lucas."

His hands tightened on the steering wheel. "You've met my grandmother. Being raised in the Devereaux family, life and death, heaven and hell, were always just part of living. We took it for granted that God and Satan existed. My grandmother told me when I was just a boy about the special gifts certain family members were born with."

"Did she know you were one of them?"

"I'm not sure if she knew at the time. It's more common on the female side of the family. Mine came through my mother. Maybe my grandmother suspected. Perhaps that was the reason she occasionally took me with her. I think she wanted me to understand, to see the possibilities. Back then, I was far more interested in girls and cutting school. As I got older, I had too much money and too much time, which only managed to get me into trouble. You know how those years ended. I didn't really understand the nature of my gift until I joined the priesthood."

"That's when it started?"

"That's when I realized I was one of the people my grandmother had told me about."

"What happened?"

"I was working in the garden when one of the older priests came to see me. He said he had a feeling about me. He said if he was right, I could be useful to the Church. I knew Father Bartholomew performed exorcisms." A faint smile touched his lips. "Turned out performing an exorcism takes a lot more than just an innate ability to communicate with unholy beings. It takes hours of study to learn the necessary rituals. Combined with the gift I'd been given, I was extremely successful."

"But you're no longer a priest."

Lucas pulled the Lexus around a Toyota with dented fenders. "The Church makes allowances for people with the ability to perform the necessary tasks. They give them dispensation, even if they're not members of the priesthood."

Lucas being born with a special gift didn't surprise her. There was something extraordinary about him. She felt it every time he was near.

"I keep thinking of Aunt Rachel," she said. "After what happened at the gallery, I'm worried Simone might hurt her."

Lucas cast Nicole a speculative glance. "I'll call my grandmother again, get her out to the house as soon as possible."

"Rachel won't like it," Nicole said.

"I'm afraid we're past that point. We'll just have to make her see how important this is.

"Simone is clearly a danger."

"Yes," he said. "As soon as we get back, I'll make the call."

"What about Sean? It's Friday. I'll be picking him up after school." For Sean's sake, they were still keeping their relationship as quiet as possible.

"We can wait until next week," Lucas said, "but we're taking a risk."

Nicole lifted her hair away from the nape

of her neck as she leaned back in the passenger seat.

"Sean already knows some of it. He helped you dig up Francois's grave. He knows Aunt Rachel believes Belle Reve is haunted by Francois's ghost and that you have a special talent when it comes to dealing with spirits."

Lucas nodded. "I think it's important we move forward on this."

Nicole thought about what had happened in the gallery and that someone could have been killed. "I think so, too."

As they drove through St. Francisville, Lucas took a left onto Old Ferry Road, then turned onto Belmond Place and drove down the lane to Belle Reve.

Next to him in the passenger seat, Nicole sat up straighter at the sight of an Onyx Pest Control Management truck sitting in front of the old white-columned mansion. "I don't remember making an appointment for the house to be sprayed."

Lucas cast her a glance. "Maybe your aunt did."

"Maybe."

He turned off the engine and both of them got out of the Lexus. Lucas followed Nicole around to the back of the house to find Rachel sitting at the wrought iron table on the terrace. She rose as they approached.

"What's going on?" Nicole asked. "I didn't think we had anything scheduled with pest control today?"

"A problem came up," Rachel said.

"What kind of problem?" Lucas asked.

Rachel sighed. "Cockroaches. Thousands of them, if you can imagine. I found a cluster of them under the sink in the hall bathroom." She shook her head. "I've never seen so many, all of them crawling around on top of one another."

She shuddered. "I started looking, and they were everywhere. The bathrooms, under the sink in the kitchen, the laundry room. Under the bar sink in the den." She crossed her arms and hugged herself. "I hate bugs, especially roaches. I called the exterminators and they came right over."

Lucas glanced up as two men in white suits carrying spray canisters walked out the back door from the kitchen: one was bone-thin, his suit baggy around his long, skinny legs; the other was chubby enough to stretch the waistband of his suit to the limit.

"You've got a real mess on your hands, Ms. Belmond," the thin man said. His name, Lenny, was embroidered in blue on his uniform. "We've done the best we could for now. We got a good percentage of 'em, but there were thousands. We'll need to come back the end of the week and spray again — probably more than once. In the meantime, you best hire someone to clean up all the dead ones. You don't want 'em to start smelling up the house."

Rachel's face went pale. Nicole looked as if she was about to throw up.

"What caused this?" Lucas asked. "We live in Louisiana. In this climate, we're used to bugs, but thousands of cockroaches? That isn't normal."

"No, sir," Lenny said.

The chubby man, Waldo, agreed. "Never seen anything quite like it, but they're here just the same." He pulled a billing pad out of his uniform pocket, filled in the information and the charges, tore off the page, and set it on the wrought iron table. "A check for the full amount would be appreciated."

Nicole picked up the bill, her eyebrows arching at the amount.

"Emergency fee," Waldo said.

She looked back down at the bill. "How about a credit card?"

"That'll do."

Lucas resisted the urge to pay the damned bill. He knew better than to offer. Eventually they might be able to discuss Belle Reve's money problems. From the fierce look on Nicole's face, he knew that time wasn't now.

She retrieved her purse from the Lexus and handed Waldo a credit card. He wrote down the billing information, then shoved the pad back into his uniform pocket. "Call us the first of the week and we'll set up another appointment."

"Thanks for your help," Rachel said.

Lenny smiled. "Happy to be of service, ma'am."

## Chapter Thirty-Five

Nicole sat down at the wrought iron table next to her aunt. "We need to talk to you, Aunt Rachel." She glanced around, but Lucas seemed to have disappeared.

"What is it, dearest?"

"Something happened at the gallery showing. The painting of the woman above the old cabin? The one we think is Simone?"

"What about her?"

"She showed up at the gallery. She was angry. She tore the place apart and nearly hurt some of the patrons."

Both of Rachel's black eyebrows shot up. "She could do that? Somehow show up in New Orleans?"

Nicole nodded. "I think she might even have been able to influence the weather. It was terrifying."

Lucas reappeared on the terrace. "A spirit can attach itself to you and follow you wherever you go. That's the reason dabbling with the occult can be so dangerous. You can bring the spirit into your life."

Rachel shifted nervously in her chair, her gaze going from one of them to the other. "So you think Simone followed you to New Orleans?"

"I think that's exactly what happened," Lucas said. "But Belle Reve is where she's most powerful, on her own home turf, so to speak."

Rachel's gaze went to the house. "Do you think it is possible she set the bugs loose in the house?"

"It's possible," Lucas said. "You can't imagine what a strong entity is capable of doing."

Nicole thought of the thousands of roaches crawling around inside the house, and her stomach roiled.

"In this case," Lucas continued, "I don't think that's what happened."

"Wait? What?" Nicole stood up from her chair. "After what happened in the gallery, you don't think —"

"I took a look around," Lucas said. "Someone broke into the house last night. Looks like they were able to get in through a window in the den."

Color rose beneath the sculpted bones in Rachel's cheeks. "I know I'm not as careful about locking up as I should be. I've lived here most of my life. It's never been a problem."

"Until now," Lucas added.

"What about the bugs?" Nicole pressed. "Are you suggesting the person or persons who broke in last night are responsible for the cockroaches? It's not like someone would just happen to have thousands of roaches on hand."

Lucas pulled out his cell phone and brought up Google. "I looked it up. It's not as difficult as you'd think." He held out the phone for both of them to see. "There are a dozen websites that breed roaches and offer them for sale."

He clicked on one of the links. "They aren't even expensive. You can buy five thousand roaches for $43.98 and have them shipped right to your door."

Rachel's face looked pale. "I don't understand. Why in God's name would anyone want to buy cockroaches?"

"They use them to feed other creatures," Lucas explained. "Fish, chickens, frogs, even bigger insects."

"I think I'm beginning to see where you're going with this," Nicole said to him.

"Think about it. Belle Reve has suffered crippling water problems. Dangerous electrical fires. Now the house has been invaded by thousands of bugs. All of this is costing money, time, and stress. What's the easiest solution?"

"Sell Belle Reve," Nicole answered flatly.

"No!" Rachel shot up from her chair. "I'm not selling!"

"It's all right, Rachel," Lucas said. "We're not suggesting you sell. We're just saying there's a very good chance your problems aren't all in the spiritual realm."

Nicole's lips tightened as the answer hit her with the force of a blow. "Phillipe Villard."

Rachel sank back down in her chair. "I have to admit I've wondered. I tried to convince myself it couldn't be true, but . . . you really think he wants Belle Reve that bad?"

"Maybe there's more to it than we know," Lucas said. "I have a friend. As a teen, Nathan was arrested for hacking into a government database, spent nearly a year in juvenile detention. Nate's all grown up now, a big supporter of the youth center, has a fancy job with a computer company in New York — still a computer whiz."

"You think he'll help us?" Nicole asked.

"I helped his younger brother a few years back. I think Nate will be glad to return the favor. I'll call him, get him to take a deep dive into Villard and his companies, see if there's more to him wanting the property than we know."

Rachel gave him an appreciative smile. "Thank you, Lucas."

"There's something else we need to discuss." His intense brown gaze pinned Rachel where she sat, and the tension returned. "We need to talk about what's happening with Francois and Simone. Simone is getting stronger. We need to find out more about her, about both of them, and about what happened in the past. We need my grandmother's help."

"I . . . I'm not sure I'm ready," Rachel said.

Nicole reached over and caught her aunt's hand on top of the table. It felt icy cold. "If you had seen what happened in the gallery, you'd understand how urgent this is."

Rachel inhaled a deep breath. She hesitated for several long moments, then sat up straighter in her chair. "All right. Do whatever you think is best."

Nicole looked at Lucas.

"I'll make the call. I'll let you know what my grandmother says."

On Saturdays, Sean liked to work on his

model cars and play games in his studio. He was feeling good, back to normal after the shooting — no headaches, nothing like that. Outside, the rain was falling, pattering on the roof. He liked it out here when it rained.

He glanced up at the sound of a knock on the studio door, walked over, and pulled it open.

"You got a minute?" Lucas asked.

Sean was getting used to calling Coach by his name when they weren't at school. "Sure, come on in. You want a Coke or something, Lucas?"

"Sounds good."

Sean headed for the small fridge, next to the old microwave oven his sister had bought at a secondhand store, and took out a couple of ice-cold cans. They each sat down in a chair at the battered table, not far from the foldout sofa bed he had been sleeping on. The studio wasn't fancy, but it was his own personal space and he loved it.

Lucas studied Sean's latest project, a scale model of Senna's McLaren MP4 race car. "Looks like it's coming along really well."

"Yeah. I think it's gonna be one of my best."

Lucas nodded. "You do nice work. You take your time, do it right." He tipped up the can of cola and took a long swallow. "I came out here to talk to you about what's going on at Belle Reve."

Sean toyed with his almost-empty Coke can. "I heard about the cockroaches. Yuck."

"That's part of it. We think someone may be sabotaging the house."

Sean straightened. "Villard? If that bastard —"

"We don't have any evidence that links him to the mishaps so far. Just keep your eyes open for any unexpected trouble."

"You bet I will."

"What I came to talk to you about is something else."

Sean's interest sharpened. "Ghosts?"

"That's right. You already know some of what's been going on — you helped me dig up Francois Villard's grave."

"You think they'll put his bones back in there now?"

"I think they might, once they're satisfied it's really him."

"Aunt Rachel thinks he's haunting the house."

"I know spirits aren't something most people believe in."

"But you do."

"I've seen things, Sean. I believe your aunt is right about the house. Finding the old bones seemed to be the catalyst for all of this. Tonight my grandmother is coming over. Her name is Gabrielle, but everyone calls her Grandmere."

"That's French, right?"

Lucas nodded. "My grandmother was born with a special talent. She can communicate with spirits."

Nicole had told him that, though he wasn't sure he believed it. "My sister says your grandmother can figure out why the spooks are here."

"We research ahead of time, try to find out as much as possible about what happened to them. So she knows a lot before she goes in. Grandmere can often tell us the rest."

"She tries to help them get where they're supposed to be after they die."

"That's right," Lucas said.

It gave Sean the willies to think of it. Dead people hanging around the old house. "I've never seen a ghost. It would be scary, for sure, but also freakin' amazing."

"It definitely is that. Unfortunately, dealing with the occult can be dangerous. Not all spirits are friendly. I'm afraid you're going to have to stay out here."

"What?" Sean jumped up from his chair. "No way!"

"You could be seriously injured, Sean. It's

too dangerous."

"I just got shot. It can't be more dangerous than that."

Lucas smiled. "You have a point, but there's no way your sister is going to take the chance."

"Won't she be in danger, too?"

"Your aunt refuses to leave. Nicole wants to be there in case Rachel needs her."

"Let me be in the house, Lucas. It'll be an experience I'll never get the chance to have again."

"If you're lucky," Lucas grumbled.

"Please? I promise I'll stay out of the way." Sean considered his options. He could always agree, then sneak over and watch through the window, which, by the look on Coach's face, Lucas had already guessed.

"Even if I say yes, you'll have to clear it with your sister, and that might not be easy."

"What might not be easy?" Nicole stood in the open doorway. The old door usually squeaked a warning, but not this time.

"Sean wants to be there tonight."

Sean managed a pleading expression. "Please, sis. I'll never get another chance like this. Think what I could learn."

Nicole shook her head. "It's too dangerous, Sean. You can't believe what happened at the art show."

"What if the ghost comes out here?" he said. "It's possible, right? Back when the Villards owned the property, our house used to be the carriage house, and they used to keep horses and wagons out here. Maybe one of the ghosts will come out here and do something bad. It could happen, right?"

Nicole flicked Lucas a glance.

"It's possible," he said.

Nicole sighed. "Anything's possible. Okay, you can come over to the house."

"You have to understand there's a chance nothing will happen," Lucas said. "They live in a different dimension. They choose the place and time."

Nicole looked at Sean hard. "You can come over, but if things start to happen, you do exactly what Lucas tells you. Agreed?"

"Yes!" Sean punched a fist into the air.

Lucas finished his Coke and tossed the can into the trash. "Take a nap. Looks like you'll be staying up late tonight."

## Chapter Thirty-Six

The storm continued throughout the day and into the evening, the clouds growing thicker and blacker, the rain getting heavier, an occasional flash of lightning.

As the brass hands on the tall grandfather clock in the front parlor moved toward midnight, it was dark and quiet in the old mansion. A pair of ornate rose glass kerosene lamps glowed on the sideboard, another burned on the bow-legged Queen Anne coffee table between the two velvet settees that faced each other in front of the marble hearth, the only illumination in the room.

Lucas introduced Sean to his tiny, silver-haired grandmother. Gabrielle, who loved children of all ages, immediately wrapped a protective arm around him and led him over to one of the settees, and they sat down, side by side.

Nicole and Rachel sat on the opposite

velvet seat, Nicole holding on to her frail aunt's hand.

Once everyone was comfortable, Lucas took a place in an antique French armchair facing the fireplace.

They all waited anxiously, the minutes slowly ticking past. When the clock struck midnight and still nothing happened, Sean began to fidget. A stern look from Grandmere and he settled back down.

More time slipped past. At the stroke of one, Grandmere's lips began to move. Apparently, she had waited long enough. Lucas didn't know exactly what she was saying, only that she was trying to communicate with the spirits in the house, to learn more about them, find out why they were there.

In the shadows cast by the glow of the lamps, Rachel looked pale and worried, her hands clasped tightly in her lap. Sean perched on the edge of his seat, unsure what to expect, his expression one of youthful anticipation mixed with a trace of fear.

Lucas's gaze went to Nicole. Fine lines creased her forehead. Her green eyes were filled with concern as she held her aunt's hand. She glanced at her brother and her eyes filled with the same worry for him. She looked at Lucas as if he were the only man in the world she trusted to help them.

Something tightened in his chest. Nicole needed him. She hadn't come to accept that, but he prayed that in time she would.

And the truth was, Lucas needed her. The journey he was on wasn't easy. Nicole was the woman he wanted by his side, the woman he had been searching for, though he hadn't realized it until now. She was smart, kind, and caring, with an ability to communicate her thoughts and feelings through her work.

Nicole trusted him, but he needed more than that. He needed her to believe in him as a man. Believe in a future for the two of them.

He wasn't sure he could make that happen.

Lucas forced himself to tune back into what was happening in the house. He watched his grandmother's lips continue to move as she silently spoke to the spirits. She was beseeching them to tell their story, listening, telling them she understood, trying to make them see it was time for them to move on. She told them they no longer belonged here, that it was time they continued their journey to the place they were supposed to be, instead of remaining earthbound for eternity.

Outside the wind strengthened, heavy gusts slamming into the side of the house, brutally shaking the windows. A flash of lightning sliced through the ink-black sky; then a vicious crack of thunder rattled Rachel's valuable collection of Meissen porcelain figurines in the bow-front glass display case against the wall, undoubtedly the most valuable antiques remaining in the house.

Nicole had told Lucas that Rachel refused to sell them, but the bills were stacking up. The time was near when she would have no choice.

Grandmere rose from the settee and picked up the kerosene lamp on the coffee table, the flame flickering as she started walking. Her lips still moving in silent entreaty, she began to wander around the parlor, pausing here and there as if she searched for something.

When she reached the doorway, she disappeared out into the hall. Lucas could hear her footsteps on the stairs, climbing to the second floor. With every step, the air in the parlor seemed to thicken, the light grow more dim. A sour odor drifted into the room and a heavy pressure settled in his chest.

Both glass lamps on the sideboard flamed, then suddenly went out. Rachel gasped. The silence returned. The darkness became so dense, it felt as if he could reach out and touch it. The temperature dropped to an icy chill; it was so cold it penetrated deep in his bones. He could feel her now, feel the evil that surrounded her as Simone's presence swelled and grew until it filled the parlor.

"Coach?" The fear in Sean's voice was unmistakable.

Lucas rose and quietly crossed to Grand-mere's empty place on the settee and sat down beside him.

"Take it easy. The entity would have to go through me to get to you, and I won't let that happen."

Some of the stiffness eased in Sean's shoulders. Lucas cursed himself for allowing the boy to be there. They should have waited until Sean was back in school, would have if it hadn't been for Rachel and what Simone might do.

Something shifted in the atmosphere, and he could feel the entity's presence, a thick, greasy stain of evil that lurked in the darkness, waiting for an opening, a way to hurt someone.

Grandmere's lamp glowed in the doorway as she returned to the parlor, illuminating the interior. There was just enough light to see a foggy white mist following in her wake, crawling across the floor, roiling and drifting, growing thicker. Ectoplasm building, taking the form of a ghostly presence.

Lucas squeezed Sean's knee, reminding him to keep quiet as the faint outlines of a person began to take shape near the empty hearth. A man, dressed in old-fashioned clothes: a frock coat, white shirt and stock, tight breeches, and a pair of knee-high riding boots.

As the image materialized, Lucas could see he was tall and black-haired, a good-looking man with intense blue eyes.

"Francois . . ." Rachel's voice was barely a whisper, but the semi-translucent figure turned at the sound and moved toward her. He spoke to her in French, telling her how beautiful she was, speaking words of love and devotion. Rachel began to weep.

Sean trembled.

"Easy . . ."

A deep rumble under the house slowly grew louder, until the floor trembled beneath their feet. Lightning flashed outside. Thunder cracked and rolled over the landscape for long, protracted seconds.

A woman's harsh laughter split the air, and the house shook so hard the glass cabinet with the Meissen figures toppled over, smashing the curved glass front, spilling the contents onto the floor, shattering the valuable porcelain figures into bits and pieces.

Rachel shot to her feet. "You evil witch! Leave us alone!"

"Sit down, Rachel!" Lucas feared for her. It was dangerous to draw Simone's attention as much as she already had. The entity was powerful and growing even stronger. Dammit, he wasn't ready for this. He would have to deal with her soon, but it had to be in his own time, on his own terms.

"Rachel!" he commanded. She dropped back down on the settee and Nicole gripped her hand to keep her there.

Something flashed in the dim light in the parlor. A brilliant white orb appeared and began to circle the room. Lucas could feel the purity of the orb, the fierce will to protect. The circle of light hovered over Rachel, then began moving again, circling faster and faster, growing larger, until the entire parlor filled with a fierce, blinding white light.

Simone's shrill voice, viciously swearing a stream of filthy words, sliced through the quiet. Her ghostly, nearly transparent figure appeared, along with the smell of evil, dense and foul, unmistakable.

Lucas recognized the beautiful face, the

woman in Nicole's Spirit painting *Simone*. Then the image began to change, the features twisting into a grotesque semblance of a woman, empty sockets for eyes, blood welling in their black depths, spilling over onto her bony cheeks. Her lips parted, and a thin, serpentlike tongue slithered out.

Sean made a sound and Lucas gripped his knee in warning. Above the ghastly image, the brilliant white orb exploded with the sound of a gunshot, scattering bits and pieces of sparkling light over the room. Simone's murderous scream sent chills down Lucas's spine an instant before the hideous creature disappeared.

The room fell silent, the quiet stretching from seconds into minutes. Little by little, the heaviness in the atmosphere dissipated and the ghostly male figure began to fade. In seconds, the man had disappeared completely.

"Francois, wait!" Rachel called after him.

"He's gone," Lucas said, rising from the settee. "They're both gone — at least for now."

Sean rose beside him.

"You okay?" Lucas asked.

"I don't know. I feel kind of shaky." He glanced around at the room, which had returned to normal. "I can't believe what just happened."

"It's not your everyday occurrence, that's for sure."

"None of the guys are going to believe me when I tell them what I saw."

"You might want to give it some thought before you tell them any of this. You're right — friends or not, they probably won't believe you. You might not like the consequences when that happens."

Sean made no reply.

Lucas went to Rachel. "Are you all right?"

Rachel bit her lip. "He was here. You saw him — Francois was here. Then *she* came."

Lucas nodded. "They're gone, but they'll be back."

He reached for Nicole, drew her up from the settee and into his arms. "How about you? Doing all right?"

She swallowed and he could feel her trembling. "I'm okay. It's hard to believe what just happened, but . . . in a way, I'm beginning to accept this is just part of the circle of life and death."

He led her over to where his grandmother stood next to the broken display case.

"She's very strong, Lucas." Grandmere lifted her gaze to his face. "And completely evil. She was that way even as a young woman."

"And Francois?"

"Exactly the opposite. He's a strong man with a kind heart. From what I could gather, he was supposed to marry Simone, but he grew suspicious of her. One day, he followed her to the family hunting cabin out on the bayou and caught her in bed with his brother. Francois and Jules had a violent fight. Francois went home and ended his unofficial betrothal."

"Did Francois love Simone?" Rachel asked.

"It would have been a marriage of convenience arranged by his father, certainly not a love match. His father tried to convince him to forgive her, but Francois refused."

"I didn't think he could remember," Rachel said.

"When he first returned to Belle Reve, he couldn't. But little by little, he began to recall what had happened. He says Jules was younger, jealous of him and infatuated with Simone. She manipulated his brother into killing him. He says Simone was with Jules the day they murdered him."

Rachel wiped away a tear and Nicole reached for her hand.

"What happened to Jules?" Rachel asked.

Grandmere's shoulders straightened. "He's exactly where a man who murdered his own brother should be. The place Simone needs to be."

Rachel stiffened. "If he's in hell, I'm glad. I know it's wrong to say, but it's true."

Nicole leaned over and hugged her. "I know you love him, Aunt Rachel. I have no idea how any of this could happen, but the way he was with you tonight . . . I believe he loves you, too."

Rachel's lips trembled. "I want him to stay."

Grandmere looked at her sadly. "He has to go on, Rachel. There's a place waiting for him on the other side. He needs to go there."

"You couldn't convince him to leave?" Nicole asked.

"I tried, but he refused. He's worried about Rachel. He's staying here to protect her."

# CHAPTER THIRTY-SEVEN

Nicole couldn't sleep. Even after Lucas's skillful lovemaking, she lay awake, thinking about what she had witnessed in the house, thinking of the danger her aunt was facing in the evil spirit Simone.

Lucas slept fitfully beside her. She knew he was worried, too. At dawn, she finally gave up, slipped quietly out of bed, went into the kitchen, and brewed a pot of coffee. Lucas followed a few minutes later, looking nearly as tired as she was.

"I saw a light on upstairs at Belle Reve," he said. "I'm going over to check on your aunt."

Nicole felt a twinge of guilt. "I probably should have stayed with her last night."

"I don't think she was in any danger last night. No matter how strong a spirit is, once it expends its energy, it has to recharge. Kind of like a battery. Simone expended a lot of energy last night."

"Rachel didn't want me to stay. I think she was hoping Francois would come to her."

"He would have been facing the same problem. I don't think he would have been able to return last night."

"Rachel loves him. How is that possible?"

"Anything is possible," Lucas said, repeating the same words he had spoken a number of times before.

Nicole sighed. "Sean's still sleeping. I'll go over with you. I promised to help her clean up the broken figurines."

"I understand they were very valuable."

"I wish she'd sold them. Now they're gone — and the money, along with them."

Lucas made no reply, but his jaw looked tight. They pulled on jeans, T-shirts, and sneakers. Once they reached the house, Nicole used her key to get in through the back door.

"Aunt Rachel?" They made their way through the kitchen into the hallway. "It's Nicole, Aunt Rachel. Lucas is with me." They climbed the stairs to the second floor and saw the light under Rachel's door.

Nicole knocked. When she heard the weak whisper of her aunt's voice, she opened the door and rushed in. "Aunt Rachel!"

"Not feeling . . . well." Rachel looked

weak and pale, and worry jolted through Nicole.

"I'm calling Dr. Marlowe."

Rachel merely nodded, which made Nicole even more worried. She flicked a glance at Lucas as she pulled out her phone and called the doctor on his personal cell. Dr. Raymond Marlowe had been the family physician since Nicole was a little girl. Always there when they needed him, he picked up on the second ring.

"It's Nicole Belmond, Dr. Marlowe. I'm sorry to call you so early on a Sunday, but Rachel needs to see you. Is there a chance you could stop by this morning? Maybe after church?"

"I'll stop by before church, go to a later service. Tell Rachel I'll be there as soon as I can."

"I'll tell her. Thank you so much." She hung up and turned to her aunt. "He's coming over this morning."

Rachel just nodded. Her breathing was labored, the pulse at the base of her throat beating faster than it should have been.

Nicole moved to her aunt's bedside and looked down at her pale face. "I should have stayed last night."

"I thought . . . Francois would come, but he . . . didn't."

"He couldn't come, Rachel," Lucas explained. "He expended a great deal of energy in the parlor. He would have needed to recharge. That's the way it works."

Rachel's shoulders relaxed and a hint of color rose in her cheeks. "Thank you for . . . telling me."

"I should have mentioned it last night," Lucas said. "With so much going on, I wasn't thinking as clearly as I should have been."

Rachel's voice sounded reedy, but she managed to force out the words. "I guess I wasn't thinking . . . too clearly, either, or I wouldn't have . . . gone head-to-head with Simone."

Lucas moved closer to the bed. "She's dangerous, Rachel. If she shows up again, keep that in mind."

Rachel nodded, but her eyelids were drifting closed.

"I'll stay with her," Nicole said.

"You've got your phone. Call me if you need me."

Nicole watched Lucas walk away, thinking he was the first man who had ever said that and actually meant it. If she needed him, he would be there. She knew it deep in her heart. And yet there was a part of her that still needed convincing.

■ ■ ■ ■

The doctor arrived within the hour, a tall man with slightly stooped shoulders. As thin as he was, in his black suit, with his graying hair, he looked a little like a cadaver.

"I'll be right outside," Nicole told him.

She forced herself not to pace the floor of the hallway, rose from her seat when the doctor walked out of the room, closing the door softly behind him.

"How is she?"

He released a slow breath. "I gave her a mild sedative, which will help with her breathing. I called in a new prednisone prescription. Unfortunately, her heart rhythms are growing more and more erratic, and her muscles continue to weaken. That's just the way the disease progresses. She needs to rest and regain some of her strength, not push herself too hard."

"I'll talk to her. A lot of things have been going on around here lately."

The doctor nodded. "In a couple of hours, she'll feel better, but the truth is, she's failing, Nicole, declining more and more rapidly. Her heart is fragile. There is no getting around it. She could suffer an attack at any time."

Her throat tightened.

"I know that isn't what you want to hear, but she's already beaten the odds. Rachel's been alive far longer than anyone expected."

Nicole's eyes stung. "I know."

"She still has the strength to make it up and down the stairs, to spend a little time in the garden. It won't be long before that ends."

Nicole inhaled a steadying breath. "I have a woman lined up to take over her care when the time comes. She's a friend of Rachel's, a home care nurse named Maggie O'Conner. We have a place fixed up for her down the hall, not far from Rachel's room."

"I know Maggie. She's very reliable. You won't need her just yet." The doctor rested a fine-boned hand on her shoulder. "But the truth is, Rachel could suffer an attack at any time. You need to prepare yourself, Nicole. The disease affects the heart muscle. It could be months, or only a few weeks. Or a heart attack could strike completely out of the blue."

"But she's been doing so well. I thought it would be a long way off."

"It's entirely possible. On the other hand, it could happen any day."

Her throat ached. She wasn't ready to accept such a terrible loss.

"Your aunt has no regrets," the doctor said. "She told me she's been very happy — especially lately."

Nicole swallowed past the lump in her throat. She didn't tell the doctor that a handsome blue-eyed ghost was the reason Rachel was happy, that she was in love with him.

The doctor checked his watch. "I'm afraid I have to go."

"Thanks for coming over on such short notice, Dr. Marlowe."

He smiled. "Probably better not to tell her, but I've had a crush on your beautiful aunt for years. If she needs anything at all, just give me a call."

Nicole managed a watery smile. "I will." She walked the doctor downstairs and out the front door, watched as he climbed into his older-model Chevy Malibu, turned the car around, and drove away.

She planned to skip church this morning and let Sean go with Lucas. She had promised her aunt she would pick up the pieces of the broken figurines in the parlor, saving any of them that survived, and she wanted to be near if Rachel needed her. It was good to know her aunt would be able to maintain her independence for a while longer. Perhaps Rachel would have a little more time with Francois.

Nicole thought of last night and what had happened with Simone. The evil entity haunting Belle Reve was definitely a threat. Nicole prayed Lucas would be able to make the threat go away. He was preparing himself, she knew. She didn't understand how that worked, but she prayed it would happen soon.

She thought of Simone, and a chill crept down her spine. Lucas would be taking on a demon. She'd had a glimpse of what an entity like that could do. She prayed God would keep him safe.

It was Sunday evening. Lucas was putting away the last of the supper dishes. By now, Sean would be back at the youth center, Nicole on her way home. Lucas figured the boy was probably debating whether to tell his friends about the night he had spent in a haunted house.

He almost smiled. It would be a tough decision for the teen — and a risky one. It was fun to be the center of attention for a while, but kids could be cruel. Lucas trusted that Sean would make the right call.

He was putting the last dish into the cupboard when his cell phone rang. Grabbing it off the kitchen counter, he recognized Nathan Silvers's number and pressed the phone against his ear.

"Hey, Nate. What's up? I hope this means you've found something useful."

"Hello, Lucas, and yes, I did." Nate was thirty-two years old, olive-skinned, dark-eyed, scary smart, and a computer genius.

"It was buried deep," Nate said. "I hit a couple of dead ends, had to make a few U-turns and backtrack a little, but once I found the path, everything fell into place."

"I'm listening."

"Phillipe Villard is in financial trouble — big-time. For the last three years, he's been illegally siphoning profits from Villard Investments. Every dime he could beg, borrow, or steal is tied up in his Belle Reve Resort project. His investors don't have a clue, but sooner or later, it's bound to come out. If Villard can't get his hands on Belle Reve, he's going down in flames, maybe even going to prison."

Lucas's jaw tightened. "I had a hunch it was something like that. Rachel refuses to sell the property. From what you've said, I think Villard is behind a series of problems costing her money she can't afford to pay. Broken waterlines, electrical fires. His last effort was to release thousands of cockroaches into the house, forcing her to pay for major pest control work."

"I hate damn bugs, especially roaches."

"No kidding," Lucas said.

"If you can get me a name, I might be able to track down the guy Villard hired to do his dirty work."

Lucas's mind was already jumping ahead. "I'll see if I can find out. Anything else I should know?"

"Maybe. It isn't something I'm willing to talk about until I have proof."

"How long will that take?"

"Not sure, and it might turn out to be nothing. I'll let you know as soon as I can."

"Thanks, Nate. I really appreciate it." The line went dead.

Lucas's next call went to Remy. "I've got a problem. I'm hoping you can help."

"What's going on?"

"Someone's been breaking into Belle Reve, sabotaging the house, running up a fortune in repair bills." He told Remy about the flooding, the electrical malfunction, and the bugs. He told his friend about Phillipe Villard's financial trouble, and Lucas's belief that Villard was the man behind everything that had been happening to Belle Reve.

*Villard.* Remy spat the name. "I never liked the *batard.* How can I help?"

"Villard's interest in the Golden Spike gives him access to the kind of people willing to do his dirty work. I figure you might be able to find out who the guy is."

"Perhaps. I know people at the Golden Spike. I will see what I can do."

"Thanks, *mon frere*." Calling Remy his brother was truly the way Lucas felt; he ended the call.

Thinking of Villard, Lucas's temper morphed into cold, hard fury. He looked up to see Nicole walking into the house, stopping in the doorway at the dark look on his face.

"What is it? What's wrong?"

Lucas clamped down on his simmering rage. He reminded himself he wasn't that man anymore.

"Sorry. I just found out there's a more than likely chance Phillipe Villard's responsible for the trouble at Belle Reve."

"We already suspected, but what have you found out?"

"Apparently, Villard's in very deep financial trouble. The Belle Reve Resort project is his last hope of extricating himself from disaster. He desperately needs the project to succeed in order to repay money he took from Villard Investments. If he can't pay it back, he could wind up in prison."

"Wow. Is there any proof?"

"Not enough, but I'm pretty sure Villard paid someone to sabotage the house to force Rachel to sell. Remy and my friend Nate Silvers are working on getting the proof we need."

She set her purse on the kitchen counter. "It's hard to believe Villard would go that far."

"Really?"

She stiffened, inhaled a deep breath. "You're right. In a way, I'm not even surprised — the rotten bastard."

He smiled at her use of the same name Remy had called him.

Nicole sighed. "And to make matters worse, the house is haunted by at least one very evil spirit."

Calmer, he eased her into his arms. "I'm working on that problem as well. After Grandmere's visit, I think we know enough to see what can be done about Simone."

Nicole looked up at him. "What are we going to do?"

Lucas's features hardened. "Exorcise the bitch. It's time for her to go."

## Chapter Thirty-Eight

They spent the evening laying out a plan. Sitting around the kitchen table, they went over their options. Lucas was the expert, of course, but Nicole had seen enough to know that exorcising an entity as powerful as Simone was going to be extremely dangerous.

"I can't face her in the house," Lucas said. "What you saw the other night was only a sample of what she can do. She's not going to want to leave. She's going to fight us with everything she has."

Nicole thought of the violence in the parlor, the terrifying scene at the gallery, and a shudder ran through her. Fear for Lucas painfully contracted her stomach. "What about you? If you go against Simone, you could be injured." *Could she actually kill him?*

"I won't lie. She's a bad one. I can feel her strength. Over the years, her power has grown immense. When Francois's bones were found, all of this was set in motion. We have no choice but to deal with her or abandon Belle Reve. Even that might not be enough, though."

"What do you mean?"

"Francois has clearly chosen Rachel over Simone. Even if your aunt left Bell Reve, Simone might hate her enough to follow."

Nicole's chest squeezed. "It all seems so impossible — and yet I know it isn't. What are we going to do?"

"We need a place to deal with her. A place she's linked to where she'll feel she has the advantage."

Nicole knew instantly where Lucas was heading. "The old shack on the bayou."

"Yes," he said simply.

Nicole nodded in agreement. "Even if she tears the place apart, it won't matter."

"Exactly. The cabin's linked to her past, as well as to Francois and what is happening in this place and time."

"This place and time," she repeated. "Simone died long ago, but she's here in the present. How does that work?"

"Years are merely instants in God's domain, *cher*."

The endearment washed over her as it always did, settling her a little. She had never thought of time that way, just a flicker in the rhythms of the universe.

"I'll make a couple of calls," Lucas said. "Arrange to take the week off from school. First thing in the morning, I'll go over to the cabin and take a look inside, see if it'll work for what we need. Maybe I can use the old pirogue at the dock to cross the bayou to the other side."

"It's still sturdy. Sean's floated around in it. But the shack is falling completely into ruins."

"If it's safe, I can clean it up enough to make it work. The problem is, if we're going to use the cabin, we'll have to find a way to lure her out there."

Nicole's mind sifted through everything that had happened and how they had put the pieces of the puzzle together. Her paintings were a large part of it.

An idea sparked. "I know how to get her there, Lucas. I'll go over to the cabin with you and do a painting of her."

Lucas firmly shook his head. "No."

"I think it could work. She followed us to New Orleans. If I go over and start painting her portrait, there's a very good chance she'll show up."

His gaze pinned hers, his jaw hard as granite. "No way in hell."

Nicole knew better than to smile at the pun. "It's a good idea. At least admit that much."

"The painting might draw her, but it'll also leave you vulnerable. You could be badly injured. I won't allow that to happen."

Nicole walked over and slid her arms around his waist, leaning into him. "You can't control everything, Lucas. Unless you can think of a better idea, if the cabin is in good enough shape to use, I'm going with you."

Very early on Monday morning, using the pirogue to cross the water, Lucas managed to forge a path through the heavy foliage to the cabin, which sat on a slope, propped up in front by stilts. The place was in shambles: half the corrugated tin roof torn away, the moldy interior as bad or worse than he had imagined. Still, the construction was basically sound. He was sure he could make the cabin work.

Returning to Belle Reve, he went in search of Nicole and found her in her studio.

She turned at his approach. "So, what did you think? Are we going to be able to use the place?"

"It's got to be cleaned up, but it'll do."

"How can I help?"

"You work on the painting. I'll handle the physical labor."

Nicole smiled. "So we lure Simone into our trap, and you take care of her — once and for all."

Lucas couldn't quite muster a return smile. Nicole had no idea how difficult the task was going to be.

Leaving her in her studio, he went out to the toolshed to collect the implements he was going to need for the task ahead: a broom, shovel, rake, hoe, and a pair of long-handled gardening shears to hack away enough of the heavy foliage to forge a path to the back door.

He carefully loaded the equipment into the car, along with a push broom and whatever miscellaneous items he thought he might need and drove down to the dock. The flat-bottomed boat was solid and well-balanced. On the other side of the bayou, he unloaded the pirogue and went to work.

By afternoon, as the heat continued to build, he had worked up a major sweat and exhausted a variety of different muscles that hadn't been tired in years. Satisfied with the progress he had made, he returned the tools to the boat and poled back across the bayou to the dock, leaving the cabin ready for the next phase.

With that in mind, he drove to Baton Rouge to collect the spiritual tools necessary to fight a malevolent being. Back at Belle Reve, he hauled much of the gear back across the bayou to the cabin. Evening was approaching by the time he returned to the carriage house.

Nicole looked up to see Lucas walking into the studio in a pair of worn, faded jeans that outlined his hard thighs and the masculine bulge beneath his zipper. A ripped, sweaty khaki T-shirt stretched over his sculpted chest, which made her mouth water. She smiled at the amount of dirt, leaves, and cobwebs that covered his clothes. Even his dark hair had a layer of fine, powdery dust.

"Looks like you've been hard at work," she said.

Lucas glanced down at himself. "I'm on my way to the shower. The good news is, I got enough done that we'll be able to use the place for what we need."

"That's great."

She watched him disappear down the hall. A few minutes later, he returned in clean jeans and a dark blue T-shirt, his hair still slightly damp. His gaze ran over her painting.

"Nice work. You think you'll be done with it in time? If not, I might be able to use the painting you took to the gallery opening."

"You could try that. It might work. It might not. My way is better. I'll be ready to go when you are. Once we're there, I'll flesh out the details, make it compelling. She'll want to watch me work on something that involves her. She's vain. Destructively so. That's why she's so angry that Francois chose Rachel over her. She'll come to watch, I know she will."

Lucas started to shake his head. He was worried about her, she knew.

"Belle Reve is going to be mine one day," she said. "Like it or not, I'm going with you."

He looked at her hard. When she didn't relent, he sighed. Bending his head, he took her mouth in a soft, but thorough, kiss.

Lucas's big hand cupped her cheek. "You're a stubborn woman, Nicole Belmond."

"I am," she said proudly.

And she intended to be there in case Lucas needed her. She wasn't sure what she could do, but she might be able to help in some way. He didn't want her getting hurt — well, she didn't want Lucas getting hurt, either.

She took the lead this time, went up on her toes and kissed him. She had never really desired a man. Lucas stirred a hunger deep inside, made her want him to do wicked things to her.

Lucas gently ended the kiss. "You, Ms. Belmond, are a temptation few men could resist, and I'm certainly not one of them. Unfortunately, now that we've made the commitment, there are things I have to do, protocols I have to follow." He tipped her chin up. "Promise you'll give me a rain check as soon as this is over?"

When she didn't answer fast enough, he bent his head and kissed her. "Promise me," he said, more a command this time than a question, and it filled her mind with all sorts of fantasies.

"I promise."

Lucas pulled her close and Nicole's heart squeezed. She fell a little deeper in love with him every day. She wished she could read his mind, know his true feelings for her. Wished all her doubts would fade.

She couldn't think of it, not now, not until Belle Reve and her family were safe. She would deal with all of it later. It was the only sensible thing to do.

On Tuesday, Nicole continued to work on

her painting, careful to sketch only a vague outline of the picture she intended to finish at the cabin, nothing that would attract Simone's attention until Lucas was ready to face her. He planned for that to happen before Sean came home on Friday.

"One thing you should know," he said. "No matter how much I prepare, it doesn't always work."

"But I thought —"

"My successes far outnumber my failures, but it's happened. I wanted you to know just in case."

Worry trickled through her. "What do we do if she won't leave?"

"Figure another way to attack the problem and try again."

She felt a little better. Lucas wasn't going to give up. She probably should have guessed that. The man was steadfast — a rock she could cling to in the roughest storm.

*When he leaves —*

She broke off the thought, refusing to give in to her fears.

Instead, she picked up her brush and carefully returned to working on the painting: the image of the cabin and a vague, indiscernible outline of the beautiful woman who had betrayed, then ruthlessly murdered, the man she hoped to marry.

Satisfied the cabin was ready for the next steps, Lucas began his spiritual preparations. Driving down Ferdinand Street, he headed for Our Lady of Mount Carmel, his mind on the task ahead. Until the exorcism was over, he would fast, remain celibate, and pray.

He parked the Jeep and walked past the bubbling fountain into the small wood-framed white church, with its tiny boxlike steeple on top. Father Donovan, a stoop-shouldered man with gray hair, wise eyes, and a gentle smile, walked toward him. His white-collared black cassock swayed from side to side as he walked up the aisle in Lucas's direction. Sunlight streamed through the stained-glass windows. A handful of people sat in pews facing the altar.

Father Donovan came to a halt in front of him. "It's good to see you, my son."

"Thank you, Father."

"What has brought you to us today? You look as if you have come with a purpose."

Lucas nodded. "I'm hoping you'll hear my confession." He explained to the priest that he would be performing an exorcism and he needed to begin the steps necessary to prepare himself.

"You were a priest once," the old man said.

"That's right."

"I have heard of your special talents. The gift God has given you is one of great value."

"Yes," he agreed.

The priest led him a few steps out of the way, over to the side of the church. "Can you tell me a little about the situation?"

Lucas explained that the exorcism involved an entity from Belle Reve's past, a malevolent presence that had recently returned and taken up residence in the house.

"Her name was Simone St. Denis before she married Jules Villard. She was a murderer, Father, a wicked deceiver, and she gloried in it. Now she's back, more evil than ever, and a terrible danger to the people who live in the house."

"I'll hear your confession, of course. Is there anything I can do to help?"

"I need to prepare for the battle ahead. I'll be spending a great many hours here in the church. I need to cleanse my soul and absorb as much of God's strength as possible. This one won't be easy to defeat."

"Our doors are always open. You're welcome to come at any time and stay as long as you wish. If there is anything I can do to make your task easier, please let me know."

"I will. Thank you, Father."

Lucas made his confession, then took a seat in one of the pews. Bowing his head, he began to pray. He asked for God to cleanse his soul and prayed for assistance in his coming confrontation with one of Satan's minions. He asked that when the time came, God would send his warrior, the Archangel Michael, the defender of humankind against evil.

He remained in the chapel for the next twelve hours. It was late and he was tired when he got back to the carriage house. He'd considered driving back to Baton Rouge and staying in his condo, but things were unsettled at Belle Reve. Josh wasn't there, and he didn't like Nicole and Rachel being alone.

Nicole was already in bed when he arrived. As he had warned her that morning, he would remain mostly in solitude. After a meal of clear vegetable broth, he went into Sean's room to sleep. Tomorrow he would return to the church for another day of prayer. Tomorrow night, he would be ready.

He prayed for God's grace and the strength to defeat the evil he would be facing. He prayed that while the battle raged, everyone around him would be safe.

# Chapter Thirty-Nine

When Lucas's cell phone rang on the kitchen counter the following morning, Nicole set aside her easel and left her studio to answer it. She'd been working on the painting, careful not to put anything in it that would draw Simone's attention.

Lucas was in town at church. He had left his phone so she could answer and he wouldn't be disturbed. She knew he was praying, clearing his heart and mind for the confrontation ahead.

Seeing Remy's name on the screen, she forced aside her fears and picked up the phone. "Hi, Remy. I'm sorry, but it's not Lucas, it's Nicole. Lucas isn't available at the moment. Can I give him a message?"

"I have information Lucas needs, *cherie*. Ask him to call me."

"He might be a while." Did she dare say it? "He's . . . umm . . . getting ready to exorcise a demon."

Remy made an unpleasant sound in his throat.

"Any chance you could give the information to me?" she asked.

For several seconds, Remy didn't answer. "Tell him the name he wants is Joseph Mercer, the man who has been breaking into the house. He calls himself Jupp."

"Mercer works for Villard?"

"That is the word on the street."

A chill went through her. The house was being purposely sabotaged by Villard, just as Lucas believed.

"Tell Lucas the government is investigating Villard. It is not something he can repeat, but perhaps he will be able to find a connection that will help the Feds."

Nicole's chest felt tight. Everything they had thought about Villard was true. "Thank you, Remy. Thank you for trusting me."

"I know you will keep our secrets, *cherie*. I see the way my friend looks at you. He sees inside you. He knows the person you are. It is part of his gift."

Her throat closed up. She thought of Lucas and how much he meant to her. *How much she loved him.* She wondered if he knew.

"I'll give him the message. Thanks for being such a good friend."

"These are dangerous people, *cherie.* You both need to be careful." The call ended. Nicole picked up the notepad on the kitchen counter and wrote down the name Remy had given her.

She tapped a finger on the notepad. Lucas had told her about Nathan Silvers. Nathan was willing to continue his search for information on Phillipe Villard. The name Remy had given her could be crucial.

She looked down at the cell phone in her hand. Nathan's name would be in the contact list. Should she wait for Lucas? Or should she call his friend Nathan and give him the name?

She thought of the demon Lucas would be facing. She thought of Phillipe Villard and his plan to destroy Belle Reve. They were surrounded by danger. She punched the contact button. It must have been Nathan's private line because he picked up on the second ring.

"Lucas," Nathan said, reading the caller ID.

"Hello, Nathan. I'm afraid this isn't Lucas. My name is Nicole Belmond. I'm Lucas's . . ." She started to say *friend,* but the word stuck in her throat. *Lover? The woman who had stupidly fallen in love with him?* "I'm

Lucas's girlfriend." *Am I?* She wasn't really certain.

"Nicole Belmond," he repeated.

"That's right."

"You own Belle Reve."

"Technically, my aunt owns the property."

"Has something happened to Lucas?"

"No, he's fine, but . . . he isn't available at the moment, and this is important. I need to give you a message."

"This is a message from Lucas?"

*Well, not exactly.* "Yes," she said. "There's a man named Joseph Mercer. People call him Jupp. Lucas is hoping you can help us find out if there is a connection between Mercer and Phillipe Villard."

For several seconds, Nathan said nothing. "Lucas and I have discussed this. Tell him I'll look into it. Tell him to call me as soon as he gets the chance."

She could hear the censure in his voice. "I will."

The line went dead. No one was happy with her today. They wanted to speak directly to Lucas. She understood. Lucas wasn't a man who could easily be replaced.

The thought sent her mood downhill. They had never discussed their relationship or any sort of future together. *If things change between us . . . If Lucas decides I don't have a place in his life . . .*

Nicole clamped down on the painful thought. She didn't have time to indulge in self-pity. Besides, if anyone backed out of their unofficial relationship, it would probably be her.

Setting the cell phone on the kitchen counter, she headed back to her studio. She studied the unfinished canvas sitting on the easel, picked up a brush, and went to work.

Rachel was feeling sluggish today, the muscles in her legs weak, making it difficult to go up and down the stairs. Several times that morning, she'd become short of breath, her heart rate accelerating, beating way too fast. Abnormal heart rhythms were a symptom of the disease.

She felt tired and depressed, missing Francois, who hadn't come to her since before the terrible scene with Simone in the parlor. The weather was overcast and humid, the air dense and unpleasant. Dressed in a loose-fitting flowered dress, she walked down the hall into the kitchen, needing something cold to drink.

Engine noise coming up the lane drew her attention and she detoured to the entry in time to see a car pulling up in front of the house. A black Mercedes sedan. She didn't recognize the vehicle, but she recognized the two men inside: Phillipe and Christian Villard.

After her first few encounters with one or the other of the men, they had begun going directly to Nicole with their efforts to purchase the property, certain they could buy her assistance in acquiring the estate.

Rachel scoffed at the notion. Her niece was not someone who could be swayed from her principles with money. Nicole was a Belmond. Belle Reve would one day be hers. Rachel was certain her niece would do everything in her power to protect the land that was part of her heritage. Part of the heritage that belonged to St. Francisville and the people who had lived and died here so long ago.

She watched the men get out of the car: Phillipe, dark-haired, lean, and elegant in a cream linen jacket over a pair of black slacks; Christian, blond, blue-eyed, and handsome in khaki slacks and a light blue short-sleeved pullover, with what was undoubtedly a country club emblem on the pocket.

Instead of heading for the carriage house, father and son crossed the gravel drive and started up the walkway to the house. Rachel waited as they climbed the wide porch steps; then, figuring she had dodged trouble as long as she possibly could, she opened the ornate white-painted front door.

"Gentlemen, what an unexpected surprise." She forced her lips to curve upward. "To what do I owe the pleasure?"

Phillipe gave her one of his phony smiles. "Good afternoon, Rachel. It's good to see you."

"Ms. Belmond," Christian added, with a polite nod of his head.

"It's quite a drive for you, coming all the way up here. What can I do for you, Phillipe? If you're here to purchase Belle Reve, I haven't changed my mind. I have no intention of selling the property."

Phillipe's smile remained in place. "It's a warm day. May we come in? Perhaps you have some of that wonderful homemade lemonade you always seem to keep on hand."

Nicole would probably have said no, but Rachel had been raised in the South, so there was no polite way she could refuse. And she was curious to see what new tactic the Villards had planned to employ to get what they wanted.

She took a step back, allowing them into the house. "Why don't you take a seat in the parlor, and I'll bring us something there."

"I'm happy to help," Christian said.

Rachel managed to smile. "Fine." Turning, she led the way down the hall to the kitchen, while Phillipe took a seat on one of the settees in front of the Queen Anne coffee table in the parlor.

Christian slowed his stride to allow her to walk into the kitchen first. He paused as she opened the refrigerator and took out the pitcher of lemonade.

"I saw your niece in New Orleans," Christian said. "At her opening at the Winston Gallery. I assume she's somewhere painting today."

"Yes." She didn't say her niece was working in her studio, not out in the countryside as she often was. It was none of his business.

Rachel filled three glasses with ice, then poured them full of lemonade and set them on a silver tray, which Christian carried back into the parlor and set on the coffee table. They each took a glass and seated themselves, Rachel across from the two men on the opposite settee.

She took a sip of lemonade. "Now that we're all comfortable, what can I do for you?"

"We've been hearing rumors," Phillipe said. "Problems with the house. Just the usual occurrences, I imagine, in a house this age. Plumbing issues, electrical fires, insects. The place is more than a hundred fifty years old and badly in need of repairs. Those repairs are costly. Our offer would eliminate having to deal with those problems and leave you with enough money to live out your life any way you wish."

He pulled a sheaf of papers out of his coat pocket and unfolded them. "This offer is a little different from the last. It accepts the property as is. No repairs needed. Just the house and land in its existing condition. It also increases the sales price to reflect higher property values."

Rachel said nothing.

Phillipe took a drink of lemonade and set the glass back down on a crocheted coaster on the table. "Along with that," he continued, "we'll give you a life estate in one of our newly built condos. You can choose the floor plan, the carpet, the appliances. We'll even give you an allowance for furniture." Phillipe flashed a smug, self-satisfied smile. "It's our final offer, Rachel. But it's one you'd be a fool to reject."

Rachel hated to admit it, but the man was right. Taking Villard's offer would be the smart thing to do. Instead of leaving her niece with the heavy burden of keeping up Belle Reve, Nicole would be free to do whatever she pleased, live wherever she wanted.

"Your family built this house," she said. "It's withstood the test of time for a century and a half, and yet it doesn't bother you in the least to destroy it."

"Life goes on," Phillipe said. "Times change. You have to be willing to change with them."

Rachel looked at Phillipe and in her mind saw the image Nicole had painted of Jules Villard, the man who had killed his own brother. She thought of Jules's wife, the scheming murderess, Simone St. Denis, who had killed not only Francois, but Grandma also believed had murdered his parents.

These two men were just like Simone and Jules, completely ruthless, willing to do anything to get what they wanted. They didn't deserve to own the beautiful old house Pierre Villard had built for his beloved Therese-Louise.

Rachel rose from her place on the settee. "I'm sorry, gentlemen, my answer hasn't changed. The house will remain in the Belmond family, as it has for the past hundred years."

Christian shot to his feet, fury distorting his features. "You really think we're going to let you stop us?" He started toward her, rounded the coffee table, and kept on coming. "You bitch! Our family built this place! It belongs to us!" He loomed over her. "We'll do whatever it takes to get it back!"

Something stirred in the air, whipping the draperies, sliding the silver tray across the surface of the coffee table. One of the half-empty lemonade glasses lifted into the air, then sat back down with a thud.

"What the hell?" Christian glanced nervously around the parlor. Phillipe rose from where he sat on the settee.

Rachel felt the shift, felt Francois's unmistakable presence as he moved to her side. His unseen nearness gave her strength. She forced a calm into her voice she didn't feel.

"Since there is nothing more to say, I think it's time for you gentlemen to leave."

Christian's face turned beet red, and his lips thinned into a furious line. "You're going to regret this. It's only a matter of time until you have to take our offer. When that happens, it'll be far less money than it is today! We'll gut this house, turn it into a modern showplace our family can be proud of!"

Christian stormed into the hallway. He had almost reached the entry when something halted his movements as if an invisible wall had dropped down in front of him. His gaze went to his father, his eyes big and round. He tried to speak, opened his mouth, but no words came out. He tried to move, but his feet seemed rooted to the floor.

The sound of a woman's loud, harsh jeer of derision sent a chill down Rachel's spine.

*"You. Will. Not. Destroy. Belle Reve!"*

Christian's body started uncontrollably shaking. He jerked sideways, then toppled over onto the floor.

"Christian!" His father raced toward him, but before he could get there, a powerful force blocked the way. He tried to go around, but it was no use.

Phillipe's gaze shot to her. "Rachel!" Terror filled his eyes. "What's happening?"

Rachel just stood staring. There was nothing she could do. No explanation he would believe.

"Rachel!" Phillipe called out again.

"It's her," she said. "Simone Villard. She murdered people to become mistress of Belle Reve. She won't let you destroy it."

Christian continued to convulse on the

floor, his teeth snapping violently together, while his father stood watching in horror a few feet away. Rachel had no idea what to do, or even what more to say. Relief swept over her at the sound of Lucas's Jeep on the gravel driveway, rolling toward the house.

Skirting Christian, she hurried to the front door and raced out onto the porch. "Lucas! Come quick!"

Turning off the engine, he jumped out of the car and started toward her, long strides carrying him across the drive and up the walkway. "Whose car is that? What's going on?"

"It belongs to Phillipe Villard. He and Christian threatened to destroy Belle Reve. Simone isn't having it."

Lucas rushed past her into the house to find Christian lying on his side in the hallway, his long body jerking back and forth. His eyes were open and staring. The foul stench of sulfur tainted the air. Rachel gasped in horror as bite marks appeared on the side of Christian's neck and an ugly purple bruise formed on one of his cheekbones.

Phillipe stared down at his son. "My God, what is happening?"

Just then, Christian's body lifted several feet off the floor, hung suspended, then dropped heavily back down. What looked like long fingernail scratches oozed blood on his cheek, while a frothy white substance foamed out of his mouth.

Lucas focused on the unseen presence attacking Christian. "Leave him! In the name of the Lord God Almighty, be gone from this person, from this house!"

Harsh female laughter rang loud and long, echoing through the house, vibrating across the parlor. Lucas started praying the Lord's Prayer in Latin, began again in English, then went back to speaking Latin.

Chills rushed over Rachel's skin as a serpentlike hissing began. Then the grating laughter returned, echoed, continued eerily, grew louder before it finally began to fade. Light, receding footfalls sounded, followed by a violent *whoosh* that seemed to suck all the air from the room.

Silence fell. For a brief instant longer, Rachel felt Francois's presence beside her, felt the touch of his hand against her cheek; then he was gone.

Phillipe rushed to his son, who lay moaning on the floor. With Lucas's help, the two of them lifted Christian back onto his feet and helped him over to the settee in the parlor.

"What happened?" Christian asked, his

words faintly slurred. He reached up and touched the scratches on his face. "What is . . . What's going on?"

Phillipe looked at Lucas. "It isn't possible. You did something. That was some sort of charade to stop us from moving forward with our project."

"I'd advise you to keep an eye on your son. She may not be finished with him yet."

Phillipe's face went pale. "You're talking crazy. Rachel did something, put something in our lemonade. None of that was real."

"Let me know if you need my help. With luck, she'll continue to focus her energy here and we'll find a way to handle it."

*Yes, with luck,* Rachel thought. But after what she had just seen, she was afraid it would take more than luck to cleanse the evil that had descended upon Belle Reve.

# Chapter Forty

Lucas made a quick check on Rachel, who seemed worried and somewhat fatigued, but all right. He looked up to see Nicole walking through the front door.

"What's going on? Christian looks like he's been in a fistfight and Phillipe was as pale as a ghost."

"Very apt comparison."

She was wearing her paint smock, a dab of yellow ochre on her cheek. With her auburn hair pulled back in a bouncy ponytail, she looked so appealing, he had to tamp down a rush of heat he couldn't allow himself to feel until all of this was over.

"I wasn't here when it started," he said. "But according to your aunt, Christian threatened to destroy Belle Reve, so Simone attacked him."

"Oh, my God."

"Bites, scratches, bruises, levitation of the body — it's called demonic vexation. The entity can cause severe burns, even broken bones. Christian was in pretty rough shape when he left, but it could have been a lot worse. Phillipe was in complete disbelief. I don't think they'll be back for a while."

"What about Aunt Rachel?"

"She seems to be all right. I think her friend Francois was here, at least for a while."

"I'll check on her and meet you back at the carriage house."

Lucas watched her walk away, trying not to notice the sexy curve of her behind. The woman had his number — that was for sure. He blocked the image and was waiting in the carriage house when Nicole walked back in.

"Rachel seems a little shaken, but okay. She would never admit it, but I think she got a kick out of seeing the Villards bested, even if it was by a ghost."

"Speaking of which, after what happened, we're going to have to postpone the exorcism. We can't attempt it tonight."

"What? Why?"

"Considering the amount of energy Simone expended, I don't think she'll be able to make an appearance at the cabin. No use going through the motions if she isn't there."

Nicole's shoulders slumped. "Dammit. I really thought after tonight, maybe all of this would be over."

"No such luck," Lucas said.

Nicole looked up at him. "I . . . umm . . . need to talk to you about something. I hope you won't be mad."

Lucas went on alert. When one of the kids at the center used that line, it was never good. "Why would I be mad?"

"While you were in town, Remy called to talk to you. He had the name of the man who's been sabotaging Belle Reve. I asked him to give the name to me."

"Who was it?"

"A guy named Joseph Mercer. Calls himself Jupp."

"Mercer works for Villard?"

"That's the rumor, according to Remy. He said the Feds are investigating Villard. He said it wasn't public knowledge, but maybe you could find some connection to something that would help them."

"Interesting. Anything else?"

"Remy reminded me that these were dangerous people and we needed to be careful."

"No question of that." Lucas studied her face and frowned. "Why would you think that would make me angry?"

"Because I didn't just take the message. I called your friend Nathan and gave him the name." Big green eyes looked up at him.

Lucas bit back a smile. If she had any idea how much she could get away with, he would be in very big trouble. "What did Nate say?"

"Nathan said he'd look into it. He said for you to call him as soon as you got the chance."

"I'll do that."

"So you're not mad?"

"Come over here and I'll show you how *not mad* I am."

She took a step toward him and he pulled her into his arms. Since the timing was wrong, he ignored the sweet temptation she made, gave her a quick soft kiss, and eased her a little away.

"I'm glad you called Nate," he said. "With luck, he'll already be digging for information that can help us."

"I don't think he liked me using his private line."

"He'll get over it."

Her eyes remained on his face. "Lucas, what are we going to do about Simone?"

*What indeed?* "By tomorrow, her energy should have returned. How's the painting coming along?"

"I was ready to work on it at the cabin tonight."

His jaw tightened. "After what happened to Christian, the last thing I want is for you to be involved."

"If I stay close to you, will you be able to protect me?"

He scrubbed a hand over his face and released a slow breath. "I don't know for sure. That's what worries me. A demon of that power can do a lot more than it did to Christian. A demon can take control of a person, make the person speak and act as it wishes, make the person an instrument of its will."

"You've seen this happen?"

He nodded. "More than once. Demonic possession has been happening since before the birth of Christ."

"Were you able to help the person?"

"I was. But it's not a sure thing. I couldn't stand for you to get hurt."

Her gaze didn't waver. "I trust you, Lucas. And I want to be there."

He didn't want her to go. He wanted her safe, but staying away wouldn't necessarily protect her. Rachel had Francois. Working through Lucas, God was Nicole's best protection.

"You wouldn't just have to trust me, Nicole. You would have to put your total faith in God. Could you do that?"

Her eyes slowly filled with tears. "I think God might have sent you to me, Lucas. So, yes, I can do that." The tears spilled over onto her cheeks. "God and you, Lucas."

His chest clamped down. His heart thumped painfully as he reached up and wiped away the wetness with the tip of his finger. He wanted to tell her he loved her. He'd known it for a while, but he wasn't sure if she was ready to hear it, and now wasn't the time. People were depending on him. God was depending on him.

He let her go and moved away. "I need to stay focused. I'll text Nathan, tell him I'll be in touch in a day or two. Then I'm going back to church."

# Chapter Forty-One

The weather worsened, a downpour that turned the ground outside to thick, oozing mud and battered the stained-glass windows of the church. Lucas spent the rest of the day and late into the night in prayer. After what had happened to Christian Villard, he was more worried than ever, certain the entity he would be facing was even stronger than he had believed.

Knowing he would need every ounce of his strength, he returned to the carriage house, sometime around two in the morning, for some badly needed sleep. Nicole had left a note on the kitchen counter, saying that her aunt had been feeling ill and that she was spending the night in the main house. After what had happened earlier with Villard, at least for now, Simone wouldn't be a threat and the women would be safe.

Lucas hoped Rachel's condition improved and that Nicole could come home, but in some ways, it was easier being away from her. Where Nicole was concerned, his celibacy came at a price. He needed to keep his mind clear and his thoughts pure.

Lucas slept a deep, dreamless sleep, then awoke to find the rain had lessened, but the air remained thick and humid. Heavy gray clouds hovered ominously overhead, and the hours ticked past. Determined to stay focused, he left a note for Nicole that he would be returning to church, but would be back that afternoon.

As he walked into Our Lady of Mount Carmel, he felt rested, his strength and energy returned. He felt God's presence, and he felt connected.

The hours passed and the afternoon slipped away from him. He left the church and returned home. Strangely, he had begun to think of the place that way, though being with Nicole was the reason he felt as if he belonged there. It worried him to imagine how he was going to feel if things went wrong between them.

She was standing in the doorway when he pulled up in front of the carriage house.

"I wasn't sure when you'd get back," she said as he climbed out of the Jeep and walked toward her.

"How's Rachel?"

"Much better. I tried to get her to let me call her friend Maggie and ask her to come over, but Rachel refused. She said she was feeling her usual self and wasn't ready to have a babysitter quite yet."

Lucas felt the pull of a smile. "I'm not really surprised."

"I guess you're beginning to know her."

"Rachel deserves to live her life the way she wants. I can't help but admire her for that."

Nicole nodded. "I just worry about her."

"You love her. Rachel's lucky to have you." They headed for the front door.

"I thought you might not be home until later," Nicole said.

"It's time I got started. I've done the basics, but there are other things I need to do. I want to be ready to start the exorcism as soon as it gets dark."

"What else is there to do?"

"To begin with, I need to anoint the walls of the cabin with holy oil, drawing the shape of the cross. Normally, I'd say the Epiphany Blessing of the Threshold, asking that peace and grace surround the doorways and all that pass through them. But this case is different. The entity doesn't reside in the cabin — we're going to have to lure her there. Which means I'll have to leave a path open for her to come in through. After she arrives, I can move things along as I should."

"If she comes, won't she realize what you're planning to do?"

"She'll know."

"Then why would she stay?"

"She's a demon. An exorcism is a battle between good and evil, God and the devil. She'll be driven to win the battle."

"Can she?"

"Depending on what happens, it's possible."

Uncertainty flashed in her eyes. "In that case, what would happen to you?"

"I have to put my faith and trust in God to protect me. That's how it works."

Her chin firmed. "If you're going to be in danger, then I'm glad I'll be with you."

Just the thought made his stomach burn. "You're still determined to go? There's nothing I can say to discourage you?"

She just shook her head. "I have to go in order to finish the canvas."

"You could finish it here, and I could come back and get it."

"I can give it more authenticity if I'm there, and I think watching me work is what's going to draw her."

He took a deep breath, knowing Nicole was right. They needed to confront Simone at the cabin. Playing to her vanity was the best chance they had of getting her there. If Simone didn't appear, this wasn't going to work.

Resignation settled over him. "All right. You can work on the painting while I'm finishing what I have to do. There's no way to tell how long it will take before Simone arrives — if she shows up at all. Assuming this works, I'll start the exorcism as soon as I feel her presence. At that time, your part in this will be over. Take the pirogue back across the bayou and wait for me at home."

"I'm staying."

"You don't understand how much time this could take. It could last several days, even longer. During my last exorcism, things got so out of hand, people's lives were in danger. I had to stop. I couldn't return until several days later. I'll admit, it was an unusual circumstance involving more than one demonic entity — and I don't think that's the case this time — but I want you to understand, anything could happen."

"I'm not leaving you there by yourself. I don't care how long it takes."

He could read her determination — and her fear. She was afraid for him. He wanted to hold her, reassure her, tell her how much she meant to him, but until this was over, he had to keep his emotions in check.

He thought of what had happened to Christian Villard. Even if Nicole stayed someplace else, there was no way to know what Simone might do.

He forced the muscles in his jaw to relax. "I hate to say this, but as much as I'd like to see you somewhere safe, there really is no such place. Simone is totally unpredictable. No matter how bad it gets, you're probably safer with me."

The smile she gave him made his chest clamp down. "Okay, then."

Lucas nodded, resigned. "I need to collect the last of my things. Round up whatever you need to finish the painting and we'll head on over."

He grabbed the hard-sided wheeled suitcase he had brought from his town house, while Nicole gathered her painting supplies, a canvas bag that carried miscellaneous personal items, and the partly finished canvas.

They loaded the stuff into the Jeep, and Lucas drove down the gravel lane until it turned into a dirt road that followed the meandering, muddy, barely moving water of the bayou.

He pulled to a stop in front of the wooden

dock and started unloading the Jeep. Nicole pitched in and they loaded their stuff into the pirogue.

"You sure you have everything you need?" Lucas asked.

"I hope so. I think I have it all."

He took her hand and helped her aboard and waited for her to get settled. The heavy, waterlogged wood tipped only a little as he climbed aboard himself. Picking up the long pole, he slid the end into the murky water and began to push the pirogue toward the opposite bank and the vine-covered, tin-roofed, ramshackle cabin on stilts across the bayou.

## Chapter Forty-Two

Nicole sat in the bottom of the pirogue, her unfinished canvas carefully perched in her lap. It took only minutes to cross the muddy brown water to the opposite side. Lucas poled the flat-bottomed boat up on the shore next to the ruined shack, and jumped down onto the bank.

Both of them were in sneakers, but Nicole wore lightweight khaki pants and a burgundy T-shirt, while Lucas was dressed more respectfully in the crisp dark blue jeans and white button-down shirt he'd worn to church. His sleeves were rolled up, exposing his muscular forearms, and Nicole could see the powerful muscles under the cotton fabric bunching as he pulled the pirogue farther up out of the bayou.

He took the painting, then helped her out of the boat. Mud squished beneath her rubber soles as she jumped and landed on the bank.

Nicole had only seen the dilapidated structure from the opposite side of the water. Lucas led her up the bank, around to the back, and she saw that he had hacked a path through the weeds, foliage, and vines to the door at the rear of the building.

They climbed the rickety wooden steps and Lucas handed her the canvas. The old screen door scraped as Lucas pulled it open, and Nicole walked past him into the screened-in porch that surrounded the back of the cabin.

While Lucas returned to the pirogue for the rest of the items they'd brought, Nicole carried the painting into the moldy interior of the ruined shack, all that remained of what had once been a secret lovers' rendezvous for Jules Villard and Simone St. Denis.

She glanced up at the ceiling, at the corrugated tin roof that had collapsed into the living area, allowing heavy vines to creep down inside. Rain from last night's storm formed puddles on the floor. An old sofa lay on its side in the water, the stuffing coming out, mostly eaten by rats, and the springs exposed.

The rough wooden floor had been swept, something Lucas must have done. He had knocked down most of the spiderwebs, leaving only those high up in the corners.

She wandered into what appeared to be the only bedroom and stopped at the sight of the altar at the opposite end. Lucas had constructed it from a narrow wooden table covered by a white lace cloth. Above the table hung an ornately carved wooden crucifix, which looked very old.

Beneath the figure of Jesus on the cross, a framed painting of the Virgin Mary and one of the winged warrior, the Archangel Michael, stood on the white lace cloth. For several long seconds, the beautiful artwork held Nicole in thrall. The paintings were exquisite, an ancient treasure that had managed to survive through time.

Her gaze moved over the rest of the items on the table, a pair of gilt candlesticks, a silver basin filled with holy water, and a leatherbound Bible, with the word printed in gold. It looked to be old, yet it was in perfect condition. Next to it was a prayer book draped with mother-of-pearl rosary beads. White, the color of purity.

A portable lamp sat on the floor in front of the altar. It would soon be dark. She turned to survey what had once been a bedroom. The tin ceiling was still intact, so the walls and floor weren't water damaged. One of the bedroom windows was cracked, both were completely clouded with dirt and grime. She was surprised to see two folding chairs Lucas must have brought, a place to sit or to set things up off the dirty floor.

There was an old iron bed, with a set of rusted metal springs, resting on what remained of a tattered carpet woven in what she barely recognized as a hunting scene. Nicole couldn't help wondering if Jules and Simone had made love in the old iron bed.

She looked up to see Lucas walking into the room carrying her easel, which he set up in a corner near the altar. He took the unfinished canvas from her hands and carefully positioned it, then used one of the folding chairs as a place to hold her painting supplies.

Next he began the preparations he had told her about, anointing the walls with holy oil in the shape of the cross, repeating the Rosary in both Latin and English as he worked.

When he finished, he popped open the hard-sided suitcase and took out a long white cassock. As he lifted it over his head, Nicole moved to help him, straightening the robe over his broad-shouldered frame.

As it floated out around him, she saw the wide gold band that slanted in a vee from his shoulders to form a single line down the front. A heavy gold cross on a long chain went over his head to dangle against his chest. She could see his quarter-size St. Michael's medallion in the vee at the neck of his white shirt.

Lucas caught her shoulders. "Are you sure you're ready for this?"

She thought of the vicious spirit Lucas would be facing, a murderer who belonged in the fires of hell. "More than ready."

His dark gaze met hers. "The greater your faith in God, the greater your trust in me, the stronger I'll be."

It hit her like a blow. In that moment, Nicole realized that she had to set aside all her doubts, all her fears, and trust Lucas completely. Lucas's life might depend on it.

Could she do it? She looked into his beloved face and all her uncertainties slid away. She struggled to find the words to tell him, but in the end, she just nodded. She looked into his eyes and a feeling of rightness settled over her, lifting off the heavy weight she had been carrying for so long.

She loved him. And she trusted him completely. She hoped Lucas could sense the huge step she had just taken.

He bent and brushed a light kiss over her cheek, then turned away and settled in to do his work. Lucas took his place in the room, his back to the altar, and made the sign of the cross.

Nicole fixed her attention on the unfinished canvas. It was time. She was finally free to complete the image of the beautiful, treacherous woman who had done murder more than once and come back to haunt Belle Reve.

Nicole picked up her brush and in minutes was immersed in her work. She needed the painting to compel Simone's appearance, make certain the entity was captured by her own vanity. Nicole's thoughts filled with the images in her mind that she had held back, no longer hazy, but fully formed.

The brush seemed to move of its own accord. She had a job to do, and she intended to do it.

Time passed. Nicole had no idea how long she had been working, several hours, maybe longer. It was the sound of Lucas's voice that drew her from her trancelike state. Outside the grimy windows, darkness had fallen, a weighty blackness that shrouded the dilapidated cabin and heightened the tension scraping along every nerve in her body.

Lucas had turned on the portable lamp, giving her enough light to work. In his white and gold cassock, he stood in the light, the altar behind him, white candles flickering in the gilded candelabra.

A Bible lay open in his big hands; a string of glossy jet-black rosary beads, interspersed with tiny beads of gold, draped over his palm. He was speaking Latin.

*"Pater Noster, qui es in caelis, sanctificetur nomen tuum. Adveniat regnum tuum. Fiat voluntas tua, sicut in caelo et in terra. Panem nostrum quotidianum da nobis hodie, et dimitte nobis debita nostra sicut et nos dimittimus debitoribus nostris."*

He began again in English, and she recognized the Lord's Prayer. Lucas had started the exorcism.

A chill went through her. Simone was there.

Nicole took a shaky breath and forced her attention back to the painting, adding even more details to Simone's beautiful face, enhancing the color of her incredible blue eyes, deepening the ruby red of her lips. Every brushstroke made the face looming above the cabin more compelling. Nicole prayed the painting would hold Simone's attention long enough for Lucas to do his work.

She could hear him speaking Latin again, his voice deep and strong.

*"Kyrie, eleison. Christe, eleison. Kyrie, elei-*

son. Christe, audi nos. Christe, exaudi nos. Pater de caelis, Deus, miserere nobis. Fili, Remptor mundi, Deus, miserere nobis. Spiritus Sancte, Deus, miserere nobis. Sancta Trinitas, unus Deus, miserere nobis. Sancta Maria, ora pro nobis."

He repeated the words in English. She thought it was the Litany of the Saints. He started again in Latin, prepared to take whatever time was necessary to defeat his satanic opponent.

The wind picked up, began to blow through the trees. Inside the cabin, a noise reached her, the faint hissing of a serpent's forked tongue. Her shoulders tightened. The slithering, sliding, of the unseen serpent's body moved toward her across the wooden floor, and fear slipped down her spine.

Nicole battled down her fright, trusting in God, trusting in Lucas. She quietly eased toward him, sat down on the folding chair he had placed behind him near the altar.

Lucas started reading from the Bible lying open in his hands. " 'In the beginning was the Word, and the Word was with God, and the Word was God. All things were made through Him, and without Him nothing was made that was made. In Him was life, and the life was the light of men. And the light shines in the darkness, and the darkness did not comprehend it.' "

Outside the dirty windows, lightning flashed in the distance as the storm slowly crept back in. Lucas kept speaking.

"*Ave Maria, gratia plena, Dominus tecum. Benedicta tu in mulieribus, et benedictus fructus ventris tui, Iesus. Sancta Maria, Mater Dei, ora pro nobis peccatoribus, nunc, et in hora mortis nostrae. Amen.*"

The windows began to rattle. The air in the room turned thick and heavy. The screen door swung open, then slammed closed. Lightning cracked and thunder rumbled. Nicole's fingers curled around the seat of the folding chair as a powerful gust shook the cabin.

Lucas's deep voice didn't waiver. "Hail Mary, full of grace, the Lord is with you; blessed are you among women, and blessed is the fruit of your womb, Jesus. Holy Mary, Mother of God, pray for us sinners now and at the hour of our death."

More Latin followed. "*Gloria ria Patri, et Filio, et Spiritui Sancto, sicut erat in principio, et nunc, et semper, et in saecula saeculorum. Amen.*"

The old iron bed began to hop up and down, making a loud, wheezing sound, sending fresh chills down Nicole's spine. The iron legs pounded on the floor and the wheezing noise grew louder. Nicole's heart raced. Her breath sawed in and out. She kept her eyes fixed firmly on Lucas. In the circle of light, he exuded calm, control, and strength.

Something shifted in the air. The moldy smell in the cabin disappeared beneath the foul odor of sulfur mixed with a repugnant smell that, at first, she couldn't name. Burning flesh, she realized, the bile rising in her throat.

She swallowed, fought down the nausea. Nicole heard it then, a woman's shrill voice, spouting a torrent of foul, disgusting language. The demon Simone was there, not the beautiful woman in the painting, but a grotesque creature with empty eye sockets in a skull-like white face. Her bony mouth opened, and a thin, serpentlike tongue slithered out.

Nicole trembled, locked down the scream that tried to escape her throat. Chills swept over her skin. Lucas's voice seemed distant, coming from somewhere far away. She looked at the creature that was pure evil and feared she was going to faint.

Fighting down her panic, Nicole took a deep breath, clearing her mind, forcing herself to concentrate on the man standing in the circle of light. Lucas's voice grew deeper, more intense.

"In the name of the Father, the Son, and the Holy Spirit, I command you, demon, to depart this place. St. Michael, the mighty Archangel, defend us in this battle. Be our protection against the wickedness and snares of the devil. May God rebuke this demon, we humbly pray; and you, O Prince of the Heavenly Host, by the power of God, cast into hell, Satan and all the evil spirits who prowl the world seeking the ruin of souls. Amen."

Lucas repeated the words in Latin, calling for St. Michael to help them. In the other room, she could hear the rain pounding against the tin roof, pouring in through the hole in the ceiling.

Nicole's spine jerked upright at a noise in the distance that seemed to be rushing toward them, a sound like the wild beating of wings.

Adrenaline hit her as a black swarm of bats swooped into the room through the open bedroom door. Fighting to hold back a scream, she ducked and covered her head with her arms while the swarm circled the bedroom — once, twice — then flew back out the door.

Her heart fluttered as madly as the wings of the bats. A headache pounded behind her eyes.

"In the name of God, I cast thee out, unclean spirit, along with the wicked enemy, Satan, and every phantom and diabolical legion. In the name of our Lord Jesus Christ, depart and vanish from this house of God and all of its surroundings."

Nicole focused on Lucas. She could feel the solid strength of him that continued unchanged. The candles behind him still burned, the heavy wooden crucifix still hung on the wall above the altar.

She could do this. She had to. Lucas was in danger. Her family was in danger. She rose from her chair and kept her attention on Lucas.

"Pay heed, Satan, you foe of the human race, you carrier of death, you robber of life. Thou are the root of all evil, the fomenter of vice, the seducer of men, the traitor of nations, the instigator of envy, the font of avarice, the source of discord, the exciter of sorrows. In the name of the Father and the Son and the Holy Spirit, I command you to leave this place!"

The floor of the cabin began to violently shake beneath her feet. The walls seemed to expand, then contract; expand, then contract. A whimper slipped from her throat. Nicole gripped the back of the folding chair.

"St. Michael, the Archangel, defend us in this battle, be our protector against the wickedness and snares of the devil. Great Prince of the Heavenly Host, by the power of God, cast into hell, Satan and any of the evil spirits who prowl this place."

Something was happening. She could feel the presence of someone else, someone entering the room from above. She watched in awe as a huge, winged warrior with long, gleaming blond hair floated down and hovered above the crucifix, a heavy golden sword in his hands.

"Archangel Michael, Prince of the Heavenly Host, by the power of God, cast into hell, Satan and all the evil spirits who prowl the world seeking the ruin of souls."

The demon Simone swelled to a being twice its size, and the next instant, the cabin exploded. Nicole screamed as Lucas tackled her to the floor and covered her body with his. Wood and glass rained down on them. Bits of metal and rusty nails fell like iron confetti.

The crackle of flames reached her as pieces of wood caught fire. Unable to believe her eyes, staring over Lucas's shoulder, she watched the massive sword in the warrior's hands swing down, neatly severing the head of the demon, sending it flying. A shriek that seemed to come from the very depths of hell shook the room, rattling the remnants of the tin ceiling.

In an instant, the demon vanished.

The huge golden-haired warrior disappeared.

# Chapter Forty-Three

Shaken to the core, Nicole sprawled on her back on the floor, Lucas's heavy weight on top of her. Rain continued to fall through the hole in the roof, putting out the small blaze; then the rain suddenly ended.

"Lucas?" But Lucas didn't move. Blood oozed from a cut in the back of his head. More blood soaked through his cassock, where a six-inch piece of metal protruded from his back.

"Lucas!" Fear gripped her and she started to tremble. "Lucas, please wake up!"

Nothing. She could feel his heartbeat, feel his breath feathering against her cheek. "Lucas . . . please . . ."

Lucas groaned, and some of her panic eased. He lifted his head, then managed to straighten away from her and slowly shove himself to his feet.

Nicole followed him up. "You've been in-injured, Lucas." Her voice trembled. "You have a piece of metal in y-your back. I don't know what will happen if I . . . pull it out. We need to get you home and get you some help."

Lucas swayed, then steadied himself. Reaching behind him, he took hold of the piece of metal and pulled it out. A gush of bright red blood followed.

"Lucas!" Nicole grabbed the cassock, where the sharp piece of metal had sliced it open, ripped it apart, then shoved the robe off his shoulders. "Please, honey, just hold still."

Tearing off a piece of the rain-wet fabric, she folded it into a pad and wiped away enough of the blood to see how badly he was injured.

"It's hard to tell, but the cut looks pretty deep. We need to get you home."

Lucas didn't argue as Nicole draped his arm over her shoulder and began to guide him toward the door. She wished she had her cell phone, but there was no place in an exorcism for modern-day inventions.

Lucas stumbled, but Nicole kept him upright. They made their way out of what was left of the cabin, across the screened-in porch, down the rickety wooden steps. He swayed as she led him along the path back to the pirogue, then helped him climb in and settle in the bottom.

The jeans and white shirt he'd worn under the cassock were red with blood, and her worry increased. Her feet slipped on the slick, rain-soaked grass, but it helped her slide the heavy pirogue off the bank into the muddy water. Nicole jumped aboard as the boat slipped into the bayou. Grabbing the long pole, she plunged it into the water and began to push them toward the wooden dock on the opposite side.

Lucas stirred and tried to sit up.

"Please, Lucas. Just lie still and take it easy. We'll get back to the Jeep and I'll drive us home. Okay?"

His eyes drifted closed, but he nodded. She thought of Sean's head wound and prayed Lucas wasn't injured as badly. It occurred to her that she had been right to insist on going with him. He'd needed her. He needed her now. She felt the same sense of rightness she had felt before.

In minutes, they reached the dock. Working together, she helped him out of the pirogue, down the dock to the road where the Jeep was parked. She settled him in the passenger seat. He had left the keys in the ignition and their cell phones in the glove box. Nicole reached in and grabbed her phone to dial 911, but Lucas's hand shot out to stop her.

"Hang up," he said. "I'll be all right. Just get us home."

"You probably have a concussion and you have a bad cut in your back. You're going to need stitches. We need to go to the hospital."

"Just get us home. We can talk about it when we get there."

She could see arguing wasn't going to work. Nicole hurried around the hood of the Jeep and climbed in behind the wheel. It didn't take long to make the short drive back to the carriage house.

Lucas seemed stronger by the time she helped him out of the vehicle, and they made their way inside. Nicole urged him over to one of the chairs at the breakfast table, and he sat down heavily.

"Let me call an ambulance," she said. "You're going to need stitches, at the very least."

"Tomorrow," he said. "Can you do a butterfly bandage?"

She glanced at the wound on the back of his head, which was still oozing blood, but had slowed to a trickle. Biting down on her lip, she hurried into the bathroom to wash her hands, then gathered gauze bandages, adhesive tape, peroxide, and a washcloth.

Returning to the kitchen, she found Lucas

sitting up a little straighter. She wet the washcloth and sponged his back and poured peroxide over the gash. As Lucas had said, it wasn't as deep as she had first thought.

"Have you had your tetanus shot?"

He just nodded.

She didn't know much about patching up cuts and scrapes, but she knew she should tape both sides of the wounds together. When she got that done, she pulled out a big gauze square and taped it in place over the cut.

"What about your head?" she asked. "You've got a lump the size of an egg and you're still bleeding." She wet the rag and washed away the blood to get a better look. "You blacked out for a second, so you probably have a concussion."

His lips faintly curved. "I've had some experience with this kind of thing. Head wounds always bleed like the devil."

Nicole slanted him a look.

"I'm not seeing double," he continued. "No fuzzy vision, nothing like that. Just a bit of a headache. I'll be okay."

"I don't like it. Maybe I could get Dr. Marlowe to come over."

Lucas caught her hand and brought it to his lips. She felt the warmth of his kiss against her palm, and her eyes stung. After all he had been through, she couldn't stand to see him hurting.

He looked into her face. "The last thing we need is to be answering questions about how this happened."

She hadn't thought of that. She nodded.

"The good news is, we're both okay and Simone is gone. She's burning in hell, exactly as she should have been before, and she won't be coming back."

He pulled her down in his lap and she leaned against him, tucked her head into his shoulder. "Oh, Lucas, I was so frightened."

He pressed a kiss on her forehead. "You were amazing. Even under attack by a satanic demon, you didn't waver. I could feel your resolve, and it added to my strength."

The tears she had been fighting welled in her eyes. She managed to keep them from falling. Lucas tipped her head back, turned her to face him, and very softly kissed her.

"Everything is going to be all right," he said.

She nodded, the promise in his words washing over her, but the tears hovered close to the surface.

He kissed her again, a little deeper. "Do you think we could go to bed now?"

She swallowed. "I don't think you should go to sleep, not until we make sure your head is okay."

A slow smile curved his lips. "Maybe you can think of a way to keep me awake."

An unexpected laugh hit her. There was no way they were making love tonight. Both of them were mentally drained and physically exhausted. Lucas was injured and likely had a concussion.

But Nicole appreciated his effort to lighten the mood.

She managed to smile. "You never know, maybe I can."

Getting a faint smile in return, she took his hand and led him toward the bedroom.

# CHAPTER FORTY-FOUR

The wind still raged outside, tearing through the branches, the leaves scratching against the windows, but the rain had stopped. Rachel had heard Lucas's Jeep returning from the bayou to the carriage house. The glowing red numbers on the nightstand read: *3:00.*

Some of her tension eased. Lucas and Nicole were home and safe. She knew where they had been, knew Lucas had gone to the old cabin to destroy a monster, to exorcise the demon Simone. Rachel was certain they wouldn't have returned unless Lucas had succeeded.

Rachel closed her eyes and willed herself to sleep, but her restlessness would not leave her. She kept thinking of Francois, wondering if he had left, too; wondering if she would ever see him again.

Yearning for him.

Her heart ached. She had worn her white

silk nightgown to bed and left her hair unbound, hoping he would come to her. All night, she had felt as if he had been somewhere near, watching over her, protecting her, but perhaps she had only imagined it.

She blinked back tears. Maybe none of it was real. Maybe this longing for a man she had never known was nothing more than her imagination. Perhaps it was only a sweet delusion.

Finally giving in to the sadness that wouldn't leave her, Rachel tossed back the covers and climbed out of bed. She crossed to her dressing table and sat down on the faded velvet bench in front of the mirror. Thinking to plait her hair into the single long braid she usually wore to bed, she picked up the silver-backed hairbrush and began to pull it through the long black strands.

As she looked into the mirror, movement caught her attention, and in the mirror, she saw him, Francois, in his full-sleeved white shirt, snug black breeches, and knee-high boots. A beautiful man, with thick black hair and beautiful, long-lashed blue eyes.

Her heart squeezed. She turned and worked to hold back tears as he approached. "Francois."

He simply took her hand, brought it to his

lips, then drew her to her feet and into his arms.

*My love.*

She heard the words in her mind as clearly as if he had spoken them aloud. He felt solid and real as she leaned against him, and her arms went around his neck. Tears clogged her throat. *I prayed you would come.*

His hold tightened, pulling her closer. *I have searched through time, looking for the woman meant to be mine.*

The beautiful words washed over her, and she knew in her heart he was right. Francois was her destiny, as she was his.

She felt his lips on hers, tender and sweet, a kiss that held the promise of so much more. In her mind, music began to play, violin and piano, the lovely pulsing of a harp. Francois took one of her hands and placed it on his shoulder, settled his own hand at her waist. She recognized the beautiful notes of "The Blue Danube" the instant before he swept her into the waltz.

Rachel closed her eyes and let the music wash over her; it was so real she wondered if the orchestra was actually in the room. Perhaps none of it was real, but it didn't matter. For now, Francois was there, and she was in his arms, her white silk nightgown floating around her, her hair flying around her as he made a turn and she followed, as if they had danced together since the beginning of time.

Rachel closed her eyes, feeling free as she never had before. They glided about the room in a world all their own; Francois pulled her closer as the song played out. Too soon, the music ended. She worried that he would disappear, as he had before, but he lifted her against his chest and carried her over to the bed.

Their clothes quickly disappeared, and Francois's mouth took hers, his kiss no longer gentle. This was the man who had come to her in dreams, the demanding lover who knew just how to please her. He touched her as no man had, stirred her as no man had. When he joined with her, she felt a rush of desire so intense she cried out his name.

Hours passed in a haze of passion and deep, timeless love. In their final release, they reached the peak together, Francois's body straining toward hers, his kiss powerful and unforgettable.

Her eyelids felt heavy as he lay down beside her, but she refused to fall asleep. She wanted this time with Francois. Wanted to feel his powerful presence for as long as God would allow.

She didn't see him rise, just felt the emptiness swelling inside her. As she sat up in bed, her gaze went frantically in search of him. He was there, she realized, standing next to the bed, dressed once more in his shirt, breeches, and boots, but his image was growing fainter.

*Mon amour, now that you are safe, it is time for me to leave.*

*No . . . please . . . Francois.* Rachel's eyes welled with tears. *Please don't go.*

His image was barely visible as his hand reached down to cradle her cheek. *I must obey my destiny. There is no longer a choice.*

The tears in her eyes spilled over, leaving a trail of wetness. *I love you so much.*

He leaned down and brushed a last kiss on her trembling lips. *My heart.* When the soft kiss ended, all that remained of Francois were the bluest eyes she had ever seen, filled with love for her, the same love reflected in her own eyes.

"No!" she said into the darkness. But it was too late. Francois was already gone.

# Chapter Forty-Five

It was almost noon, the heat building along with the humidity. White clouds floated overhead, but last night's storm was over. After the long, stressful night, they had slept late. Lucas had awakened with Nicole draped over his chest, one of his arms wrapped protectively around her.

As he lay beside her, wanting her as he always did, his mind replayed the events of last night. He kept seeing Nicole's beautiful face as she looked a demon in the eye, terrified, yet standing her ground, determined to remain by his side, no matter the danger.

She was a true warrior, everything a man could want in a woman, everything Lucas had ever desired. He wanted to tell her, to say the words that had been in the back of his mind for weeks.

But he had to be sure. Was Nicole ready to trust that he would not fail her? That he would stand by her and the family she loved?

He had loved a woman once, had believed that she loved him in equal measure. Her betrayal had stolen something from him, left a hollow place inside. It had taken years for him to trust enough to love again. He prayed he was right in trusting Nicole.

Nicole climbed out of bed and headed straight for the shower. The aroma of freshly brewed coffee was almost enough to lure her into the kitchen, but she needed to check on her aunt. A shower would purge the faint remainder of the noxious odor left by the creature Lucas had faced last night.

She thought how magnificent he had been, staring into the face of what had truly been Satan himself. Calling on the power of God and the Archangel Michael to destroy the demon Simone.

Nicole's heart swelled with a surge of love for him.

She had always protected herself from the kind of deep emotions she felt for Lucas, had fought against them from the first time she had seen him. Now it was too late.

By the time she stepped out of the shower, worry about her aunt also filled her mind. Nicole hurriedly dressed in khaki shorts and a sleeveless print blouse, which tied up in front, and breezed into the kitchen.

Lucas, in jeans and a black T-shirt, held out a cup of coffee, which Nicole accepted with a grateful smile.

"Thanks." She took a sip and sighed as she walked behind him and lifted his T-shirt to assess the gash in his back. There was no new bleeding, thank God.

"How are you feeling?" she asked.

"Pretty good, considering."

"I don't suppose you're ready to go in for stitches."

"I don't suppose."

She wasn't surprised. Lucas was as tough as he was compassionate. "I need to go over and check on my aunt; then I'll come back and change your bandage."

He nodded. "I'll go with you."

It was still fairly early, but she didn't want to wait any longer. Nicole thought of what the demon had been capable of doing. She thought of Francois and his feelings for Rachel.

*Anything is possible.* Lucas's words rang in her head and her worry kicked up. She wished she could have gone to see her aunt last night, would have if the hour hadn't been so late and Lucas hadn't been injured.

Nicole took a last swallow of coffee and

set her cup on the kitchen counter. Crossing the gravel lane, they made their way around to the back door of the house, and Nicole used her key to get inside.

"Aunt Rachel, it's Nicole and Lucas!" she called out.

"I'll take a look down here," Lucas said when they got no response. "You go on up."

Nicole hurriedly climbed the stairs and headed down the hall to Rachel's bedroom. The door was closed. She rapped lightly, then turned the knob, found the door unlocked, and walked in.

Rachel lay in bed, her black hair unbound, a stark contrast against the snowy-white pillow. Her face was pale and her eyes red from crying.

Nicole hurried to her bedside. "What happened, Aunt Rachel? Are you all right?"

Tears rolled down Rachel's cheeks. "Francois is gone."

Nicole thought of the last time she had seen the two of them together and felt a tug in her heart. "Are you sure?"

Rachel sat up in bed, bracing her back against the headboard. Using her embroidered handkerchief, she sniffed back tears and wiped the wetness from her cheeks.

"Francois came to me last night. He told me I was the woman he had been searching for. He said that I was meant to be his." She dabbed the handkerchief against her eyes. "But he couldn't stay." She swallowed. "He said, now that I was safe, he had to leave." Her words trailed off as fresh tears rolled down her cheeks. "The hours we spent together last night were the best of my life."

"Oh, Aunt Rachel." Nicole sat down on the edge of the bed and pulled her aunt into her arms.

"I'll always love him, Nicole. Always . . ."

Nicole thought of Lucas and the heartache she would feel if she lost him. She glanced up to see him standing in the open doorway. Rachel sat up as Lucas strode across the room to her bedside.

Lucas reached down and took hold of her icy hand. "I can see how much you're hurting, Rachel."

A faint sound came from her throat and fresh tears welled in her eyes.

"Sometimes the things that happen to us seem completely unfair. It feels as if the pain is unbearable. But God works in ways we can't understand. I don't know what He has planned for you, but you have to trust that He knows best. Your Francois is in the place God intended. He's at peace, Rachel. You gave him that. Always remember that."

Rachel swallowed back more tears. "Thank you, Lucas."

He turned to Nicole. "If you need me, you know where I am."

Nicole just nodded. She stayed with Rachel until she had wept the last of her tears, then left her sleeping, sure she'd gotten little if any rest last night.

Nicole had no more words of comfort. Rachel's pain made her think of Lucas and the terrible pain she would suffer if she lost the man she loved.

Lucas left Nicole with her aunt and returned to the carriage house. A faint headache throbbed behind his eyes and his back was sore, but no longer bleeding. Nicole's butterfly bandage was holding. Since he wasn't going in for stitches, he'd have another scar, but it would be minor, just another marker along the path of life he had taken.

The coffee had been sitting a little too long, but he poured himself a cup and sat down at the kitchen table. It was getting late in the day, and he had to head to the youth center to pick up Sean for the weekend. But first he still had some business to attend.

Pulling his cell phone out of his pocket,

he hit Nate Silvers's number.

"Lucas," his friend answered, a little too cheerfully to suit Lucas's mood.

"Sorry to take so long getting back to you. Something came up that needed to be dealt with."

"Actually, your timing's perfect," Nate said.

"That so? What's up?"

"I guess your lady friend told you she called me."

"She did. She was afraid I'd be mad."

"Were you?"

"It would take a lot more than a phone call to make me mad at her."

He heard the chuckle in Nate's voice. "So that's the way the wind blows," Nate said.

"With any luck, yes, it is. I look forward to introducing the two of you."

"I look forward to meeting her."

"So, what have you got?"

"I managed to get a look at Villard's bank accounts. I found payments to his henchman, Jupp Mercer, the guy who's been destroying Belle Reve."

"How do we prove it?"

"I don't think we'll need to. There's a chance Villard is connected in a major way to the auto theft at Casino Rouge Chateau."

Adrenaline suddenly coursed through

him. "What makes you think he was involved?"

"While I was digging, I stumbled across a couple of Villard's offshore Cayman accounts. I noticed some fairly recent deposits and there was something about the dates that rang a bell."

"Go on."

"As you know, Villard owns an interest in the Golden Spike Casino. The gaming business attracts a criminal element, which means Villard would have the kind of connections it would take to pull off something like a million-dollar car heist."

Exactly the way Remy had found Jupp Mercer.

"The theft was big news all over Louisiana," Nate continued. "Turns out, the Cayman deposits were made just a few days after the thefts."

Lucas nodded to himself. "Enough time to get the cars sold."

"That was my thinking."

Lucas's jaw hardened. He thought of Sean and Nicole and what Villard had done to them; he had to clamp down on his temper.

"Nicole's brother was blackmailed into stealing one of those cars," he said. "More trouble for Nicole means more trouble for Belle Reve. The question is, how do we prove it?"

"I'm working on it. I just need a little more time."

"Thanks, Nate. I owe you a big one."

"You helped me, I'm helping you. For the moment, we're even." Nathan ended the call, and Lucas set his phone back down on the table. He rarely swore, but several foul words hovered on his tongue.

If Villard was connected to the car thefts, he was also connected to Ollie Martinez and Mickey Dugan, the men who had attacked Nicole.

A swear word slipped out. Last night had ended the ghostly problems that had been haunting Belle Reve. It was time to tackle Villard. When Phillipe had gone after Nicole and Sean, he had crossed the line. From now on, Villard was fair game.

One way or another, the man was going down.

Lucas drove Sean from Baton Rouge back to Belle Reve for the weekend. Sean had handled the situation that was becoming clear to his friends. Their coach, the owner of the school, was dating Sean's sister. Apparently, Sean had convinced them that Lucas's intentions were entirely honorable — though Lucas wasn't exactly sure what Nicole's intentions were.

As he drove the Jeep toward Belle Reve, Lucas tackled the topic of the exorcism, and that Belle Reve was once again free of any spiritual entities.

"Wow," Sean said. "That must have been something."

"If you want to know what happened, ask your sister. I imagine you can convince her to tell you what it was like."

Sean said nothing for a few more miles, digesting a subject few kids his age had to deal with. "So Francois is gone then, right?"

"That's right. He remained on the earthly plane to find out the truth of what had happened to him. He and Rachel met, and he stayed to protect her. He was a good soul, so once she was safe, he went on to the place God had ordained for him."

"What about his bones?" Sean asked as the Jeep rolled toward home. "They belong to Francois, right? We need to put them back in his grave."

Leave it to a kid to cut to the basics. "You're right. I should have thought of that. I think we've done enough research to convince the sheriff the bones belong to Francois. If he agrees, we can return them to his grave."

"What about Aunt Rachel? She really

liked Francois."

"She's sad that he's gone. In time, she'll feel better."

*Or maybe not,* Lucas thought. Rachel and Francois were soulmates. Most people didn't believe in such things. Lucas did. He could see the pain Rachel suffered.

His smile slowly faded. He'd be back at work, but his problems would be far from over. He still had Villard to deal with.

And it was past time he found out where he stood with Nicole.

## Chapter Forty-Six

It was Monday morning. Lucas and Sean were back at the youth center and Nicole was painting again, a feeling of freedom she had sorely missed.

Over the weekend, Detective Mark York, the man who had worked with Sean after his arrest, had called to tell them Joseph Mercer had been brought in for questioning. The police discovered that Mercer was wanted for assault in Mississippi and manslaughter in Texas, where, driving drunk, he had caused a collision that had injured four people.

In exchange for a shorter sentence, Mercer, who worked at the Golden Spike, had admitted to breaking into Belle Reve and committing a series of acts designed to force the owner to sell. He'd been hired by the son of one of the Golden Spike investors: Christian Villard.

Mercer was finished. And Christian was

in very deep trouble.

Nicole felt a shot of satisfaction. She returned her attention to the canvas. She was painting Belle Reve from a different angle, the dawn sun rising, casting a golden glow over the majestic old house.

She would rather have taken a ride, gone on the road to explore new locations, but she wanted to stay close to her aunt.

Rachel hadn't left her bed since the night Francois had disappeared. She was crushed, her heart completely broken. Nicole had phoned Rachel's friend Maggie and asked her to come stay at the house. Sadly, Rachel had made no protest.

Dr. Marlowe had come to see her, but after his examination, he had simply shaken his head.

"She's slipping away, Nicole. I'm not sure what happened, but something has sent her into a major decline. Perhaps you could get her to see a psychologist. If she won't leave the house, I might know someone who would make a house call."

"I'll talk to her about it," Nicole said, but she was certain Rachel would refuse.

"I'd be happy to prescribe an antidepressant," the doctor said, "but as weak as she is, I'm not sure it's a good idea."

Nicole's throat tightened. She knew what

was wrong with her aunt. No psychologist would believe Aunt Rachel's depression was caused by losing the ghost of the man she had fallen in love with.

"I know this is hard," the doctor said. "But if something happens, your aunt's living will makes her wishes more than clear."

*Do not resuscitate.* Nicole simply nodded.

The weekend had come and gone. Rachel was eating a little better: a bowl of soup for supper, and a croissant and juice this morning.

Rachel had promised to come down later and sit in the garden with Maggie. But Nicole didn't think her aunt would truly get well until she could accept the loss of the man she loved.

Nicole looked down at the canvas. The afternoon had slipped away, the sun shifting from east to west, the tall live oaks casting long shadows. Nicole rubbed the ache at the back of her neck. Satisfied with her work so far, she picked up her easel, paints, and the canvas, and carried them back to her studio.

Nicole had a date with Lucas tonight. He was taking her to the St. Francisville Inn, where they had gone before. After everything that had happened, he'd said they deserved some quiet time together.

She chose her clothes with care, a slinky black dress and very high heels she hoped would make Lucas drool. He had called and said he'd be there at seven-thirty to pick her up. When the car door of his silver Lexus opened, he stepped out in a perfectly tailored navy-blue suit, French-cuffed white shirt, and black Italian loafers.

She smiled. She'd wanted to make him drool, but it was working in reverse. She gave him the once-over, head to foot, and heat tugged low in her belly.

"For a onetime gangbanger and former priest, you sure know how to style."

He laughed, bent, and kissed her cheek. "You look beautiful."

"Thank you."

It didn't take long to reach the lovely historic inn on Commerce Street. The beautifully appointed old porches and parlors were charming. When Lucas gave his name, the hostess smiled and led them to a quiet, linen-draped table in one of the more intimate dining rooms.

Lucas ordered a bottle of Dom Perignon.

"Special occasion?" Nicole asked, smiling.

"It could be," he said mysteriously.

The waiter popped the cork, filled two

chilled flutes, and set one in front of each of them.

Lucas lifted his glass. "To God's warrior woman."

Her heart tugged. She clinked her glass with his. *To the most amazing man I've ever met.* But she wasn't sure she should say it.

They talked through supper: how well Sean was doing in school, the painting she had just started, the weather, stories Lucas told about his past, a story from her years in boarding school — which Nicole had never told anyone.

They finished the meal. The table was cleared, and they sat back to enjoy the rest of their champagne.

"We've talked about a lot of things tonight," Lucas said. "But not the most important one."

Her nerves kicked up. Nicole made no comment.

"I brought you here, not only because we deserved a night away from the problems we still need to solve, but because I wanted to tell you what a wonderful woman I think you are."

Her heart rate kicked up.

"I'll never forget the way you looked standing next to me while a demon threw everything in its power against us."

Her eyes burned.

"I've known for some time that you were the woman I wanted to share my life with. What I need to know is if you feel the same way." He reached into the pocket of his navy-blue coat and pulled out a blue velvet box, flipped it open to reveal a stunning diamond solitaire engagement ring.

"I love you, Nicole. I want you to be my wife. Will you marry me?"

She swallowed, trembled. Her stomach knotted. She loved him. There was no doubt. But if she married him, she would be giving him the heart she had guarded for so many years, trusting him with her very soul.

The tears in her eyes rolled down her cheeks. What would happen to her if things didn't work out? How could she live with the pain? What if he decided she wasn't enough for him? Even her parents had left her.

With every particle of her being, she wanted to say yes. She also wanted to turn and run out the door, to keep going and never look back.

She could feel his eyes on her and, for the first time, glimpsed his uncertainty.

"Nicole?"

She brushed the tears from her cheeks. "I

wasn't expecting this. I don't know what to say."

He sat back in his chair, his features closing up. "It's simple, really. Do you love me, Nicole?"

"Yes, but . . ." Her words trailed off; she was unable to explain.

"You love me," Lucas repeated, "but not enough to marry me?"

"No . . . Yes . . . I don't know. I wasn't expecting this. I just . . . I need a little more time."

"Funny, those are words I've heard before." Lucas shoved the velvet box into his pocket and rose from his chair. "Time won't change the way you feel, Nicole. I want a woman who loves me enough to commit to me, to share the burdens and joys of my life. As I'll love her enough to share the burdens and joys of hers."

He rounded the table and pulled out her chair, helping her to her feet. "The bill is taken care of. It's time for us to go."

"Lucas, please . . ."

He made no reply, just guided her through the restaurant and out the door to his car.

All the way back to Belle Reve, Nicole's heart throbbed painfully. She loved him. He was everything she wanted, and yet when she tried to tell him, the words stuck in her throat.

He walked her to the front door of the carriage house, used his key to open the door, then walked her inside. He left his key on the kitchen counter. "I'll be back to pick up my things. I'll call before I come."

Tears washed down her cheeks. "Lucas, no . . . Please don't go."

"I can't do it again. I'm sorry, *cher.*" Turning, he made his way back to the Lexus and started the engine. He turned the vehicle around and headed back down the driveway.

Nicole watched him until the car disappeared. Fresh tears rolled down her cheeks. *What have I done?*

Lucas loved her, but he had taken a chance on a woman before, a woman who had betrayed him.

Just as Nicole had done.

The night was long and empty. Tears soaked her pillow. Nicole reached for the man who should be sleeping beside her, but he was gone. She absolutely understood the terrible depression her aunt had fallen into after losing Francois.

Nicole prayed for morning, and eventually her prayer was answered. She sat at the kitchen table, listless and fighting fresh tears. Lucas was gone. He would never take her back, even if she went to him and told him she had changed her mind. He wouldn't be able to trust her again.

She loved him — that was the cold, hard truth. But was there really a man who loved her enough to stay with her through all the years? She thought of her parents — her mother, who had left her father for another man. Her grandparents were divorced. She didn't have a friend who was still married to the same man.

She hoped the shower would wash away some of her sadness, but she felt as dull and depressed as she had before. Every time she remembered the look of desolation on Lucas's face, she wanted to cry all over again.

Dressing in jeans and an old T-shirt, she forced herself to eat a bran muffin to settle her stomach before she went over to check on her aunt. She hoped Maggie had been able to coax her downstairs and out on the terrace.

The two were old friends, but Nicole didn't think Rachel would confide the truth of her heartbreak, that she was in love with a ghost.

Nicole left the carriage house and had almost reached the main house when she heard a car driving up the lane. For a moment, she thought it was Lucas and her heart took a leap. The black Mercedes pulling to a stop was unmistakable. Phillipe Villard had arrived.

A fission of nerves slipped through her. Jupp Mercer had confessed to sabotaging Belle Reve, and Christian had been arrested. What was Phillipe doing here?

She gave him a fake smile as he approached. "I'm a little surprised to see you."

His jaw looked tight. "Is that so?"

Her own lips tightened. "What do you want, Phillipe?"

"I thought it was time we had a little talk."

"Neither Rachel nor I have anything to say to you."

"Then let me make things perfectly clear. My son is in jail. My business is destroyed. The police arrived at my home this morning to arrest me. You and your aunt are responsible for everything that's happened."

She kept her phony smile in place, just to taunt him. "Really? You did everything in your power to force my aunt to sell. You even paid a man to break into her home. It's a miracle no one was hurt. I'm surprised the police released you so soon."

"They came to the house. With the help of my housekeeper, I managed to elude them."

One of her eyebrows went up. "You think that was wise?"

The expression turned hard, his eyes glittering with barely suppressed rage. He took a step toward her. "I want to know what you did to my son."

Nicole forced herself not to take a step back. "I don't know what you're talking about."

"Christian hasn't been the same since the night we came here. He's been volatile and moody, constantly lashing out. Now he's under arrest. I told him not to talk to anyone, but he wouldn't listen. He has the police convinced I'm involved in any number of crimes." He moved closer, and she did move back.

"It's you," he said. "You and this house. The things I saw that night . . . What are you, some kind of witch? What did you do to him?"

"I don't know what happened to Christian, but I know that what's happening to him right now is exactly what he deserves."

Phillipe moved closer, forcing her backward until she came up against the side of the house. "You're going to pay for what you've done. You and your stubborn aunt. And then I'm going to burn this place to the ground."

Nicole gasped when she saw his hand move; she caught the flash of metal and felt the barrel of a gun pressing into her ribs. She swallowed down a rush of fear. Damned if she would let this man intimidate her.

"You think things are bad for you now? Add murder to your crimes and you'll never see the light of day again. You'll spend the rest of your life in prison."

Villard roughly gripped her shoulders and spun her around. He pushed her toward the back door, shoving his gun into her back. Nicole prayed Maggie and Aunt Rachel weren't on the terrace, but were upstairs or somewhere else. Unfortunately, luck wasn't running her way.

As they rounded the corner, Maggie saw the pistol and pushed to her feet, while Rachel sat immobile, every drop of color vanishing from her face.

"What's going on?" the buxom woman asked.

"You'll have to ask him," Nicole said.

"Shut up and get in the house, all of you." He waved the gun in that direction.

Maggie helped Rachel up from her chair, and the women made their way inside. Nicole followed, Villard's gun still in her back.

"Into the parlor," Phillipe demanded, and they moved in that direction, Nicole's mind frantically working to figure a way to stop whatever Villard had planned.

Rachel and Maggie sat down next to each other on one of the velvet settees.

"You don't need to do this, Phillipe," Rachel said. "I'll sell you the house. It's nothing but a few acres of land. I'll sign whatever papers you want. It isn't worth someone's life."

The pistol swung, aimed in Rachel's direction. "It's too late for that. You should have taken my offer when you had the chance."

Nicole thought she heard a sound outside, a faint engine noise, wheels on gravel, but it was too far away for her to be sure. The police would be after him. Would they think he might come here? If there was a chance, she needed to keep him talking.

"You want to know what happened to Christian? I'll tell you."

The gun returned, pointed straight at her heart. "What did you do?"

Nicole took a steadying breath. "Christian has always been a good son, hasn't he?"

"Of course. He loves me and his mother." The barrel didn't waver. "You're trying to distract me. I should kill you all right now." A twisted smile curved his lips. "The trunk of my car is full of gasoline. Maybe I'll lock you inside while I burn the place down."

Cold dread slipped through her. "Before you do that, don't you want to hear what happened to your son?"

Villard made no reply, but she clearly had his attention.

"You remember what happened the night of the gallery opening?" Nicole continued. "The terrible storm that blew up outside, the painting that flew off the easel and sliced across the room, barely missed cutting off someone's head?"

"It was just an accident caused by the wind."

"It was the woman in the painting, the same woman you saw the night you came to Belle Reve. She's a demon, Phillipe. You saw with your own eyes what she did to Christian the night he was here."

"That's insane."

"Put the gun down, Phillipe — or we'll call her back." She didn't dare look at Rachel or Maggie. Simone was burning in hell. She would never hurt anyone again. "You can't begin to imagine what she can do."

The gun shook in Phillipe's hand. Looking into her face, he lifted it until the barrel pressed against her temple. "You're lying. There are no such things as demons."

Her chin firmed. "Actually, there are."

She could almost feel his finger tightening

on the trigger. Maggie screamed as a shot rang out, and Nicole closed her eyes against the pain of death she was sure would follow.

Instead, half of Phillipe's head exploded, spraying blood and gore all over the far side of the room. There was a hole in the parlor's front window, where the glass had splintered. The front and back doors crashed open, and police in camouflage uniforms with SWAT on the back poured into the house.

Nicole spotted Lucas racing toward her, and then she was in his arms.

# Chapter Forty-Seven

"Everything's all right, love. You're safe. He can't hurt anyone now."

A sob escaped as she clung to him. There was blood on her clothes, but she looked away from the body on the floor.

"How did you know?"

"Detective York called. He said the police tried to execute a warrant for Villard's arrest, but he managed to escape. From what they knew of his animosity toward you and Rachel, and from what Christian had told them, there was a very good chance he would head for Belle Reve. I arrived outside at the same time as the Baton Rouge PD SWAT team."

Nicole looked at him through a haze of tears, loving him more than ever, wishing there was something she could say to mend things between them. She clung to him even tighter, unable to let him go. Then she turned to see Maggie bending over Rachel on the settee.

"Rachel!" Nicole rushed to her side. Her aunt's breathing was little more than a whisper, her hands icy cold, her face sheet white.

Lucas pulled out his phone and dialed 911 for the medics, spoke in quiet tones to the dispatcher. "They're on their way."

The parlor was overflowing with armed police and the scene was one of blood and violence.

"She needs to be somewhere else." Lucas bent and scooped Rachel into his arms.

"The den!" Nicole led the way to the room, off the kitchen, with the big-screen TV and overstuffed leather sofa. Lucas carefully rested Rachel on the sofa and Nicole hurried to her side.

Reaching out, she took hold of her aunt's cold hand; Rachel's pulse was so weak it was almost nonexistent.

"Everything's going to be all right, Aunt Rachel. The ambulance is on its way. Just hold on until it gets here."

Rachel forced her eyelids slowly open. "Take care of yourself . . . and our family."

Nicole swallowed past the tears clogging her throat. "Save your strength. The ambulance will be here any minute."

Rachel's gaze went to Lucas, and he

moved to her side.

"I know you . . . love Nicole," Rachel said. "And she . . . loves you. She's just . . . afraid."

Lucas's features softened. "I know."

Rachel took a shallow breath, the effort to speak too much. Lucas eased away, allowing Nicole to move closer. Rachel's breathing was no more than a whisper of air, barely enough to lift her chest. Then a last sigh feathered out and the movement stopped altogether.

"Aunt Rachel, no!" Nicole could hear the blare of the siren as it grew louder, but Rachel's wishes were firm, as the doctor had reminded her. Rachel was ready to accept whatever God had in store for her.

A sob caught in Nicole's throat. She felt Lucas's arm go around her, gently lending his support. Maggie wept quietly in the background. Tears burned Nicole's eyes, but Aunt Rachel was no longer struggling.

Something stirred the air in the room. Nicole looked up to see a shadowy figure hovering near the ceiling. It was the vague image of a man in breeches and knee-high riding boots. He was tall and handsome, with the bluest eyes she had ever seen.

It couldn't be happening, but it was.

Rachel's eyes opened and her face softened into a smile. Her transparent image lifted upward, out of her body. No longer in jeans and a T-shirt, her white nightgown and long black hair floated around her. Francois took her hand, and a look that could only be love passed between them. An instant more, and then they were gone.

Nicole bit back another sob, her heart aching. Lucas's arms tightened around her, holding her close.

"She's where she wants to be," he said. "Francois came for her. They're together now and she's happy."

Nicole's heart ached and yet she believed Lucas was right. She nodded against his shoulder and Lucas kissed the top of her head.

He drew her a little away. "I love you, *cher*. If you love me, too, you can have all the time you need. I'll be waiting whenever you're ready."

Nicole swallowed past the tears in her throat. He was taking a chance on her, a chance on both of them. "I don't need any more time. I've seen love in its purest form. It lasts through time and beyond. I love you more than life itself — and I'm not afraid anymore."

Lucas pulled her back into his arms and buried his face in her hair. The ambulance arrived, and silently he led her out of the den. The house was a crime scene now. Lucas led her past the EMTs, who rushed into the room; past the police, who were yellow-taping the building.

He left her long enough to speak to Maggie, who stood on the terrace, wiping her eyes. He explained that he was taking Nicole back to his town house in Baton Rouge; then he stopped for a moment to speak to the officer in charge, telling him where they could be found to give their statements.

Weaving their way through the maze of police vehicles, they headed for the carriage house. Lucas waited while Nicole packed a bag; then he helped her into the Jeep for the ride to Baton Rouge. Instead of starting the engine, he reached for her trembling hand and brought it to his lips.

"I love you, *cher*. So much." Lucas pulled out the blue velvet box, took out the beautiful diamond engagement ring, kissed her, and slipped the ring on her finger.

The pain in Nicole's heart eased. Lucas was there. Everything was going to be all right.

# Epilogue

It was Sunday, October 20, Aunt Rachel's birthday. Sean, Nicole, and Lucas stood in front of the headstone on her grave:

Rachel Juliette Belmond
October 20, 1980 — May 7, 2024
A Beautiful, Beloved Soul

Next to her, a much older stone read:

IN LOVING MEMORY
Francois Etienne Villard
Beloved Son of Pierre and
Therese-Louise Villard
Born February 18, 1843
Died 1878
Finally at Peace

The last line had been added to the original marker. There was still no record of the exact date of Francois's death, but his bones had been placed in the grave, where they belonged, and Rachel had been buried at his side.

The cemetery sat on Belle Reve land. It was Nicole's decision, and she knew without doubt it was what Rachel would have wanted. What she and Francois both would have wanted.

Nicole set a bouquet of white roses on top of the grave and wiped a tear from her cheek. They stood there awhile in silent prayer, the wind ruffling her hair and the skirt she had worn to church that morning.

"You ready to go home?" Lucas asked.

Nicole nodded.

"Sean?" Lucas asked.

His gaze remained fixed on the graves. "When I think about everything that's happened, sometimes I still can't believe it."

Lucas glanced back to the graves. "Maybe it's better that way."

Nicole reached over and took hold of his hand, reached over and took hold of her brother's, and they made their way back to the Lexus for the return trip to Baton Rouge.

A lot had happened in the five months since the shooting at Belle Reve. Nicole and Lucas had been married, just a small ceremony at the little white church in St. Francisville, exactly what she wanted. Nicole no longer doubted her husband's love for her, or the deep love she felt for him.

Lucas had sold his town house and bought a much larger home at the edge of the city, with plenty of room for Sean, including a separate shop he had already converted into his man/boy cave. Her brother still had time left on his sentence, but he was getting along without a problem.

Christian Villard was serving a two-year sentence for his part in the attempted destruction of Belle Reve. With his father dead and the company bankrupt, Nicole believed the sentence was harsh enough.

The biggest change was in Belle Reve. Nicole and Lucas had discussed what should be done with the property — now that she and Sean no longer lived there — and it certainly wasn't turning it into a resort.

The house was a beautiful historic landmark. With Aunt Rachel gone, and Nicole the owner, they decided to donate the property to the State of Louisiana Division of Historic Preservation. Under the jurisdiction of local authorities, Belle Reve would be repaired, maintained, and opened daily to visitors for guided tours. A caretaker would live on-site in the carriage house.

Belle Reve would remain the Diva, majestic as she had been since the day she was built.

And though Nicole felt a pang as they drove away, Belle Reve would always be a part of her, along with the families resting for eternity in the graveyard up on the hill.

# ABOUT THE AUTHOR

**Kat Martin** is the *New York Times* bestselling author of more than sixty books across multiple genres. Sixteen million copies are in print and she has been published in twenty-one foreign countries, including Japan, France, Argentina, Greece, China, and Spain. Her books have been nominated for the prestigious RITA award and won both the Lifetime Achievement and *Reviewer's* Choice Awards from *RT Book Reviews*. She and her husband, the author L.J. Martin, live in Montana and spend their winters in Ventura, California. Visit her online at KatMartin.com.

The employees of Thorndike Press hope you have enjoyed this Large Print book. All our Thorndike Large Print titles are designed for easy reading, and all our books are made to last. Other Thorndike Press Large Print books are available at your library, through selected bookstores, or directly from us.

For information about titles, please call:
  (800) 223-1244

or visit our website at:
  gale.com/thorndike